Christopher Ransom was born and educated in Colorado, but moved to New York and then LA with his wife to pursue various careers such as selling ads for media magazines and screenwriting. They then bought a 140-year-old birthing house in Wisconsin, where he wrote his first novel.

Also by Christopher Ransom

The Birthing House

THE HAUNTING
OF
JAMES HASTINGS

CHRISTOPHER RANSOM

sphere

SPHERE

First published in Great Britain as a paperback original in 2010 by Sphere

A CIP catalogue record for this book
is available from the British Library.

ISBN 978-0-7515-4375-9

Typeset in Caslon by M Rules
Printed and bound in Great Britain by
Clays Ltd, St Ives plc

Papers used by Sphere are natural, renewable and
recyclable products sourced from well-managed forests and certified
in accordance with the rules of the Forest Stewardship Council.

Mixed Sources
Product group from well-managed
forests and other controlled sources
www.fsc.org Cert no. SGS-COC-004081
© 1996 Forest Stewardship Council
FSC

Sphere
An imprint of
Little, Brown Book Group
100 Victoria Embankment
London EC4Y 0DY

An Hachette UK Company
www.hachette.co.uk

www.littlebrown.co.uk

To you, my good-hearted father,
for all the beanstalks.

reader advisory sticker

This is not a Ghost story.

After spending three years in his employ, I could write that book if I wanted to, for it was I who shadowed the bard of pharma, serial killers and boobies, the man *Rolling Stone* called The Biggest Rapper in History, the lyrical genius and pop culture scourge all the kids wanted to be like, be with or simply be – Ghost.

Of course there were times when I was not allowed backstage, under the velvet rope, into the blacked-out limo. But I could provide you with very detailed, often salacious reportage from behind these scenes too. Page Six-worthy events whispered and texted to me. Guest-house gossip, bitch-slapped Twitter kittens drowning in pity, a dope opera in snippets. I could offer such a tale because his bodyguards, his trainer, his manager and even his psychotic ex-wife, Drea-Jenna, pinned his dirty laundry on the clothesline strung between my ears. And in one way or another, all three of his personas – the artist known as Ghost, his alter ego Snow Flakey and Nathaniel Eric Riverton, that scared white boy from St Louis – let me into their shadow world.

It was not a pretty place.

But unless you haven't read a newspaper or a magazine or watched MTV or paid any attention to pop culture for the past seven years, you already know that story –

Five multi-platinum albums that sold forty-six million copies worldwide, tours through twenty-two countries, seven Grammys, addiction and predilection, acrimonious matrimony, nubile groupies, divorce, club fights and fight clubs, first class stabbin' cabins, three stints in rehab. Blood oaths, gun smoke, media storms, trials for assault and attempted murder both by and against Ghost, squabbles in Houston, Denver and Miami, the beat downs always overhyped and true. Hair bleach, tatts, wife beaters, forties and sneakers. Beats, bass, tempo. Rhyme, spit, verse. Uppers, downers, roofies, poppies and snow. Gunshots, pills, journals and worm holes. Hollywood film sets and Scarlett starlets, Oscar noms, broken-hearted moms, lyric sheets, dedications, shout-outs, endorsements, VIP rooms, cocaine brooms, name-drops, cops, race cards, turf wars, record execs and all the excess that made Ghost public enemy number one and, for a time, the One.

Yes, yes. But you don't know my story. Which is, in a way, funny. Because without Ghost, his excess and success, I wouldn't have a story. He would never have needed a body double, and I, James Hastings, born with eerily similar genetic cues, would have gone into a different line of work. I would not have washed my hair in peroxide and dressed like him for Halloween. Strangers in the bar that night would never have said *Oh my God it's him!* Stacey would never have urged me to enter that radio station contest. I would not have landed in the local paper, then the AP wire and *USA Today*'s annual celebrity lookalike feature, where I caught the attention of Ghost's manager. I might have followed a more traditional path for an aspiring actor, serving lettuce wraps at P. F. Chang's and taking heroin to cure my blues. If I had not pretended to be someone else, my girl might never have left me, in which case we could have gone on to a brighter future, any future, together.

If only. I would gladly choose heroin addiction to . . . this.

But Ghost needed a double, I needed the money, and – I can barely admit this now – it sounded like a lot of fun at the time. Being a part of his world, imagining that his career was my career, his lifestyle my lifestyle. I fell for all of it, and it felt good to be looked at the way they looked at him, always with that mixture of fear, lust, need. He never needed me more than when he was on top of the world.

To tell the truth, by then I think Ghost was sick of looking at me. This is understandable. I was sick of looking at him, too. No one wants to go around being shadowed by his *doppelgänger*. In a way, that's what I was doing all along. Watching the bigger, bolder, more talented version of myself, the self I would never be. Not that I ever had the chops, or even wanted to be a rapper. But a somebody, a superstar? Who doesn't want to be one of those for a day?

A possible irony: in the year that has passed since I terminated my employment, Ghost has pulled another disappearing act. Retirement, rehab, hiding in Bulgaria. No one knows. Or maybe they do know and I just haven't been paying attention. And so what if he did retire his jersey? There may never be another rapper, of any skin color, to equal him. But he's made his mark. The work stands. He will always be remembered . . .

I hope the foul-mouthed white motherfucker is dead. I hope his death was not a peaceful one. If his reaper came in the form of so many pills, I hope they dissolved him inside out over a period of days, leaving a slug trail of his blood on the linoleum where he screamed his last. If the black curtain descended on him in the form of jealous star or enraged record executive, I hope his murderer scooped his eyeballs from his skull with a cantaloupe baller, severed his limbs with a dull machete, made a gasoline pyre of his remains and salted the earth where his ashes were buried.

If he's not dead and he does come back, he can tell his own wretched story.

We are in the aftermath. It's my turn to serve it up. But I'm not writing this to gain your sympathy. I'm not even writing it for you, whoever you may be. In fact, unless something terrible and irreversible happens to me, unless something worse than death comes for me, this growing document will never see the light of day.

I'm laying it down for the same reason he wrote all those mad thumping addictively dark songs. I have to get it out of me. I don't know if such a thing is possible, but I have to try. I can't live like this. I can't live with the black holes in my memory, the negative spaces that host the demons and invite the waking nightmares in.

I'm writing this because I need to remember. I need to remember Stacey.

Now I have a ghost story to tell you.

disc 1

the husband

1

The first thing, though, is that my wife didn't really leave me.

Stacey left the house for work, back when she was on mornings at the garden center in the Marina. She was scheduled for only fifteen hours a week or so, just enough that she didn't have to ask me for money to pay for her flowers and the little bird baths and crystal balls she collected for the gardens in our backyard. She developed interests abruptly and obsessively, changed jobs accordingly, and for the past nine months she had approached gardening like a combat soldier, all biceps and lip dew, wading in wearing surplus shorts, Kevlar kneepads, a paisley bandana on her head and the serrated, Japanese bayonet-like Hori-Hori strapped to her thigh. In lieu of a paycheck she brought home hundreds of dollars' worth of flora. She liked to lose herself in the labor, sometimes coming to bed with dried soil on her legs, her nails grimy for days at a time, which I found kind of sexy, I admit. Hot wife getting dirty and all that. I thought she took the job to maintain a sense of independence, but now I understand it was a reason to get out of the house, away from me.

To get from our home in West Adams to Marina del Rey, she had to take the alley behind 21st up to Arlington, Arlington to Washington Boulevard, follow Washington westbound for about seven miles, then slide down Lincoln, all of which, at 8 a.m., can eat an hour. Of course the Ten is another option, but though it is a five-lane Interstate in each direction, at that hour traffic is so bad it makes you want to join the Taliban.

Stacey didn't like using the alley. But I told her to keep her car in the garage for security reasons, and the alley was the quickest route in and out of the neighborhood, so she used it.

The night before, we'd been fighting. Actually, Stacey and I never really fought. We had extended silences. A cold, hard distance had grown between us slowly, over a period of months. After a couple years of living here, Los Angeles was too much for her. The noise, the pollution, all the usual problems. Kids who grow up in the City of Angeles, it's like a second skin, their natural reef. They learn to surf the city like those stoned turtles in *Nemo*. But Stacey and I grew up with land. Trees, hills, the Arkansas River. Tulsa was the Big City. She was depressed, but it seemed somehow worse and simpler than that. I just thought she had bad mood swings, boredom.

This dimming phase followed the latest backlash from Ghost's final studio album, *Snuffed*, the tour for which I was not invited to join and which he cancelled halfway through, seeking treatment for 'exhaustion'. I was held back in Los Angeles, positioned to throw off the media.

My job was to make them think he was here, bopping around town, not checked into Brighton or wherever he decided to take his spas and counseling that year.

When I wasn't out doing faux-cameos at clubs or letting kids with their iPhones snap photos of me at malls in Topanga or Long Beach, I worked on the play I planned to direct (it was a hunk of shit). I knew my run with Ghost was coming to an end and Trigger, my manager, was throwing out lines for casting directors, trying to convince them I possessed a range that extended beyond the one-note performance that was scowling like Ghost and slinking away from fans who couldn't tell us apart. Pining for the role of a *Law & Order* perp, I would have accepted a commercial pouring that blue piss into a diaper.

I usually didn't fall asleep until about four or five in the morning and slept on the couch so I wouldn't wake her. I rarely heard her leave the house. I'd rise at eleven, drink coffee, catch up on email, check the casting newsletters and boards. The afternoons were spent working on my play until Stacey got home from work or spending the day with her friends over in Los Feliz.

Perhaps it is my fault she wound up with such friends. I was the one who encouraged her to make the effort. Her friends back in Tulsa were a diverse group, waitresses, bartenders, musicians, art geeks and other school acquaintances making their first forays into the corporate machine before doing the non-profit pull-out and segueing into early motherhood. The LA friends she made through the art gallery and through my end of the business were, like us, transplants, aspiring toward something rarer, with a drive that Stacey found off-putting. They were louder, effervescent to a clamoring degree, hungry for It – and if It demanded becoming the kind of club habitant who lets strange men snort illicit powders from her nipples in the bathroom stall, well, that was just part of the ride.

Whereas Stacey was quiet and never seemed to abandon herself to the giddy cocktail of whatever scene she enjoyed watching, her new LA friends operated as if downing martinis and shrieking at waitresses was the secret to being noticed by the A-list set. They popped pills, chased married men, shoplifted out of boredom and stabbed each other in the back more or less weekly. I think they adopted Stacey as a corruptible country girl, and maybe she was an uncomfortable reminder of how much of themselves they had shed since getting off the bus from Tacoma, Denver, Boise. And they wore her down. Rowina Daniels, the kleptomaniac from North Carolina, she was the one who got Stacey into shoplifting. I'd already been to the police annex in the Riverside Outlet Mall twice that year. Found a tiny pair of cable cutters in Stacey's purse. That's not right. Maybe when your girl is fourteen. Not when she's thirty-one and your wife.

That morning, *the morning of*, as the police later called it, I didn't see her leave the house. She didn't call. By evening I was worried. I called her friends, but they hadn't seen her. I called the garden center, then the art gallery, but she wasn't scheduled for either that day.

Finally I was standing over the sink, watching the day give way to dusk. I looked through the window, not really even looking for anything, just thinking maybe it was time to call the police. That's when I noticed the garage door was open. The detached garage was a drive through, so there were two doors, one inside the yard that opened onto the driveway, the other into the alley. I had the sick feeling then, looking at that door. This shadowed hole, calling me from across the yard. I pretended she had just forgotten to shut it, or maybe the battery in her garage door opener had stopped working, but deep down I knew something bad was waiting for me in there.

I drank a glass of water and went out. I didn't run. I just sort of ambled across the yard, annoyed. And about halfway there I saw her white Audi deep in the garage.

Time jumped a bit.

One second I was standing in the yard. The next I was standing beside the S5, the driver's side door open, her keys dangling in the ignition. The engine was off. In the console cup holder was a tall plastic tumbler full of her iced coffee. Cubes melted, the creamer floating in white clumps. The car was set too deep, its ass end sticking out into the alley.

My first thought was, *Oh dear God, some psycho in a van snatched her, he's on his way to Utah with her right now. Just like that Ghost song, 'Take My Wife'.* The gravity of this, and the evil images that came with it, made me pant. Then I imagined she had left me. I almost wished she had some other man on the side, because I knew whatever was coming would be worse.

'No,' I said in the garage. *This is not a crime scene*. 'She got distracted.'

Once again time seemed to slip.

I was standing in the alley. I looked both ways. And there was a couch I didn't remember, a riot orange thing with velvet upholstery and great gouts of dirty foam sprung from the cushions. It was the color of insanity. Someone told me that, once – orange is the color of insanity. But I never gave it much thought until I looked at that couch. It wasn't a little rip or one bad cushion. The fabric was shredded, the wooden frame splintered. Springs pulled so hard they'd gone straight as knitting needles. I have seen some fucked-up shit in that alley, but that couch looked like some four-hundred pound Mongoloid with one eye and a heart full of PCP had come at it with a Samurai sword and just didn't stop until his arms fell off.

There were candy wrappers and trash piled around it. And there was a roll of dark brown carpet behind it, folded over like a tortilla, with fresh weeds stuck to it. I traced the drag marks, which formed a long trail, and noticed tire tracks, fat and wide patches of bald dirt where someone had skidded. Another twenty feet back, on the other side of the garage, the weeds had gone dead-fish white from being covered for months.

I walked to the carpet and my hand just reached down and pulled it off, easy as pulling a clean flat sheet from a mattress. I stared down at the broken body and the face

14

with the eye looking at me, and the weeds and sludge layers of caked purple blood in her snow-blonde hair and it settled on me, a heavy black pair of stinking leather wings that embedded themselves, becoming a part of me.

'Oh, sweetie.' I fell to my knees beside her. I began to brush the road from her hair. 'Oh, my sweet girl . . .'

I was afraid to touch her and hurt her. Make her worse. But I couldn't leave her. I pushed my hands under her back and legs and scooped her in my arms. I carried the woman I had known since fourth grade through the garage and over the yard. I held her until we were inside, where I rested her on the couch. The house was empty, ten thousand miles from civilization. I made a support of the pillow under her head and pulled a blanket up to her neck and I kissed her. We were sixteen the first time we kissed and never had made the decisions that brought us here. I lowered my face onto her stomach and it went through me like cold blades.

There was a sound in the air, like a tea kettle reaching steam. For a minute I thought it was the sirens, but there were no sirens. It was just this awful high-pitched piping sound, a screaming coming through the walls, closer and closer until it was drilling into my ears. It made me sick and I ran from her, into the kitchen, where I bent over the sink and heaved until my legs gave out.

Time was no longer slipping. At this point it was scattering like sheets of dirty newspaper in a high-velocity wind tunnel.

I lost track of things. A lot of things.

15

What I remember next is being in the upstairs bathroom. I was looking up at the paintings of the rabbits on the bathroom wall, Stacey's rabbits, the morose paintings she loved, God knows why, and then I was reeling away and running into the hall, back down the stairs and I might have been screaming for somebody to help me. I needed to call somebody. The little red Motorola she had given me for my birthday was sitting on the dining-room table, not fifteen feet from the sun room where I had been working all afternoon. I rarely checked this phone. I was always busy checking The Leash. That's what she called the BlackBerry phone Ghost, Inc. used to communicate with me. I opened my red cell and started to dial 9-1-1 and that's when the little voicemail envelope popped up on the screen.

You have one voice message.

I stood there wondering if I could go back in time. I was afraid to turn around and see her on the couch. Everything in me slowed and I listened to the message she had left me at 9.12 a.m., almost ten hours earlier.

I don't know why she hadn't called the home phone. Maybe she was in a panic. Maybe a darker thing inside her didn't really want me to answer. But she left me the message, probably sitting in her car, right before she backed out of the garage. She had to have been sitting there, because she never got past the alley and if she had been in the house she would have talked to me face to face. I'd have heard her crying. She was crying so hard and I was sleeping on the couch, less than a hundred feet away from her. Did I hear it ring? I might have. I might have heard it and rolled over, pulling a pillow over my head and going back to sleep while she was begging.

'Where are you? James, where are you? You're never home and I'm so scared, I can't, I can't, I don't understand what's happening any more. I . . .' Her crying faded for a few more seconds and then the message ended.

She must have started to back out then. I don't know who or what gave her pause. All I know is who didn't stop her that morning, the night before, and all the nights when she was drifting toward oblivion – the man who had made a vow to protect her for the rest of her life.

So, my wife didn't really leave me, is the thing to remember. I left her, not the other way around.

I left my little rabbit all alone.

The detective who worked Stacey's case, Tod Bergen, took me for a drink a couple weeks after. He was a burly guy with tight hair and a pink face behind clear-framed glasses, a near-albino you might find managing a Swedish furniture boutique. He was a good cop as far as I could tell, and a smart one. He'd been on the job for sixteen years, said this kind of thing happened in Los Angeles more often than anyone wanted to admit. Ten million people. Too many cars. Enough pedestrians and cyclists thrown in to keep things interesting. You'd think with so many people crammed into so few square miles, there'd always be a witness.

But this was not so, Bergen explained while I sat beside him at the bar, numb and mute with contempt for

17

everything that breathed. 'Last year we worked a case up in Bel Air. Male jogger, fifty-eight, not the guy on top of the studio, but one of the big guys in line. He was run over by a Corolla, both the car and the jogger abandoned. Mr Mogul'd been lying under the Toyota for two days when someone finally called to have the car towed. They don't like Corollas in Bel Air. The driver had it attached to his wrecker before he noticed the running shoe . . .'

'She was accepting,' I said. My head felt like the machine that turns cabbage into coleslaw. 'I keep trying to find the right word to describe her. I should know by now. But accepting is the only one I can think of.'

'Well, it happens,' Bergen said. 'That's all I'm saying. You can't look for a reason, or blame yourself. Don't even start down that road, son.'

'She accepted me. She accepted this life. The whole world.'

'That's a rare quality,' Bergen said.

The takeaway – she had stepped into the alley at the wrong time. Maybe she was saving a cat or picking up trash. Maybe a drunk behind the wheel, some working stiff coming off the third shift. The severity of the damage to her torso suggested a truck, but no one saw a truck, if that's what it was. No one heard the brakes. No one saw a fucking thing.

Maybe if we had leaked my connection with Ghost to the press, we would have come up with something. But his people and the police advised against this, suggesting it would only clutter the phone lines with bullshit tips, a bunch of loonies trying to get in on the excitement. Stacey's parents blamed me, and left me out of their own investigations, if they pursued any. Her father, Roy, was just broken, reduced to a shard of dry chalk. Linda, her mother, told me I deserved to rot in hell, which I guess I did. My parents, both older, retired evangelicals back in Oklahoma City, had written me off years ago. My mother said I had sold my soul to Satan, which I guess I had. I didn't want it to become a tabloid item, one of those forty-word snippets in *US Weekly*: Celeb Lookalike Loses Wife. I didn't fight this advice to let it go. I wonder now if that was a mistake.

I don't wonder if it was more cowardice on my part – I know it was.

Stacey was cremated, her ashes sifted into her garden behind our home. I emailed a letter of resignation to Trigger, which he forwarded to Ghost's business manager. It went unchallenged. I stopped dyeing my hair platinum blond and let it grow. I visited a dermatologist in Hollywood for two hours of laser tattoo removal three times a week until the most visible copies (on my arms, my neck, stomach) were reduced to raw pink baby flesh (yes, it is just like going to bed on fire). I grew a short beard and saw an optometrist who would prescribe a new pair of tortoise-shell frames to further disguise me as plain old me, and learned that I actually needed a prescription.

'You have astigmatism of the left eye,' the rotund, white-smocked man told me, patting my thigh with a small plastic paddle. I think his name was Robert

Bryans, or Brian Roberts. One of those two first-name names. 'It's not serious, but you should wear glasses at night, especially when driving. You will also enjoy going to the movies a lot more now. The screen won't look so out of focus.'

I didn't respond. Her left eye was the one that had burst from her skull. *It's okay, darlin'. I'm with you in spirit, or maybe you are with me. With any luck I will go blind in sympathy.*

I boxed up my Vaporware threads and the pairs of signature Converse Ghost had given me for Christmas every year. I bought some regular clothes and soon looked like every other nobody on the street. I went to the liquor store and spent eight hundred dollars. I shed his gestures, the strut, pose, tics. I dropped his speech patterns and twangs, minimized the gangsta slang. I kicked the Ghost habit once and for all, put him in a box six feet under and pissed on his proverbial grave. I dropped out of his world, and this one.

Eleven and a half months passed before I saw her again.

2

The night death came back to West Adams I wasn't spying, though it's true that by then I had developed a habit of watching my neighbors. Sometimes with my naked eye, but more often through the 80mm Zhumell spotting scope I gave Stacey for her twenty-eighth birthday. She had been in a photography phase. I had hoped the Zhumell, which could be used as a telescope or digiscope attached to a camera, would encourage her to turn her gaze skyward when she inevitably tired of taking pictures. Upon presentation, she pretended to be thrilled with her gift. But after a few days of lugging her two Nikons, gear bag, the scope and its folding tripod around the backyard, trying to turn pigeons roosting under Whitey's gables into urban art, she lost interest.

Playing the role of optimist, I moved the scope and tripod to the second-story balcony and spent fifty bucks on astronomy books. Over the next month, we shut off the TV and pretended the balcony – with its little arched roof, recessed decking and short spindled railing almost hidden in the house's façade – was our private observatory. We shared bottles of Beaujolais and discussed the possibility of alien life forms. But eventually our lives turned busy, the weather cooled and the entire rig was abandoned.

Architecturally West Adams could be Anytown, USA, which is why so many scenes for movies and television shows are shot there. The banking- and commerce-heavy Koreatown lies north; South Central's bludgeoned ghettos adjacent, you guessed it, south. The skyline of downtown Los Angeles lies east, the blur of afro-centric Crenshaw and industrial Culver City to the west.

Situated in the middle of them all and cut in half by the ten lanes of infinite traffic that ride the Santa Monica Freeway, West Adams is a roughly ten- by twelve-block enclave of historic homes that varies wildly, a little pocket of a neighborhood where nine-hundred-thousand dollar Victorians were steps away from run-down apartment buildings with diapers on the lawns. The same seventy-foot-tall skinny palm trees swayed in front of squalid one-bedroom crack houses and restored Queen Anne mansions owned by clothing label upstarts. A five-color painted lady might sell for seven hundred and fifty thousand despite her crumbling brick foundation; a plain six-bedroom bungalow two blocks south might be had for three-fifty due to its proximity to the church/liquor store/porn video/fried chicken shack/nail salon strip mall.

We were attracted to the neighborhood because it was on the way up, was being improved by the refinancing Hispanics and blacks who had never left, was being slowly gentrified by the young and upwardly mobile, those self-anointed artists and entrepreneurs like us, the ones who weren't content with a condo or a ranch home in El Segundo; we wanted *character* and damn the risk, the gunshots, the gangs . . . those were just rumors.

After the accident, I retreated to the balcony out of respect for Stacey, who didn't like it when I smoked in the house. The tripod seemed to be waiting for me, beckoning my sozzled eye. After four hours of stargazing, Stacey's scope had become my scope, and I had my first night of real sleep in months.

I furnished my nest with a lawn chair, a small table for my ashtray and a green metal Coleman cooler my father handed down, to hold my beer. I kept a pair of flip-flops on deck, and mounted a hook under the eave to hold my black windbreaker and one of Stacey's scarves (the thick purple one of cable-knit cotton), and thus my little self-pity station was complete.

When I wasn't dreaming of launching rocket-propelled grenades at SUVs on Arlington, I saw remarkable, sometimes unexplainable things in the sky: flashes of green too slow to be comets, a jetliner whose red and green flashers blanked out under a cloudless sky, a red eyeball which seemed to vibrate looking back at me from light years away (more likely I was tanked and that one was just a stop light on Venice).

But like Stacey I soon lost interest in the stars. I learned to watch the people instead. Junkies staggering from fix to fix. Catholic schoolgirls walking home holding hands. Realtors hustling nervous newlyweds, like we had once been, into the latest remodel. Single mothers sorting credit card bills at dining-room tables. Upper-class fighting (silent candle-lit dinners which resembled aspirin commercials) and lower-class fucking (lights on, loud, dog-style). Up there on a balcony you see the life of your neighborhood, good and bad.

It was not a total escape.

Sometimes I stayed too late and drank too much, slewing dangerously close to the edge. It was a twenty-foot drop and our porch was surrounded by a concrete walk. Had I fallen, I probably would have spent the rest of my days drinking whiskey from a sippy cup. As dusk turned to true night (and my tipsy turned to true inebriation), often I would urinate off the side, into Stacey's bougainvillea. Sometimes I would stand there naked and laughing and waving my arms, waiting for someone to call the police. They never did. Spend enough time twenty-five feet off the ground, you realize no one walking or driving by ever really looks up.

I can see now that I craved human company. I had spent so much time playing the role of Ghost, a larger than life character to whom people flocked, I didn't know how to be James Hastings. I certainly did not know how to be a grieving husband. I would have liked a manual. Most of our real friends were still back in Tulsa. I didn't know how to make new connections in cafés or bars. So it wasn't long before I learned the optimal night, hour and angle to view each of my neighbors in their natural habitat, and my attentions were particular to three: the Gomez's handsome bungalow to the west, into Mr Ennis's stucco eyesore to the east and

Officer Lucy Arnold's brown Victorian across the street and three houses west.

Watching Euvaldo Gomez and his children, grandparents, cousins and their teenaged friends popping in and out was like watching a family sitcom with the sound off. There were patriarchal outbursts aimed at the calamitous dining-room table, and fits of playtime laughter on the living-room floor. Mrs Gomez was always cooking and serving food. The kids were always spilling fluorescent green or red punch. Euvaldo was an accountant with one of the firms downtown. At the end of each day, he would remove his jacket and collared shirt and tie, but not his pinstriped trousers or wingtips. He spent his evenings in his armchair while his children provoked him. I cast him as a Latino Archie Bunker, and learned to read his moods by the set of his eyebrows and the vigor with which he stabbed the remote control. They were a happy family – hardworking, celebratory, always in motion right up until bedtime, when the household would collapse into deserved peace.

With a swivel of the wrist, it was onto the next house.

Officer Lucy Arnold and I had history. She was a tall brunette, athletic with sinewy arms and almost imperceptible breasts, a bicycle fuzz prowling Venice Beach. Of all things for a cop to be, she was shy. She claimed to be the ugly duckling from high school, but she was all right. Proximity and professional courtesy opened the door for her, I welcomed her offer to help, and soon Officer Arnold became just Lucy. A casual friend and inside line to the department, my wallflower mole.

As the updates on Stacey's case lost any new wrinkles, Lucy and I entered a routine of twice- or thrice-weekly happy hours which consisted of drinks on my porch, banter about her day and tender inquiries into my 'process'. Now and then, when the Friday margaritas were blended a little too strong, Lucy would make some sort of flush-faced overture, usually a hug, or the wiping of a tear (hers) in amazement at my stoicism (numb drunkenness) in the face of such loss. We fumbled our way through a couple of her sports bras and somehow, as we crossed paths one afternoon in the kitchen – me emerging from the bathroom, she turning from the fridge with two cold beers – she wound up giving me a handy in front of the stove. But she wouldn't let me reciprocate just then, perhaps sensing I had nothing to offer. The clumsy tangle of our increasingly sad happy hours became too much for me to endure. She understood. She would be there if I needed someone to talk to.

I didn't believe she was being opportunistic, trying to land a vulnerable man now that his wife was out of the picture. She was just a nice woman with the misfortune to be on the receiving end of my mixed signals. *Help, thank you for dinner, now leave me alone.* We cooled off. Six months passed. Our exchanges on trash day or in the produce aisle at Ralph's were still pleasant, but I seldom watched her any more.

By the time the incident with Mr Ennis happened, I had stopped thinking about Lucy Arnold altogether.

If the Gomezes were my sitcom, Mr Ennis was my still life. I never learned his real station in life, but my money was on lifelong bachelor or early widower, because I never saw anyone pay Mr Ennis a visit. No minivan arrived to spill grandkids onto his lawn, no old bag in her housedress ever vacuumed around his feet. He was like a grandpa silverback gorilla, the one you see at the zoo with half a dozen bananas lying around him because he no longer gives a shit and just wishes someone would shoot a dart into him. His living room was a diorama of mid-century couches, home-made lamps of cut-bottle glass, a vinyl ottoman and brandy snifter terrarium filled with peat moss and a tiny rubber turtle resting on a log. Sometimes Mr Ennis leaned over the terrarium and spoke to the turtle. I would have paid large sums to hear these conversations. I nicknamed the turtle Tiny Mr Ennis.

Mr Ennis lived a life of solitude and grunt sustenance, appearing magically in his chair around seven with a frozen chicken dinner still in the tin. He set these meals upon a folding TV tray and watched an hour and a half of local news, then *Wheel of Fortune*, the letter blocks shining bricks of white light across his chest and face and the oily sofa that propped him up like a short, meaty mannequin. After Vanna and Pat said goodnight, it was cop shows, heroic high drama until bedtime at ten sharp.

Initially there was something comforting in his isolation, a reminder that I was not necessarily the loneliest soul in our corner of the city. But toward the end I watched him with a gnawing hopelessness, too aware that if I continued on my present course his fate would soon be mine.

27

That evening, when the one-year anniversary of Stacey's death was less than two weeks away, I checked in on all the usual suspects, but there was scant entertainment to be had. The air turned cool for March and I smelled rain.

I ducked back into the house and descended the stairs, on my way to retrieve another beer from the fridge. The wide landing was covered with a floral runner. Above the landing's center, at eye level, was a porthole window that faced east. There wasn't much to see out this window, except for the wild tangle of juniper bushes that threatened to overtake Mr Ennis's shitbox abode and, I suspected, played hell with my allergies every summer.

As I passed the window, a pale face with a great yawning mouth swam over its surface. I startled and turned quickly, the way you do when someone on the street bumps shoulders with you. The face that confronted me was my own. Just a reflection created by the chandelier hanging in the foyer below me, and the outer darkness pressing itself against the house. I exhaled and rolled my shoulders before moving on.

Except that I hadn't been yawning, I realized. The image I glimpsed had been yawning or stretching its jaw in some demonstration of power. Also, there had been a wave of blonde hair above the pale face. I have dark brown hair and it's messy, but it doesn't fall in any sort of wave over my face.

This kind of discrepancy does not usually trouble your average drunkard. We see spots, doorways tilt. But

28

maybe by then I was conditioned to sense a new opportunity for spying, always looking for the parted curtain, the inviting figure walking by a narrow pane. Whatever the reason, I was compelled to press my face against the glass, cupping my hands around my cheeks to block the light behind me while I squinted into the encroaching darkness.

There were Mr Ennis's juniper bushes, forming a long scraggly wall along the side of his house. Above them, about halfway back, was a frosted window with rusting metal louvers. That would be his bathroom. But by craning my neck to the left, up the lane of my driveway and toward our front lawns, I could see into his living room and kitchen.

The old round fluorescent light in the kitchen made the yellow Formica countertop glow like cartoon butter. Next to the brown, latching handle fridge and stainless steel toaster was a rack of wooden pegs with red and white checkered dish towels hanging from them. I couldn't see the table in the kitchen, but there must have been one, otherwise the vase full of flowers would have been hovering in mid-air. The vase was transparent crystal and contained half a dozen green stems supporting a bright arrangement of violets. I was thinking it rather unusual that tired old Mr Ennis had fresh flowers in his kitchen when a pale hand came into view and clasped the bunch in a knuckle-whitening fist. A long flat blade sliced and the heads of the violets toppled over. I want to say that my eyes shifted, but that's not right, because they didn't have to. It merely felt like I

29

was looking down as the woman crouched and looked up, seizing my gaze. Her face was puffy, her features blurred, the whole pie of it waxy, the color of Chèvre. But I knew the platinum hair which hung to her neck, ending in a choppy shelf. I recognized the blurred pools of icy blue where her eyes should have been, and they found me. From the corner of Mr Ennis's kitchen, across his darkened living room, through his window and up to our little porthole, Stacey looked at me.

I gasped and, as if hearing me (impossible), Mr Ennis jostled on his couch and looked over his shoulder, staring into the darkness between us. My entire body tingled and the house seemed to quake. I clutched the window frame and, when I looked back to the kitchen, she was gone. I did not see her vanish. One second she was there, the next she wasn't.

Mr Ennis heaved himself from the couch, but made it only one step before going immobile, as if deciding he didn't really need another glass of grape soda, and sank back into his couch. He continued watching his television as if nothing had happened.

I staggered away from the portal window and tripped down two steps before catching myself on the banister rail. I looked over my shoulder, down into the foyer, my mouth moving in silence as I realized there was no one around to confirm what I had seen. I considered going over and knocking on his door. But what would I say?

I returned to the couch and sat staring at the walls, a chill seeping into me. I was drunk, I decided. I never felt drunk any more, but I drank all day, steadily, continuously, so I must have been. I must have let my anxieties get the better of me. Your own reflection does strange things to you. I repeated assorted explanations to myself until I dozed off on the couch.

In the morning a slow warbling siren disturbed me from my fugue. I leapt from the couch and swerved into the foyer. I peered through the front window and Mr Ennis was just a white shape. The medics were wheeling him down the steps of his front walk on a gurney. Even before I yanked the door open and crossed my lawn to confront the police and Lucy Arnold and the firemen who could do nothing except hold back the rest of the gawkers, I understood Mr Ennis would not be coming home.

3

'How are you holding up?' Lucy Arnold said.

'Real good.' The shock was still rippling through my system. 'You want a beer?'

I counted the cases stacked beside the fridge. One, two, three, four, five, six, seven, eight, nine, ten, eleven, twelve, and most of the thirteenth. A God-blessed ocean of beer. I'd tired of having to leave late at night to buy more, so I went to Ralph's every Sunday and bought five or six cases. Tecaté, Corona, Dos Equis, whatever was on sale and Mexican. Always cans. No limes.

'It's not quite ten, James.'

'Don't mind me, then.' I loaded twenty warm Tecatés into the produce drawers, removed a cold Modelo. My hands were shaking as I gestured toward the living room. 'Have a seat.'

Lucy moved like a statue coming to life. For all her fitness activity – patrolling the boardwalk on her LAPD-issue Trek, jogging in Hancock Park, screwing Match.com buddies to the wall – she had an unnerving ability to come off stiff, always prying herself from counters or leaning tiredly against doorways. She hadn't had her shower this morning (the hair was mousy, a fleck of sleep still clung to the bridge of her nose) and her yoga pants and black t-shirt showed too much of her frame. I was reminded of Stacey, if for no other reason than Lucy was in matters physical her polar opposite. Whereas Stacey had been just over five feet tall, voluptuous in her compact frame, and – until the last year – vibrant with a contained energy that somehow fit her playful manner, perpetually grinning, Lucy was hips and elbows and clavicles, a heron at the arms and neck, always on the verge of frowning.

I sat in my Scandinavian recliner. Lucy glanced around to see what I had done with the place since her last visit, saw the answer was nothing and became a geometry problem on the couch.

'So, what's up?' she said. 'You seemed pretty shaken up out there.'

'It's been a bad week. Though obviously not as bad as Mr E's.' I poured a little beer on the floor for him.

Lucy looked at the puddle, then at me, as though I were a dog who has just lifted his leg in the house.

'It's a black thing,' I said. This did not put her at ease.

'Did you know him?' I once confessed to spying on her and she had been flattered. But that was another time, and I never told her my habits extended to the rest of our block.

'Not at all.'

'Oh.'

'That what's sad. He was just this lonely guy.'

'He was old, James. Maybe he wanted to be left alone. Is there something else bothering you?'

I remembered Stacey's face. First in the porthole window, then in his kitchen. I wondered where she was now, the question itself causing me to shudder. *It was the booze.*

'No more than usual,' I said. Lucy stared at me.

From the moment the officer in charge greeted me at the dividing line between our properties, I made up my mind that I would not tell anyone what I had witnessed.

'Coronary event is the early read,' the stone-faced cop had said. 'If you're not a relative I need you to stand back there, on your property, sir.'

Nothing I could have told the police on the scene, or the one now sitting in my living room, would have helped Mr Ennis or his family, if he had any.

'Is it the timing?' Lucy said. I didn't know what she was talking about. 'It will be a year next week, right?'

Oh, that. 'A week from Sunday,' I said. 'You don't think it's going to have any significance. It's just another day on the calendar.'

Lucy frowned. 'Of course it does. You wouldn't be human if it didn't. We're conditioned to recognize anniversaries, dates.'

I swallowed half my beer.

'Do you have plans?' she said.

'Like what?'

'Someone to spend the weekend with. I guess if it were me I would want to get out of the house, go do something good for myself.'

'No, I'm not seeing anyone.'

She sighed. I guessed I was being an asshole.

'Tell me about you. How's life on the beat?'

Lucy filled me in on a couple of her recent arrests,

34

including the apprehension of a handsome Korean masher who proved so charming she found herself jotting her number on her notepad and slipping it into his pocket before the cruiser arrived to take him in for booking. She regretted this after further inspection of his record (the previous mashees were *young*), and eventually had to change her phone number. She received a small promotion for hitting her five-year mark with a clean record. I congratulated her and the conversation veered back to actual relationships, as it tends to between single people who have been knocked out of the major leagues but haven't given up hope of receiving one more call from the front office.

'There's a guy,' she said. 'He's fine, but I knew by the second date it wasn't going anywhere.'

'He's no good in bed?'

'There's more to it than sex, James.' But she was blushing.

'Uh-huh.'

'I'm a cop. Why does every guy think this is a green light to break out the handcuffs?'

'We're always looking for the new play.'

She laughed. Okay, there was still a little something there and neither of us flinched. Despite mucking up everything I touched, there still existed in this woman some goodwill toward me. With feeble effort I could parlay it into something comforting, maybe even something real. On any other morning, but not this one.

'You look good, Lucy,' I said. 'Happy.'

She tilted her head. 'Thank you.'

A moment stretched between us.

I said, 'Now you're supposed to say how good I look.'

She cupped a hand over her grin. 'Oh, James. You look like shit.'

'See, that wasn't so hard.'

'What's going on with your hair? And the beard's getting a little unruly.'

'I'm going for a kind of nineties grunge thing.'

Neither of us could tell if I was joking.

'So, are you looking?' she asked. 'For the new play?'

'I'm a fucking mess. It never ends.'

'Do you want it to end? Because I think that's part of it. Wanting to move on.'

I finished my beer. 'What else do you know about him?'

'Who?'

'Mr Ennis.'

'Oh.' She looked disappointed I had returned to the subject of our deceased neighbor. 'Not much. I remember him mentioning a son in Barstow or Reno, I think.'

'You talked to him?'

'A few times. I invited him to that pot-luck Thanksgiving I threw two years ago. He was polite but declined. I didn't press him.'

'Could you confirm the cause of death?'

Lucy frowned. 'He had a heart attack. Didn't Troy tell you?'

'Troy?'

Lucy spun her finger in a circle. 'The officer who spoke to you before I led you home.'

'Oh, right. Did he seem, you know, at peace?'

'I don't know what you mean.'

Did he look terrified out of his fucking mind? I wanted to scream at her, but of course did not. 'Can they tell if he went quickly or if he suffered?'

'Like more than a heart attack suffered?'

'Never mind – oh, shit, wait.' I sat forward. 'The flowers. Did they find a vase full of flowers in the kitchen?'

'Flowers?'

'Yes, purple ones, with the heads cut off.'

'I have no idea.'

'Will you check?'

Lucy's patience was nearing its end. 'If it's important. Are you sure there's nothing you want to tell me? Because if you saw something—'

'No, no. I'm just . . . I had a bad dream, maybe. It's cool. I haven't slept well for a few days.' I looked at the couch. 'Thanks for coming by, though.'

She stood, not meeting my gaze. I followed her to the front door. Why did I feel like I was disappointing her again?

'Hey.' I touched her shoulder. She flinched, then regarded me with her mistrusting deer eyes. 'This weekend. Maybe we can go drink some bad Chianti and have a sing-along at Cheese & Olive's.'

She smiled. 'I'd like that.'

I nodded. 'Cool.'

'Yeah, cool.' She tensed up, debated it, then awkwardly kissed me on the corner of my mouth.

I watched her scuttle across the lawn. She glanced back as she met up with the sidewalk and waved.

I waved back. 'What do you make of that one, Stace?'

In the silence that followed, I regretted addressing my wife aloud.

Four days after Mr Ennis was wheeled out of his home, two men dressed in gray work pants and shirts emptied his belongings into a moving truck. The commercial cleaning crew – six Hispanic women and an Asian guy with a clipboard – swept through after the movers. A forty-something white man who may have been Mr Ennis's son appeared, pounding a For Rent sign into the lawn with a rubber mallet. As he was doing this, his cell-phone went off. He removed it from his pocket and spoke to someone for fifteen minutes. He clamped his phone shut and slipped it into his pocket, shaking his head and smiling ever so slightly. He then removed the For Rent sign and hucked it into his truck bed, not bothering to wipe the dirt clods from its legs.

I slept in late the next morning and missed a phone call from Lucy. Her message said, 'Hey, James, I know you're sleeping but I just wanted to let you know I spoke to the ME. Our friend died of a heart attack. He had a history of heart disease, so . . . yeah. No flowers, either, but that doesn't mean you can't bring me some. Just kidding. I don't need flowers.' Snorts and snickers of embarrassment. 'Okay, looking forward to Saturday, so I hope you're warming up your vocal chords. Call me.'

I meant to. I really did. But other developments averted my attention, and I did not call Lucy Arnold back.

This turned out to be another mistake, one of the bigger ones.

4

The era of the balcony was over. I began to wonder how much I could get for the house. I guessed I had about seventy thousand in home equity, and half as much in my checking account, where it was earning all of one point in annual interest and shrinking by five thousand a month. Three thousand went to the mortgage, the other two to bills and beer. I had enough to start over somewhere decent, and I decided I would call our realtor, David, the next morning.

I was on the covered front porch, having a smoke and a beer, when I noticed a small silver and orange U-Haul van parked in front of Mr Ennis's house. The cargo hold was bare save for a pile of gray moving blankets and a wooden rocking chair resting on its side. The metal gangplank was up, jutting from the truck's tail like a bladed tongue, suggesting the movers were done for the day. Or the new owner, since U-Haul implied you were not sipping martinis while a paid crew took another year off their backs. The sun was setting tiredly. There were no lights on inside the house. If the new residents were unpacking boxes or hooking up the television and dialing for that moving day pizza, I couldn't see them.

I blew a stream of blue smoke at a fly and swallowed the last of my beer. I was turning to go spend the rest of the night on the couch when I heard a screen door creak and then spring back into place with an obnoxious clang. On the heels of this racket, a woman's voice –

'Ow, watch it. For fuck's sake.'

Ooh, an angry one.

I waited, expecting her husband or some kid in tow to trot back to the truck and retrieve her rocking chair. But the woman who materialized on the small porch only stood and stared at the quiet street. Her chest, shoulders and hair were just a shape above the ragged juniper bushes until she listed to one side and twirled slowly into the porch light. When she stretched her arms above her head, I was able to make out a loose tank top over her snug t-shirt, one breast in the shirt bulging from the tank. Though covered, the breast gave the impression of an accidental spill that had yet to be noticed by its owner. It was a purposeful wardrobe malfunction, designed to attract attention. This was very Los Angeles, like the whale tail thong that 'accidentally' rides above the waist of the pants.

She bent over and raised a bottle of wine, pulling a respectable measure down and wiping her lips with her forearm. She hiccuped in silence and looked down as if just now realizing it had come to this. I could not see her hands. With the slightest quiver of her arm, the wine bottle shot into view, arcing high over the porch railing

40

and into the polluted pink sky before falling back to earth where it disappeared into the juniper bushes. A damn good-looking broad, littering like it was the seventies.

Oh baby, feeling my buzz, *I just fell right the fuck in love with you*.

Her need came at me in a warm pulse. Somehow I knew she was alone and not thrilled to be here. Someone had driven her from her last home and this was the last stop before things went from bad to beyond redemption. I imagined a boyfriend with four motorcycles and a fierce left jab.

She turned, facing me across the expanse of grass and driveway between us. I waved my beer can at her half-heartedly. 'Hello,' I said too quietly for her to hear. My porch light was not turned on, so I guessed she had no way to know I was smiling.

She slumped and turned away. Her screen door creaked and slammed itself home for the night.

Nice roll, Hastings. Another gutter ball.

Inside I flicked on every light as I floated through the main floor: dining room, living room, gallery, sun room, laundry, both first-floor bathrooms and kitchen. Light was good, light was essential. The house was too large to live in alone, and the downstairs had become my domain. The bathroom had a shower, I kept a basket of clothes in the laundry room, and the living room lived up to its name spectacularly. I made my bed on the couch and dozed off.

*

41

The home phone trilled, startling me awake. I don't answer the phone most days, but I arose with the hope it might be Lucy Arnold calling to chat about the arrival of our new neighbor. I was hoping to draw out some gossip on the son from Barstow, why he had cleaned the house out so quickly, and who this new tenant might be. I marched over and stared at the cordless cradle on the end table. The time was 1.28 a.m. and the small gray screen read CALLER UNKNOWN. On the fifth ring I picked up.

'Hello.'

The connection was there, but no one spoke. I thought it might be one of those automated bank reminders that dials through a database of customers and patches a service representative through only after the machine has recognized a voice. Were the computers calling in the middle of the night now?

'Hello?' I repeated.

Normally I would have clicked off after three or four seconds, but something told me to wait. I sensed a person there, listening, huddled in a darkened room.

'Can I help you?'

'I want her back,' a man said. The voice was as thin and lifeless as any I had heard, the voice of a disgraced violin tutor after three glasses of Chardonnay.

'Who is this?'

'I want her back.'

'Who?' I said. 'Who's calling?'

'I want her baaa-*aaack*.' The voice cracked, on the verge of tears. 'Please bring her back to me, please. I'll do anything you want.'

One of Lucy's cast-off suitors? The rejected masher or some other nut job who'd been stalking her? Had some psychotic lover seen us together again and decided to turn his aggression on me? Was he even now watching her, me, the house?

'Oh, Stacey,' the man wailed. 'I'm so sorry I wasn't there, please come back—'

I slammed the phone down, jamming the OFF button with my thumb until the handset skittered off the cradle and fell to the living room's hardwood floor. I was shaking, and almost regurgitated the dregs of my Mexican beer dinner. I recognized the voice on the other end of the line.

It belonged to James Hastings.

I stared at the machine that had just reproduced my voice as if it were a small vessel sent to earth, designed to deliver an organic evil that was even now waiting to hatch in my living room. Black molded plastic, some microchips and wires, a fibrous speaker pad and microphone. It was only a cluster of dead matter, chemicals and compounds, things dug from the ground and brewed in a lab. I knew this, and yet it might as well have been a giant black spider with gleaming red eyes. I felt . . . *invaded*.

I stared at the caller ID screen. It was blank now, of course, because no one was calling. But there were two little plastic arrows next to the gray screen, one pointing up and the other down. I pressed the down button and stared at the number. 310-822—

'Bullshit,' I heard myself say. It was our home number, my home number.

The time stamp was 1.28 a.m., precisely one minute ago.

How do you dial yourself? I remembered playing that game as a teenager. You did a sort of double click thing with the hang-up tab, waited for the second dial tone, then dialed your own number and hung up. No, that wasn't it. You didn't even have to dial your number. Back then, all you had to do was double-tap the hang-up tab and then leave it depressed and after about three seconds your own phone would ring. Could phones still do that?

I picked the handset off the floor and set it on the cradle and waited for ten seconds. I lifted the handset and pressed TALK twice, heard the pause and the second dial tone, then hung up. Thirty seconds passed, then a full minute, then two. The phone did not ring. I tried it again. The phone did not ring. Maybe cordless phones didn't work that way, or maybe the phone company had discontinued the feature due to too many pranks. I was considering calling the phone company to ask how I could call myself when the phone rang again.

I rocked back on my heels and reached for it, but hesitated. I checked the caller ID screen again. It was my number. I picked up the handset and pressed TALK. I held the phone to my ear. I did not speak.

There was a connection. I could not hear anyone.

After half a minute or so, my mouth unglued. 'Hello?'

No one replied.

'Hello?'

You were only imagining it. You're still drunk.

'Who is this?' I said. 'Are you recording me? Listen—'

A woman sighed heavily, and for a long time. 'AAAAaaaaaaahhhhhhh . . .'

It was not a sigh of pleasure or distress. She sounded as though she were being forced to make some ill-defined vowel sound for an instructor, or a doctor holding a wooden depressor on her tongue, shining a light down to her tonsils – and it made the skin of my arm crawl.

The line went dead, and immediately following the barely perceptible click there was a single *thunk* above my head. Something had just fallen to the floor. Or been dropped. Something that might have been a phone, my phone, the one I never used any more and which had been charging in the darkness of the master bedroom for almost half a year.

Someone was in the house.

I took four steps with the phone in my hand, then realized I was a coward and was not going to march up the stairs and confront anyone. I did not own a baseball bat or any other weapon. The police. Call the police, I thought. Call Lucy Arnold and tell her to round up her brethren, we have a situation.

I pressed the TALK button again. There was no dial tone. I pressed it twice, waited and tried the line again. It was flat, dead. I was frightened, and then angry as well as frightened. Angry for being such a coward. Ghost wouldn't stand here like a little bitch. Ghost would march up there with a butcher knife and shred anyone who dared to trespass in his castle.

I went to the kitchen and yanked open the utensil

drawer. I found a long meat fork with a thick black handle. I shoved the phone into my back pocket and walked to the stairs. I went up at a steady pace, determined not to slow down or panic. I made it to the landing and flipped on the hall light. I listened for any movement and heard nothing. I squeezed the meat fork handle and began my circuit of the halls, which formed a rectangle around the ballroom – a space smaller than it sounds and might once have been a library or large study of some sort, but which Stacey had decided would become the ballroom – at the house's center.

The first longer leg of this rectangle, immediately off the stairs, was flanked by a linen closet, then the main bathroom, followed by another closet and finally the master bedroom at the end. I checked the bathroom and the closets, opening and closing the doors with delicate precision. None contained a person. I continued to the master bedroom and found the door closed. Had I left it open or closed? I could not remember, and it didn't matter much because Olivia, the woman who cleaned the house every two weeks, might have shut it after her dusting or whatever she did in there nowadays. She could have left it open, too, and the fact was I had no way of knowing. The master bedroom was maybe halfway across the house from the living room. It might have been the bedroom phone that had been dropped, but the noise I heard had sounded closer than that, toward the center of the house.

I decided to check the other rooms first and finish my inspection in the master. I walked around the ballroom's doors, into the second long hallway. I checked the three smaller bedrooms, the second half-bathroom and the wider closet where we stored the Christmas tree decorations and other boxed junk we rarely used.

All of the rooms were empty. I backtracked, passing the ballroom's double doors again, and suddenly wanted to be in the master bedroom and done with this distraction. I twisted the knob and barged in, the meat fork at my side. I flipped the light on.

The bed was made. Everything was neat, ordered, just as I had left it. Olivia had kept it clean, ready for my return. It was like a hotel room, the sheets folded back, the pillows plumped. The walk-in closet harbored no trespasser.

On the nightstand was a square lamp with a clear glass base, the clock radio and the telephone. The handset was standing appropriately erect on the cradle. No one was here. No one had used the phone. No one was in the house. The *thunk* sound was just one of those random old house sounds.

Unless the thing that made the random old house sound is in the ballroom. Go on, you big pussy.

No, I wasn't going in there tonight. There wasn't a phone in the ballroom, and this inspection was about the phone, the caller. Nothing more.

So, who had called me? And how did they manage to replay my voice? My voice, repeating things I said months ago, back when I spent a good portion of the evenings drunk and bawling and talking to myself so that I didn't have to listen to her voice in my head – or

47

worse, the vacuum of silence when she refused to talk to me? Had I used the phone then? Had I called someone in my misery? Could they have recorded me and played it back to taunt me? Who would do such a thing?

No one called me these days, except for Lucy. Everyone else had stopped calling months ago, when they realized I wasn't going to leave Los Angeles until I was good and ready. *It's better to leave him alone*, they said, though they couldn't understand how I could stay in *that house*.

This house. This bedroom, our bedroom, the room I could no longer sleep in. I went to the dresser and opened a drawer. Stacey's socks. Little balls of pink and yellow and white. And then her 'winter' socks, the plain athletic socks that used to bunch up in piles at her ankles as she padded around the house when January subjected us to fifty degree mornings. I closed the drawer. The next was packed tightly with what I had come to think of as house shirts, old t-shirts that began their life as mine, were adopted by Stacey, and eventually belonged to both of us. The kind of shirts you put on to paint a chair on the patio. I unrolled a black one featuring a cheesy airbrush-type painting of a nude woman standing on a tree limb in a mystical forest, her back to me as the full moon swelled yellow in a faery sky. Wolfmother, it said. One of Stacey's favorite bands. I pressed it to my face and inhaled. It smelled like dust.

I dropped it and closed the drawer, opening another to the top right. Here was a collection of my underwear. I stared at them, trying to make sense of the order, the neat way they had been folded and stacked. Did a certain portion of women in the world fold boxers in thirds, sides in, and then in half, top to bottom, until they were a perfect square? I always thought Stacey wasted her time folding my underwear this way.

'Just wad them into a ball and shove them into my dresser,' I had told her on at least a dozen occasions. 'I don't care how they look, save yourself the trouble.'

And she would always frown at me as she continued folding, her movements growing more graceful and yet somehow robotic as if she were defying me by playing the role of laundry geisha. 'It's nicer this way, James,' she would say.

That was another of her Stacey-isms I had forgotten about.

It's nicer this way.

Stace, why do you always put the same Otis Redding CD on when we have company over for dinner? *It's nicer this way.* I would catch her using her special bottle of lemon polish on the wooden coffee table-trunk despite the fact that Olivia had sponge-cleaned it earlier that day. Why don't you just tell Olivia to do that next time? And Stacey, my wife, my little imperfect, white-haired wife would double-wrap the cloth around her middle and pointer fingers and massage the oil into the dark knots and, almost beneath her breath, say, 'It's nicer this way.' I made fun of her for the way she misted the bedspread with her pouch of jasmine water right before we crawled in to have the sex (that one was a James-ism, 'the sex'), treating our ordinary, Crate & Barrel bedroom like some boudoir, and she would lift her chin and look away from me and say, 'It's nicer this way.'

I realized that I was holding a pair of my boxer shorts, the orange paisley one that only days ago I had worn and left in the plastic basket that served as my downstairs hamper, and I realized that I was crying again. Somehow, in the past three days, they had made the trek from the laundry room to this dresser, where they were folded into thirds, then in half, a perfect square. That was some kind of magic, a trick that broke my heart even as I began to shake with fear.

She had been right. Always.

It was nicer this way.

5

Saturday I bought a gun.

Actually, I didn't buy it. My neighbor, Hermes, gave it to me. He worked out of his Navigator at the end of the block, on the corner in front of his green shingle. The house was in his mother's name, but it belonged to Hermes. A man named Jaysun kept an office with a view out the third-story turret, where he could spot po-po coming from six blocks in any direction. The rest of the crew usually clustered in a circle, dealing, texting, chilling, waiting for the action, soaking up the heat and arguing about sports.

Before our driveway was repaved and the garage rebuilt, Stacey and I had to park on the street. This meant that when we came home from late dinners or clubs, back when we still went out on Sunset and pretended we were somebody, we often had to park two or three blocks from our front door. We had noticed Hermes and his crew, and the cars that slowed, the handshakes through the window before they sped off.

'Do you think they're dealing?' Stacey had asked.

'They're not waiting for the school bell to ring,' I answered.

We were two frightened white kids from Tulsa, progressive but still essentially Middle American. But the idea of crossing the street, in our own neighborhood, to avoid threading our way through a pack of six black men blocking the sidewalk, seemed wrong. The first time we met them, it was after midnight and the block was dead silent. Dew on the lawns, a gritty mist in the air. When we were ten feet away, I cleared my throat.

'Hey, guys, how's the night?'

'What up, dawg,' one of them said very slowly, exhaling a raft of blunt smoke over our heads.

'Late dinner, drinks,' I said as we stopped and joined them. 'We're in the white house up on the left. Just moved in a few months ago.'

'I'm Stacey, this is my husband James,' Stacey cut in. 'You guys should come by some time for a cocktail tour. We're still remodeling but you're welcome anytime.'

I tried to mask my alarm at my wife's invitation.

'Right on,' the tallest one said, his eyes going up and down Stacey's one-piece Adidas dress. He was built like an NFL linebacker and handsome enough to make a black dress shirt and track pants look formal. He had long dreads and his eyes were the color of a dragon's. 'Hermes,' he said, offering me the other blunt making the rounds.

'I'm good,' I said. 'But thank you.'

Stacey stepped up, hit it and quit it. Hermes grinned in approval, first at her, then at me. That was my girl. Neither of us liked to smoke pot. We were bar kids, kept to the sauce. Later Stacey discovered pills, for different reasons. But leave it to my wife to go the extra mile in order to bond with our neighbors. To her, this small act was no different from the yellow chocolate cake she had baked and delivered to the Gomez's two weeks earlier. It was the right thing to do.

'Yo, Herm,' a man leaning against the Navi said. 'Dis nigga look like Ghost.'

'I get that a lot,' I said. I did not feel like explaining my job just then, though that would prove useful later. The black community respected Ghost, and some of that respect naturally spilled over to me, even after they learned I was his *fugazi*.

'You the ones with that howlin' diggy?' one of the others said. He was short and his Lakers jersey fell to his knees.

'That's Jaysun,' Hermes said

'Henry is Stacey's beagle,' I said.

'Rawr-ooo rawr-ooo!' Jaysun said, and we all laughed.

Hermes and Jaysun came by a few weeks later and had a beer on our porch, filling us in on some of the local flavor. I confessed my role as Ghost's untalented twin and hooked them up with some tenth-row tickets to a show at the Hollywood Bowl. It was all good. No one – from within our sketchy neighborhood or trolling from another part of the city – ever fucked with our house or the car. This was something, considering I had just bought Stacey a loaded S5, the down payment for which came from that skit Ghost and I did on MTV. The one where it appeared as though Ghost was performing an autopsy on himself, before returning from Heaven with a machete to carve up those who dared to try and take his place. The skit was later licensed by one of the 'edgy' soda companies, became a hit in Japan. Hastings gets a bonus.

So when I decided I needed a gun – just for some added security – there was no question of who I would turn to. I just took a short walk down to the corner and waited by the hydrant, chinning in his direction. Hermes's driver, a grinning man who weighed at least three hundred pounds and went by Salaucey or just Sal, leaned out the window and waved me forward.

I stepped up to the window. We made small talk for a minute. Then they recognized the look on my face.

Leaning across the Navi's console, Hermes said, 'Whatcha need, G?'

I made my request. Hermes didn't ask why and refused to accept my four hundred dollars.

'You take good care of this block, Hastings. Shit, my house gone up sixty K, all the home improvement you done.'

'You been looking at real estate comps?' I said. 'You can't move out on me, Herm. Not now.'

'Nah, man. I ain't goin' nowhere. This here my home. But I talk to the brokers same as everybody else. I know what I'm holdin'.'

'So, what do I do now?'

'Now you go home and chill. Give it an hour, then check your recycle bin. Come see me you run into any pro'lems.'

'My recycling bin?'

Hermes looked at me. 'The big green bucket in your driveway.'

Salaucey said, 'The blue one's for recycling, black is for trash, green is for grass and tree shit.'

'Oh,' I said. 'So, you mean the grass bin?'

'Yo, Herm,' Salaucey said. 'I use the green, we gonna get grass all up in dis boy's gat.'

'Blue then, mothuhfucka,' Hermes said to Salaucey.

'Blue,' Salaucey said to me.

Hermes pointed as if trying to tap me on the chest. 'But don't leave 'at shit for the garbage mens to pick up. 'Morrow's trash day.'

'Got it. Thanks, Herm.'

I went home and waited. Nervous. Wired. Then bored. An hour passed and I dozed off on the couch.

I jolted awake, looked at the clock. Five hours had passed. I went out the kitchen door, to the bins in my driveway. There was a rolled brown lunch bag in the blue container. I carried it inside and opened it in the kitchen. There was a box of .40 Smith & Wesson 165 grain cartridges, two nine-round clips and a Glock 27. I'd seen Ghost play with guns many times, of course. But when he and his boys started messing with hardware, I left the room. I was always worried one of them might mistake me for him. A beef erupts and I get wet while he gets away, like he always does.

The clips were full. I inserted one, ready to rock and roll. Taped to the grip of the semi-auto was a folded note, in surprisingly clean cursive script. The note, which could have been one of Ghost's lyrics, said –

Remember,
Bitch on a psychological safety
Finger off trigger = safety on

Finger on trigger = safety off
Drop the Glock on the floor, relax
you aint gonna blow yo motherfucking
toes to kingdom come.

Sunday morning. Stacey had been dead for a year.

As I lay on the couch thinking *today is the day*, I realized that unless I was looking at a photo of her, I could no longer remember my wife's face. The face I had seen in Mr Ennis's house had been a blur, one I was trying hard to forget. I recalled her firm thighs and rounded calves. Her yard-tanned belly with the ruby stud in the navel. Her fingernails painted blue, green, black, never red. I was still able to summon her hair, the choppy white shelf of it. I knew that her eyes had been blue but could not recall the calming life in them. The set of her jaw, the line of her nose, the contours of her ears – all of these details eluded me, and thus their sum.

For the first time in months I regretted putting away the photos. All I could see when I closed my eyes were the after-shots, the fractured doll, and today was no day for that.

I spent the morning at Target, looking at waffle irons. Stacey had always wanted one and I never bought it for her, my argument being that a waffle iron is just another one of those appliances you use once and then realize it's a pain in the ass to clean up. It goes into the cupboard until you have a garage sale fourteen years later. I decided I would make Belgian waffles with fresh strawberries (her favorite breakfast) and eat them today, in recognition. I carried the most expensive Braun they had up to register twelve.

A beautiful black girl with a cleft lip or some unfortunate facial irregularity rang me up. Her nametag said Naomi. She might have been nineteen or thirty-two.

I could ask her out, I thought. She probably doesn't have a boyfriend. And because I was in my misery a shallow and deluded idiot, I did not stop there. If she did have a fella, he was similarly maimed, a club foot, was cruel to her, because he could be, because they had no one else. They lived in a one-room apartment with a hot plate. She had gout. Standing here all day was agony for her. I had a house, money in the bank. I could rescue the shawty in a weekend, move her in and buy her a whole new wardrobe, a new convertible whip, get her on a health plan to cover the surgeries so that, having nothing left to complain about, she could go about the business of saving me. *Oh, Naomi, don't you see? We're perfect for each other. Damn, girl, I think I luh you.*

And perhaps most indicative of my deteriorating state of mind that day, I found myself regretting letting my Ghostness go to hell. If I still had the hair, the clothes, the tatts, she probably woulda . . .

I didn't remember leaving the store, and it took me almost fifteen minutes to find the Audi in the parking lot. On the way home I stopped at Dennis's Tap Room, which is probably the worst bar in West Adams. I sat in a red leatherette booth and consumed eleven whiskey sours, occasionally caressing the waffle iron at my side. The bartender came around and asked me if I wanted a hot dog or 'something to anchor the juice'. I said no but could he bring me a couple more sours, and make them doubles? He obliged but said that was it, after those I had to leave. I did as I was told and stepped outside and discovered the day was almost gone.

When I got back to the house, I drove in from the rear, idling in the alley. I stared at the spot by the telephone pole for a while, waiting for it to make me scream or cry or feel something, anything other than dead. It didn't.

I pulled into the garage, hooked the bag with the waffle iron over my elbow, and leaned my way across the lawn. I spent almost half an hour setting up the waffle iron and reading the instructions. I debated going back out for strawberries, but realized I was too drunk to say the word 'strawberry' let alone navigate the produce section at Ralph's.

I did not bother checking the phone for messages. If I had, I would have heard Lucy asking if we were still on for dinner at C&O's.

I grabbed a cold beer from my arsenal, opened it and fell onto the couch, passing out instantly, the Dos Equis gurgling across the floor. A little more than five hours later I stirred as something in the air around me changed. The sensation was always the same. It was the feeling that someone was standing at the end of the couch, tugging a cool fleece blanket over my bare toes.

I rose to find myself in darkness, all the lights out. I was no longer drunk, merely intoxicated back to a semblance of sobriety by cold, undiluted fear.

6

If every house comes with one special feature – a turret made for reading in a shaft of sunlight, a gentleman caller's bench with the suitor's initials carved into the seat – the clincher that convinces her she cannot live anywhere else, then Stacey's special feature was the ballroom. It wasn't as grand as a hotel ballroom, of course, but we made it splendid. It was a thing to stumble upon, its main entrance being two floor-to-ceiling doors at the end of the second-story hallway. It was architecturally and metaphorically the heart of the house. I guess that made Stacey the soul.

During our first tour, Stacey said it would be a great space to throw a party, and we proceeded to throw our share. Euro Cinema Tuesdays, Halloween costume parties, and formal black and white New Year's Eve bashes, most of which descended into something approaching a garage band bacchanal.

The ballroom was thirty feet end to end, sixteen wide, with a pitched ceiling that met the spine of the roof some fourteen feet above the floor. At the time of closing, everything in between had been a shambles. The plaster walls were crumbling, there were holes in the bar and the crown molding curled like strips of flaking skin. Some shameless resident from 1976 had installed hideous vinyl over the original wood floor. I tore the bubbling vinyl out and refinished the wood; Stacey tiled the sunken center, making a checkerboard of brushed Italian marble that still had chips in it from wedding dancers one hundred years ago. Her uncle Steve was a restoration pirate in New Jersey. He had crow-barred one hundred and sixty marble tiles from some wannabe gangster's home in Newark and paid a guy to truck them out as a wedding present to us. Stacey had set them one at a time until her knees bled. She couldn't walk right for two days after, and I'm pretty sure there are still drops of my wife's blood in the grout.

At the far end, opposite the entrance, was the long mahogany bar with a brass foot rail and a massive mirror behind it. The mirror was a single pane some twelve feet wide and four feet tall. The gilt-stenciled glass was smoke-gray with age and all the more charming for it, so we left it as is.

Hitting the estate sale circuit, Stacey spent the better part of a year and almost ten thousand dollars picking out the benches, fainting couches, glassware and other set pieces. I hired a guy to rewire the Art Deco shell sconces and another to install the antique turntable, which delivered Dory Previn, Glen Miller, Edith Piaf and, occasionally, Neil Diamond or the Chili Peppers, and sometimes Ghost to the B&W tower speakers. We had danced there with as many as fifty friends, and sometimes alone.

On our fifth wedding anniversary, Stacey called me up to the ballroom and greeted me wearing nothing more than black heels and a pair of silver satin elbow gloves, the ballroom lit with candles. As I had moved to her and she to me, both of us playing out roles in some romance channel movie of the week, she twisted her ankle and fell down. I burst out laughing, she started crying, and after slapping me for laughing, she laughed too. I ended up carrying her to the bedroom where I packed her ankle with ice, which in turn made her shiver and more or less killed the sex. Somehow the whole catastrophe of her seduction being thwarted by her clumsiness made me happier than any sex would have, or maybe it just touched me somewhere deeper. *This is so Stacey*, I remember thinking. Innocent, not cut out for the dark side, but willing to try. Always trying to make me happy.

I hated the ballroom now.

It was windowless, hot and musty – no matter how many times I asked Olivia to clean and air it out. The last time I had stood in the ballroom in the middle of the night, I experienced an undercurrent of longing and anger so deep it seemed almost limitless. It was a hot flare, feminine, not from me. It crawled over my shoulders and scratched my skin. I might have been in a bad mood, but the last time I had been in the ballroom, I fainted. It was last Thanksgiving, after the Lions lost another one by three touchdowns. I went in to look for a shot glass behind the bar and just blacked out. I came to in the garage, sitting in the Audi with the keys in the ignition. I did not remember exiting the ballroom, walking down the stairs, stepping out the back door. Something in me just snapped, a circuit overloaded, and there I was. The garage doors open, the alley beckoning.

I hadn't been back to the ballroom since.

Until the night of her death anniversary, when I was disturbed from my drunken sleep on the couch by the familiar cold sensation at my feet. Time slipped – and I was standing in the ballroom's absolute darkness, enveloped in the familiar vacuum of silence as I waited for it to begin.

A minute passed, but nothing happened. No visions assailed me. I was merely standing dead center in the room, my head bowed, swaying on my feet.

'Hello?'

I hated the sound of my voice when I was alone. In there, at that hour, it made my heart beat erratically. Windowless, the ballroom was so dark I could not see my hand in front of my face.

'What do you *want*?' I said, now angry as well as frightened.

No one answered. I sat on the floor, tired and disoriented and needing a moment to get my head around this pattern. It had ceased when I moved downstairs, but now it was starting again.

Perhaps I am not here, I thought. *I might still be sound asleep, down on the couch. But how would I know? I should set up a camera, one with a motion detector and night vision. Anything larger than a rat moves in this old ballroom, bingo.*

I imagined watching a recording of myself sleepwalking, the screen grainy and green from the night-vision lens, and wondered what else I would see in the ballroom that I couldn't see now. What if I filmed myself and the next morning, watching the footage, noticed something in the corner? A shadow that stood out in the darkness like a jacket hanging in a closet. A pair of white orbs, like boiled eggs, hovering five feet off the floor. *On second thought, no, let's not do that. Let's not film anything that may or may not be happening in Casa Hastings. We've seen that movie and it didn't turn out well.*

I rubbed my eyes and my hand fell to something hard and misshapen on the floor. I closed my palm around the handle. It was my new toy, the Glock 27.

Without pausing to consider how it had gotten there, I gripped the gun, stood and headed for the door. But after only a couple of steps I halted, paralyzed by the need to make a decision. It seemed important that I make up my mind about something. I had been afraid of living in this house for too long. I was tired of waiting for the main event. It would be nice to return to the bed for a change. The couch was fine and in a surprising way good for my back, but if I avoided the upstairs much longer, the house would continue to shrink around me until my . . . neurosis . . . had gotten the best of me, and then there would be no place to sleep at all.

I turned in the dark, my eyes adjusting. I could see my hand now, and the black outline of the gun in it. The vague furniture shapes, the hulk of the bar. The smoky mirror a tunnel of welcoming darkness, reflecting nothing. James Hastings wasn't even here. The meaning came to me then, the message I was searching for. It was as clear in my mind as her face once had been, and it would be my deliverance back to her. I wrapped my finger around the trigger and set the muzzle to my temple. My teeth clenched. My muscles tensed, tensed, and a cold hand wrapped around my bare arm.

'James, wait,' Stacey said. 'You're not alone.'

7

I jerked away and the trigger went *click*. A thousand tingling pins pushed into my skin. The cold pressure of her fingers lingered on my arm as I whirled, swatting the air, touching nothing as I fled. Somewhere in this panic, the gun fell to the floor.

I made it to the ballroom's double doors, yanked them open and ran down the hall, to the front landing. I stormed down the stairs and leaped over the last four, landing in the foyer with a slam that made the chandelier twinkle like wind chimes. I backed myself into the kitchen, my heart aching as if it were trying to pump marbles. What I had been on the verge of in that room – I never intended that. But for a moment there, something had gotten inside me. Something had made the prospect seem not only sane but . . . comforting.

She wants me to join her.

I was clawing my car keys from the counter when the footsteps began to thud above, continuing at a leisurely pace toward the back of the house. I knew Stacey was dead and that her body (her broken, discarded body with its obscenely bulging eye and contorted pelvic bones) had been cremated almost a year ago. I also knew that I had heard her voice, close enough to my ear to feel her breath, not two minutes ago.

The footsteps approached the top of the stairs. There were fifteen stairs. I'd counted them many times. I tried and failed to count the footsteps coming down them now, but there couldn't be more than a couple more to go—

Thump, tha-thump, stop.

Whatever it was had reached the bottom. I imagined it standing there, cold, eyes adjusting to the light, tracking my scent. I watched the short hall between the foyer and the kitchen, giving me a clear view to the front door. Even if it went through the front door, I'd see whatever this turned out to be.

The footsteps scraped over the foyer oak. The brown rug bunched at one corner. A flat leather sandal came into view, smoothing the rug. A woman cleared her throat. The sandal became a shiny pale leg under denim cut-offs, a black t-shirt smeared with powder-blue paint, a mess of strawberry hair. She walked to the mouth of the kitchen and stopped. I was looking at her, a face, not Stacey's, a stranger's face. The woman was pale with wide goldfish eyes and a soft flared nose, everything rounded and smooth. She stood with her arms a few inches from her sides, posing in a manner that was almost masculine, cocky.

'I'm sorry, James,' she said. 'I didn't mean to scare you.'

Her voice was rich, just shy of assertive, and oddly

66

calm. I had never heard it before. I was immediately disarmed by dual emotions. First an almost overwhelming attraction. She was not beautiful in the model sense, but comely, possessing the kind of strangely ordinary features that become harder to look away from the longer one regards them. The second was the disorienting feeling of familiarity, the kind which makes men in bars say, 'Haven't I seen you somewhere before?' and mean it. I was frightened by her unexplained presence in my house, and yet I wanted to look into her eyes, sink into the glossy green wet of them.

As a consequence my mouth seemed to fill with wool. She was still twenty feet away but I noticed how she flushed, as if she were reading my admiration and it embarrassed her, or excited her. She pulled a strand of hair over one ear and clasped her hands in front of her waist, mockingly prim.

She said, 'I'm here now. I'm your wife.'

The word 'wife' was a tight band of leather around my neck, shunting my circulation. For a moment her voice echoed Stacey's, but Stacey's had been softer, younger. It wasn't my wife's voice this woman used.

'You're not my wife,' I said. 'My wife left a year ago.'

Her charm deflated, and there was sadness now. 'No, I said I'm here . . . about your wife.'

Had I heard her wrong? I was certain I had not, and yet I must have.

'I've been watching you for a little while,' she said. 'I was worried I would be too late.'

'For what?'

'To keep you from doing whatever it was you were thinking about doing upstairs.'

I felt shame, and was once again at a loss for words.

'This is going to be hard,' she said. 'Can we sit down?'

I stared at her in wonder.

'My name is Annette Copeland. I just moved in next door.'

My new neighbor? The shadow on the porch? Was that why she looked familiar? No, I hadn't seen her well enough to explain the intensity of my feelings now.

'I know how your wife was killed,' she said.

How your wife was killed. Not 'how she died'. Adrenaline blasted alcohol through my veins, pushing it through my pores in a cold sweat. In an instant I was sober.

'I didn't know what happened until a few weeks ago, otherwise I would have come sooner. It was an accident. A terrible—'

'You . . .' I said, short of breath. 'You were there?'

'No. My husband was involved. His name was Arthur. He ran into her with his truck.' She was clutching the hem of her shirt. 'He took his own life twenty-six days ago.'

'Good,' I said. 'I hope he's rotting in hell.'

Annette Copeland began to cry.

We were seated in the living room. After she started crying in the kitchen, I needed a beer and offered her one. She held it in front of her unopened as she followed me, shuffling like a frightened child. A hundred questions in my mind fought to get to the front of the line. She was on the couch, cowering at one end. The severity of her crying was the only thing that prevented me from screaming, throwing her out or binding her to a chair with an extension cord.

'I'm sorry for your loss,' I said, not really feeling sorry at all but wanting to get on with it.

She wiped her nose with her t-shirt. 'I'm sorry. That's disgusting.'

I nodded. Everything about this situation was disgusting.

'He couldn't live with it,' she said. 'He didn't tell me what happened. But a year ago he came home early from work. He was drunk, in shock. He told me he was sick and went to bed. Every time I begged him to tell me what was wrong, he just said he was depressed. It was his job, he said. I thought it was a midlife. Our marriage was not the best before it happened, and it fell apart after.'

'If you're looking for sympathy—'

'No, I'm not.' She looked me in the eye. 'I'm just trying to tell you. He hid it very well. He started drinking heavily. He was always a drinker, but he quit his job a few months ago. I told him I would leave him if he didn't get some help. A month ago I went to stay with a girlfriend for the weekend. I was going to make a decision, intervention or separation. When I came back he was dead. The note he left explained what he had been hiding.'

'He never turned himself in,' I said, stating the obvious, maybe because I had to. 'He killed my wife and just left? What kind of people are you?'

'I'm not going to argue,' she said. 'I'm not here to defend him. It was unconscionable. I'll do whatever you want.'

What did I want? My wife back. That wasn't going to happen. Her husband's head on a plate would have been nice, but that wasn't going to happen either.

'What do you want?' I said. 'Why are you here?'

'I thought you deserved to know the truth. I kept driving by and when I saw the house for rent, I just thought . . . it was almost like a sign. Fate, as stupid as that sounds now. I needed to go somewhere, and I thought maybe if I was closer to you, I could think things through a little better and figure out the best way to . . .'

'What?'

'Approach you. Help in some way. I don't know. I don't have anything left, but whatever I have is yours.'

This angered me further. 'What did this note say?'

Annette nodded. 'He wrote it on a yellow legal pad and left the news article beside it, the item about Stacey.'

'Don't say that. Don't say her name like you know her.'

'I'm sorry. Your wife. He said he was sorry he had lied to me and hurt me this way, but there was no other way he could live with himself, even if he went to prison. He said that he was on his way to work that morning and traffic on the freeway was backed up, so he exited at Western Avenue. He sometimes used Western or La Brea to get to his office in Century City. When he got to the light at Western and Washington, there was construction. He was

70

late for an important meeting. I knew he had been under a lot of stress because of his company. They packaged mortgages for commercial and high-end residential real estate and were attached to that whole sub-prime mess, like the other banks. He was late for a meeting with new investors, another bank who was preparing to offload Arthur's company's toxic portfolio. He lost his temper in traffic. He was trapped there and then he spotted the alley. He decided to cut through the alley to where it met up with Arlington. He said he was going almost sixty miles per hour when she stepped out of the garage.'

I couldn't look at her. I had my hands over my eyes. I was leaning over my knees while she told it.

'He stopped too late. He got out to help her, but she . . . it was instant. He said he looked around for help but there was no one. No one had seen him and it was too late and he knew it would ruin . . . he would lose the company and go to prison. He was scared. He gave in, in a moment of weakness.'

'A moment of weakness. He murdered my wife.'

'I'm sorry. I'm so sorry.' She started to cry again.

I hurled my beer at the wall. It crashed against a framed still from *Purple Rain*, cracking the glass right below Prince's signature. Stacey had given it to me for my twenty-sixth birthday.

Annette reared back in terror.

'Stop crying!'

She pulled into a tighter ball and, after another minute or two, composed herself. Very softly she said, 'Do you want to hear the rest?'

71

No, but I had to know. I nodded.

She recited the rest of his note from memory. 'He said, "I behaved like a monster. If another man had done the same thing to you, I would not hesitate to end his life. I have seen the core of myself, and I cannot live with what I have seen. There is no place for me in this world. I do not deserve to be forgiven for my crimes. But if you can, please try to forgive me for leaving you. I hope that one day we will be together again. Arthur."'

I felt as if my head was going to explode, and I hoped it would. All this time I wanted know, but knowing was worthless at that moment.

'You still haven't been to the police,' I said. They would have told me if she had, of course.

She shook her head. 'But I will. And you should. I can give you the name of the officers who handled Arthur's . . . I'll show you the note, if you want.'

Something was wrong with that. 'You didn't show *them* the note? This note that spelled it all out? What else aren't you telling me?'

'What? No.' She appeared hurt by the accusation. 'It wasn't like that. I, I was scared. I was still in shock. I was afraid they would take my home away. I had nothing. And then later I wondered if I would want to know, after a year. I waited a few days and then I was scared that I had held it back, that it would be worse since I waited, and it got harder to think and, and – I was paralyzed. I know I was wrong, but I didn't know what to do except come see you first.'

'You've been watching me for a month?'

'No. Only a week or so. Maybe two.'

'And you just decided to rent the house next door? Sort of insinuate yourself into the swing of the neighborhood before you divulged this? Lady, are you out of your fucking mind? Who does this?'

'I know how it sounds,' she said. Her face was dirty with tears. 'I was confused. I tried to imagine what your life was like now and I was afraid of making it worse. The lease is only month to month. I thought I could help you in some other way, if I got to know you first, maybe I could do something to make your life better, and then I realized I wasn't acting rationally and I just – here I am, okay? It's not up to me.'

I could not stay seated. 'You stupid woman. You keep saying these things. You think this is how it goes?'

'It was an accident! I don't have anybody left!'

I watched her, waiting to see if she would hyperventilate. She rocked back and forth on my couch and cried with the force of an emergency room. I got up and walked into the kitchen. I stared at the window above the sink. After a few minutes she quieted down again. I went back in and glared at her.

'What I am supposed to do with this knowledge?'

'What I said,' she hiccuped. 'Anything, whatever you feel is right. I'll do anything you want me to do. It's your right.'

'What is this, your idea of some tribal custom? Your people are responsible for my loss, you're my compensation? Is that what you think I need? Bullshit. You're lonely. You have nothing left. Your life is shit and now you want me to make it better. You want forgiveness for your husband and that's not fucking going to happen.'

Her eyes never wavered from mine. 'I will do *whatever you want*.'

I watched her for a moment. I wanted lots of things from her. Good things, bad things. Mostly bad.

'All right,' I said. 'What I want is for you to leave.'

She didn't move.

'Get out of my house. Right now.'

She stood, fighting the urge to try one more time. Then she saw that if she were to stay, if she were to go against my wishes in this moment, I would hurt her.

'I'll be next door,' she said. 'Whatever you . . .'

She walked quickly to the front door and exited, leaving me to decide her fate.

8

'She answered all my questions,' my old friend Detective Bergen said. His hair was shorter. All his blond curls except the little baby pompadour at the front of his forehead had been buzzed off. 'I reviewed the report. I referenced the husband's note with his bank signatures. I reviewed her original statements to the officers who responded to the call. She offered to let us poly her. I told her that was up to you. I can arrange that, if you decide to go that far. But it's rare for someone to come forward like this, especially considering she had to know that if we hadn't found the truck or a witness after a year, we weren't likely to. She's smart enough to know we're going to double-check everything, make sure it fits, which I have. The only crime she's committed is with-holding evidence and knowledge, which she did for, what, three weeks? Not quite a month anyway. We could push that, but given her state of mind, what she's been through, I'm not sure the DA's going to go to bat for us in any meaningful way. I'm not sure what else I can tell you right now, James.'

'Her story checks out,' I said.

'Looks that way.'

We were seated on the deck at Johnny's, the patio bar overlooking Venice Beach, where firm, barefoot waitresses with ratty braids were used to serving me cheap beer and cheap oysters. The morning after Annette's magical appearance, I called Bergen and told him her story. He didn't seem surprised. I guess he'd heard stranger things. Two hours later I watched through the window as he rolled up to speak with her next door, unannounced. She stepped out on the porch. He showed her his badge. She invited him inside and then I couldn't see anything. Her shades were drawn. He was in the house for an hour and a half. When he finished, he headed toward his car, paused as if remembering me and then walked across my lawn. I opened the front door. He told me to sit tight, avoid talking to her until he could go over everything. He said he would get back to me in twenty-four to forty-eight hours, and here we were.

'How'd he do it?' I said.

'The accident?'

'Kill himself.'

'Blew his head off in the garage. Had a forty-four he used for target practice. That was . . . uncommon, being that he was a little guy. Forty-four is a cannon, more at home in a set of mitts. Arthur had little lady hands, but ballistics tested positive for powder and it was registered in his name. The signature matched. He was wearing a light blue suit. A funeral suit. That's a delusion, there. The preparation without thinking about the mess.'

I made a face. 'She found him like that?'

Bergen nodded. 'Bad, bad deal all around.'

We took a moment to drink our beers and stare at the waves. The sky was overcast and the waves were the color of liquid pewter. The beach looked dirty. No one was lying in the sand. I could see Bergen was relieved, even if I wasn't. He got to close another case, though I guess compared to the rest of his load it hadn't really been much of a case to begin with.

'What am I supposed to do now?'

'Up to you. Could hire an attorney. I'm sure you could find one who'd be happy to file a civil. Try to prove she knew about it a year ago and helped cover it up. Go after his auto policy. I don't know what her assets are, but a jury would probably give you most of them, plus something for punitive.'

'Punitive,' I said.

'You spent a year wondering what happened. Grieving, without closure. A psychologist might argue that you will now have to start over. The clock has been set back. I'm not saying that's true – I'm not a shrink. How you deal with it is up to you. But as far as what a jury will believe, yeah, you're the victim here.'

'I could profit from Stacey's death.'

Bergen snorted. 'Hey, you asked.'

'I'm sorry.' The idea of courtrooms and trials all for some money made me feel ill. 'What I meant was, what am I supposed to do about her, this Annette?'

'She took out a month to month lease. She seemed confused about why she moved in the first place, but it's guilt. Call it a nightingale effect. She thinks she can help

77

you, which will of course make her feel better. I told her that is not her job and she should refrain from further contact. I made sure she heard me.'

I nodded. This all sounded so reasonable.

Bergen leaned forward conspiratorially. 'You don't want her for a neighbor, we can make her go away. Easily.'

This was, I admit, comforting. I imagined her packing up her U-Haul again, the LAPD escorting her out of West Adams, probably over the hill to the Valley.

'Do you think she's nuts?' I said. 'She's got to be, right?'

Bergen grinned. 'No more than most of the beautiful women in this town.'

'Is she dangerous, Tod?'

'She's been through the wringer. My take is she's honestly trying to do the right thing, and that's something. But if you decide to let her stay – and, really, it's up to you, you're calling the shots here – my advice would be to keep your distance. I'm not saying she's dangerous, but you don't need the headache.'

I didn't quite understand what he was getting at.

Bergen put his hands out. 'No offense, but between the two of you there's enough trauma and bad juju to feed a shrink for decades.'

'You're saying don't get involved?' I scoffed. 'Don't worry about that.'

'People don't meet this way, James. Not happy people. And when they do, they don't get any happier.'

I pushed an oyster shell like a little sled around the dish of ice. 'I know.'

'Good. Have you met anyone? You at least get laid since last time we spoke?'

'No.' I thought of Lucy Arnold. 'But I have a few feelers out.'

A ringtone I recognized as the opening bass line to Aerosmith's 'Sweet Emotion' began to play from under the table. Bergen flipped his clamshell and said, 'Bergen'. He stood and I was given to understand someone else needed his investigative skills more than I did. 'Tell Hayden to look at the AA files and call me as soon as he can. I'm on my way.'

The clamshell clammed. 'Sorry, bud, gotta motor.' He dropped a twenty on the table and put on his Michael Mann sunglasses.

I stood. We shook hands. 'Thanks for the help.'

'Call me if you have any problems with her,' Bergen said. 'But unless you go looking for it, I don't think you will.'

'Okay.'

He hesitated before leaving. 'James.'

'Yeah?'

'You're young. You served your time. No one else is holding the keys to the cell now. Understand?'

I did.

I considered the situation very carefully and waited a whole week before I went to see her again.

9

As I stood on Mr Ennis's porch and she opened the door without a greeting, I was reminded of those adorable but mildly hardened sitcom wives, the kind married to such a lovable schlub you think if he could land her maybe you could too. Given what she had been through, she should have looked worse. But maybe she was still in shock.

'I just wanted to thank you for cooperating with Detective Bergen,' I said. 'He's a good one. He looked out for me last year.'

She nodded solemnly. An awkward moment stretched between us. When it seemed it would not pass, she stepped back.

'Come in, have a seat.'

I heard Bergen's warning in my head as I stepped inside. I wondered what had happened to the turtle, Tiny Mr Ennis.

'I would imagine you have more questions,' she said, turning to the refrigerator.

The living room, kitchen and hallway had been painted sunny shades of blue and yellow. She had moved in a set of wooden chairs and a round dining-room table, a bookshelf (still empty) and a few other tastefully out of place things: a roll-top desk with pigeon holes and a green leather surface, an expensive piece of exercise equipment, a small wafer-thin television standing on a wine cabinet with chicken-wire doors. I guessed she was serious about this.

'I do,' I said. 'So many I don't know where to start.'

'Would you like something to drink?'

'A beer if you have one.' I pulled a chair from the little breakfast table in the kitchen, right about where the flowers would have been floating.

She returned with two bottles of Budweiser. I accepted reluctantly. The King of Beers gives me headaches. She sat across from me, waiting for me to start.

'I guess we're neighbors,' I said, tilting my bottle at her. 'Cheers.'

'Is that all right?'

'For now. But I'll be watching you.' I wanted that to be laced with humor. It wasn't.

A minute of silence passed. I wondered what her husband had looked like. I made him bald, thin, hirsute. Sweaty.

'You don't sound like you're from Los Angeles,' she said.

I did not like to be reminded of my pre-Ghost accent, the slight Oklahoma drawl that was one-third southern, one third western, the last third some kind of corrupted surfer cadence that stemmed from my slow metabolism and generally mellow vibe.

'We moved here from Tulsa.'

'For jobs?' She was going carefully, her shoulders tense.

'Sort of.'

'Are you an actor?'

'Close. I was a double.'

'I'm not familiar with the movie business. Is that like a stuntman?'

'More like a stand-in.'

She cracked a thin smile. 'You mean like for butt shots?'

'Nah. I used to look like someone famous. He paid me to do appearances, security precautions. I was a wooden duck to fool the public.'

'You do look a little familiar,' she said, searching my face. I waited, hoping she wouldn't get it. She shook her head, smiling at my embarrassment. 'Come on. You have to tell me now.'

Oh, what the hell. 'You listen to rap? Hip-hop?'

'No, sorry.'

'Don't be. I didn't either. But you know who Ghost is, right?'

Annette blinked and swallowed hard. I could see it click, and I wished I'd just told her I was another aspiring actor.

'You mean the serial killer guy?'

Here we go. 'He's not actually a serial killer. He just raps about serial killing people.'

'Wow. You really work for him?'

'Used to.'

She stared, trying to see Ghost in me.

'You have to picture me with a blond Caesar cut and a tracksuit,' I prompted.

'One of my boyfriends used to listen to his music. Is all that stuff true about him and his wife?'

'Show business,' I said. 'He never beat her.' I didn't know this, actually, but I doubted he really had. 'He loved Drea-Jenna. Tragically.'

'He's kind of scary. Weren't you afraid?'

She obviously wasn't getting this. 'Okay, let's say you have a stage. You want to do a disappearing act, like David Copperfield. Live audience. Ghost is rapping, doing a skit. The bad guys come on stage and pretend to take him hostage, tie him up, gag him. Right?'

'Okay.'

'Suddenly there's a trapdoor in the floor, Ghost falls through the hole. The bad guys are surprised, how'd he get away? A loud boom. Gunshots, bombs, smoke. The bad dudes look up – here comes Ghost, dressed like Jason from *Friday the 13th*, swinging machetes in each hand as he glides down from the ceiling.'

'This is a movie?' Annette said.

'No, live performance. It's all choreographed.'

'Oh.'

'But here's Ghost, fake heads rolling across the stage, fountains of blood. How did he get there? Where'd he come from?'

'After he fell through the floor,' she said.

'Exactly. But less than five seconds later, he's back, in another costume, unleashing hell.'

'There were two of you.'

'You got it,' I said.

Annette smiled weakly. 'I'm sure it was quite an experience.'

'It was, at first. But then it got old, the need to shock.

Very tiring. There was always a controversy, outraged parents and censorship groups. It was all very overblown. People are so . . .'

I was talking too much. She seemed disinterested.

'Like I said, that's over now.'

Annette seemed to sense it was time to change the subject. 'Do you know anything about plumbing?'

'Not really. Why?'

'My hot water isn't working.'

I got up and went to the sink. I ran the hot water for a minute. It stayed cold.

'Your water works,' I said. Obviously. 'Did you have the heat switched over in your name?'

'I called them. It was working yesterday.'

'Your pilot light is probably out,' I said. 'Do you know where the hot water tank is?'

She shook her head.

'Probably outside the house. Mine is. Want me to check?'

'No, that's okay. I'll find it later.' Her hair was limp and she looked waxen.

'Have you been taking cold showers?' I said.

'I've been working here around the clock. I don't sleep much.'

'You can use mine.'

Even before she blushed I realized how wrong that sounded. And how unwise all of this chit-chat was. Bad enough we were even speaking, now she thought I was hitting on her.

'Sorry. I didn't mean—'

'Oh no,' she said. 'That's very nice of you. I just don't want to impose.'

I set my beer down. 'This was a mistake,' I said, walking toward the door. 'I'm sorry but I need to leave now.'

'It's okay.' She moved quickly around the table. 'I won't bother you. I just wanted to say I'm available if you need . . .'

I crossed the room and we met at a point and she stopped when I stopped and now we were blocking each other's path to the open door. Up close I noticed the fine lines around her eyes, the dusky crescents under them. I couldn't think of anything to get me out of the way.

I turned toward the door.

'Tell me,' Annette said.

'Can't bring her back,' I said softly.

She didn't respond and probably didn't hear me. Outside, a squirrel stood up on his hind legs and blinked, then darted across the street in jerky steps before leaping onto the grey folds of a banyan tree and spiraling out of sight.

I turned around and my hands went to the sides of her face. She was terrified, her green eyes very wide, but she did not resist. I kissed her and she pushed her tongue into my mouth. I hadn't kissed a woman in more than a year, not even Lucy, whom I had always approached with my head turned away in shame. Annette left her arms hanging by her sides but I could feel the need rising up in her. I bit her lip and she breathed harder. I kissed down her neck and shoulder and I could have crushed her. I tasted her tongue and she placed her hands on my chest without pushing me away. Her hands moved down, over my stomach, to my crotch, and I felt something in me threatening to spin off like a hubcap on the freeway.

I backed away panting. I backed into the doorway. She removed her t-shirt and her breasts barely moved. She had lots of freckles and her nipples were wide and smooth, almost featureless, the same cocoa shade of her lips. She backed deeper into the house, standing on the balls of her feet, swaying, ready to flee.

I shut the door behind me. I came at her and she made as if to run and then stopped, letting me collide with her. She grabbed my head and let me kiss her and I did so, rougher, in a hurry now. She ground her hips into me and then bent away to unfasten my jeans. I reached under her cut-offs where she wasn't wearing anything and found her with my fingers. She was trimmed short, roughly, and wet to her thighs. There was nowhere to go. She didn't own a couch. She turned her back to me and began walking, dragging me behind her. She fell forward on the table, pushing her ass up. I held her hips up and slipped inside her. She gripped the sides of the table and moaned as I fucked her. 'Like that,' she said. 'Just like that, James.' We heaved against the table, scraping the legs across the floor, through the vacant space where Stacey had cut the flowers. Annette gasped and I came inside her. I locked against her and she reached back to ball my shirt up in her fist, keeping me there, pushing and pulling me. She was loud, her hair spilled across the table, moving her hips up and down until she came in withering contractions that pushed me out.

I fell away from her, fumbling my pants and plopped into one of the chairs. I held onto the table to keep from sliding to the floor and hung my head, out of breath. She pulled her shorts up, staggered away slowly and leaned against the wall. Her neck and face were blotchy, Rorschach patches of pink forming over her brown freckles. Her knees bent and she slid down to the floor, looking up at me.

'I'm sorry,' I said.

'I said anything.'

I shook my head. This was wrong in at least five different ways. Either that, or it was exactly right. My tribal right. And maybe hers, too.

'I might need to take you up on that shower now,' she said.

The water ran audibly through the pipes in the walls. I went to the master bedroom, flicked a light on and changed into a fresh white t-shirt and a pair of jeans I hadn't worn in a year. I walked around the ballroom, to the smaller bathroom. I brushed my teeth, washed my face and tried to clear my eyes with little geysers of Visine. The left one looked like something had burst, spilling red ink in the corner that was supposed to be white. *Lay off the booze, James.*

Carrying a glass of water, I padded along the hall, wondering what the hell we were going to do now. I felt a strange elation. She lived next door, we could do this anytime. What if we were a perfect match? What if that miserable bitch called fate brought us to this point and we were meant to be each other's salvation? Other than Lucy Goosey, Annette was the first woman I had been intimate with, and to be honest, the two experiences were so different there was no way to compare them. One was a lighting bug, the other was light itself.

Lucy. A pang of guilt – I was supposed to have dinner with her last weekend. Not cool, James. I would call her tomorrow and apologize, but not reschedule. But if having Annette here felt like I was on the precipice of something, so too did it already feel like a betrayal. I forgot to make waffles for Stacey's anniversary. I had done nothing in the way of commemoration. I had done the opposite, losing more of her in the arms of another woman. As I passed the ballroom doors, the sound of creaking hinges danced up my back and flicked at my ears.

I stopped. I turned around.

The left door had opened inward, as if inviting me. I was certain both had been closed when I passed them only minutes ago. Now there was a gap just wide enough for a body to pass through, a column of blackness between the white doors. Around the corner, the shower water hummed. I sipped more water, staring at the open door. Old house, floors that weren't so level. The tectonic plates under California, always shifting by tiny degrees. Maybe a draft. Except I knew those were excuses. I hadn't felt any tremors and there were no drafts up here. The ballroom was a sealed, windowless vault within the house.

I went toward it with every intention of kicking the

doors wide open and flipping the lights on. I would give the room one last inspection just to be sure. But as I approached the open shaft my heart rate increased and I could feel the thing inside the ballroom sweeping across the floor to greet me, her pale white hand ready to dart forth and take my wrist as I gripped the knob—

I gasped, yanking the door closed and spilling water on my bare feet. The doors bowed into the hall as if a trapped force were attempting to escape and settled into each other, latching firmly.

I walked quickly to the stairs. I did not look back.

Back down in the living room I felt slightly more at ease. The shower water hummed in the walls. Annette was taking her time. I just wanted her to go home now, so I could sleep. It was only nine or ten, but I could not hold a conversation in this state of emotional depletion. My eyelids became lead drapes. I nodded off in my chair uneasily.

I snapped forward and looked at the clock. Almost twenty minutes had passed and the water was still running and Annette had not come back downstairs all refreshed. But this didn't mean anything necessarily. Women take long showers. At least, Stacey had. How long had Annette been in there, really? Twenty minutes? Half an hour?

I was already climbing the stairs. I slowed as I neared the bathroom, hoping she would finish before I was forced to intrude and begin an interrogation.

I cleared my throat loudly. 'Did you find a clean towel?'

People go deaf in showers, I told myself. Steam was seeping into the hall, heavy with the aroma of citrus shampoo.

'Annette?'

The door was ajar, a two-inch gap affording me a fogged view of the slate floor and low-slung Bond car of a toilet. The Hastings commode was Japanese-manufactured and equipped with a bidet, heated dryer, derrière perfumer and some sort of miracle fan. The only thing missing was a tiny man inside to sprinkle the talcum powder and hand you a mint. Stacey had test driven one at a friend's house and fallen in love with it. I was appalled but if toasty cheeks and a whistle-clean asshole made your wife happy at a time when so little else did, you plunked down the four grand and called yourself lucky until the next prescription wore off.

I knocked. No one answered. I knocked again.

'Hey, Annette? Hello?'

The only sound was the drone of water on porcelain. I knocked harder, pushing the door open a little wider. The shower curtain was flapping open and three of the brass rings dangled freely from the hoop above the claw-foot tub.

'Oh, shit.'

The fine ropes of her wet hair were hanging over the tub, dripping pink water onto the floor.

It's nicer this way.

10

I shoved the door, pushing the wall of steam. Annette was splayed on her back, knees tented, head tilted to one side like she had cut her wrists or someone had come in and dropped a brick on her. Her eyes were closed, her lips parted. The shower head was sprinkling her torso with now-cold water. A puffy, open wound above her left ear was trickling blood down her neck and shoulder until it became a pink ribbon swirling around the drain. I bent into the spray and felt for a pulse along her neck.

'Annette! Wake up, wake up!'

I thought I felt air coming from her mouth but it was difficult to tell with the spray. I shut the water off. I raked the curtain aside and tried to straighten her, using her armpits for handles. One of her legs flopped over, twitching.

'Can you hear me?' This was a sliver of the rescue I had never been able to perform and I almost screamed my wife's name. 'Annette, wake up!'

Her eyes fluttered. Her head swiveled tiredly. She put her hands out, trying to grab me or ward off something.

'Ohhh, bit, abbit,' she mumbled, and coughed. The coughing made her tighten with pain.

I grabbed a towel from the same basket and wrapped her front. I lifted her to a sitting position in the tub. 'Can you hear me?'

She blinked water from her lashes. '. . . don't let rabbits.'

'What?'

When she tried to stand her left hand slipped along the tub's rim and she fell on her ass with a thud.

'It's okay, slow down,' I said. 'Here.'

We got her legs under her. She was still bleeding from the lump above her ear, staining my shirt, but it wasn't too bad. I hugged her as I walked wide-legged and deposited her on the toilet. I handed her a second towel, which she let fall on her lap. Her eyes opened all the way for the first time and she looked through me as I pressed a cloth to her wound.

'Are you with me?'

She looked around the bathroom, up to the small twin paintings in thick black frames beside the lone window of frosted glass brick. Each painting featured a black and white adult rabbit, crouched on the ground like it was sneaking under a fence, but there was no fence. The rabbits weren't munching carrots or grinning in some falsely anthropomorphic manner, just hunkered down on their bellies, caught in profile before a fuzzy green backdrop of grass and white flowers. They had green eyes and were aimed in opposite directions, as if about escape their frames and dart over and under one another. They were just some generic paintings Stacey found in one of her catalogs, neither cute and cuddly nor valuable, but she had loved them in her weird way. I had never given the banal renderings much thought, but Annette was staring at them like a little girl in a pediatrician's office, grinning through gritted teeth. Her eyes widened and she twitched violently and looked away, squeezing her eyes shut.

'What is it?'

'I'm sorry, I'm so sorry,' she whined. 'Don't let the red rabbit get me.'

Red rabbit? There were no red rabbits here. Only two black and white ones.

'It's okay,' I said. 'You have a small cut on your head.'

'Just let me . . .' She was steadying herself with one hand on the wall.

I backed away, waiting to see if she would fall off the toilet. 'Where are your clothes?' Annette had left her place with a small leather backpack of clothes and her make-up, but it was not in the bathroom now. 'Where's your bag?'

'In my room.'

That didn't sound right. She must have tossed them in one of the spare bedrooms. She was confused. She thought she was home.

'Don't try to walk yet.'

I went to the master bedroom and removed a pair of Stacey's blue Dodger sweatpants and sweatshirt, pink-rimmed ankle socks. When I came back she was on her feet, attempting to dry herself. I set the clothes on the toilet lid.

93

'You're going to need a couple stitches.'

'No. I just . . . gimme a minute.'

'I think we should call someone.'

Annette finished stepping into the pants and pulled the sweatshirt over her head. She held the towel rack for support. She kept closing her eyes but every few seconds they would slowly roll open again, as if she were on a boat in the middle of the ocean.

'Do you remember your name?'

'Annette.'

'Annette what?'

'Copeland.'

'Do you know where you are?'

She nodded but was frowning.

'You could have a concussion,' I said.

'I have to go home,' she said, meeting my eyes. 'Now.'

Her hands were still trembling. She tried to go it alone but was listing to the right, so I walked her down the hall, to the stairs and down, out onto the porch. I felt terrible and had no idea what to say. When we reached the lawn she freed herself from my grip and began to walk faster.

'We should see someone,' I called after her. 'It's not safe—'

'I'm fine,' she said, hurrying away. 'Don't worry.'

'You have to wake up every hour—'

She was almost to Mr Ennis's walk. I gave up my pursuit.

'Okay, I'll stop by tomorrow.'

She mumbled something but I was too far away to hear it.

I went inside and removed a blanket from the trunk. I stretched out on the couch, trying to find a label for the evening. What a magnificently fucked-up turn of events. Exhaustion set in until the only thing keeping me from sleep was the vision of her fallen in the tub, a freckled bowl of cream.

For a minute there, I thought she was dead. I closed my eyes and saw Stacey's rabbits, black and white-spotted in their frames, their walleyes staring at me lifelessly. What had Annette seen? What had Stacey seen? Why did she love the paintings? Why was Annette frightened of them?

I didn't know. I felt as though I should remember something about the rabbits, but my head ached and I was tired. For a minute there she looked up at me like a . . .

Is there a dead woman in my house?

This was my last coherent thought for the night.

I woke up hot and panting in the sunrays beaming down through the west side windows. I had slept well into the afternoon. When I sat up and planted my feet on the living-room floor, I glanced to my left and my heart stopped for a few seconds, then began to make up for lost time. A pair of Stacey's heels was sitting on the floor, caked with dirt and dried mud. A sense of wrongness bordering on cruelty stole into me and I crawled backward hastily until I was sitting on top of the couch's backrest, gulping for air.

Those aren't supposed to be here.

95

I was able to give Annette a set of Stacey's sweats last night because I had never finished boxing up her clothes. Last August I made it about halfway through that important grieving ritual before I broke down and cried so hard I thought one of my organs was going to snap like a rubber band. So, yes, there were some casual clothes, a stack of t-shirts in a drawer, sweaters on the top shelf of the walk-in, and a few jackets still hanging in the closet off the foyer.

But not her shoes. Her shoes being somehow more personal and painful to see every day, I had packed up every single pair, from flip-flops to motorcycle boots, including this gold patent pair of heels she had bought for the Grammys we had almost but never been invited to, and locked them all in the storage bay I had rented over on La Brea, some three miles away.

But now they were back, streaked with mud, as if she had gotten all dolled up and then walked through a cow pasture during a thunderstorm. One was standing up, the other fallen on its side.

'I'm finished, James,' a woman said.

I yelled in surprise, jerked my head up and quickly deflated. My maid was standing in the kitchen doorway, holding a tray with her rags and cleaning supplies in it. 'Jesus *Christ*, Olivia.'

'I thought you were awake.'

'I was awake but I didn't hear you. My heart can't take this.'

She was a fit woman nearing forty, with thick, strong arms and narrow hips. As always, her hair was pulled back in a bun, her face rosy and shiny from her labors. In front of her ears were little wisps of black hair that reminded me of baby cowlicks. She offered no apology, or an explanation about the shoes. I realized she just wanted her check so she could go home and watch her shows.

I went hunting for my checkbook in the sunroom just around the corner. On my way I pointed to the dirty shoes and said, 'What do you know about that?'

She didn't answer. When I finished signing the check and came back in, Olivia was staring at me, lips pursed in disapproval. I offered her the check but she just let it hang there between us. I looked around, realizing the house had not actually been cleaned.

'I cannot accept this,' she said. 'I did no clean today.'

'What's wrong?' *And if you no clean today, why are you sweating?*

She shifted on her feet. I looked at the shoes, then back at Olivia.

'I do no think I can clean this house no more, James.'

'Oh? Why not?'

She looked away. 'I . . . I have other obligations.'

'Okay, look. Sunday was the one-year anniversary. I've been drinking too much. Whatever I did, I'm sorry. I really value your help, Olivia.'

Olivia stared at me. 'Please. It's better not make a fuss. I am very tired.'

'I understand. I'm not upset. But you can tell me why, can't you? We're friends.'

I realized how dumb this sounded. We were not friends. She was my maid. I liked her, she worked hard.

I had never made a pass at her and had no idea what she thought of me. I was her boss, probably not much else. And yet this was like one of those minor dating relationships where you don't really love the person but now, when she's breaking up with you, your pride makes it seem like you cannot live without her.

Olivia almost spoke, then clamped her mouth shut.

'Try me,' I said. 'Whatever it is.'

She became agitated and then her eyes lighted on me. 'Something is wrong, James. It's, it's no *natural*. Can't you see that?'

I looked at the shoes. 'I don't know how those got here.'

'I found them in the bathtub!' she cried, her eyes scaring me more than the shoes now. 'I clean for two years and you leave me this?'

I wiped my face in frustration. 'No, no, Olivia, listen to me. I did not put the shoes—'

'You dig them up in the yard! Like a dog! I am out back sweeping the patio and everywhere I see the holes. Her shoes. More shoes! What kind of man are you?'

'What?'

'You need to see a doctor, James. You're sick.' Her cleaning tray was shaking and a brush with metal bristles fell to the floor. She ignored it, her eyes wandering around the ceiling, the corners of the room.

'Olivia. What is it? Is it something in the house?'

Her nostrils flared. 'It is tainted. You need to let her go.'

'What does that mean? What happened?'

'If you do not make peace with her, others will follow her home. She will bring evil into this house and there will be no peace for you.'

'What—'

'Goodbye!' Olivia left her brush on the floor and slammed the front door on her way out.

After her little Nissan truck's engine faded away, I walked through the kitchen and out the back door. I stood on the patio, surveying the lawn. At first it was almost funny, and then it was everything but. There were eleven holes, each one dug out about a foot wide and a foot deep, the little piles of dirt next to them still moist as if freshly turned. Next to at least half of the holes were additional pairs of Stacey's shoes, similarly dirtied. Her little green Chucks. Her black velvet clogs. Her pink espadrilles. Others I had forgotten about but which pierced my heart anew. Off to one side of the lawn was a dirt-caked shovel. Someone had been digging for gold. Gold patent pumps, it would seem.

Olivia thought I had gotten drunk and buried my wife's shoes and then, in some form of daze last night, when I was sober, dug them up?

I had not. Would not, could not, never would.

But did I know this for sure?

In my hand was the check I had made out for one hundred dollars. In the upper left corner, above my address, it said JAMES HASTINGS & STACEY HASTINGS. We still had a joint checking account. A psychologist might suggest this was further evidence that I was holding on to her.

But digging holes in the yard. What kind of sleep-walking would this require?

Someone else was messing with me, and, when I found out who, they would regret it. I ripped the check into pieces anyway, making sure the first tear went between our names.

11

Ever since Stacey died, I was terrible with keys, sunglasses, remote controls. Anything pocket-sized and losable, I lost it. Which is why I had no way of knowing if someone had broken into my storage locker at the Self-Store-It Center, where I had installed a junior high kid's combination lock on my unit instead of the kind that you can blast with a shotgun. Those babies come with two little brass keys, and I would have lost them. The combo lock was still there, though – locked. There were no signs of forced entry, but someone with scintillatingly brilliant powers of deduction just might have figured it out. It was the date of our wedding, for one. For another, there was a card taped to the floor of my desk's center drawer which read, in large red felt tip, STORAGE LOCKER COMBO. And below that: 09-04-04

I opened the lock, put it in my back pocket and slid the metal door up. I saw nothing out of place, but this didn't stop my stomach from clenching, my skin breaking out in the same nervous itch. I was a junkie in the presence of my favorite fix.

Stacey's things.

I had stacked the boxes along the walls, leaving a slot in the middle so that I would not have to empty the whole damn lot just to find one of her old mixed CDs, a photo of us at the lake house, the rugby shirt she had stolen from me in college, any old thing. As if tending a version of her grave, I had stacked and labeled everything in a tidy fashion, going so far as to place a small hand-woven rug Stacey had been fond of and half a dozen scented candles in this metal cage. The carefully drawn block letters from my Magic Marker on the boxes – STACEY'S SWEATERS, STACEY'S BATHROOM TRINKETS, STACEY'S JACKETS (SPRING) – now seemed to mock me, the me I was back when I had decided establishing this shrine was healthier than a drop off at Good Will. Someone should have taken me aside last summer and stamped FRAGILE on my forehead.

Problem: there was only one box labeled STACEY'S SHOES. I pulled it down and inspected the top. The packaging tape was still intact. The cardboard around it had not been ripped or tampered with. But there had been three boxes of her shoes. Stacey was no Imelda, but she liked her shoes. Which meant that two were missing. Someone had been in here.

'Hey,' I said to the dust. 'It wasn't me.'

I put the box on top of the others, scanned everything once more and turned away and reached up to drag the metal door down. But I paused, forgetting something. I lowered my arms and turned. I tried to remember what was in each box. How much of her remained, and what I had thrown out or given away. I was drawn to one of the boxes in the right corner, a smaller carton with a blue band of rubber packing tape around the base. Without knowing why, I kneeled and began edging it out from under the stack. It scraped across the concrete floor and popped free, leaving the heavy pillar of boxes above it to canter and tumble down at odd angles. I pulled it to the center of the bay and crouched, peeled off the tape and opened the box.

Inside were three shoeboxes but no shoes, and I remembered how Stacey used to save shoeboxes for other storage purposes: letters and stationery, discarded perfumes, knit hats and mittens she might have worn twice a year. I opened the top shoebox, a shiny black Nine West job now splitting at the seams. Inside this was a small Christmas present. The paper was frosty blue with ice crystals and foil twinkles, tied off with a scissor-permed silver bow. I knew Stacey had wrapped it; that had been her favorite part of wrapping presents, using the scissor blade to strip the ribbon so that it sprung back into a coil. She had loved the texture of it, the *rheat-rheeeeeat* and pop of each strand. The present, or pressie, as Stacey would have called it, had no label, no 'To: — and From: —' tag.

Had I packed this up? I didn't remember ever seeing it. I had probably found it buried in some closet and thrown it in before moving on. I might have been drunk, angry, in a hurry to get it over with.

I opened the present, crumpling the paper into a ball.

Under the paper was yet another box (this was starting to feel like a game of Russian dolls) and I ripped that open too, at last removing from layers of lemon-colored tissue paper a silver photo frame with a glass front. Behind the glass was a photo of Stacey in Cabo San Lucas, leaning against a wooden sign in front of our favorite taco stand, a cold Corona in one hand, a fried shrimp taco in the other, smiling at me, the photographer. Then, to my astonishment (and momentary revulsion), the photo changed.

Now I was staring at a photo of Stacey at home, standing over the sink, looking over her shoulder at me, one hand in dish suds, the other flipping me the bird. Her hair was mussed, she hadn't wanted me to snap this one. The photo changed again, and again, and I realized I was holding one of those digital frames that scrolls through dozens or hundreds of photos.

I fell back on my ass and leaned against the boxes, holding the frame with both hands as the photos phased in and out, one image of her replaced by another, and sometimes – though much more rarely – with the both of us. I realized this had been intended as a gift for me. A gift from Stacey last Christmas, the Christmas she never had. I hadn't turned it on. She might have meant for it to be scrolling as I opened the carefully wrapped box of silver and blue. Amazingly there was life in the battery yet, and I sat numb against the boxes of her possessions as the digital frame played through the entire chronology and started again, progressing from younger to older, elementary school to the high school years to college and her twenties, daytime, napping, nightlife, bartending, singing into a wine bottle, laughing, watching me, standing with me, ignoring me, each a photo I had admired or taken, and some I had never seen, ones she might have borrowed from her parents or friends in order to scan them for me. It was, I realized with deepening, almost unbearable weight in my throat, the story of Stacey since I had known her, her every mood and the rise through our history together playing now like a sad synopsis of the first third of what should have been a lovely life.

Stacey at sixteen, the braces have just come off, white spaces on her teeth. So proud.

Stacey at seventeen, pale with nerves in her blue prom dress. Ruffled sleeves, her big hair, so pretty then, so embarrassing in retrospect. I'm next to her and look worse.

Stacey bowling in senior year gym class. Gutter ball. She actually looks sad about it.

Stacey in her Chili's uniform. Her blonde hair in a ponytail. She had smelled like fajitas and quit after only two weeks, but still gave the restaurant two weeks' notice.

Stacey riding a mountain bike near the Arkansas River. She is wearing a pink helmet and pink gloves, holding on for dear life. Not talented athletically, but game for the activity.

Stacey and her dad by the U-Haul on moving day. He looks like he wants to kill me for whisking her away to Los Angeles. She looks too young to go. The amount of trust and faith she put in me is staggering.

Stacey in front of Barney's Beanerie, drinking a Bloody Mary, doing a bad metalhead thing with her finger horns. Our first week in Los Angeles. Her snow-blonde hair is long and straight, almost long enough to reach the top of her butt. God how I loved her hair. Look at her. She's coming out of her shell.

Stacey with Viggo Mortensen. Spotted him at Starbucks and couldn't help herself. She looks drunk with lust. Viggo looks embarrassed for her. She loved *The Lord of the Rings*, the books and the movies. Called them her guilty pleasure. I never understood the guilt part.

Stacey painting the ballroom, her brush extended, she's too short to even reach halfway up the wall. The optimism of the new move. The endless energy for redecorating. Where did it all go? Into the house, or just away?

Stacey in a puffy parka and knit cap blowing on a cup of coffee, somewhere cold, mountains in the background, maybe Colorado, a road trip I can't remember. I was probably traveling for work. She looks chapped, cold.

Stacey and her friend Heather Keinzle from Redondo Beach, sisters in pedicure. Happy. She had been in a real funk after learning that Heather was moving away, a new best friend that was not to be.

Stacey eating a bowl of Frosted Flakes on the couch, Henry in her lap staring at the spoon like it is God. Thus begins the stay-home phase, where Stacey would rather spend all day with her dog than go out and be with people.

Stacey staring into her own phone taking her own picture with her pearly white teeth bared, this one taken and attached to a text reminding me to get my teeth cleaned. She always made the appointments, and kept them. She wanted me to take better care of myself. I thought she was nagging me.

Stacey lighting a candle on the dining-room table that is set for Thanksgiving, her chef apron hanging over the stemware. So serious, the pressure of her first holiday meal enormous.

Stacey in the passenger seat of her car on the drive to Pismo Beach, her hair golden and flying in the wind and the Pacific Ocean out her window. We had been fighting. This was one of those make-up trips. She was a downer, unable to summon the false enthusiasm. I don't remember what we did for two days.

Stacey with a towel around her waist, one arm covering her breasts, shouting at me to stop it. We haven't had sex in almost two months. This was not the way to get the ball rolling again.

Stacey leaning back on someone's green Vespa in Santa Monica, posing with a cigarette. For the first time she looks hardened. Something in her has been lost. Is she depressed now? Really? Or was she just annoyed with me this day?

Stacey walking Henry on the path in Laurel Canyon, her floral print sundress tilting off her hips as if an invisible hand were tugging the hem, her gait tight, anxious, scurrying ahead of me.

Stacey looking up from her pillows, flat on her back,

her eyes wide and her forehead lined as I stand over her taking this photo in bed, minutes after The Sex. We must have recovered somewhat. Sometimes the sex was still good. But it was like she wasn't really there.

See them all again. Stacey happy, happy, happy, cool, sometimes surprised, sometimes chagrined, but almost always a crack of a smile, the eyes glinting with mischief. A normal girl becoming a woman. Two dozen photos, three dozen, four. Sixty, seventy photos in, the cracks begin to appear. More blank expressions than smiles. Her cheeks sucked in, her face drawn in some of the photos. In others, her normally natural white blonde hair a little off, one too many bad highlights, ashen. The forced smile. A tension in the shoulders. In later group photos, she was never quite looking at the camera. Her eyes seemed to be drifting, unfocused. It wasn't obvious until the second pass, but a presence began to make itself known, the invisible cloud hanging over her. Is it the pall of adulthood, the party ending, or something worse?

Stacey with four friends at Coachella Music Festival, tailgating. She is fucked up in an unhealthy way, worse off than her friends. Muddy boots, someone's baseball hat askew on her head. She looks miserable.

Stacey napping on the couch with Henry at her feet, balls of wadded tissue on the coffee table beside her. Her eyes puffy, rounded with dark moons. She might have dozed off crying, or was battling the flu. Who would bother taking these? Had I?

The last shot:

Stacey in the backyard at dusk, standing in the fence's shadow, in that sundress again, a dark shape without a face. Her arms hang limp at her sides. The photo grainy, the light all wrong. She is just a flat cut-out, a negative space too far away. I am nowhere there with her, only angry here. Who took this? Why would she show me these things? What is she doing out there in the dark all alone?

What happened to her eyes?

In this final photo they are but smudges of gray. As if the blue had been stolen. As if they aren't even real.

12

I rang the doorbell. I knocked. I waited, turning in little circles and watching for movement inside Mr Ennis's house. Either Annette was not home, which meant she was feeling better and went out for something, or she was not feeling better and was in fact comatose in the back bedroom or wherever she had collapsed last night. I knocked harder. Maybe she had called a friend to come by to take her to a doctor. I didn't have her phone number. The only thing left to do was walk around and peek into the windows, but I could do that just as well from my balcony, with the scope, without looking like a peeper.

I remembered the lock on Stacey's storage locker, my fingers spinning the green-faced dial. And I realized it was too late to check for fingerprints. If I asked Bergen or Lucy to have it dusted now, they would find no prints except those which belonged to me.

I stepped off Mr Ennis's porch and shuffled over to my mailbox. I removed two bills, some home décor and clothing catalogs, and one shrink-wrapped issue of *Allure* from a subscription I had tried to cancel but which kept arriving month after month.

I was halfway to my porch when a deep voice said, 'Freeze, *muchacho*!'

I ducked, genuinely alarmed until the last arc of flying cold water slopped over my feet and wetted the cuffs of my pants. It was about a pint. I turned toward the Gomez place and was greeted by the sight of my neighbor's son and daughter pumping their bazooka sprayers at me.

'*Yo soy disparo!*' I cried, miming a bullet wound by pressing the mail to my crotch.

Another line of cold water slapped a diagonal line across my chest and Emilia and Fernando ran away in a fit of giggles. Their father, Euvaldo, was leaning back against his truck, braying in such a way that his gold crowns twinkled in the sun. His dress shirt was untucked and he was running the garden hose over his chrome wheels. A can of turtle wax sat on a cloth rag on the truck's hood. When we had moved in, the Gomez's roof had basketball-sized holes in it and the house was up on stilts, waiting for a new foundation to replace the hundred-year-old bricks. The short hedge delineating the property had been something out of Tim Burton, and the Gomez mobile at that time had been a brown Dodge minivan held together with baling twine and duct tape. Now the house was immaculate, the hedge tighter than a nun's ass, the GMC a $35,000 twin cab with lots of chrome. Euvaldo Gomez was running laps around me and both of us knew it.

'You working hard today, James?' His English was clear and he spoke with the clipped cadence of a wrestling coach.

111

'Not really, *jeffe*. How about you? You gonna retire this year? Buy Lupé that beach house on Majorca?'

Euvaldo tossed his head back and emitted another series of jowl-rattling *gya-gya-gyahs* before cutting himself off as quickly as he had started. 'I will stop working when I am dead, James. Not one day before.'

During this neighborly ritual, Euvaldo worked his way across my yard sideways, a man walking the ledge of a tall building. This meant home improvement advice or neighborhood gossip.

'James, James,' my neighbor was saying, 'you have a new roommate?'

'Roommate?'

'Yes, my friend. A lady friend. It is time for you to get back on the horse, no?'

I did not want to tell the story of how I had met Annette. 'No, not really.'

Euvaldo was having none of it. 'Oh, si, *cabrón*. Bring her to my barbecue Sunday. She can meet the rest of the family.'

Lucy knew the Gomezes, so he must have been refer-ring to Annette. But why was he acting like Annette and I had something going, after only one night? What had he seen? 'That is very kind, Euvaldo. Maybe a little soon.'

'You are a young man, James. It is never too soon for love.'

I chuckled. 'She's having trouble with the plumbing. I don't even know her.'

Euvaldo scowled. 'Why must you hurt me this way?'

'What?'

'You can't keep a secret from me, James. I've seen this girl in your house many times. She is very beautiful, *amigo*.'

Half of the blood in my body dropped to my feet. 'Hey, come on.'

'*Que?*'

'You're joking.'

'About what?'

'You've seen her? In my house, before yesterday?'

The *señor* must have noticed his *gringo* neighbor's change of color, because he stepped closer and spoke in a lower voice. 'You just met her yesterday?'

'You're messing with me, right?'

Euvaldo squinted up at my house, then back to the Ennis place. 'Maybe I exaggerate a little sometimes, but no, I am positive. This girl, I've seen her five, six times, James. Last week, and at least one week before that.'

'Inside my house?'

'I thought she was your girlfriend?'

Euvaldo was not only a vigilant member of the neighborhood watch, he was on the board that approved modifications to the historic homes and led various efforts with the city to fund restorations and improvements. He took an interest in people who were not invited guests in his hood.

'Who is she, James?'

'I—' *don't know!* I almost screamed. Maybe I was desperate to deny what Euvaldo was suggesting. Maybe I didn't want to make trouble for her, scare her away. But there had to be an explanation. Euvaldo could be mistaken, a little too vigilant in his neighborhood watch. Lucy might have filled his head with strange ideas.

'Forget it. It's a misunderstanding. I'll talk to her.' I smiled. It was important to put my neighbor at ease. 'I'll tell you about it later.'

Euvaldo let it go, but he looked skeptical.

'No worries. Thank you, *jeffe*.'

'If you say so.' Euvaldo edged back to his lawn and picked his garden hose up, turning the flow toward the property line. 'You need to water your lawn, James. Your grass is turning to shit.'

'I know, I know.' I climbed my porch steps, biting my cheek.

'Anything you need, James. We are here for you.'

Last call, over the shoulder, 'You too!'

This is unacceptable, I thought, slamming the front door. I threw the mail at the nearest wall and stormed into the kitchen. What if she was here, watching me for weeks, snooping around my house? She said she had been trying to decide how and if to approach me. But *in* my house? Why would she let herself in? What the hell was she planning to do here? I was livid, as much with myself as with her.

You dumbass, I could hear Bergen say. *Didn't I tell you to stay away from her?*

I would ask her what the hell was going on, she would explain it, end of story. And if it wasn't a convincing story, one phone call and Mr Ennis's house would be vacant by the end of the week.

Problem was, she'd disappeared.

*

114

Overnight I picked up the habit of walking around the neighborhood, circling back and passing her house four or five times a day. I didn't see her for three days, but the walks seemed to revive me. My legs were embarrassingly stiff and tired after the first two of these outings, but my head began to clear. I had been drinking less since her arrival. I shaved my beard. Got back on the Grape-Nuts. Cleaned the house. Looked out the window every half-hour.

On the fourth or fifth day after Annette's shower injury, I returned from a good two-mile stroll to see the sun setting on a forest-green convertible Mustang parked in front of Mr Ennis's house, its black rag top down. It was a '69, I could tell from the raised and rusting haunches. I don't know how I knew it was her car, but I did. Maybe that first night I had glimpsed something rebellious and shambling underneath her veneer. Maybe it was a lucky guess, but it proved correct when she waved at me from the steps of my front porch. She stood, her hands in her back pockets, smiling.

I halted on the sidewalk and almost screamed. Her hair was blonde. Not lighter in the sunlight. White blonde, platinum blonde, snowbird blonde, neckbreaking blonde.

It's nicer this way.

13

'Where you been, stranger?' she said. Then she noticed my expression. 'What's wrong?'

I walked toward her slowly. 'Your hair.'

'Yep,' she said, doing a little shampoo commercial flip. 'Can't even see the cut now, can you?'

'I hardly recognized you.' With her blonde hair, her rusty freckles seemed . . . wrong.

'You should have seen the bruise. Ugh, the purple under my hair, I might as well have taped a magnifying glass to my head. And it was time for a change anyway. I hated my hair.'

'It's pretty,' I said. *Pretty fucking strange.* 'I thought maybe you were in a coma by now.'

'Aw, you're sweet,' she said. 'I must have given you quite a scare.'

'Do you remember what happened?'

She squinted as if she couldn't quite see me. 'I slipped. I barely ate that day. Probably just fainted. It's really not a big deal.'

'I keep thinking about what you said, though. "Don't

let the red rabbit get me." Like you were scared of the paintings.'

She smiled. 'Really? I don't remember any rabbits. Maybe you can show me later and we'll see if anything comes back to me.'

I knew she had seen something. She just didn't want to discuss it. I tried to think of a way to frame what was going to be, no matter how I framed it, an accusation.

'Is everything all right?' she said. 'You look pale.'

'No, everything is not all right.'

Annette crossed her arms over her chest.

'My maid quit, after finding a pair of my wife's shoes in the house.' I waited, got no reaction. 'Euvaldo Gomez seems to think—'

'Oh!' Annette lunged forward and took me by the arm. 'Hold that thought. Can we talk about this over dinner? I got some shrimp at the market and left it soaking. I wanted to do something to make up for the other night. Do you have dinner plans, or is this too weird?' Her eyes took on a vacant glaze. 'You don't owe me anything,' she added, her jubilation gone. 'I'm such an idiot.'

'No, no it's fine, but . . .' Her hair threw me off again. Why not black? Black hair would cover a wound better than blonde, wouldn't it?

'Around eight? I want to hear all about whatever's going on.' She was already twirling away. 'Oh, I bought a good bottle of Scotch, for after!'

I wanted to rush across the lawn and take her by the arm and ask her what she had been doing hanging around my house, what she saw in my bathroom that made her fall down, if she owned a shovel. I wanted to shake her and ask her if she had ever seen a photo of Stacey. But she was already gone.

Instead I went inside and crawled onto the couch and rested my arm over my eyes. *Maybe I should start drinking again. Sobriety is screwing up my perceptions.*

She acted as if we had already put the wreckage behind us, or at least made one hell of a start. The first encounter, the one that ended in sex, could still be written off as a freak turn of events. But I knew that if I accepted this dinner I would be guilty of encouraging more than friendship. Dinner could only escalate things.

Is that really what she wants? Is that what I want? A romantic involvement made possible by our dead spouses? I'm sure history is littered with such death-born entanglements, but Annette wasn't a Boleyn girl and this wasn't the Ming Dynasty. This was my life.

Shouldn't there be a period of plutonic comforting, walks in the park, coffee-shop conversations? A consultation of friends and family, the tribal elders? Shouldn't we be taking this more seriously? True, I had been lonely for a year. *You're young*, Bergen had said. *You've served your time.* But what had the last year of her life been like? The last thirty days? How could she jump into this?

We didn't have to have sex tonight. We could talk, just have dinner. Dinner was okay, wasn't it? What's that dating service called? *It's Just Lunch!* Yes, and it was just hair color. No, I shouldn't go see her. And yet I had to know if she had been in my house – before we ever met.

I had a few hours to kill before dinner. I decided to locate the missing gun. I would have to return it to Hermes. Having the Glock in the house only made me feel like there was a little black cloud following me around, waiting for me to get drunk again so a lightning bolt could blow my brains all over the walls. I looked around the first-floor rooms before remembering I had dropped it in the ballroom.

The house was cut with afternoon sunlight. As I mounted the stairs, every corner in the hall shut off another pane of light streaming through another window, and by the time I got to the ballroom's double doors I was standing in quiet shadows.

I pushed the doors open and strode in as if I owned the place, which of course I did, and flipped on the lights. Why hadn't we hired a contractor to install a few skylights in the ballroom? Three slits in the roof would have striped the room in warm light, and at night the view of the stars would have been a nice touch. But the sconces and overhead chandelier with its eight-candle flame bulbs lighted the room adequately, and my new-found sobriety helped me see the space for what it was: a hipster couple's attempt to impress their friends and re-create a past era they never lived through in the first place. The ballroom no longer felt ominous or musty. The evil presence I had sensed had been ventilated. Expelled for good, I hoped. Now it was just a big room with some second-hand couches along the walls and a pretty cool bar at the back.

The gun was not on the floor.

I looked under the couches and the settee and end tables. I checked the shelves behind the bar and the drawers underneath it. No Glock. This is the problem with big houses. Even when you live alone, it's too easy to leave something in a room on the other side, far from where you spend the bulk of your time.

I shut the doors behind me, and made a complete circle of the second story – or four left turns, actually, since the hallway is one big rectangle. I glanced into the spare bedrooms and the small bathroom as I went. One nice thing about owning a big house – there's plenty of room to spread out when your spouse can't sleep. Sometimes Stacey would toss and turn, and tear herself out of bed at four in the morning, exasperated by her insomnia and my utter lack thereof. She never admitted it, but I know it angered her to see me snooze through the night while she obsessed over petty grievances with one of her friends, resented my next trip or simply emerged from the balm of her last Ambien too soon.

She liked the small guest bedroom in the corner, the one with the tiny trundle bed and baby-sized rocking chair – items that would never be used by a Little Lord Hastings and which I now found too depressing to be creepy. Whenever I woke early to discover she was not in bed with me, I almost always found her in this tiny corner room with Henry, our beagle, who now lived somewhere in Burbank with a girl of ten who probably pulled his ears and let him sleep in her bed. Waking alone on such mornings, I used to stop and stare at my wife and her dog, curled into a ball with his butthole aimed at her face, and I would wonder why she never slept so soundly with me. Another question I probably should have stayed in therapy to answer.

The child's rocking chair was not empty.

I stared at the large teddy bear and tried to remember which one of us bought it, when and where. No, this was not a slip of the memory. I wouldn't have forgotten this bear. He was fat and rough with a sharp snout, modeled after a black bear, not the cuddly type you find in toy stores. His glass eyes were beady and brown, his fur paws padded with real leather and – my favorite feature – his claws were not little nubs of felt, but honest-to-god talons. Made of plastic, yes, but they were hard, and marbled like they had dirt in the grooves underneath. Two inches long, sharp enough to put an eye out. This 'toy' could maul Paddington in two or three quick strokes, yanking his stuffing out like Stove-Top before taking a big shit in that yellow hat.

Lovely. Just the thing to prop up in the crib with the mewling nipper.

He must have been expensive, I realized. He was a serious bear, the kind some energy consultant father might bring home to his son when he returned from Ukraine. I crouched in front of him. The bear wore a plaid collar with a gold tag attached to a small brass ring. The tag was engraved. It said

Kenneth B. Bear

Nope. Total blank. If Stacey had bought it, I would have noticed it at some point during the past twelve months. I guessed B was for black, but whose idea was it to name a stuffed animal Kenneth? It sort of fit his humorless expression, but still.

'Where did you come from, Kenneth?' I said, flicking his hard black nose.

Kenneth did not answer. My fingernail hurt. The gun wasn't here. I shut the door. My temper flared again. Someone was taunting me and I didn't care for it.

The closet and dresser in the master bedroom yielded no firearms.

The gun was not upstairs, nor – let's start facing facts, James – in the house at all. Either I had left it in the car (unlikely) or someone had stolen it (possible; not pleasant to dwell on). Then again, maybe Annette had taken it away when I fled, just in case I blew up at her. She might have hidden it to protect me from myself. One more thing to ask her, and, while I was at it, I decided to take the bear with me. I backtracked to the corner room and picked Kenneth up by the ear. He was heavy, so I hefted him under one arm.

Evening was setting in. The hallway was darker than when I came up just a few minutes ago. My footsteps seemed too loud in the hallway. All the doors were closed and this irritated me. So many useless rooms. Why did I stay? Who needed this house? It was absurd. Half a dozen paces from the front stairway, the air behind me whooshed and someone slapped me on the back. Kenneth tumbled to the floor and I stumbled after him. My right hand shot out to the wall for support and my feet landed hard, close together. The sting radiated from the center of my back, the crack of flesh against flesh still movie-slap-loud in my ears.

I tottered, surprised and angry as I turned, instantly reduced to a bully's victim in the elementary school hallway, filled with an anger that was replaced by a quickening, immense fear. There was no one standing behind me and no footsteps echoed in the silence that lingered.

'Oh, god damn you.' My voice was meek, and once again I hated the sound of it, not least of all because I didn't know who I was talking to.

I tried to rub my back but could not reach the spot. A wide patch of my skin was still stinging. I entered the bathroom and flicked on the light, which seemed to come to life slower than usual, a delay I attributed to the energy-saver fluorescent bulb. I glanced at the rabbit paintings on my way to the basin. They were the same as always. Plain, uncaring, flat and annoying in their dumb insignificance.

I twisted, I turned. I used Stacey's handheld mirror to get the angles right as the bathroom seemed to drop twenty degrees. With the proper positioning of mirrors, my shirt pulled up to my shoulders, my neck stiff and my heart rate climbing, at last my pale skin revealed the unmistakable pink shape of a woman's hand.

14

When she opened the door and saw me standing there with the Kenneth bear, she simply looked at it with a trace of a smile, then looked up at me expecting an explanation, which I did not offer.

'Is that a gift?'

I half threw the bear at her and it bounced off her knees and fell on the porch between us. 'You tell me.'

'Oh!' She started, then looked at me like I was crazy. 'Hello?'

I stared at her.

'Why do I feel like I'm missing something?' she said.

'Come on. Enough.'

'What?'

'You don't know anything about it?'

'About a giant stuffed bear?'

I threw my hands out – *well?*

'James? What? I don't understand.'

I told her where I found it, but I left out the part where someone or something slapped me on the back. 'Is there something you need to tell me?'

'No. I wouldn't do that.' She seemed hurt by the accusation. 'Do you want to come inside or . . .'

'Look, have you been in my house or not? Because Euvaldo Gomez saw someone in my house. A woman.'

'You think it was me.'

I cleared my throat. 'You said you were watching me.'

Annette rolled her eyes in frustration. 'I was checking out the neighborhood. I toured the house, walked around the property. I might have strayed into your yard. I like to know who my neighbors are and this isn't exactly Westwood, is it?'

'No, but—'

'If I really wanted to break into your house, why would I tell you I was watching you first?'

'He's pretty observant, Annette. Anyone else, I wouldn't have thought twice about it. But Euvaldo is sharp. And then I thought about the night we met, how you walked in and just sort of announced yourself . . .'

Annette took my hands and pulled me toward her. 'I'm sorry. I know I shouldn't have. I told you that, though, right? The first night. I said that I had been trying to decide if I should contact you.'

'Right, and I appreciate your honesty.'

She released my hands. 'But you're still wondering if I was in your house. Planting teddy bears. Running a game. That's what you think?'

'No,' I said. 'Yeah, pretty much.'

'I lost my husband, James. I'm not really in the mood for games. I don't know who Euvaldo saw in your house before we met, but it wasn't me.'

We had a little stand-off. I blinked first. 'Must have been a misunderstanding, then.'

She sighed. 'So, are you still coming in for dinner, or was this just an interrogation?'

I felt sufficiently foolish. She looked at the bear, then back at me. She laughed. 'Oh, James. A bear?'

I left the bear on the porch and went inside.

'Well, don't leave him outside. He looks expensive.'

'He's mean, is what he is.'

Over dinner I kept staring at her eyebrows. They were blonde too, and thicker than I remembered. Had she done them before dinner, or had I been too stunned to notice earlier? What else had she dyed blonde, and did I really want to know?

All she did was pink some shrimp in a skillet with butter, cayenne and the juice of two lemons before dumping the contents into a larger pot where she tossed it all with fresh linguini, but the result turned me bow-legged. I hardly touched the salad and bread, and limited myself to one glass of the spicy red wine she poured with the meal.

'What are these little bits of grass?' I said.

'Chives. I found them growing in the backyard. You like them?'

'Uuuuhhh.' I leaned back in my chair. 'You shouldn't have gone to all this trouble. I'm easily impressed.'

'I think that was a compliment,' she said.

Annette wore leather clogs, faded jeans and a blouse that might have been spun from green cotton candy. The top only made her freckles darker, their background whiter. Radiant is not a word I use to describe most women, but she really did seem to be glowing.

'So how was the rest of your week?' she said.

I had decided to lay the rest on her. 'Someone buried my wife's shoes in my backyard. When, I don't know, but that same someone, or maybe someone else, went ahead and dug them back up.'

Annette's eyes went wide. 'Really? My God, why?'

'Don't know.'

'Who would do that?'

'I have no idea.'

'Is there anyone who would want to mess with you that way?'

'Like who?'

'I don't know. Anyone you used to work with, an ex-girlfriend, delinquents in the neighborhood? You know, some kids stole all my patio furniture once. I searched the neighborhood for a week and then Arthur went up to mount a satellite dish and found it all on top of the garage.'

She'd lost me on that one. I stopped hearing her when she said 'ex-girlfriends'. I was thinking about Lucy Arnold. The girl 'friend' I still hadn't called back. She had at least one reason to be mad at me, but would she really lash out by burying Stacey's shoes in the yard? I doubted it, but you never knew in this town.

Annette sensed she had hit upon something. 'What?'

'I thought of someone, but she's not like that.'

'Was she your girlfriend?'

'No, not really. Just a friend.'

Annette laughed, and there was on top of the laugh

something of a sneer. 'You might want to chat with this "friend". I've seen our half of the species do some pretty nasty stuff after a break-up.'

'We didn't break up.' I didn't want to discuss Lucy now. 'Forget it.'

She fell quiet. I asked if she minded if I smoked. She suggested we go out back. I followed her, and as I lit up she took one for herself. We smoked and sipped more Cabernet. It was around ten, the night warm, the hum of the near but invisible freeway soft around us. I felt sated, sober, normal. Annette looked glossy in her buzz, dreamy-eyed. We stood beside each other and every few minutes she would lean into me, our shoulders pressing into each other.

'So why do you stay?' she said, looking over at Whitey. 'I only ask because that's a lot of house for a single guy.'

'Just having a hard time deciding where next, I guess. This is a lonely city now. Or maybe it always has been. I've never felt like myself here, but I don't want to go home. They'd all be trying to make up for lost time, wanting to talk about it.'

Annette stubbed her cigarette on her heel and flicked it into the bushes, the little litterbug. 'If you think Los Angeles is lonely, you should see my place.'

I waited.

'It's one of those gated developments in some made-up town, out by Palm Springs, but not very Palm Springs.'

Hadn't she said her husband worked in Century City? 'I thought you lived in Los Angeles.'

'We did, a few years ago. I couldn't stand the traffic, so we bought a place in Sheltering Palms and Arthur kept an apartment in town. He commuted in Sundays, back out on Friday evenings.'

'Must be nice out there. Quiet, clean.'

She stared up at the stars, what few we could see. 'Most of the houses are abandoned now, with all the foreclosures. It's another ghost division.'

'A what?'

'Ghost division. That's what the paper calls them now. Catchy, isn't it?'

'It's really gotten that bad?'

'Oh, yeah. It's worse in Florida. Las Vegas, Phoenix. But there are some here, too. I saw a thing in the *New Yorker* about these entire developments across this country right now that are, like, evacuated, and I said, oh, swell, that's where I live. It's like they didn't stop building until every single penny dried up. I didn't even realize ours was emptying out. Not that it was ever really full. Sheltering Palms was mostly investment properties, second and third homes, and those got dumped first. The people who are left, they're in denial.'

'Stuck, huh?'

'One of my friends, Rick Butterfield, he's an ex-cop. He has one of those unmarked cars, got it from an auction, the kind with the spotlight. He drives in circles around the neighborhood all night, shining his light into the empty houses. Sometimes he goes snooping around inside, to see what's left behind.'

'Sounds like a real charmer.' *We should set him up with Lucy. We could double-date.*

'He's not so bad, I guess. He means well. And I love the house. I'm trying to find a way to save it, but Arthur's insurance doesn't cover . . . well, obviously they don't pay out on, you know, suicides.'

'He didn't leave anything, asset-wise?'

'I'm finding out more and more everyday his money – our money – was all tied up in bad deals. He put it all in real estate, most of it in Sheltering Palms, which his company was helping to underwrite. He was a broker for four years and suddenly thought he was Don Fucking Trump.'

'What will you do?'

She shook her head. 'I just need to hold on for a few months until I find a job. Another year or two, they'll all come back. That house will be worth a million, a million two again and I can sell it. But I don't know if I would go back and live there. Too empty, out there in the hills. The last couple days, I realized how much I missed this.'

'This?'

'People, neighbors, civilization. Five minutes from the grocery store. Bagels.'

Civilization killed my wife. 'Well, now you have the Ten for a backyard.'

She stood and wiped her hands on her jeans. We looked at each other. Calculations were made. I decided to quit while I was behind.

'Thank you for dinner,' I said. 'I was worried this would be—'

She got up on her tiptoes and kissed me. It didn't last too long but it was soft and warm, with just the tip of her tongue. When she lowered her heels, her hand dragged down my chest and hooked over the waist of my pants. She looked down and tugged my belt once, as if securing a piece of luggage.

'It's been a long time for both of us.' She said this matter-of-factly, not in some hushed seductress tone.

'Four days?' I said.

She slapped my arm. 'Being with someone.'

'Less for you.'

She began unbuckling my pants. 'Arthur and I weren't a real married couple for years. I lost him a long time ago.'

'I'm sorry.'

'I don't want to talk about them any more.'

She was somehow clumsy and innocent, like a girl playing doctor. Her parents and teachers hadn't told her this was a no-no. Then she kneeled on the concrete patio and my fly fell open. I glanced around, feeling exposed. Oh, Lucy? Lucy Goosey? Are you watching me now?

'Inside, maybe?' I said.

'No. This is better.'

I swayed on my feet. I closed my eyes. I thought of Stacey, but Annette wasn't like Stacey in this act. Stacey had been very straightforward yet sensual, intimate, with a measure of shyness. Annette was conducting a little piece of performance art. She understood that men are visual, that visual is another thing in this. For her it was

131

less an act of love or even affection than a challenge to outperform all the others who came before her, to wipe away memories of the last or best one. She used me like a wand with the power to restore youth, and I felt pervy for watching but could not look away. I was hypnotized by her freckles, her blonde hair, her skin almost translucent, a little blue vein that ran over her temple, under the surface of her skin, to her forehead. She was warm, alive, her hair so white . . .

I covered my mouth with my arm. She turned her head as I ejaculated into her hair. I shuddered and sank to the ground and she began pulling me around, on top of her. She bunched the back of my shirt and dragged me up, then down, her fingers scratching behind my neck as I found her with my mouth.

She didn't move much for a minute or so, and then she began to arch her back. She said, 'Mm-hm. Yes, that. Do it how you used to.'

I raised my head in shock. I blinked at her. She continued to roll her hips, then realized I wasn't doing anything. She sat up and looked at me.

'What?'

'Ah . . .'

'What's wrong?'

I tried to smile. 'What did you just say?'

She gave me a confused expression. 'I didn't say anything. You don't want to—'

'No, no, it's fine,' I said, embarrassed now. Must have imagined it. *Had* to have imagined it.

I kissed her stomach and she leaned back, relaxed. I

moved lower, it got better. She was sweet and smooth, like kissing a salted cantaloupe. I did it the way I used to, because when you have been with the same woman for fifteen years that's about the only way you know how and she clamped her thighs around my head, moaning through it and shaking, ending with a sigh. I crawled up, absurdly proud, and we lay breathing, looking up at the dimmed stars, the whole hot mess cooling quickly.

'Sorry,' she said. 'I forgot the Scotch. Sort of lost control.'

'Sort of,' I said.

I wanted a cigarette and a cold beer. I did a slow sit-up, then stood to pull my pants off my ankles and buckle my belt. I was facing my house, toward the door to my kitchen. I had left the patio light on, which shone down on the walk that led to the garage and the alley beyond. Standing just outside this cone, in a black patch of grass, was a boy of eight or ten. His face was pale and featureless, a blurred mask under a crop of dark hair. He was maybe thirty feet away, wearing a dark jacket over a white dress shirt and tan slacks, the outfit of a boy who attends private school. He was standing motionless with his arms at his sides, watching us with blacked-out eyes. His mouth sagged open in an oval, but he produced no sound.

'*Holy shit.*'

Annette clutched my leg. 'What's wrong?'

I glanced down at her. 'Don't move.'

'Is someone there? James? What is it?'

I scanned my backyard, and hers, the driveway. The boy was already gone.

15

For the next week the list of things my neighbor Annette Copeland and I did *not* do grew longer. We didn't
date or sleep together or have sex. We didn't talk on the
phone, email, text or hide from one another. Instead, we
pressed against the membrane between our homes, spotting each other in the yard while we went about our
business. I threw away Stacey's shoes, filled in the holes,
mowed the lawn. Annette brought home an umbrella
table to spruce up the patio, plus a kettle grill and a side-
board on wheels.

It was just a rental for her, but she really seemed to be
pouring herself into it. A few days after the patio began
to look like a Hammacher Schlemmer catalog set, I
heard her speaking to someone in the yard, followed by
the *beep-beep-beep* of a truck reversing. I looked out the
porthole above the landing to watch her waving a flatbed
truck down her driveway. Annette was decked out in her
cut-offs, a form-fitting tank top, gold-tinted Aviator
shades and a blue paisley bandana around her head. She
had donned new orange calfskin gloves, and her feet
were anchored in heavy brown work boots, also new. I

couldn't see her thumb, but it sure did seem to be turning a bright shade of green.

The truck bed was loaded with trays of flowers and vegetable starters, more plants in plastic pots, annuals of every color, plus bags of mulch and fertilizer. While her driver-helper (she told me later his name was Mel Larkin, a chemistry teacher turned casualty of the California budget crises whom she'd hired in the Lowe's parking lot) unloaded these to the back patio and skirt of gravel around it, Annette returned to the Mustang's trunk and began unloading the hardware. A shovel, a spade, a rake, hoses, sprayers, feeders – everything you would want if you woke up one morning and decided to create an instant garden.

'Chicks dig flowers,' I said to the window. 'It's like a domestic spring fever.'

Two days later she had cut a twenty by ten square in the grass, tilled and mixed the soil, put everything in, then roped it all off with green mesh and wooden stakes to keep the vermin out, the woman gone territorial.

In the evenings, we waved and made faces at each other from our front porches, she on the phone, unwinding with wine, me smoking or grabbing the mail. We had entered a test of will power. Come see me anytime, but don't pressure me. I need to settle in, you need to sober up. Here's a plastic box of leftover lasagna for you – eat up and think of me. Yes, that was me who trimmed your juniper bushes yesterday while you were out shopping. Thank you. Don't mention it, I hated the fucking things. I see you, I want you, but I'm not going anywhere, and neither are you. You're watching me? Or am I watching you? Goodnight, sleep tight, don't let the Kenneth bear bite.

I slowed my drinking to a trickle.

I got nervous again. I wanted her, I feared her. Push-pull, push-pull.

Why had I let myself get into this again? The point where you don't know how much is too much, too little. Is this what regular people go through in regular life, all the time? No wonder people snapped it off the minute it got difficult. Breaking up is easy. Sticking around after the quick score is hard.

I was falling, but was I falling for her or the idea of her?

After a week of this dancing around the obvious, I went back to her. She answered the door in the same cut-offs and paint-stained t-shirt she usually wore. She looked piqued. I had intended to invite her to lunch, but seeing her in the same clothes and this sad little house gave me an idea.

'Are you busy?' I said.

'Not really. What's up?'

'I thought you would like to come to the Farmers' Market with me for lunch.'

'Oh, I just had a sandwich,' she said. 'But I'll keep you company.'

'What kind of sandwich?'

'Bologna and mustard.' She forced a measure of enthusiasm. 'My favie.'

My favie. That was one of Stacey's. Not the bologna sandwich. The childish way of abbreviating things. She was always ending words with –ie, and sometimes –y. When I cooked pork chops, they became porkies. When the house got cool in winter and she wanted me to fetch her sweatshirt, she would say, 'Honey, will you grab bluey on your way back from the kitchen?' This is how we came to name our house. We were the only white couple on the block, the house was white, Stacey named it Whitey.

'We need a break from this scene,' I said. 'Come on, let's get some dessert.'

She grabbed her purse and slipped into a pair of sandals. We took the Audi up Arlington, through Hancock Park, then over to 3rd. We parked and waded into the patchwork maze of tents and shops and restaurants that make up the odd mecca next to CBS Studios known as the Farmers' Market. It was a weekday, which one I am not sure, but I could tell by how little foot traffic was there. I bought a cheese crêpe at the crêpe stand and Annette ate most of it, as I'd guessed she would. She looked a little gaunt from her gardening, but she seemed happy, grateful to be out doing something. There were a lot of trinkets and tourist t-shirts, not much in the way of good shopping. While Annette perused a newsstand I bought a large iced tea and a gyro at another counter. We shared the pita sandwich as we walked from the Farmers' Market into the more upscale, adjacent Grove shopping promenade.

'Are you looking for something?' she said. 'Or are we just walking?'

'Just walking.'

We were holding hands and it did not feel awkward to do so in public. Up ahead, the fountain spurted in synchronization with piped music and a dozen or so people watched it as if it were Old Faithful. A man in plaid shorts and a yellow piqué shirt took a photo and urged his children closer, as if he wanted them to climb in and bathe with the coins glittering beneath the pool's surface.

The Anthropologie store was coming up on our right. I used to call it the Apology store, thinking they should apologize for charging $350 for a blouse. But their bohemian couture interpretations never seemed to go out of style and made just about any woman look good. I thought Annette would not be able to resist slipping in to browse. Stacey hadn't been able to, and as we neared it I couldn't help feeling like the goose walking over Stacey's grave.

Annette hadn't noticed the store, but at the last second she turned toward the window displays and her pace slowed considerably. She stopped. She made a little sound like a purr crossed with a sigh.

'You want to go in?' I said.

'Do you mind?'

'Not at all.'

She let go of my hand and was swallowed by the colorful fabrics. I walked aimlessly while she dug through racks of dresses and blouses. The details changed but the fashions had not. Everything seemed to be of the same calculated vintage on display two years ago. I thumbed a beautiful pair of gray huaraches on a pedestal, the leather wraps thick as rulers. The tag said $650.00. I walked on.

I circled around the cashwrap counter and glanced back at Annette. She was holding up a yellow sundress with blue and pink flowers on it and I could almost see her through it. She looked at the tag, threw her head back and returned the dress to the rack. I sidled up to her testing bolero sweaters in front of a mirror.

'See anything?'

'Plenty,' she said, dropping two hangers on a stack of leather books. 'Ready to press on?'

'You liked the dress.'

She gave me a questioning look. 'James, no. Let's go.'

'I want to.'

She protested but I won. We couldn't find a saleswoman, so I pushed her into an unlocked dressing room. I stood outside while she put it all together. She exited in a pink camisole beneath the yellow sundress, the sweater on top, the huaraches below. While she was inside, she had let her hair down and fluffed it loose, messy.

She posed, doing a side-to-side runway move. There was a gentle fear in her eyes. 'Well?'

'Leave the cut-offs here.'

She laughed. The total at the register was north of sixteen hundred. She carried her raggedy clothes in the bag and we stepped into the sun.

We were seated on the patio at the patisserie across from the Grove Cineplex, sharing a bottle of French wine. We nibbled at a croissant and shared another bottle of French wine. The sun was low enough that most of the promenade was in shadow, and the air was perfect. We watched couples and families walking by and she thanked me for her new clothes every fifteen minutes. After Anthropologie, I'd bought her a cheap pair of black sunglasses from one of the cart kiosks. They had little fake diamonds on the rims and she didn't want to take them off.

'Do I look famous?' she said.

'Better than,' I said. 'After we finish this wine I'm going to take you home and . . .'

'And what?' She leaned into me, biting my ear.

I was distracted by a couple walking toward us. I sat forward.

'Hey, it's Trigger.'

'Who's Trigger?' Annette said.

'My manager. One sec.' I half stood, bumping the table in my excitement. 'Trigger! Yo!'

Annette's grip tightened on my hand as Trigger glanced around, looking right over us. At six-six, two-forty, with curly brown hair that he allowed to grow dangerously close to a white-man's 'fro, Travis Metzger was hard to miss in any crowd. My manager was based in Austin but came to Los Angeles for meetings every couple weeks. I hadn't spoken to him in months. The last time we had talked he said all I had to do was pick up the phone, he'd find me something, anything, to get the ball rolling.

He leaned toward a jewelry cart and tugged a woman's

sleeve. She turned, and I recognized her as Blaine, his wife. She was a striking brunette with locks that fell in oiled curls. She had a deep Texas tan, and – per Trigger's hook 'em horns *modus operandi* – naturally large breasts. She had appeared in the *Playboy* Girls of Starbucks issue while in college; that's how Trigger found her. He was getting his hair cut one day, saw her photo, called her agent and closed another deal. The only time Stacey and I had them over to our house, Blaine had still been a marketing major at the University of Texas, which made her almost ten years Trigger's junior. Despite their age difference, she and Stacey had hit it off. I hadn't seen her since the memorial service, but she was a sweetheart through it all.

'I guess you should invite them over for a glass of wine,' Annette said, releasing my hand. I sensed a resignation in her withdrawal.

They were finishing her purchase. 'Trigger, over here!'

I felt several of Hugo's patrons turning to see what I was shouting about. Finally, he saw me, smiled, and pulled Blaine away from the jewelry cart. They cut across the flow of pedestrians. I kicked out two chairs and sat down. Blaine wore a leather jacket and translucent t-shirt above blue jeans fashionably sandblasted white. She was attempting to install the bracelet she had just bought and her head was down until they arrived at the short canvas and steel rail fencing Annette and me in.

Trigger flashed his smile. 'Ghost Dog, my man, look at you.'

'Thanks for calling to tell me you were in town, you bastard,' I said.

'Spur of the moment, cheem. How you livin'?'

'Good, man, good. Trigger, this is Annette. Annette, this is the man who makes sure I don't starve.'

Blaine got the bracelet to click and looked up, already beaming her big white smile. Annette stood to shake hands and Blaine's eyes darted from me to Annette.

Blaine screamed.

She caught herself before it became a real scream, covering her mouth as she wobbled on her heels and fell into her husband, but it was loud, a shriek that made everyone around us jump. The color drained from her face and her lower lip quivered.

'Are you okay—' I started to say.

'Whoa, girl, easy.' Trigger did a double-take at his wife, then looked at Annette and he saw it too and his smile faltered.

'Pleased to meet you, Trigger,' Annette said without enthusiasm.

Trigger bobbed his head. 'Likewise. This is my wife . . .' He was still staring at Annette, his cheeks puckered.

'Blaine,' I prompted.

'Excuse me,' Blaine said, shaking her head. 'I wasn't paying attention.'

Trigger and I exchanged the kind of hopeful and scared look men share when they don't know if their wives are going to hit it off or tear some stockings.

He recovered first. 'So, what are you two up to?'

'A little shopping, a little wine,' I said.

'James spoiled me,' Annette said, thumbing the strap of her dress. She leaned over and kissed my ear. 'Num num num. Didn't you? Didn't you?'

I grinned, stealing at glimpse at Blaine. She was looking away, too uncomfortable to even participate in the conversation.

'Sit down,' I said. 'Let's order another bottle of wine.'

Blaine shot her husband a nasty look.

'Ah, no can do, partner,' Trigger said. 'We're late for a dinner as it is. But I'll call you tomorrow. We got to put you back to work.'

'That'd be good,' I said. 'I'm ready.'

Blaine was still pretending to be interested in the Puma store display windows to our right. Annette was staring at Blaine's waist or stomach with . . . interest.

Trigger nodded and looked at me like he really wished I would explain myself. 'Hastings, what a surprise.'

Annette was still staring at Blaine's waist. I followed her gaze up. Blaine's cheeks had taken on a sickly pallor, despite her deep Texas tan. Her mouth curled into a grimace and she doubled over, clutching herself.

'Whoops,' Annette said.

Trigger caught his wife, keeping her from falling over the canvas fencing. 'Babe? You okay?'

Blaine held one hand over her diaphragm. 'I'm fine, I just . . . we're really late.'

'Oh, honey,' Annette said softly, pointing subtly at Blaine's waistline. 'I think you have a visitor.'

I glanced down. It wasn't her waistline. A red stain about the size and shape of my thumb was spreading through the crotch of Blaine's sandblasted jeans.

'Oh, God,' Blaine said, placing her shopping bag in front of her crotch. 'Shit, I forgot what day it is.' She looked like she was about to cry.

Trigger was still clueless. 'What? What'd I miss?'

'Travis, let's *go*.' Blaine threw Annette the most artificial smile I have ever seen. 'Nice meeting you.' She shot me a look. 'Bye, James.'

'Tomorrow,' Trigger said as his wife dragged him away.

'Call me,' I said. 'We need to put Ghost to bed for real, man.'

'Right!' Trigger waved.

I couldn't be sure, but when they were about thirty feet down the promenade, I thought I heard Blaine say, 'Are you kidding me . . . it's sick!'

When they had disappeared into the crowd I sat down with Annette. 'Jesus, that was awkward. The poor thing was mortified.'

'He seems nice,' Annette said. 'But she's got issues.'

'They must be fighting. She's not always like that, really.'

I turned and looked at her tousled blonde hair, her big-framed glasses perched on her little nose, the yellow sundress. She was perfect, except for the tears sliding down from behind her sunglasses.

'They weren't fighting.' Annette's voice was so frail it was almost a whisper.

144

'To hell with them,' I said. 'They're just used to seeing me miserable. I'm so sick of people looking at me like I'm a victim.'

But even as I said so, I wondered who I was defending. I felt exposed in public, the eyes of the other shoppers and patrons prying into my affairs.

Annette seemed to read exactly what I needed.

'Let's go,' she said.

16

There is a period where things are missing, hidden behind a wall of white noise. No matter how hard I concentrate, I can't bring them back. This period was as short as two days or as long as two weeks. The in-between is snow static, a dead television channel, unpleasant to stare at. What did we do during this outage? What did she do to me? What deals were struck? How much did I give away? I don't care to guess.

The next thing I remember is being in her bedroom. It was late. We were just in from the night, still dressed in street clothes. My cheeks felt cool, rosy from wind like we had been running through the yards and alleys of West Adams, kicking over trashcans and batting down mailboxes, giddy as truants. We weren't drunk and I don't remember being full or tired from a meal. I was wound up, ready to run another ten miles or solve a physics problem. We seemed to be in a groove, careless, sliding further into the music of each other. On her nightstand was the giant snifter terrarium, the one with Tiny Mr Ennis inside, resting on his little branch of driftwood. She had found him when she moved in and decided to keep him because he was cute.

'Good night, Tiny Mr Ennis,' I said, falling into her cool arms.

'Who are you talking to?'

'Your turtle.' I turned off the lamp, plunging us into darkness. 'That's his name.'

'Oh, you two know each other?' Her voice was already laced with lust. When she went, she went quickly.

'No, but I've seen him around.' We began to grapple playfully, in synchronization, a dance so familiar I didn't have to think of my next move.

'What if Tiny Mr Ennis wants you to leave the light on?'

'Is he afraid of the dark?'

'No, he wants to watch you fuck me.'

I laughed. She didn't. She turned the light on and plowed back into me. She was becoming frantic.

'Will you fuck me, James? Will you fuck me until I say stop?'

This was a little too much. 'I guess so.'

'But I don't want you to stop,' she said. 'Even when I tell you to stop, keep fucking me. I want it to hurt. I want to be sore. Promise you'll do it.'

Did she seek punishment? Did she still feel guilty? Yes, but not for Arthur and his evil deeds. Her darkness came from a colder place.

'I'll try.'

When we had been going for a while, I told her I wasn't going to last much longer.

'Slap me,' she said between breaths.

'What?' I was on top of her, eyes closed, nearly winded.

'Slap my face.'

This struck me as so absurd I actually laughed a little. 'No, don't think so.'

'I need it. Slap me. Come on. Slap my face.'

Whose voice speaks to you in the darkest moments? When someone invites you to do bad things? Invites – and then begins to beg? Who do you turn to when your Jiminy Cricket is out to lunch and you begin to believe she really does want it?

Smack the bitch, Ghost said. He was cackling, drunk on Henney. *She's a freak, give her what she wants, faggot. If you don't, I will.*

'No,' I said. 'Stop.'

'Pleeeeease, oh God, do it.'

'What's wrong with you?'

She kept panting, even as I stopped moving altogether. 'Can't,' she said. 'I can't feel anything. I'm dead inside, James. I'm all cold and hungry in here.'

I rolled off her, disgusted. 'God damn it, stop talking like that or else I'm out of here.'

She scooted across the bed and clung to me. My back was turned to her and she was crying against my shoulder. After a while I rolled over and looked at her. She was a cocktail of at least seven emotions, her eyes shimmering as she writhed against me.

'I'll leave you,' I said. 'This will be all over.'

This.

What is this?

'No, you can't leave. You have to stay,' she said, clenching me. 'Don't ever say that. I won't let you leave. You can't ever leave me again.'

Something in me seemed to dissolve, then. I wanted to say, 'I never left', but I couldn't form the words. The idea that this had been a game now seemed dangerously naive. I wondered at that moment who I was speaking to. I closed my eyes and let it happen.

Static.

White fuzz on a black screen.

I let her do what she wanted, whatever she wanted. She was insatiable. I could not keep up. I tried, but she was always one step ahead of me.

Toward the end of that week she began to rise before me. She would have coffee early out on the porch, and sometimes I heard her talking on the phone, discussing business details, money, her house. *There has to be a way, Dan. Find one. I don't care, I'll find a job if I have to.* I would drift off for a few more hours and then come out of her bedroom to find her with a yellow legal pad on her lap and a pencil between her teeth. Seeing me, she would set her calculations and plans aside. Sometimes she would have breakfast ready, or we'd make the short drive up to Roscoe's Chicken and Waffles. She let me drive her drop-top and the clutch took some getting used to, but it was a nice change from the Audi. Nice to have your head up in the air like that.

'What's going on with the house?' I said one morning, pushing a chicken wing around a pool of maple syrup.

'There's hope.'

She was starting to get antsy, but she wasn't ready to tell me the details yet. I didn't pry, but I began to worry that she might get the house back. She might get the magic call from her lawyer or find enough money to avoid foreclosure. She might decide to peel. Out of Mr Ennis's house, out of West Adams, out of whatever thing we had going now, this thing that was getting heavier and stranger every day. I decided it was time to go home. I couldn't think straight around her. I would slink back to the house, to give her some space for a day or two.

I think it was June. You don't expect horrible things to happen in June, but they do.

Sunday morning was unusually cool, overcast. The house had two furnaces but I never used them. I awoke early with a chill on my leather couch gone cold. While I was microwaving a cup of yesterday's coffee, wondering if I was coming down with the cow flu or geese flu or whichever one it was now, I realized I had forgotten to check my voicemail since coming home from Annette's.

There were eleven messages. The first five were hang-ups. That's strange, I thought. The sixth was from Trigger. My throat locked up. I *knew* it would not be good news.

'Hey, James. Trigger. Call me sooner than later. Thanks.'

That was it. No 'My man, Ghoster' or '*amigo*', just 'Hey, James'. The tone was . . . well, it wasn't any Trigger I had heard before. The Trigger I knew said things like,

'I want to make you a *cock*load of money!' and, 'You beautiful monkey, why you won't give me no love?'

I scrolled through the caller history and dialed back. His assistant, a young man named Renny, gave me a quick 'hiya, James' and put me through.

'James? That you?' Trigger sounded like a moist wrinkled shirt stuffed in a wicker hamper.

'Trigger, hey. Sorry, I was away for a few days. Everything all right?'

Trigger cleared his throat. 'I don't have anything urgent here. No jobs, I mean. I didn't want to get your hopes up. I'm just giving all my clients some notice.'

I had wandered into the kitchen and stood over the sink. The sink was where I took the bad calls.

'Aw, shit,' I said. 'You're getting out?'

'No. Not permanently, anyway. But I'm taking a few months. Things are, ah, pretty hectic around here. At home. I can't put myself into work. I'm hoping to ride out the year and kick off with a new plan in January.'

January was seven months away. This was not a vacation.

'No problem, T. I'm not starving here. Do what you need to do. But you don't sound like yourself, boss. What's going on?'

We'd talked about our finances, our most embarrassing bedroom encounters, petty crimes we had committed growing up. Guy stuff. Friend stuff. So when he didn't speak for nearly a full minute, I knew. I knew right then that whatever was bothering him had something to do with me. With us.

151

'It's Blaine. Blaine's in trouble.'

For a terrible moment I was relieved, and then felt like an asshole for being relieved. 'What happened?'

'That day we saw you at the Grove. You remember?'

'Yeah, she seemed uncomfortable,' I said.

He lowered his voice, as if not wanting colleagues outside his door to hear. 'We were driving back to the hotel and she was in serious pain. I'm talkin' . . . screaming pain. So, I take her to the emergency room. They're short-staffed, of course, there's a line of wailing people going out the door. She was in a state, and the blood, it wouldn't stop. She almost bled out, James. Another five minutes and she would've fucking died.'

I closed my eyes. 'I'm sorry, Travis. Is she okay now?'

'She's not okay, no.'

'What—'

'They still don't know – that's what's so fucked up. Whatever started it, one of her ovaries collapsed. They think it was a cyst or something, a blockage that just blew up, but they don't know. It went all the way into her fallopian tube.' Trigger was on the verge of tears now. 'It just – something inside her, it just wrecked her. She went into cardiac arrest from blood loss. She's stable now but she's been through two surgeries. I still don't know if something went wrong during surgery or what. But when she came out she was worse. She had a stroke.' He wasn't on the verge any longer. He was crying. I had never heard Trigger cry and it was a terrible sound. 'She can't talk right, James. She's fucked up. My baby's all fucked up.'

He sobbed heavily for a moment. I was thinking about Annette. What exactly had transpired when the four of us met? I really didn't know, and I wasn't sure I wanted to know.

'I'm so sorry, Travis. She's going to be okay, man. You'll be with her and you guys are going to get through this. She's a strong girl.'

'Look, I gotta go. You never know how much stuff there is to do, taking care of somebody. You don't think about it.'

'Is there anything I can do? Do you want me to come down and keep you company? Annette would understand.'

That came out wrong. What did I even mean by that?

'No. *No*. That's not going to help. I just wanted you to know.'

Something in me hardened. I knew I wouldn't go to Austin. We were buddies, but the relationship was business first. We had acted like old friends, but were we, really?

'Annette, huh?' Trigger said. 'I don't know about that woman, James. I don't know about Annette. Where'd you meet her anyway?'

'Hm? Oh, she's my neighbor, believe it or not.'

'Huh.'

'She felt bad about things. That they were awkward,' I added, wishing for the call to be over.

'Right. Well, it *was* pretty fucking awkward, James,' he said. He did not sound like he was making the same connections I was, but he was sifting through it, mulling something over. 'I got to tell you, for your own good, I think. It was more than awkward. It was fucking weird, man. It was creepy and sort of sick, James.'

He's distraught. Let it go. There's nothing wrong with Annette. This is all just a coincidence. Blaine got sick. Annette surprised her. The two are not related. Trigger's just jealous. Jealous that I'm moving on and happy with someone when he's stuck. Stuck with a woman who's never going to be normal again.

'Sick?' I felt sick to my stomach. 'I don't, I don't know what to say—'

'You know,' Trigger said. 'You know why. Jesus, man, you got yourself a real replacement there, huh?'

'What? No, it's not like that,' I said. 'The hair maybe, but—'

'The hair, the dress, the make-up. For Christ's sake, she nuzzled up to you, talking like Stacey. What *is* that? What kind of moves are you teaching her? It's almost like she never fucking left.'

'My wife is dead!' I said. 'Stacey's been dead for over a year. I think I'm entitled to meet someone. You know nothing about her, so please, leave her out of it.'

The connection between us was silent, just dead quiet.

At last he said, 'I know Stacey's dead, James. I was there when they cremated her. The question is, do you know she's dead?'

'Fuck you, Travis.' I slammed the phone down.

After finishing two beers in the kitchen, I went back to check the other messages.

They were worse.

17

I've only had one manager and, until that day, believed I would never have another. Trigger was the one with the vision, the one who had the faith that we could turn this lark into something bigger. He had saved my ass by convincing Ghost's people to put me on a salary and benefits, back when I was working fifty then a hundred days a year for him, at his beck and call at any hour. You wouldn't think there'd be much money in double work, and usually there isn't. But when Ghost's popularity – and thus his paranoia – was at its peak, I was sent on more deadbeat missions at opposite ends of the country than I can remember. My salary – before special events, bonuses, expenses, per diems, and countless other perks – was a hundred and seventy thousand.

This is not to say money buys happiness, not when you spend a third of your days on the road, living in motels that smell like ghee and embalming fluid, walking aimlessly through public places where no one gives a fuck whether you are Ghost or Jesus Christ. And when you did accidentally get caught by a swarm of fans, you would be relieved, thinking, it's about time, this ought to break up the monotony ... until they realized you weren't Ghost, just some freaky fan-employee-spin-off dude pretending to be him. And don't bother explaining you work for him, it's cool, you, like, party with him sometimes. For one they don't believe you, and for two, if you get caught divulging the arrangement or in any way trying to profit from it, you will get fired. If you're lucky. If you're unlucky, you will be sued by a team of lawyers who eat platinum records and shit downloads for a living.

Nevertheless, the salary and benefits kept Stacey and me financially secure for those years. It also had a habit-forming effect on Ghost. I became his habit. Once he and his team had me on the bankroll, it only made sense to get their money's worth. What could have been a six-month escapade turned into a three-year career with no end in sight. Until the accident, anyway. Until Ghost went into hiding. I wondered if Ghost had someone else to take my place now. Another James Hastings asking how high when Ghost said jump. If not for Trigger, who would I be now?

I realized I was on the verge of tears. The number of good people in my life had just decreased by one, and there weren't many left. I pressed the NEXT button again.

Of the five remaining messages, two more were hang-ups, my caller ID reading PRIVATE above the time stamps. Wednesday at 9.12 a.m., and again Friday, also at 9.12 a.m. No message, just a dial tone by the time the greeting segued to the beep. Whatever. These were probably robo-calls from my bank. I was probably delinquent on a credit card or the DirecTV.

Next.

'Hi, James, it's Lucy,' she began, upbeat. I braced myself. 'I just wanted to thank you for dinner. I had a really nice time, and I'm so glad you've decided to move on with your life and start letting your friends help you . . .'

She didn't pause, but at this point I was frightened, wondering if I actually had gone on that date instead of blowing her off again. I decided I had either lost my mind or had a doppelgänger roaming around (*ha ha! Maybe Ghost was fucking Lucy Arnold now!*), keeping Lucy's hopes alive while I moved onto the suicide blonde.

Then I heard the rest.

'. . . oh wait, I must have dialed the wrong number,' Lucy continued, shifting to an icy screed. 'Sorry, dickface, for a minute there I had you mixed up with a real man. I forgot you are a little boy and a pretender and, we know this by now, *a fucking alcoholic loser* and a truly inconsiderate prick. I hope you find someone to rock you in her arms while you spend the rest of your life drinking yourself into the ground.' And here she did pause, chuckling in a way that made my bowels twist before finishing in a controlled, delicate tone. 'Don't call back, don't wave, and don't peek into my house with your creepy fucking telescope again or I'll have you Tazered until your dick glows like a Maglight.'

Slam.

'Whoa,' I said to the machine, deleting the rant. She

must have spotted me going in and out of Annette's house. Only jealousy and rejection would push Lucy to such extremes. After hanging up on Trigger, I didn't think anything could make me feel worse, but this did.

Like the two that had come before Lucy's, the final message was time-stamped 9.12 a.m. Three calls at 9.12 a.m. The last one did not list a numerical date. It read simply TODAY.

Today? But I was home, and hadn't heard the phone ring. My head began to throb, the pain radiating all the way down the back of my neck.

There was the usual click, followed by a long silence. The line was clear but no one spoke. I glanced down at the phone's digital clock. The green LCD now said 9.24 a.m., which meant this final call had come through minutes ago, most likely while I was talking with Trigger. Had I missed the call waiting signal? Call waiting doesn't sound like it used to. It doesn't make that loud *ta-DOO-do* sound from the eighties, the one that was impossible to ignore. Now it just goes *dun-dun* very politely, meek as a kitten's last two heartbeats. But I hadn't even heard that.

The message should have begun by now. I stood in my living room listening to the silence. I don't know how many minutes passed, but the line stayed open longer than it should have. What was it with these 9.12 a.m. calls? The rusted gears in my head began to grind, the effort of remembering physically painful. Yes, there had been more 9.12 calls, months ago. They had come once a month or so, I was sure now, just often enough to stick in my mind, not quite often enough for me to think they were anything other than a telemarketer.

The hissing silence extended into a white static abyss.

9.12

9.12

9.12

I arrowed back through the first five hang-ups.

9.12

9—

The handset slid from my grip and the living room went spotty as I began to faint. The sound of the phone clattering to the floor seemed to echo down a long metal corridor as it came to me:

9.12 was the exact time I had received *the* message, the one Stacey left me on the last day, minutes before she was run down in the alley.

My head bounced on the wood floor and I succumbed to darkness.

I once heard Ghost telling members of his entourage a disturbing story.

He was in eighth grade, he claimed, perusing the school library's issues of *National Geographic* to find an archeology feature for the report his science teacher had assigned. The article he chose concerned a two-thousand-year-old clay pot unearthed somewhere in former Mesopotamia. Hidden in a straw-padded crate within a sealed room within a larger complex of small, apartment-like structures, the pot had been almost miraculously preserved, its finely grooved texture nearly pristine, like the grooves on a vinyl record that had never been removed from its sleeve.

A hypothesis emerging from the field of acoustic archeology had been making the rounds. Scientists had known for some time that certain chambers – medieval stone sanctuaries, primitive caves and the like – were built to enhance and preserve acoustics within. The team believed they had found such a chamber and that, along with the right texturing equipment and other tools the potter had used to shape the pot, it was the perfect candidate for their experiment. The experiment was to prove that some fragment of the sounds that had been present in the environment during the original throwing process might have been captured and essentially *recorded* into the clay.

To test this hypothesis, the archeologists partnered with a team of audiophiles who were expert at the then-nascent compact disc and laser technology. This second team constructed a very complicated version of a CD player with a self-correcting laser and together, applying their collective knowledge of the culture, climate, landscape, materials and pottery-making practices of the era, aimed the laser at their clay pot – spinning on a new table that had been constructed to imitate the original's imperfections – and began the digital translations. If they were successful, they might hear the squeak of the spinning pottery wheel, the bang of a hammer or other tools from an adjacent workshop, the clomping of camel hooves outside the potter's studio, and so forth.

They did not hear the clomping of camel hooves.

But after performing hundreds of tests at different throwing speeds, they were able to unlock, record and replay two-thousand-year-old sounds. The part Ghost loved was not that the scientists had been able to 'listen' through time, but what precisely they stumbled into. As they stood in silence, holding their collective breath, watching this aged pot spin in their cluttered laboratory of cables and glass partitions, their headphones filled with the soft but unmistakable coo of a woman crying in the potter's work room – convincing them she was herself the potter. After eighteen seconds, her crying was overlaid with the quieter vocalizations of a second presence, a man who might have been sitting in the background or standing behind her. He was chuckling in a way that one member of the experiment described as 'a low, menacing fashion'.

Due to size limitations and imperfections in the pot's texture, the scientists were able to replay only a total of thirty-two seconds of the accidental recording. In the last seven seconds, immediately after the man began to chuckle, the woman stopped crying, as if surprised to learn she was not alone. There followed, another observer said, 'a tearing sound, much like the ripping of fabric. And then a sort of wet patter or splashing.' The recovered track elapsed, not fading out like a song, of course, but simply ceasing, as if someone had lifted the turntable's needle. A forensic team was brought in to inspect the clay and surface finishing materials, and tests on the faded brown streaks of organic paint taken from the pot proved positive for human blood.

'The research team might have traveled through the acoustics of time only to eavesdrop on a primitive domestic homicide,' the article's author concluded.

Knowing Ghost and how he liked to embellish the details, this was a true story right up until the woman's throat was slit. The story haunted me regardless, even though giving me and the rest of his entourage the creeps was not really even the point of his sharing it with us.

'That's how they're going to find my shit,' Ghost said at the end, just before we broke up lunch to return to the sound check. 'In another two thousand years, some space motherfucker gonna come to earth and dig up civilization we destroyed and hear one of my songs. And when he do, he gonna hear a whole lot more than a woman crying in the background. He will hear humanity from The Source' (this was another of his self-applied monikers), 'and then his fellow aliens gonna know what kind of world we made. He gonna know how Ghost's America liked to roll.'

In the wake of all that happened in West Adams, I have wondered if there is an explanation of the underlying mechanics to be found in the realm of acoustic archeology or a similar field. Something hiding between science and the supernatural. When you consider that every CD or vinyl record or downloaded song contains a ghost of the performer, you begin to accept that the soul can embed itself in many more places, and in infinitely interesting ways, than in the human body.

But no performance exists without an audience. As

the listener we become complicit, a willing participant, and our applause is the natural response to this transfer of energy, the power source that binds artist and fan, continuing the process of absorption. The rabbit was born in the painter's imagination. He or she transferred the vision to canvas, touching something in Stacey's heart, until it existed in her imagination too. How many mornings had she toweled off in front of it, casting her warmth back into its surface, into the fibers of its canvas? Did she speak to it? Did she sing in the shower? Did the steam from her showers embed the canvas with molecules of her skin?

Paintings, cassette tapes, signatures on paper. The unused film, the eyepiece of her telescope, the worn grooves in the floorboards. Compact discs, portable hard drives, soot-smoked mirrors, the insoles of her shoes. These are vessels, waiting to capture projections. What is a house but a larger vessel, a blank platter of vinyl waiting to be pressed by the recording needle of a human perception? A hard drive waiting for the software? A marriage is an opera written over months, weeks, years, a lifetime if we are lucky. When one of the performers in that opera disappears and her understudy steps in to take her place, it is only natural that the next iteration, the aria or cover song delivered by the understudy, will become warped. The audience must sense something has gone afoul, lost, rearranging the sonic landscape of the mind and the terrain of the heart. What if it doesn't require years to leave your mark on a house? What if, when the emotions running within reach a fever pitch or trauma is enacted, it can be accomplished in a year? A week? With a single act of violence?

When one important player in the scene drops out, does the house experience a vacuum to compensate for the loss? We enter a house for the first time – for a dinner party with friends, with a real estate agent showing a vacancy – and we feel its character instantly. This is a warm house, we say. Or, this house feels sad, empty. How do we know? What part of us resonates to the house so assuredly, so quickly?

The vessels are everywhere. Your wife's voice in your voicemail. The dent in the notepad from her last letter. The bits of data stored from the deleted text message, the residue of her fingerprint oil on the keypad she used to type it. The depression in the pillowcase. The memory of the bedroom, where you made love and left your heart on the ceiling. The ring around the bathtub that never comes clean, no matter how many times you scrub it.

Your wife's blood in the alley. Your wife's reflection in your new girlfriend's hair.

Whose human silence had I heard on the home phone? How had I called myself to replay my own grieving from six months ago? Had I mistaken another man's grief for my own? Or had the . . . call it an *anima*, the conspiring energy inside the house . . . translated a message from Stacey? Were these mere echoes from earlier potent events, or was Stacey reaching out to me, reminding me that I had taken a vow of forever?

If the emotions and spirits inside us can embed themselves into a house, there must be a technology, organic or manufactured, that can release them. When fate aims a laser at the grooves of our spiraling grief, what do we become? Most importantly, if Stacey was the music, which one of us was the clay pot?

The house? Or one of the people inside it?

I woke with my cheek stuck to the living room's wood flooring, which peeled away with a tacky sound as I got to my knees. There were drops of blood, but not enough to pool. I rubbed my cheek and traced a trail of dried crust that ran in a crooked line up to my eyebrow, where my fingers stumbled into a hard knob. I hissed, turning slowly, a chill setting deep into my bones. I needed a hot shower. As I shuffled through the foyer on my way to the stairs, a warm draft enveloped me.

The front door was wide open, the last of the day's light thinning on my porch.

18

I shut the door and took the front stairs without hurry. My body ached as if I had been in a bar fight. I trudged by the landing's porthole window without stopping – I did not want to see any reflections, my own or hers – and continued up the second set. The hallway was empty. Halfway to the bathroom my pace further slowed, just as it had when I found Annette conked out in the tub. I had also been very near this door when something slapped me on the back. I opened the bathroom door, half expecting to see Stacey sitting on the toilet, embarrassed and angrily waving at the closet, needing a new roll of paper.

The bathroom was even darker than the rest of the upstairs, its single window of frosted bricks a blurry charcoal shade. The flap of shower curtain still dangled free of the last three rings. Annette must have grabbed the curtain for balance as she fell. But what caused her to fall? She had blamed exhaustion . . .

The rabbits were in their frames, black and white against a green hillside. Did they have a sex? Is that why Stacey had liked them? Had she thought of them as boy and girl, husband and wife? I reached back and ran my hand up the wall, flipping the light switch. The bathroom light did not turn on. I swept up and down twice more, but the spiral fluorescent energy-saver bulb (the kind that was supposed to last five years) in the ceiling socket did not respond. An electrical short, then.

I crossed the bathroom until I was close enough to touch the paintings. The rabbit at the bottom might have been female. She had softer eyes and a bit more of a feminine aspect to her shoulders and hindquarters. The small puff of a white tail. The nearly identical rabbit above her was a tad longer, sleeker, possibly younger or male. Little green eyes on both of them, but one visible in profile. There was nothing remarkable about them. A mediocre talent had been commissioned by one of the catalog companies. The same twin paintings were probably hanging in ten thousand homes across America. Whatever had triggered Annette's reaction, it had been borne of her bruised mind, not these paintings. I was turning toward the mirror when the bathroom light began to glow.

My stomach dipped and I turned, expecting to see someone standing in the doorway, one hand on the wall switch, the other raised and ready to slap me again.

There was no one in the doorway. The gases inside the fluorescent bulb were brightening the room as they warmed. I did not remember the house having electrical problems. We had put some money into the plumbing, replacing the old knob and tube with new copper, but the electrical had been updated and passed inspection before we signed papers. I was certain of this because I recalled the inspector, a tired old guy named Robert Knapp who wore a plaid-lined Baracuta jacket, a thick class ring that seemed desperate, and bifocals over his inflamed nose. Very knowledgeable fellow, was Knapp. Helpful, polite. He had a cold that day and spoke like he had a throat full of milk. What was the phrase he had used? Oh yes, 'The electrical is up to par, or better.'

Maybe not so up to par after all, Bob.

What had I come here for? A shower? I could do that downstairs. I never used this shower any more. I allowed a minute to pass without moving or speaking and my ears began to ring in the silence. It was very faint until I tuned into it, then growing louder, a faraway but approaching whistle. The sound of a tea kettle reaching steam. Where had I heard this before? I was still trying to remember as I returned to the paintings.

I staggered back, blinking rapidly. The rabbit in the bottom painting had changed. Her single green eye had become a red marble with only a pinpoint of black for the pupil. I was certain it had been green only a moment ago, but now was the color of grenadine, darkening even as I stared at it. I kept blinking, expecting the light to stop playing tricks with my eyes, but it did not. The male above her was still black and white and his little eye was green, but hers was—

Her red eye blinked. The black pupil dilated swiftly.

I stepped back and to the right, growing dizzy, and the eye swiveled, following me. Not in the way quality oil paintings seem to meet one's gaze from any point in a museum room. The rabbit's red eye *moved*. First right and then, as I attempted to dodge its gaze, to the left, tracking me, toggling like a bearing. I moaned.

The rabbit had taken on a glossy sheen, reddening as if fresh paint were thickening upward, outward from the body, soaking the fur. I continued to back away as its coat became completely saturated, until I found myself against the wall, away from the door I had been expecting to exit. The tea kettle piping was rising up through the canals of my ears, making it difficult to string together a coherent thought. I knew that if I were to cross the room again and reach up, my hand would sink through the glass plate – the glass that wasn't really there now, if it had ever been – and come away wet, my palm smeared with her blood.

The rabbit turned her head. Her lips pulled back, revealing two needle teeth and a black nub of tongue. Her expression was that of a hissing cat, her floppy ears tucked flat against her skull. She was screaming, shrieking loud enough to wake the dead, or maybe it was the dead trying to wake the living.

I clapped my hands over my ears and jerked back, bumping my head against the wall. The collision seemed to rectify my perceptions, for in an instant the rabbit returned to her previous coloration, the effect being something of a flash card flipped by an invisible hand. Now she was black and white, her eye green and lifeless. The painting was just a painting, a false lure. The high-pitched whistle, however, did not cease, and I realized it was the sound of her screaming, and had not come from the rabbit at all.

It was coming from the woman in the ballroom.

169

19

As I ran down the hall the screaming escalated and stopped abruptly, leaving only the familiar ringing in my ears. I halted, trying to understand what I was about to walk into, afraid of continuing only to discover that I was too late. I took three tentative steps, heard no further commotion, and walked steadily to the double doors.

They were locked. I yanked the knobs, the doors flexed outward, my hand slipped and they rebounded into place. I yanked harder.

'Annette!'

I did not know that it had been her screaming, but the alternative was unappealing. She did not answer. I banged on the door, stepped back, raised my leg and kicked as hard as I could and the doors blew open with a satisfying slam. The room was dark, and I kept one arm raised to ward off an attacker, should there be one coming at me from the darkness.

When nothing did, I stepped to my right and found the switch, throwing on the chandelier flame bulbs.

Annette was standing motionless in the center of the ballroom, with her back to me, arms at her sides. Her blonde hair was whiter than ever and she wore the yellow dress with pink and blue flowers on it.

No, not quite. This dress was older but of the same style, not yellow at all, but faded pink, with green flowers instead of blue. This was the first dress, the one I had bought for Stacey at Anthropologie in the Grove two years ago. Annette's legs were bare, her skin pale all the way down to the black flats. The shoes were crusted with dried dirt. In her right hand was the missing Glock, aimed at the floor. Her finger was wrapped around the trigger.

Psychological safety. Finger on = safety off.

'Annette?'

Something was wrong with her body. She looked stiff and bigger, taller.

'Annette? What are you doing?'

Stacey laughed inside my head. *Guess again, James.*

Annette turned in a half-circle. Something about her was—

'Oh, God, no.'

Lucy Arnold had dyed and cut her hair. She had found the gun – or stolen it. Her eyes were glossy black. Her lips were trembling and a loose string of saliva dangled almost to her collarbone.

'Lucy? What are you – what happened?'

But even as I spoke, I knew. I had hurt her feelings. She had seen me with Annette, carrying on like she didn't even exist. Underneath Lucy's sweet and shy veneer there lurked a psychotic, jealous stalker. All of the incongruities made sense now, the puzzle pieces falling into place. The woman Euvaldo Gomez had seen in the house weeks before Annette arrived. The little signs around the house, my underwear folded in the dresser. Lucy could have found the combination to the storage locker.

She's wearing your dead wife's clothes. She's fucking insane.

'Lucy. I'm sorry, okay? Put the gun down now, please.'

I stepped to the side, my hands raised, and saw our reflections in the giant mirror behind her. The aged glass was hiding something. I could feel it, drawing on me, us, the energy trapped inside the room. Lucy was trembling, her face blank. What had made her scream? What had she seen in the mirror that made her scream?

The red rabbit. The real one, not the painting.

'It's okay,' I said. 'We're okay, everything's fine. Will you hand me the gun?'

No, I hit my head, is all. Annette's mumbling about the red rabbit got under my skin. The power of suggestion. Stacey is dead.

Deal with Lucy. She is a real person.

'Lucy Arnold,' I said, putting some force into it. 'Officer Arnold, put the gun down.'

She looked down at Stacey's shoes, as if just now realizing she was wearing them and did not recognize them. The first one simply lay there as she stepped out of it. The second one was stubborn, caught on her heel, until she made a swinging motion with her leg and the shoe slid across the floor, pattering dully against the wall under the settee.

Then she noticed the gun in her hand.

'You don't need that. I promise.'

172

'Sh-sh-she won't let me,' Lucy said. 'She'll k-k-ill us both.' Her expression did not change. Even with the stutter, she sounded as if she were reading the words from a script.

'No, it's not real,' I said. 'You're safe. I won't let anything happen to you.' I offered my hand and stepped closer to her.

'She m-m-made me do it . . . came to me in the n-night . . . whispered to me. Stacey's not dead. She's in the phone. She's in my buh-bedroom. Here, she's here. She's eating m-me alive.'

Beads of sweat dripped over my brow, stinging my eyes. I took two more steps, hands out, palms up. 'It's not real. You just got confused, sweetie.'

Lucy's body was rigid and the tears leaked down her face. 'She m-m-akes me wear the clothes. Sh-sh-she said she wants to c-c-come back. I'm sssss-upposed to make her come back.'

'Put the gun down, Lucy.'

'She's very, very mad at y-you.' Her lips twisted into a snarl and she raised the gun at my face.

I lunged and yelled, 'Stop!'

She screamed and the gun boomed overhead and Lucy lost all control. She clawed at me as I tried to grab her arms, but she was hysterical and slipped from my grasp. The gun dropped with a clatter, was kicked in the scuffle, and spun across the marble tiles.

'Leave me alone!' Lucy ran from the ballroom, shrieking. 'She won't leave me alone!'

I stood still for moment, amazed I had not been shot.

173

Her footsteps thudded down the hallway and pounding sounds echoed through the walls, as if she were bouncing side to side like a horse trapped in a burning stable.

'Lucy!'

I ran after her. By the time I reached the top of the stairs, the front door opened with a bang. I ran down as fast as I could and tripped on the third to last step, my heel slipping on the smooth wood as I went airborne. I hit the last stair ass-first, then the floor, and my tail bone twanged like a hot guitar chord. I rolled over in the foyer as the pain went up my spine. I was trying to stand when I looked up and saw Lucy running blindly down the sidewalk. She exited the frame at an odd angle, hewing west across Euvaldo Gomez's lawn.

I got to my feet and limped after her. I made it down the porch steps and glanced toward Mr Ennis's house. Annette was standing beside her green '69 with the driver's door open, a paper bag of groceries under one arm, the sunglasses I'd bought her perched on her forehead.

'What happened?' she said, watching Lucy trot away, then glancing back at me in dawning horror. 'James? What did you do?'

'She's out of control,' I yelled without stopping. 'Call the police! Now!'

Annette's mouth fell open and I broke west over Euvaldo's lawn where one of his children, a girl of five or six, was standing in the middle of the grass, pretending to dig with a plastic spade. She threw her spade at me as I ran by and I had the absurd idea that this toddler had buried Stacey's shoes, or dug them up.

174

Back on the sidewalk, I spotted Lucy up ahead. She had a half-block advantage as she staggered into the middle of 21st Street. She was limping, her head bobbing.

'Lucy! Stop!'

She was less than fifty feet from Arlington, the cross street. What time was it? I couldn't see traffic through the trees and over the parked cars. If it was rush hour everything would be reduced to a crawl and she would be spared. If it was not rush hour, the strays coming off the freeway ramp would be hauling ass, trying to make the light at Venice Boulevard. I gained speed and weaved onto the street. The usual line of cars were bunched almost bumper to bumper, the hundreds of commuters inching in slow surges.

'James!' a man yelled behind me.

I recognized the voice as Euvaldo's, but I did not stop. I was a hundred feet from her. She was weaving down the street like a drugged hitchhiker.

I gained ground. Seventy feet. Fifty. 'Lucy, stop!'

She was going to run into a wall of parked cars in less than thirty seconds. Then what? Someone would see her. They would have time. Someone would help her—

There was a turn lane on Arlington, a second slot to allow local traffic to exit into the neighborhood. I remembered this only after the black SUV rolling on chrome 22s leaned around the corner at more than thirty miles per hour, tires chirping as it straightened onto our street. The windshield reflected black leaves from the trees overhead. I could not see the driver. Incredibly, the

175

engine revved harder – the driver relieved, as we always were, to finally be off that fucking Ten – before he saw her.

'No!' I screamed, rushing forward with my hands thrown up.

The Navigator's bumper bit into her knees and lifted her legs a millisecond before the grill met her torso and lofted her higher, seemingly juggling her before shoving her forward like a snowplow. The driver stood on the brakes and the SUV nosed down in a crooked skid as Lucy Arnold was thrown off the hood and dragged down with a wet slapping sound. The Navigator's front left tire crushed her hips, rode onto her torso, and smeared her head into the asphalt, sending a fan of blood and other cranial fluids across my chest and face before all of us came to a halt.

A big black guy with dreads ejected himself from the driver's side, stumbled a few steps and stared at me. Hermes. He walked to the front of his car, paused and recoiled. He looked at me once more and turned away, his hand automatically putting a cell phone to his ear. He had seen this or something as bad, probably involving bullet or knife wounds. He was already calling his lawyers. He wasn't the one who called 9-1-1.

Annette did that. She told me I was screaming as I staggered to the destroyed woman's side, howling my wife's name as other residents carried me away from her. I tried to run, tripped on the curb and fell into the gutter, crying with my head between my knees as my neighbors surrounded me. I smelled Euvaldo's cologne and saw

Annette's face floating before me. Women were screaming in the street, and the Gomez children were crying as their mother led them away from what I had done.

I don't remember the rest of the week.

SHE

Trigger once told James that these types of lookalike and security gigs ran hot for a year or two at most, and that he should prepare himself for the day when it shut off entirely, without notice. Ghost's record sales might nose-dive, forcing staff cuts. He might find someone else who looked like him. He might fade away and become a pro-ducer, a clothing magnate, not a performer. He might get shot, overdose, commit suicide. Stacey and James decided that when any of these things happened, they would dive into the parenthood training program: regu-lar sex, healthier lifestyle, painting of the nursery, college savings account.

They were only twenty-eight, James reasoned. They had a few years. Stacey chose some names anyway. She did not care for the crop of currently fashionable unisex names like Alexis, Peyton, Ashton, Jude. She liked simple, early twentieth-century names. She felt it was important to go with something strong yet humble. She chose Edward for a boy, Doris for a girl, and truthfully she wanted both and probably a third. James thought privately that some women nearing thirty develop a fecund Mom-ness about them; a sensuous, earthen, biological emanation that surrounds them like baby powder. He believed Stacey had acquired this aspect while he had his back turned. He would come home from a gig and find her loose and braless in her sweats, her hair a day or two unwashed but sweet, a luster in her cheeks. Her breasts would seem to have swelled a cup size and he would experience an unimagined ache in his chest for want of filling her womb, her days, her life with something more.

He returned from a summer concert festival to learn she had adopted the beagle. Henry kept her company when James was away, and provided her with a new lifestyle. The dog beds, the training, dog parks, walks on the beach. Henry helped Stacey meet new friends, other childless, dog-owning couples and singletons that got used to bumping into her at the big park off of Mulholland Drive.

James hired a fencing contractor, and Henry had his yard. But they still liked to drive over the hill, to the hiking trail off Laurel Canyon. Every other Saturday or Sunday they would pack a small cooler with seltzer, grapes, cheese, crackers, and sometimes a book for James to read to her. He would load Henry into the car and park in the shade at the foot of the path. Stacey would leash Henry and James would throw a Mexican blanket over his shoulder, and they would go up the hill.

The last time they had made this trip, Stacey had been wearing a yellow sundress with roses on it and, in odd contrast, her silver running shoes, a chunky, no-

nonsense digital watch and a pair of marksman-yellow tinted Aviators too large around her small face and low cheekbones. Her white hair had grown past her shoulders and as he watched his wife and her dog trotting along, confident, headstrong and not wanting for much but a baby, for the first time James thought, *the girl is gone. She disappeared while I was working and she is a real woman now.* And that was good, the only real evidence he had become a man.

The paved trail was a golf cart path too steep for any golf cart to climb. After half a mile of traversing, the pavement turned to dirt, sandy in places, pebble-strewn and rocky in others. James was wheezing behind Stacey and Henry. She had done her time in the Pilates and yoga gulags. This being his final year as Ghost's double, James was going to flab on Craft Services and road grub, which might have been a problem if Ghost himself were not simultaneously falling apart and bloating in public. The artist had developed a fondness for little brown bottles of magic pills and late night drive-thru fare.

In those early years, back when Ghost was built like a whippet, James's contract stipulated a strict fitness regimen, his weight and general shape (muscle tone) not to exceed 'The Employer/Artist _____' by more than seven pounds or 8% total weight of artist and +/– 6% of artist body mass index. To eliminate any excuse for violating this clause, James was provided with memberships to three national chain fitness centers, and whenever the entourage checked into a hotel, the spa and gym package was a given. They dined on organic snacks, and the nutritionist emailed James meal plans to follow at home, where he took it upon himself to perform two hundred sit-ups and push-ups every morning and again at night just before bed. At least once a week, in addition to each of the fourteen days prefacing major events where he would be on camera, James was taken to a private dressing room and inspected, measured, framed, lighted and prodded just about everywhere but his junk, and even that was sometimes squeezed by Janey, the matriarchal lesbian from wardrobe (but only in jest, as one might squeeze the Charmin in the grocery store to see if it's really as soft as advertised). Urine and blood were taken to test for drugs, enzymes and God knows what else. Neutro-Ceuticals were applied to his skin. Exfoliation was expected.

James didn't dare test these policies, not for the first two years. He needed the job. He wanted the job. But near the end he wanted out and was letting himself go to pot. His body was rebelling and trying to force his hand at a time when he was too lazy and in denial to sack up and find a new job. Climbing that hill with Stacey and Henry was instrumental in making him face the truth.

But even if James had not been out of shape, he would have been forced to have The Talk that afternoon. Stacey had been waiting for the right moment to bring him around. James did not know it would be their last honest discussion.

'I really hope we don't see any snakes,' he said. 'Watch your step, babe.'

They had reached the first plateau and continued on

a smaller path, off the main one, into the brush. The lane was now only about a foot wide and every so often disappeared in a washout. James knew there were coyotes and mountain lions out here, things that could make short work of Henry.

'There's rattlers in these hills!' Stacey shouted back. 'Are those slither tracks?'

'Not cool.'

He knew she was teasing, but the image her remark planted in his head now had him looking everywhere for signs of The Ones Who Move Without Legs. James had a serious fear of snakes, one that could not be diluted with logic. Seeing them anywhere, in the wild or on a movie screen, touched something primal in him, as if the devil were dipping his quill pen in James's cerebellum.

When they had gone another hundred yards without seeing any humies (Stacey's word for annoying passersby), she let Henry off the leash and the dog ran ahead, sniffing everything and pissing on cacti. They found a tree and made their picnic in its shade. James kept watching the ground, checking the spaces between bushes and the blanket, ridges in the sand, waiting for that dried twig to come alive.

'Oh, James. Are you really still thinking about snakes?'

He looked back at her. 'I'm fine.'

And that was true. Being away from civilization with her calmed him. Stacey put her shoes under her head and stretched across the blanket. Her dress was riding a little high and he ran his hand over her thigh, watching the heat-scorched San Fernando go on for miles, a dry sea of man-made blight reaching to the horizon.

'I missed you this time,' he said, watching Henry dig in the sand down the hill, where he appeared to have cornered a chipmunk. 'A lot.'

She didn't respond for a minute and he wondered if she had dozed off already. But when she spoke, her voice was clearer, as if she had just found her cue card.

'Do you ever worry about that stuff that happened?'

'What stuff?'

'Back in Wisconsin?'

James tensed.

'I'm not saying that you should worry,' Stacey said. 'And I know we talked about it and you're supposed to forget about it, and I have, too. For the most part. But – do you ever think about it?'

'You mean how the parents are doing?' He knew damn well what she was talking about. 'Or the kids?'

'The kids are dead, James. The parents are ruined.'

He knew this too. But why was she digging in?

'No, I don't think about it. But you do, so why don't you tell me what you want to tell me?'

She was calm, which was more unsettling. 'I'm worried,' she said. 'I'm really scared, James.'

'About what?'

'About you. About your safety.'

'Honey, we have security. Ghost is totally paranoid. We don't go anywhere without the Secret Service.' They weren't the Secret Service, but that's what he called the dozen or so hulking bikers and thugs Ghost kept on the payroll. 'I've explained this before.'

'Exactly,' she said, and he knew he had walked into a trap of his own setting. 'Have you ever considered why he's so paranoid?'

'He's a celebrity. He's got millions of fans. He spends ninety per cent of his waking hours smoking weed and popping pills. Take your pick.'

'John Lennon had millions of fans, and he wasn't singing about kidnapping, murdering and dissecting women with power tools.'

James took a deep breath and counted to five. This did not stop the knee-jerk reaction, the one he used to deflect the fact that he worked for a man who was in some quarters as reviled as Larry Flynt and the President.

'I'm not Ghost,' James said, and immediately realized how asinine that was.

'Yes, you are, James. To them you are. That's the whole point of your job. And don't tell me you have the same kind of protection he does, not when you're out doing dummy appearances at the Viper Room and he's in St Louis holed up in his mansion. Do you know he wears a bullet-proof vest now? He won't even leave the house without it.'

'Did you read that in *Vibe*?'

'He bragged about it in the *60 Minutes* piece last November. Don't play dumb. We can argue, but please don't insult me by pretending you aren't aware of the risk.'

'It's part of his image, Stacey. Ninety per cent of the game is fiction, braggadocio. You know that.'

For the first time she began to raise her voice. 'You're not *listening* to me. I know that, you know that, Ghost knows that. But the angry parents don't. The right-wing wack-jobs don't know that, or don't care. They see him and they think, Behold, the Antichrist!'

'You're talking about a handful of people. They don't follow him around. They write letters to Congress.'

She was on her knees, leaning toward him now, her eyes watering up. 'All it takes is one. One unhinged *fuck* who mistakes you for him and, and . . .' and now she was crying. 'What am I supposed to do? What would I do without you?'

James threw a stick he had been peeling. 'You want me to quit? Just say it, if that's what you want. Tell Ghost he can keep his six-figure donations to the Hastings foundation?'

'Don't do that. Don't talk about money with me. We have plenty of money. We used to live on bar tips. I'm talking about your *life*. Our life.'

James might as well have been arguing with his mother. She had all but disowned him when he took the job.

'You're just scared,' Stacey said. 'You're being a coward.'

'Oh, I'm scared now.'

'You're afraid of moving on. You've got it so good, you're afraid to push yourself and do what you said you would do. You're so used to being him, you're afraid nobody wants James Hastings.'

James didn't have anything to refute that with. She crawled across the blanket and hugged him fiercely.

'You're all I have.'

James could not remain defensive or angry. He knew that his wife was truly scared. 'I'm sorry. I didn't know it was bothering you so much.'

Stacey composed herself. 'I'm sorry for dumping it on you all at once. I just don't see you and then you're home and I don't want to spoil it. But I can't take it any more, James. I can't. I wish I could, but I'm done with it.'

Still, he wondered how much of her fear was real and how much was just her missing him. He knew she wasn't being manipulative, but he thought that maybe, without her even being aware of it, this was her biology's way of trying to get her husband back. The first step toward making that baby, normalizing the rest of their lives.

'Are you happy?' she said. 'Do you even like what you do any more?'

James didn't have to think for very long. 'I'm tired. I'm tired of being away from home. Tired of playing the same stupid role.'

'Really?' She wiped her cheeks, smiling.

Henry came running back to them, panting and collapsing in the shade, his chest going like a little freight train. *Chicka-chicka-chicka* . . .

'I have daydreams where his career is going down in flames. It's awful, but sometimes I wish he would overdose again, or, I don't know, just get in another fight and pull his gun on somebody and wind up in jail. Or die. Then it would be over and I could walk away.'

'That's horrible, James.' She was laughing. 'But I've prayed for the same thing.'

'Three years is enough. I never expected it to last this long. Maybe I can produce a film, get into music videos. Something.'

'Yes, exactly. We have the money. I'll be your D-girl.'

They sat there for a while, thinking about the future. It was nice to remember they had choices.

'Stacey.' He said her name to hear it, to remind himself. There was power in her name, not to be taken for granted.

She kissed him. In the shade he showed her that he loved her, and she showed him that she loved him, and they decided right then to try and make a baby on the hill. But it didn't take. And he didn't quit.

He loved her, but he didn't quit until after she was dead.

20

My angel was talking to me again.

'James? James? You're awake, baby, just open your eyes.'

Slits of light stabbed my eyeballs. I clenched them tighter.

'Will you lower those?' Stacey said to someone. 'It's too bright for him.'

Things darkened. I could feel them waiting for me. I smelled bacon and coffee, and I was very hungry. There was no escape. I opened and closed my eyes in increments, a little wider each time, until I was awake, looking around. Nothing was blurry. It was just like waking up on any other morning, except the TV was bolted to the wall. If breakfast had been here, it was gone now. Stacey was squeezing my hand but I could not see her.

'I'm back here, honey,' she said.

I craned my neck. She was . . . no, she wasn't. She had the same blonde hair but her face was shaped differently. Oval like Stacey's, yes, but more severe somehow. Her cheeks were sharper, and she had freckles. Annette, of course. Annette was standing beside me, up by my shoulders, facing my feet and our audience.

But something about her had changed. She smiled down at me and winked and I realized one of her eyes was now blue, the other green. *Blue is for blondes, green is for redheads. Isn't that right? Which one had Stacey lost? The left eye, the same one of mine that developed astigmatism.* Annette had winked at me with her left eye, the one that had changed. It had gone blue and cold, too steady.

Stacey's eye, lost in the accident . . .

'There he is. All caught up on his beauty sleep and ready to confess.'

Detective Tod Bergen raised himself from a low chair at the end of the bed. He wore a smooth, almost shining gray suit and a white shirt open at the collar. With his coiffed blond hair and chrome sunglasses dangling between his pectorals he looked like an ad for menthols. There were no doctors or nurses in the room.

'Confess to what?' I said.

'Sneaking extra hits of morphine.' Bergen grinned. 'Doc says no injuries other than the bruising on your back and some raspberries on your knees. They're going to do a psych-o on you before you check out. You might have a few rounds of PTSD to go yet, but I told them you were tough. You feel up to a talk?'

'Sure.'

He looked at Annette. 'Can you give us a minute, Annette?'

Annette stroked my hair reassuringly. 'You'll be okay?'

I nodded.

'Want anything to eat?'

'Mm. Fatburger?'

Annette smiled and walked into the hall.

Bergen shut the door after her. He dragged the chair over and sat so that I was looking down at him, which felt strange. I did not have the energy to concoct a cover story.

He nodded happily, ready to eat me for lunch. 'Between your neighbors and the driver, and Annette's statement about certain events prior, we have a good picture of what happened outside the house. Want to tell me what happened inside? Can you remember?'

I took a deep breath. 'Most of it. I was about to get into the shower, the one in the upstairs bathroom. I heard someone screaming. I ran into the ballroom. Lucy was standing there in my wife's clothes, holding the gun. She stopped screaming when—'

'Where'd you get the gun?' Bergen interrupted.

He's a good detective, I thought. Don't lie. He'll read it in two seconds flat. But Hermes might be pissed when you rat on him, oh yeah. Which one would you rather have as an enemy? The LAPD or the local drug dealer?

'Hermes gave it to me.'

'You bought the gun from Herman Willocks, the driver?'

'No, he gave it to me. I offered to pay. He refused.'

'What, as a loaner? Temporary deal type deal?'

'No. More like a gift.'

'Why?'

I shrugged. 'We're neighbors. I got him some concert tickets a couple years ago.'

Bergen looked pissed for a moment. I wondered if that made it less of a crime, the fact that money had not changed hands. Is it illegal to give someone a gun? Probably.

'Why'd you decide you needed a gun?'

I told him about the weeks surrounding Stacey's anniversary, how things seemed out of place, how I felt someone had been in the house. I told him I might have been paranoid, or freaking out about the anniversary. I told him I had contemplated suicide, a truth that revealed itself to me even as I spoke it.

Bergen was frowning, checking his notes. 'When did he give you the gun?'

'A few weeks ago,' I said. 'Just before the anniversary.'

Bergen eye-drilled me.

'What?'

He read from his notepad. 'Quote, "He came to see me about needin' a piece a year and a half ago, said it was for security." End quote.'

'What?'

'That's your neighbor's statement,' Bergen said.

I was confused. 'That's not true,' I said.

'Were there two guns?'

'No.'

'Well, one of you is mistaken,' Bergen said.

Had I asked Hermes for a gun more than a year ago? Had I forgotten, somehow gotten mixed up? I didn't think so.

'No,' I said. 'I'm sure.'

'Right,' Bergen said. 'It's not important right now. I'll check on that. Meantime I'm more interested in why you decided you needed a gun. Was it because of Lucy?'

'I didn't know she was dangerous, if that's what you mean.'

'How many times did you speak to her on the phone?'

This was an easy trap to spot. I knew I had not spoken to her on the phone at all, not once. I had only heard her messages, and I told Bergen so.

'But you knew about them, right? The numerous phone calls?'

'All I heard was the one message about our dinner date, before I blew her off, and then the second one, the angry one a couple weeks later.'

'We didn't find those,' he said. 'You erased them?'

I nodded. He would have the records by now. He knew more than me about this whole situation.

'Did she threaten you on these messages?'

I thought back. 'No, she told me to stay away from her, that I shouldn't call her or wave to her ever again.'

Bergen diddled his ear with his pinky. 'Her records show she called you almost every day for two weeks leading up to the event.'

'Same time, right?'

'What do you think?'

'Nine-twelve.'

'Right. What's the significance of that? Something special between you two?'

'It's the time Stacey left her last voicemail to me. The day she was killed. I let Lucy listen to the message months ago, when we were on better terms. She might have noticed the time stamp then. I don't know.'

'So, you had a relationship with Lucy Arnold.'

'Wouldn't call it a relationship, Tod. She used to come around. We had drinks. She tugged me off in the kitchen once, if you really want to know. We never broke up. It just sort of fizzled.'

He chewed on that for a while. 'Let's go back to the ballroom.'

I nodded. Fun.

'You hear her screaming, you walk in, she's wearing your wife's clothes. What did you say or do next? Be specific.'

I took him through it as best as I could remember, which was pretty clearly, except for her exact words. I told him I was just trying to talk her down, to keep her from popping me.

'She seemed very scared, confused, not like herself,' I said. 'She said Stacey didn't want me to live.'

'She said that? She said, "Stacey doesn't want you to live"?'

I thought it over again. 'I don't know if she used Stacey's name. She might have said, "She", not Stacey.'

'But you had the impression she was talking about someone else, your wife?'

'Yeah. She was angry with me. She was crying. I kept apologizing for blowing her off, but she didn't seem to hear me. I told her to give me the gun and she said, "She won't let me." Like she was hearing another voice in her head.'

Bergen frowned. 'Had she ever appeared mentally ill to you? Unstable? In any way, however minor?'

I thought back to our sad happy hours. 'No. She was just shy. She seemed lonely but shy. She had a kind of passive way of coming onto me, whatever that means.'

Bergen shrugged. 'You never can tell. Then what?'

'Then I kept getting closer to her and she became agitated. She was sort of frozen, up until the very end. Then she pointed the gun at me. I almost had it and then she fired over my head and I collided with her. I guess she dropped the gun on her way out.'

Bergen frowned. 'That's it? She just dropped the gun and walked away?'

What was I forgetting? Lucy had said something on her way out the ballroom doors. 'She screamed "Leave me alone" and ran out. Wait, no, she said, "Leave me alone, she won't leave me alone."'

'And then she ran away?'

'Yes.'

'And you chased her?'

'No, not at first. I was stunned. I thought she shot me.'

'But you did chase her.'

'Yes, eventually.'

'Why?'

I was stumped for a moment. Why had I chased her? 'I was worried about her. I heard her banging around in the hall and I thought she was going to hurt herself.'

Bergen sat back. 'You weren't angry with her?'

'No.'

'A woman breaks into your house, dressed like your deceased wife, and puts a gun in your face.' Bergen came at me, making his hand into a gun and aiming it at my face. His fingernail was six inches from my nose and I could smell his coffee breath. 'You weren't mad at her. You wanted to help her.'

194

Something in me revolted. 'I felt guilty! You think I wanted to beat her up? I was *relieved*. I thought she was going to kill us both.'

Bergen stepped back. 'Easy, easy.'

I breathed. I was hungry. I had a hunger headache.

'Are you calm? You want me to call the doc?'

I shook my head. 'Just get on with it.'

'Did you at anytime believe you were talking to your wife?'

'What?'

'You heard me. When you found Lucy in your house dressed like that. Did you even for a minute think you were talking to your wife?'

'No,' I answered without hesitation. 'I never thought that.'

'Are you sure? Even in those clothes? You've been through some shit, all last year. You were screaming your wife's name after the Lincoln hit Lucy. Do you remember that?'

I didn't remember that, but I believed him. What the fuck was wrong with me? *At first I thought it was Annette. We've been playing dress-up. We're kinky like that.*

'James?'

'No. Soon as I saw her, I thought, holy shit, it's Lucy Arnold.'

Bergen sighed. He seemed to be considering things, which way to go. 'Man to man, off the record, James. What do you think happened?'

'What do I think happened?'

'What was her problem?'

Tell the truth, James, Stacey said. *He's trying to help you.*

'I think I led a lonely woman to believe I had feelings for her. I think she saw me with Annette, she knew we were seeing each other. I think I hurt her feelings and she got mad. I think she was in the house a few times, snooping. She might have buried the shoes in my yard and dug them up to fuck with my head, and when that didn't work she stole the gun and waited until I came home from Annette's, where I had been fucking another woman non-stop for a week, and . . .'

Bergen was staring at me in wonder. 'And then?'

'And then she snapped.'

He studied me for a moment. 'Can you think of any other reason this might have happened? No matter how ridiculous it might sound. Anything?'

Did he know? How would he know about the rest? I needed to say it aloud. I needed someone to hear it. 'Yes, I can.'

His eyes dilated.

'Either Lucy snapped,' I said. 'Or my house is . . . there might be something inside it. Sometimes I can feel her there.'

Bergen stared at me. 'Are you saying your house is . . .? That Stacey was, ah, influencing Lucy?'

I sighed. 'Maybe.'

Bergen's lips parted. He struggled to find the words. 'Why would you—' He shook his head once, then tried and failed to mask his patronizing tone. 'Why would "Stacey" want to do that?'

He's doing his own psych-o now. And maybe he's been doing it since question one.

I decided to go all in. 'Because she's angry with me.'

'For?'

'For not being home when she called. For not answering the phone.' I started to cry and looked away. 'For not saving her.'

Bergen sat down. 'You can't save people from accidents, James.'

I cried for a bit anyway.

'James? Look at me, son.'

I did.

'There's no such thing as ghosts. Your house is not haunted. Lucy Arnold was on four kinds of prescription medications. She had a history of anxiety and depression, possibly some form of mild schizophrenia. She told her therapist she sometimes heard voices, all right? I personally spoke to three of her former lovers and they all left her because she would not stop harassing them. One of them had a restraining order on her last year. Add to which, I lifted her prints from the storage unit rented in your name on La Brea. We took seven positives from the door and two from the lock. We found more of her prints in your kitchen, your living room, the bathroom and your ballroom doors.'

I had stopped crying.

'I know when someone's lying to me. This all fits, and I never saw you as the kind of guy who'd lose his temper and chase a woman down the street. So. I'm going to leave you alone now, on one condition.'

'What?'

'Promise me you'll get some counseling. Annette has the names of three good doctors. Don't drag this out. Be a man and get on with your life. You need to talk to someone about your wife. Will you do that?'

'Yeah.'

'I'm fuckin' serious this time.'

'Okay, yes, I promise.'

Bergen smiled. 'And go slow with your girlfriend, there. She might be a keeper, but you two . . .' he trailed off, shaking his head.

'What?'

'The hair, James. Jesus. Okay? That's why you need therapy, man. She's a sweet gal. She was very cooperative on all this, and you should be thanking your lucky fucking charms she answered all my questions. But just because she's willing to indulge your, what? Fantasies? That doesn't make it right. I get it, she gets it, okay? But stop being so fucking morbid, for Chrissake. Take it easy, son. Didn't I tell you this was going to be a headache? She's a looker, I'll give you that. But there are limits, right? Got to be limits.'

'I know,' I said.

'Okay. I'll check on you next week. Get your ass to the shrinker.'

He shook my hand and left.

After Bergen's interrogation, my session with the hospital's on-call psychiatrist was a cool breeze. I told him what he wanted to hear. He told me he was a big

Ghost fan and doubled my valium prescription with a wink.

Annette came back with my Fatburger, two bags of onions rings and two vanilla shakes. I ate it all in her car on the ride home. When she pulled up in front of my house I stared at it for a minute without opening the door.

'You ready?' she asked.

'I don't think I want to stay here any more,' I said.

Annette looked through the windshield. 'Where should we go?'

'Away,' I said. 'Just . . . away.'

'We can stay at my place,' she said. I looked at Mr Ennis's house. 'No, in Sheltering Palms.'

'I thought you were in foreclosure.'

'I will be soon. But we can probably crash the gates one more time. For a week or so anyway.'

'And then?'

'We'll figure something out,' she said.

I looked at her. Her eyes were hidden behind her sunglasses. Did I want to figure something out? I guess I did.

Inside I packed a week's worth of clothes, flip-flops, my toothbrush. Back in the car I found a pair of old school Ray-Bans in her glove compartment and crawled in back, put my heels up on the rear panel and rolled a sweatshirt under my head for a pillow. Annette drove and I fell asleep enveloped in a warm cocoon of sun, wind and tire hum.

disc 2

the wife

The Millennium Falcon, my rhymes jump to light speed
Han Solo smokin' bowl-o's in the land of legalized
  weed
With a wookie who taps every last Holly and never Go-
  lightly
I poke a hole in the condom, skip the K-Y and flow
  tightly
Mow the lawn with Lady Gaga's Schick
and break one off in Keira's ass Knightly
Go ahead and try, shy boy, take off this mask you most
  likely
find yourself wishin' you brought a bigger knife to the
  fight, see
When I finish openin' arteries your blood jump-starts
  my battery
And guess who's next while you text 9-1-1 and scream
  help, please
I grab the scalpel and stain the sheets like Jeezy Wayne
  Gacy
Pin your eyelids back and grab a snack so you can
  watch me

Creep down the hall, grow ten feet tall and have a ball
dibbidy-dibbidy-dee-the-that's all, folks
It's time for Ghost to wake up wifey

– Ghost, 'Red Rider'
The Habitual Offender *LP*
courtesy of Serial Nubile Records © 2008

21

I drifted in and out until her cursing at intermittent traffic woke me a few hours later. The car slowed, then surged up to highway speed again, and the sun beat into me and I gave up on sleep. I climbed into the front and buckled my lap belt and fished around on the floor until I found a bottle of water. I guzzled and cupped a handful onto the back of my neck. Annette kept rubbing her temples between angry glances at me.

'Do you want me to drive?'

'You don't know where we're going,' she snapped.

I stayed quiet for another half-hour. We were well past the Inland Empire, I realized. There were a lot of golf courses and resorts to the south and a lot more of nothing to the north. 'Where are we? Arizona?'

'A little ways past Banning. Not quite to Palm Springs.'

'We could go camping at Joshua Tree,' I said. 'Isn't that out here?'

'Just a little ways north.'

'Are we close?' I said. 'To your place?'

'Another hour or so.'

'It's pretty,' I said.

'It's obscene. This was all just ranch country in the twenties. Now it's spas, clubs, shopping malls, golf courses, sushi restaurants. Everything you could want and don't need. But we don't live in Palm Springs or Palm Desert.'

I decided to keep quiet and let her narrate when the mood struck her. We exited south, moving into the desert for another twenty-five minutes, doubling back until things turned somewhat green again, then hooked up with a road that disappeared into the low hills, winding and climbing for another ten miles through a shallow canyon (okay, it was a suggestion of a valley) before the signs for Sheltering Palms appeared, warning us to reduce our speed, Residential Area Ahead.

'Now I'm really lost,' I said.

'If there was a highway that went straight through this godforsaken land for another two hours, we'd wind up back in San Diego.'

'Really?' That didn't make sense to me.

'Actually, I don't know. Hemet is pretty close, but there aren't any roads in this direction that go there, not after the SP.'

'The SP?'

'Sheltering Palms,' she said. 'You know, like the OC.'

'Right.'

Traffic had ceased to exist. We were the traffic. This was the kind of place people mean when they say, 'way out there'. Peace. Quiet. Sand. Rocks. No sign of the humies. Hastings's idea of Heaven.

We approached two chintzy white gates leaking rust and a white-walled security booth with no one on duty. Annette removed a plastic card from her purse and waved it in front of the magnetic box. Nothing happened. She waved the card again, spastically, and said, 'Open up, you piece of shit.' After a disconcerting period of waiting, the gates began to hum, sliding on casters into pockets within the brick walls. The walls seemed excessively tall and formidable until you looked in either direction and realized they terminated after about fifty feet. At the ends were pallets of bricks waiting to be added, but no workmen. I glanced at my cellphone. It was 3.25 in the afternoon and I had NO SERVICE. As we entered, I noticed that the security booth windows were just air, every inch of glass broken out or waiting to be installed.

The roads were clean, composed of new asphalt and shallow concrete gutters so unblemished they might have been made of snow. Mature palm trees (what else?) and grass lined the medians, but the grass was crabby and browning by the minute. It must have been a hundred and five degrees, with no wind. *But it's a dry heat*, I consoled myself. The houses were big and no two looked exactly alike, but they were clearly all of one builder. Lots of white and pink stucco, some with white stone façades framed in heavy wood beams. Black tile roofs sucking solar into the grid to counter some of the AC expense, which out here would be exorbitant.

About a hundred feet in we entered a roundabout with a marble fountain at its center, which itself kept a large swan made of greening copper and whose feathers were marred by hard-water stains. The head of this atrocious sculpture stood at least twelve feet above the fat body, a grotesque miscalculation of neck and beak that undoubtedly figured in the nightmares of children who lived here. No spumes glittered in the sun, but a trickle burbled out of the swan's daffy beak, encouraging a beard of moss that hung in greasy strands. As Annette leaned the Mustang through the curve we were blanketed by a miasma of equal parts bog mud, charred metal and rotting salmon.

'I think the motor needs to be replaced,' I said.

'Is that what that is?' Annette scrunched up her nose. 'I always wondered.'

'And there's a dead horse floating in the basin.'

'Don't be a poopy-pants. I told you there'd be some rough spots, but this is a nice place. There's tons of stuff to do here. Wait till you see the bocce court.'

I appreciated her optimism.

The speed limit was posted as twenty-five, but Annette left her pony in second gear and we moved deeper into the development at what felt like a walking pace. There weren't any kids at play; she was giving me a chance to take it all in. The lawns were hardpans of baked dirt. Next to the fire hydrant was a plastic big wheel that had once been red but was now sun-bleached the color of a seashell. I counted fifteen vacant driveways before I spotted another car. It was a blue Grand Cherokee and looked to be in more or less mint condition except for the tires. All four had gone flat. Not slashed, just heat-fucked.

Annette had not been exaggerating. This was not a partially sold out community or a struggling development. It was an abandoned suburb, paradise fled, a ghost division.

The lots ranged from a tenth to half an acre, but the houses were too close together, with less than ten feet of white gravel or dead sod between them. Most were four-, five-, seven-thousand-square-foot jobs. Two-story Mediterranean and Spanish villas. Lots of terraces and archways and balconies for tanning, hosting martini parties or busting out the good old telescope. Some of the balconies were missing chunks of plaster or stucco, the fallen debris littering the driveways below, the metal caging and rebar inside exposed like snapped tendons.

'Oh, hey,' I said, pointing. 'We got a Benz at two o'clock. Someone's home.' The black E-Class was parked in front of a rather striking sherbet-pink domicile whose lawn was still green but also twenty inches high and wilting.

'That's Dr Sewell's place,' Annette said. 'The car belongs to his ex. I think he spends most of the year in Vail now. His sons go to Arizona State.'

The basketball backboard mounted above the middle door of Dr Sewell's three-car garage was missing its hoop. Where the orange plating had been bolted in, there was now only a fiberglass maw. On the backboard itself, in black spray paint, was a fairly accurate rendering of the male genitalia. Above the man junk, in contrasting hot pink, the graffitist had written DR COCKFAG SUKS BOY JOOSE and added a smiley face.

I sipped at my water bottle. 'It would seem Dr Sewell is not on ideal terms with Sheltering Palms' more artistically inclined ruffians.'

'Assholes,' Annette said. 'That was supposed to be cleaned up by now.'

'Maintenance fallen off a bit, has it?'

Annette bumped us up another ten miles per hour. 'Grounds-keeping is supposed to be on until August. Security until the end of the year. I'll call the office tomorrow.'

Annette's headache seemed to worsen. She kept squeezing her temples. I could see her right eye behind her glasses. It blinked in three-click syncopation, signaling a right turn that refused to come.

'Another headache?'

'I feel like I drank a bottle of ouzo.'

'Did they begin after you fell down in the tub?'

Annette scowled. 'I don't know, all right?'

I figured Sheltering Palms had a hundred completed homes, but the low hills were littered with lumber and dumpsters on lots that had been flagged and graded, their foundations poured, the framing abandoned. We leveled out at the bottom of the main valley, which was sort of a bowl at the neighborhood's center. A golden retriever with a ratty coat trotted along the sidewalk without looking at us, then veered over another dead lawn before disappearing between two houses. He was not wearing a collar, and somehow that bothered me more than the rest of the dereliction on display.

Oh, Henry.

'We call this the pit,' she said. 'Not the best part of the neighborhood.'

The houses in 'the pit' were smaller, tasteful but bland, the trim and exterior features scrapped in an attempt to make some of these modern blights afford-able for up-and-coming families. The Euvaldo Gomezes of the world. New money from India, maybe. I imagined a city council meeting with the Caucasian investors, rosy cheeked big-guts gathered around a table, pointing at blueprints and the glass-encased diorama. *Well, fine, fuck it, let them in. But for God's sake put them all down in the gulch where we don't have to look at them.*

More cars populated this section. Practical, no longer upscale models a year or two from becoming true eye-sores, with chirping fan belts and blatting mufflers. A nineties Maxima here, an embarrassing, grape-colored fourth generation Camaro there. A couple of big con-tractor trucks that had once been shiny and tough but were now listing to one side, their battered tool boxes overflowing extension cords, paint-spattered ladders roped to the bed walls. The real standout was a beige van with a pine tree and elk mural just below the tinted dome window, the kind from behind which hitchhikers uselessly scream.

What we were dealing with was an enclave not merely on the way down but showing the first signs of infesta-tion. Not the immigrant infestation, or the color infestation. The criminal infestation.

As in the four Middle Eastern men standing around the pimped-out Tahoe, the ones who perked up as we approached. They concealed something in a paper shopping bag and decided they were late for the early bird special down at the clubhouse, time to boogie. I looked over my shoulder as we passed. Two of them skipped up the walk and ducked inside the house. The other two hopped into the Tahoe, gunned it in reverse, then shot toward the entrance, as if we had rolled up on them with double-barrels propped on the sills. Breaking up the party like Annette was police. Like they would have been skeptical of any car, but were actually afraid of the lady in the green Mustang.

'Fucking terrorists!' Annette blurted, hands whitening around the steering wheel. I flinched, then flinched again as she called out over her shoulder. 'Go back to Iran or I'll blow your fucking house up!'

I threw myself against the door. 'Jesus Christ!'

Her scowl dropped as if she just remembered I was in the car. She reset her shoulders and faced the windshield, everything calm again.

'What the hell? You know those guys?'

'Not personally.' She nodded in acquiescence. 'Okay, I shouldn't have said that. They're just – they're not supposed to be here.'

'Friends of the Ayatollah, you think?' I bit my lip. 'Should we call Homeland Security?'

'It's not funny, James. We've had problems. Those . . . *men* don't live here. They're ruining it for the rest of us. Why are you arguing with me? Do you want to go back? Just tell me—'

'All right, all right,' I said. 'Forget it.'

I was either being exposed to a new, ugly side of her or she was just lashing out from the stress of returning home, to the site of her own tragedy. I was too tired to argue or sift through it right now. I prayed to Allah she had cold beer in the house.

Annette's turn signal eye finally worked. We took a right, then another right, into a shallow cul-de-sac. The lone house standing at the end was an unimaginative interpretation of a Tuscan villa, big and yellow with a detached gatehouse, a courtyard and a swimming pool behind bars. Annette aimed her fazer, the garage door opened and she nosed our good steed in with practiced precision. A kid's lime-green Haro Freestyler BMX bike was leaning against the back wall.

'Yay, we're home.' Annette did a half-hearted little seal clap.

I had forgotten this was where Arthur had done it, in the garage. But I wasn't looking for bloodstains. I was still looking at the bike. I had owned one just like it when I was twelve.

'James?' Annette was waiting at the door.

'Whose bike is that?' I said.

'What? Oh, the neighbor kid left it on the lawn last fall. Arthur put it inside but his family moved away before we could return it.'

I didn't say anything.

'They didn't leave a forwarding address. Maybe you can put it on eBay and find out if it's worth anything.'

I nodded and followed her inside.

213

22

Annette gave me a brief tour of her mostly empty house. She still had her bed and a few other pieces of furniture, but it looked like moving day, the blinds dangling at bad angles, geometric dust stains and dead bugs on the beige carpet. The bathrooms were nice, with lots of colorful Mexican tile, but they smelled damp, swampy, like Florida. She opened windows as we went.

In the upstairs hallway she pointed to a closed door and said, 'Arthur used this room from time to time. I haven't gotten around to it yet. It's important you don't disturb his things, please.'

'Okay.' Thinking, *it's her version of Stacey's storage locker.*

She tested the knob to reassure herself (yep, still locked). I wasn't eager to see it, but I also wondered if she was trying to Bluebeard me by going out of her way to remind me it was off-limits.

I wanted to take a swim. As soon as I'd dropped my bags in the living room and looked through the sliding glass doors, I saw myself making a real summer of it, roasting in a floatation chair, the beer cooler next to the diving board, Annette making triangle sandwiches for lunch, me manning the grill as the sun went down, the two of us frolicking in a lawn chair before passing out by nine. But the kidney pool was algae-lined and scummy with leaves, so I spent most of the next day calling around for a pool cleaner (she had been 'forced to lay Amani off six months ago').

Goldilocks didn't have so much as a bowl of porridge in the house. She said she would go to the store tomorrow and in the meantime we ordered a pizza, which took an hour and a half to arrive. She had no beer, only a bottle of white wine gone to vinegar. I pretended not to mind. The first floor had no furniture save for a couple of couches and the curtains, not even a television to pass the time.

'I had to sell everything,' she said, her shoulders slumping, voice cracking.

'Hey.' I went to her and held her. 'I can help get us some new stuff. It's okay.'

'It's not okay. I'm fucking broke!' She began to cry.

After a while I released her. 'How much?'

'How much what?'

'To stall the foreclosure.'

'I can't take your money.'

'Think of it like I'm paying for a vacation. This is a rental property for me. I don't want it hanging over us and you can pay me back when you sell it. I just want some peace and quiet for a week or two, all right? So, how much will it take for you to sleep well here?'

She deflected and I persisted. We arrived at a sum of seven thousand to make the oldest outstanding

215

mortgage payment, cover a month's worth of utilities, and give her enough walking around scratch that she wouldn't have to feel like an urchin and beg me for five dollars every time she wanted to run back to the drug-store for a new comic book.

'This doesn't feel right, James.'

'You're helping me recuperate,' I said. 'You don't have to worry about money now. I'll get a job at the factory.'

'What factory?'

'That was a joke,' I said.

She smiled thinly and then winced, holding her forehead. Her head was still aching. Coming back was hard for her. This was a swirl of grief and tension headaches.

'Why don't you take something for your head and go lie down,' I said. 'I'll go get some regular groceries and stuff.'

'You don't know where anything is.'

'I brought my laptop. I'll order a TV.'

The Wi-Fi from someone's house nearby still worked. Two days later the geeks delivered a thirty-six-inch plasma, a sound bar, Blu-ray player and a dozen or so new-release CDs and DVDs I chose without much con-sideration. Annette spent most of the first week making calls to the banks, her lawyer Dan and running paper-work back down the hill. I heard her talking sternly but quietly behind the den door, followed by apologies and possibly tears. After these calls, she would hug me and thank me and when I asked for details, why she was crying, she would brush it off. We would have sex again, right then, hot and fast in the afternoon, and later, slowly and carefully at night. I tried not to think about the circumstances that had brought us together, or the headaches, which arrived when she woke up and hung on through the afternoon, no matter how many Excedrin migraine capsules she swallowed.

'I really think you should see a doctor,' I kept telling her.

'I don't even have insurance,' she would say. 'There's nothing they can do. It will pass. I'm fine, really.'

In the evenings we took walks around the neighborhood. She told me about people who used to live here, or had kept a second or third home here. The dentist who had lost his practice for selling pharmaceutical cocaine and happy gas along with the crowns and whitening jobs. The orthopedic surgeon who rebuilt Tom Brady's knee. An Italian family we saw once, the five of them walking the dog, dressed in linen shirts and woven sandals as if preparing for the exodus. Their moving van arrived the next day. We watched TV late into the night, eating licorice and falling asleep on the couch. Sometimes I would look over at Annette and, though she was facing the screen, I was sure she was a million miles away, registering nothing of the repeat sitcom whittling away the hour.

'Everything okay?' I would ask.

And after a ten-second delay, she would answer: 'What? Oh, you can change the channel if you want.'

I stopped asking what was wrong. Ostrich. I think they call it playing ostrich.

This wasn't working, this little pretend vacation. A week into it and we were acting like a married couple with nothing left to say to each other. She got up to use the bathroom often and stayed in too long. A couple hours after going to bed, she would go downstairs in the middle of the night and open the refrigerator door, staring into it for minutes before closing it, and I would lie in bed knowing she wasn't moving and knowing there was nothing much more than leftovers and milk inside. Then she would come back to bed and toss and turn for a while, her sleeplessness keeping me at bay. Something about all of it was bothering her. She was trying to make a decision. Was it about me? About us? The house? I had no idea.

I slept for twelve, fourteen hours at a go and took naps in the afternoon. Every morning I awoke with plans to do something, get organized, read the paper, mow the dead lawn. But I was disorganized, fuzzy-headed, unmotivated. She went through a manic cleaning phase for two days. I offered to help but Annette said no, not after loaning her seven thousand dollars.

'I can clean my own house, thank you. And you need to rest.'

'No, I don't. There's nothing wrong with me,' I told her.

And there wasn't, physically. I had suffered no injuries in West Adams. Just the shock. But the hell of it was I *did* need to rest. I spent a lot of time on the couch, reading a few of the paperbacks Arthur had left behind. Manly escapist fiction. Renegades and ex-KGB trash. And one fat historical romance, *The Bronze Horseman*, consumed me for two days straight and damn near made me bawl. I asked her if she had read this and she said it belonged to 'one of his whores' and threw it out when I was done, disgusted with me for enjoying it. I sat by the pool all afternoon and drank beer. She didn't drink, didn't swim, didn't like the sun. She complained of the heat, the dead silence. She had no friends out here.

'Did you ever talk to someone?' I said one night after dinner. 'About Arthur?' She didn't look up from her plate of ribs and corn on the cob. 'I went to a doctor for a few months after Stacey,' I said. 'It didn't seem to help then, but, looking back, I think it might have.'

Annette slid her chair back from the table. She stood glaring at me, lifted her plate and threw it at the wall. The plate shattered and a trail of barbecue sauce oozed down to the carpet. She blinked, her face red, and then marched upstairs and slammed the bedroom door.

I cleaned up the mess and began to form farewell speeches in my head. If something doesn't change by tomorrow, *adios* . . .

In the morning she woke me on the couch and apologized. She didn't know what was wrong with her, could I forgive her. I told her it wasn't a big deal. I had been there.

'Do you want me to give you some space?' I said.

'No. I need you here.'

'Are you sure?'

'It's strange, but I feel closer to you here than I ever have.' She stretched out on the couch on top of me and kissed me. We enjoyed a moment of quiet pressed together. 'If we got some new furniture, we could waste the summer here.'

'I dunno,' I said. 'I'm beginning to think it would be easier for you back in West Adams.'

'It doesn't matter where we are,' she said. 'We have to get better inside first.'

'I guess that's right,' I said.

'I found a credit card in Arthur's desk. I think we should try it out.'

We went shopping for furniture. I really believed it was the grief inside her until we went shopping for furniture.

23

About thirty minutes outside of Sheltering Palms, but not yet into the nearest town (Palm Desert, I think, though I couldn't have found it on my own), we came upon a huge empty parking lot with three giant stores – furniture, carpet and tile, and a third for bathroom fixtures – connected into one supermart that defied every law of commerce by being open for business. I counted four cars in the parking lot. They had to belong to the employees. Who or what was sustaining this enterprise I had no idea. By winter these stores would be gutted.

Inside the furniture outlet we picked out a new dining-room table, a leather couch and loveseat, and a few accessories to fill the gaps in the house. Annette became more animated as we stepped into the showroom, the scent of new upholstery reviving her spirits. The salesman, an ancient whose nametag read Suzanne, introduced herself as Sue-*Zahn* and I could see most of her skeleton through her parchment skin. Her knuckles were the size of walnuts and roped with green veins. She came on like a bulldozer, though, giving us the hard sell, pursing her drawstring smoker lips and flapping her reading glasses chain when I began to balk at throwing in another matching end table or debated the merits of spending an extra $149 to Scotchguard the reading chair and ottoman.

'You want to invest in furniture to keep as you become a family together,' she said in a voice tanned by brown Moore cigarettes. 'We don't do disposable here. Anybody can fill a house. We're in the business of furnishing *homes*, and we deliver at no charge.'

Annette kept nodding, smiling. They had me boxed in.

'I'll have Derek write this up,' Suzanne said. 'And meet you over in the hutch parlor. All our native woods are fifty per cent off until tomorrow.'

'Ooh, thank you,' Annette said, pulling me along as she weaved through an obstacle course of recliners. Two boys with identical haircuts and matching clothes, one a foot taller than the other, engaged in a game of tag around us, using the chairs for cover.

'Are we really ready for a hutch?' I said. 'I thought hutch status was reserved for people with grandkids.'

Annette smiled over her shoulder at me as the shorter of the two – a squealing, gap-toothed stick figure in need of a flu shot – rounded a maroon lounger and his taller brother pursued him in shrieks of gaiety. The little one kept whipping his head from side to side as he ran, oblivious to us. As if sensing the collision, Annette whirled just in time and he slammed into her midriff. He made an *oof* sound and bounced off her as if hitting a baseball pitch-back, seeming to levitate for a moment before landing flat on his back. Annette bent over in pain, staggered a bit and then went forward and crouched over him in a concerned manner.

I glanced at the taller boy, who was steeling himself rigid beside a plaid recliner, waiting for me to scold him. I shrugged and looked around for their parents. The only other couple – a pair of heffalumps on the far side of the showroom – had their backs to us, admiring the grandfather clocks. I heard urgent whispering behind me, then heard Annette say, 'Ouch!' This was followed by a *crack*. The accomplice brother and I gaped at each other in confusion. When I looked back, she was leaning over the fallen boy, holding a wad of his shirt in her fist, whispering and shaking him.

'Breathe, just breathe,' she said.

The boy was flat on his back, his mouth locked open, emitting clicking sounds. I was gripped with bystander syndrome, trying to understand how such a simple collision had turned into this. He was choking or beyond choking, perhaps seized.

'Breathe!' Annette said, and slapped him across the face. She shook him harder and still he could not gasp that next breath. She slapped him again, this time with the back of her hand. The side of his face was turning red.

'Get off him!' I rushed in and shoved her aside.

She grunted and released him. I did not know CPR. I put my hands on his chest. His heartbeat was going staccato and his mouth hung open, so I tilted his head back as he continued to turn green. His eyes locked on mine and I nodded to him. 'It's okay, bud,' I said. 'Relax, just relax now.'

I glanced back for help. Annette was marching toward the front desk, arms limp at her sides. The older brother kept looking from me to his brother and back, terrified.

I massaged the boy's cheeks and pushed two fingers into his throat. His tongue was where it was supposed to be, but his throat was full of fluid. I lifted him into a sitting position and scooted to his side. I clapped him on the back and he immediately coughed blood that flecked his lips and dripped onto his shirt. I flung myself away in revulsion. Arms thrashing, he inhaled an enormous breath and scrambled to his feet, allowing gravity to send twin threads of blood from his nostrils to the floor in a weaving line as he fled. He went through the front doors, releasing a howling sob only after he had reached the sidewalk. Outside, his big brother grabbed him and pressed him to the storefront, interrogating him by the looks of it, and both boys kept glancing at us, their faces drawn in fear.

The two fingers I had pushed into his throat were red-tipped, as if dipped in paint. I wiped them on my pants, at a loss for what had just transpired. I assumed Annette had gone to call for help, but when I caught up to her at the payment center, she was just standing there, palms flat on the glass countertop, her expression blank.

Suzanne was printing our invoice and her confident demeanor had been replaced by a stiff urgency. She did not look at either of us. She tore the invoice from the printer and slid it toward me, then pulled her hands away hastily and fumbled with the chain attached to her glasses. Her gnarled hands were shaking, her lips curled under her teeth. She stole a glance at the couple on the other side of the showroom, possibly debating the wisdom of calling them over. I realized she did not know the extent of it, had not witnessed the collision. But she had been scolded, and she knew something in her store had just gone very wrong.

'Well?' Annette snapped at me. 'Are you going to sign for the delivery or do you just want to forget it?'

'What?' I looked into her eyes. The left one, the one that had turned blue while I was in the hospital, was dilated and open wide. The green one had gone lazy and lifeless. *Whatever is in her, it changed one of her eyes. Took control. As if they're now wired to different lobes.* She slid the delivery invoice at me and slapped it against the glass, daring me to protest.

I stood there bent over the paper, the pen hovering, unsure of my next move.

'Sign it and give her your card, James,' Annette said. 'Pay the woman, for fuck's sake, so we can get out of this pigsty.'

Suzanne jumped. I guessed the dead man's credit card hadn't worked. I handed over my Visa. Suzanne shot me a terrified glance and ran the card.

I turned and watched the two boys out on the sidewalk. The taller brother was trying to locate his parents, perhaps estimating his chances of finding them without running into us again. Annette shoved the paperwork and my Visa card into my chest and stomped off toward the front doors.

'I'm sorry,' I began, turning back to Suzanne. 'I don't know what—'

'I want her out of my store,' the old woman said. 'And I don't want to see you in here ever again. You can expect a visit from the police.'

The front doors burst open and the boys ran past Annette, shouting, 'Mom! Dad! Mom!'

Annette did not look at them. She went through the doors and crossed the parking lot. I had to go quickly or else she would drive off without me.

'Oh, dear God,' Suzanne said, staring at the one wearing a bib of his own blood. They reached all six hundred pounds of Mom and Dad, who began searching the store with increasingly angry expressions.

'I'm sorry,' I said. 'It was an accident.'

I hurried to the front doors.

'Wait a minute,' Suzanne called after me. 'Hold it right there!'

The sun hit me hard as I crossed the parking lot. I saw the Mustang's green flank reversing and ran to it, slapping the sidewall before she could speed off without me.

'Annette, stop!' I fell into the front seat and Annette rammed the shifter into park. I was panting. Sweat leaked down my sides, into my waistband. 'What did you do? What was that?'

'What?' she said. 'He ran into me.'

'He was choking on his own blood!'

Annette just stared at me.

'Did you hit him? For the love of Christ, did you slap that little boy in the face before he started choking?'

226

'He bit me!' she said. She held up her hand. There was a half-moon of purple indentations and whitish flesh cut open but not bleeding. 'That little mongrel ran into me and when I tried to help him and make him apologize, he bit me.'

'No . . .' my voice trailed off. 'He wasn't breathing. You were shaking him. I saw you.'

'I was trying to help him,' she said. 'You have no idea what you're talking about.'

I ran my hands through my hair and rubbed my eyes. 'I don't understand why he was bleeding like that.'

'Oh please,' she snapped. 'How could you think – no. You know what? Fuck you, James.'

She rammed the shifter into gear and we lurched out of the lot. We did not speak during the ride home. I told myself she was sick. Mentally or physically or both. She had hit her head and something wasn't right. She was not in control of her actions any more. She drove so recklessly I feared further argument would send us careening into a ditch.

At home, back in the garage, I stared at the bike. Annette turned the car off but did not exit.

'James?' she said softly.

I ignored her.

'James?'

'What?' I nearly shouted.

'I didn't slap him.' She looked tired, sorry for making trouble.

I waited, staring into her flat, lifeless eye. The green was dead, the blue alive. One was stronger than the other.

227

'Kids have accidents,' she said. 'Every day. People die every day.'

'What does that mean?'

'What does it mean? It means what if it hadn't been me he ran into? What if he ran into a car? What if he ran into a ditch and fell on a broken bottle?' Louder and louder. 'What if he was playing with a knife and stabbed his brother in the neck? What if he found the gun and *blew his own god damn head off*!'

'You're sick,' I said. 'You need help—'

'He could have died!' Annette shouted. Her entire face went red and the veins in her forehead pulsed. 'He could be dead! *Dead!* Do you understand me? *Do you understand me?*'

I could only stare at her, and that was difficult bordering on unbearable.

She got out of the car, slammed the door and went inside.

I sat in the garage for a while, looking at the BMX bike.

24

She wasn't on the first floor. I waited a few minutes, running a sponge nonchalantly around the kitchen counters, humming nervously. I kept seeing that boy's face. If I had not lifted him, he would have drowned in his own blood. And I could not escape the feeling that she had wanted him to die. That she had been pushing him to the edge.

In how many ways was I culpable? The store had my credit card info. The police would find my address, but not me. They wouldn't know I was here. Except, ding-dong, dumbass – you have a furniture delivery. They could be on their way right now. I almost hoped they were.

And I was guilty of riding along with her as she became a danger to others. This was a wake-up call. I needed stop her. I needed her to understand that her aggressive . . . assault, yes, it was an assault . . . was unconscionable. I would not allow it to happen again. And if she did not immediately agree to see a physician and a therapist, and acknowledge how awfully she had behaved, I would leave her. Tonight. Simple as that.

I went up the stairs. The master bedroom door was locked.

I knocked. 'Annette, open the door.'

Silence.

'Annette, we need to talk about this. The police are going to come sooner or later. I'll talk to them if they come. I will tell them what happened. Do you hear me? You're going to have to deal with this.'

If she stirred, she did so in silence.

'I'll be back in fifteen minutes,' I said to the door. 'We will talk about this. Otherwise I'm gone.'

I went downstairs and stood in the kitchen and chewed my nails. I drank a beer, and then a second beer. Gone to what? Where are you going to go? I went into the living room, hooked up the Blu-ray player and watched something starring fire.

When the movie was over, I stared at the credits, delaying and delaying. I had six or seven beers rolling around in me, but felt sober. The day was shot. Night was here and I didn't see a way out. I was too buzzed to get behind the wheel. Maybe tomorrow morning would be the better time to confront her. It was going to be a long night, the kind where I slept on the couch. Well, there was the television. I had more movies. I sat up to go use the bathroom and the doorbell rang. It was a modern doorbell, more of a muted gong, a sort of thrum deep in the house. For a moment I didn't even know what it was, then it gonged again.

I set my empty beer bottle on the floor and walked

around the kitchen, through the front hall, into the foyer. The porch light was off but the foyer light was on, creating a glare on my side of the front window. I could not see anything outside, so I stood behind the door for a moment, wondering who would ring the doorbell at almost nine thirty.

Oh, of course. The police.

I looked through the peephole. The view was fish-eyed and no one was standing on the porch. There were no police cars on the street or in the driveway. Maybe the gong wasn't the doorbell. I turned and headed back toward the hall. I turned right into the bathroom.

Bam . . . bam . . . bam.

Someone knocked on the door three times, using the side of their fist by the sound of it, with a deliberate pause in between each strike. All right. So, it was either someone short or someone had walked away and gone around the garage right before I looked through the peephole, then came back and tried again.

I walked back to the door and looked through the peephole again. Same empty porch. Same empty street. This was sort of not funny now.

I opened the door. I checked the end of the driveway. The front yard. The street. No people. I leaned to the right and flicked on the porch light. It did not reveal anything. I was closing the door when something twinkled in my peripheral vision, down low on the concrete step. I shoved the door aside and stepped out.

Annette did not have a welcome mat, or even a real porch, just the bare concrete step some four feet by four

231

feet. At the approximate center of it was a white chalk circle the diameter of a basketball. In the center was a tight formation of marbles in the shape of a V with a stem growing out of the center. Seven of the marbles were black and the one at the base was white. I stepped around it and viewed it from the other side, and realized it was not a V with a stem growing out of it.

It was an arrow, pointing at the house.

I looked up quickly, scanning the yard again. I walked down the step, along the walk, into the driveway. I checked the side of the house, the gate with the court-yard and pool behind it. I went the other way around and checked the side yard where the grass was dying and only three or four dead young trees separated ours from the undeveloped dirt lot next door. Nothing and no one. If it had been kids, they were hiding now.

I walked back to the front porch and picked up the white marble. It was heavy, about the size of a grape. I tossed it in my palm a couple times, then lobbed it at the door. It made a hollow *whock* noise that bore no resem-blance to the knocking I had heard a few minutes ago, and fell to the foyer tile and rolled down the hall a bit. I went in and started to shut the door behind me, then stopped. Something about leaving the marbles on the porch bothered me, so I went back out and scooped the others up and carried them inside. On the way to the kitchen, I bent and added the white one to the others in my palm. I set them on the kitchen counter, in a row between the tiles, watching them for a minute while nursing another beer.

Marbles. An arrow. Inside a circle.

If it was supposed to mean something, the meaning was lost on me.

Kids. God damn kids.

I set my beer down and went upstairs to check on Annette.

The bedroom door was ajar and the room was hot with evening sun that had not vented despite the late hour. A weak glare from a distant street light cut through the vertical blinds, striping the bed and her shape under the covers with dull orange light. I went to her side and sat on the bed. Her face was dotted with sweat. Her eyes were partially open but she did not blink or do anything to suggest she knew I was in the room.

'Hey,' I said. 'You all right?'

She did not respond. I moved up against the bed and wiggled her wrist. Her arm felt like a stick floating in a sleeve of gelatin. I put my hand on her forehead. I expected her to be feverish but her skin was cool, almost cold.

She's emotionally exhausted. Let her sleep.

Stacey had been emotionally exhausted, too, near the end. Those last few months before the accident, during that cold distance that was our way of fighting. She had been spending more and more time out of the house, even when I was home between gigs. When I confronted her and said she was changing, that I knew something was wrong, she denied it and said she was just 'emotionally exhausted', as if emotions were a finite resource.

What does that mean? I had asked her. I hated the phrase. It's a child's excuse. Emotionally exhausted is what celebrities tell the media when they are too strung out to perform. Ghost had used the same line every couple of years, walking off stage or canceling the last leg of his tour.

'You wonder why I'm not prancing around, happy to see you?' Stacey had responded, a deadness in her voice. She was not even arguing, merely reciting something. 'Maybe it has nothing to do with you. Since when is my whole life about you and Ghost?'

'What's Ghost got to do with anything?' I said. 'You're never here, even when you're here. I don't know where you go. What do you want me to do?'

'Leave me alone,' the sullen teenager replied without moving her eyes from the television. 'Think you can do that?'

'No. I can't. I love you and I want to know what the fuck is wrong here.'

Then she got up and calmly walked out of the house, got in her car and drove off to wherever she was going that day. Back to her friends, off to see her new boyfriend (less likely, but it had crossed my mind) or maybe just to sit in another yoga class where she could feel independent and spiritual.

Three days later I found the pills. I was looking for a cigarette lighter in her purse, not snooping. All right. I was snooping. But it was her purse, not her diary or Fort Knox, and I was her husband. I think it's fair to say that when your spouse becomes a zombie in the skin of the person you married, purses, wallets, cellphone records, dry-cleaning pockets, and, yes, email become communal property. Is this not part of the reason we get married in the first place – to have someone there to catch us when we start to fall?

Annette was still sleeping. I looked at her chest, trying to gauge the regularity or irregularity of her breathing. Was this her way of grieving? I didn't think catatonia was a natural symptom of losing your husband. Was it drugs for her, too? Torqued chemistry, à la bipolar disorder? Dissociative personality disorder? Demons lodged deep, math teacher named Chester?

Don't let Annette fall. Don't let her be like Stacey.

What if it's too late? What if she's already like Stacey? And what if there's no 'like' about it?

I didn't find a lighter or a book of matches in Stacey's purse that day. Just a bottle of Tylenol PM, the orange DayQuil capsules, some valium, Percocet, Lamicta, Ambien, Xanax, and a few others that weren't even in bottles, just rolling around at the bottom with the lint like newer, more entertaining flavors of Tic Tacs. Two of the prescriptions were in Stacey's name. One was in the name of Rowina Daniels, her kleptomaniac friend from North Carolina. The others were blank, the labels peeled off.

Is my wife depressed? I had wondered.

And then, *how long?*

And then, *is this what depression looks like, or are we dealing with something of a greater magnitude here? Has she been diagnosed?* Someone had written two of the scrips for her.

235

But what about the rest? Was she in counseling? Do doctors really think two, three, five kinds of pills are the answer to our problems? I knew she took Ambien now and then to help her sleep. *If it's a legitimate health issue, why is she being so secretive?*

And god damn it, what's so difficult about telling your husband, 'I don't feel so hot and I don't know why. Will you help me figure out what's going on?'

The fact that he's never home when you're feeling strong enough to ask for help. How about that?

I looked down at Annette, pale, shivering Annette in the bedroom. Was I attracted to unstable women? Or was this a coincidence? Half the country is on one prescription or another, I consoled myself. It's not her fault. Modern life is a nasty stretch to serve. We take antidepressants and anti-anxiety and anti-feeling human pills the way we used to take vitamins and cigarettes and martini lunches. We take one pill to wake us up and another to put us down. A simple cup of coffee and a walk after dinner have become Red Bull and vodka. We take a pill to relax so we can cross off five hundred things on our To Do list, most of which are meaningless. We take fuckpills, but do we really need to provoke and then tame an erection that lasts four hours? If we are not trying to feel more more more, we're doing everything we can to feel nothing at all. Flatly happy or just god damned sad aren't allowed any more. In the pursuit of a pain-free emotional life, we're sanding the edges off the human experience, and we'll keep on doing it until we wake up one day and realize life has become one monotonous swim in a kiddie-safe pool filled with hand sanitizer.

Your addiction is your excuse, baby. Buck up.

Yes, have another beer, James. Go sleep in another motel and spank it to more internet porn so you don't have to deal with a complex human being, you numb, hypocritical asshole.

Annette. She could be suicidal. Have you considered that? What if you leave, just bail and go back to your happy life in West Adams, pretend you never met her, and then wake up next week to Detective Bergen knocking on your door? Hiya, James. That friend of yours, the kooky neighbor? Yeah, killed herself. She went Lucy on us. Way to string another woman along. You really know how to help a woman in need, Hastings. You know what you are? A jerk-off. Another jerk-off in a city of millions.

And that was what it came down to for me, right then. As messed up as this woman was, she had come to me for help. She had lost her husband. Our fates were intertwined. She had come to me for help and I had let her in. What kind of man would I have been if I just wished her the best of luck and walked out the door?

'Annette? Can you hear me?'

She did not respond.

I closed my eyes and summoned something. In the silence, here on the hot second floor where my thoughts were hazy and her condition teased me, impossible things seemed possible. I leaned closer and spoke very quietly.

'Stacey?'

No change of expression. She merely continued to sweat.

'Is that you? Can you hear me, Stace? Are you trying to tell me something?'

The facial muscles under her left cheek began to twitch. Just three or four quick flutters, as if someone were pulling an invisible thread attached below her eye. Then it stopped and she was still. Her breathing was slow. This was insane but I had to try it. I had to know. I leaned in until I was less than six inches from her face.

'Stacey,' I whispered. 'Stacey. I'm here, love. Open your eyes. I'm right here.'

Annette's breath trickled in and out. Nothing changed.

Something in the room smelled bad. There was a new odor, subtly biting and alkaline. It was so familiar but out of place that it took another minute for me to classify – my mind leaping back to Henry's puppyhood and stained carpets – as urine. I stood up and rubbed my mouth.

Oh, I see. This is real. She is very sick now.

I reached forward and peeled the bedding back, down to her knees, and then bit my hand to keep from screaming.

25

The large wet spot that had spread around her bottom was not what made me bite my knuckles until my eyes watered. I was staring at her skin. Annette was wearing only a ribbed tank top and a pair of blue cotton panties. The rest of her was bare and pale. No, pale is inadequate. The skin covering her legs, arms, neck and everywhere else visible to me then was *alabaster*.

Like so many redheads, Annette had hundreds of freckles. I had gotten so used to them I no longer noticed them. But now their absence stood out in one great negative space. Her freckles were not faded or pale against the paler epidermis. *She had no freckles.* The very pigment that had once set them off against her already light skin had vanished as if she had spent the last twenty-four hours soaking in a tank of Clorox.

Her cheeks were the only part of her to retain any sort of color, and there she maintained only the slightest pink, but, yes, now that I studied her face, I could swear that this too was fading. I stood above her for unknowable minutes and tried to comprehend what illness could have such an effect. She had the skin of a corpse that had been floating in a lake for a week without the gaseous bloating, and yet she breathed. She was alive.

A crawling fear, one I did not know existed, slowly but inexorably claimed me. It was the fear of a child cursed with adult knowledge, discovering some terrible truth before he is mature enough to cope with it. I had nothing to compare it to. Not even finding Stacey dead in the alley behind our home, which had been a horror but not a fear. I did not know what this meant, what it was. My mind groped for reason and reference but found neither. I stood with it and it rearranged me. I was powerless and alone with an awful secret, the secret of her changing.

She's dying. Call for help. Call an ambulance.

Annette's eyelids went up in one smooth motion. Her eyes did not move to me. She only stared straight ahead, unblinking, her pupils reduced to pinhead specks. Blue. Both eyes were blue now. Her lips parted and I retreated another pace from the bed.

'He's here,' she said in a voice too quiet and soft for me to identify as her own. I waited, but nothing followed and another minute passed.

'What?' I prompted.

'He's in the house again.'

This sentence, and the ones that followed, seemed to form over a period of minutes.

'He's in the bedroom with her,' she said. 'Wearing the red suit. So red . . . it's almost wet. His skin burns. It shines with the blood from the boys and girls.'

'No one is going to hurt you,' I said.

Her chest rose and fell between the words. She displayed no sign of agitation.

'He won't stop until he eats every part. Every part of me.'

'Who?' I heard myself ask. 'Who is he?'

Her eyelids came down and went back up. Her breathing accelerated, the little gusts now audible. Her head rotated on the pillow and her eyes found me. My legs began to shake. I could not control them.

'And then he's going to get the boy, too.'

I licked my lips. 'Who? Who are you talking about?'

'Her son.' Her eyes shimmered. 'Oh, Aaron . . .'

The bicycle. In the garage. It belonged to a boy. She had a son named Aaron and she was talking about herself in the third person now. Who did she think she was then? Who was this white form on the bed?

'Who are you?' I said.

She sat up in the bed and hissed, reaching for me. 'Sssss-staaaayyy . . .'

I ran from the room, slamming the door behind me. I ran down the stairs and stumbled out the front door, into the night that had fallen.

26

I don't know at what hour I stepped out, only that it was now true night. I ran to the end of the cul-de-sac, turned right and kept running until it became obvious that she was not following me and my lungs were burning. I settled into a brisk pace and walked for an hour. I moved through the development unseen, or at least undisturbed. The windows of every home I passed were dark. I saw few cars, all of them parked, and no people walking their dogs or otherwise stretching their legs. I followed the sidewalks and at some point crossed a field of grass I did not know was a park until I almost ran into the cold, abandoned bars of playground equipment. I sat at the bottom of a slide and made trails in the sand with my shoes.

I hadn't thought about the Mustang when I ran out the front door, and now I couldn't bring myself to go back, not even to the garage. She might be walking around the house now, looking for me. She might be standing in the living room, at the window, stiff behind a curtain like a department store mannequin, waiting for me to return.

Oh, Aaron.

I did not know anyone named Aaron, and I didn't want to. I was not going back there, not tonight, perhaps ever.

Sheltering Palms was too deep in the desert to have bus service. I did not have my cellphone to call a cab. I considered walking out, down the road, into Palm Desert or whatever the nearest town was, but I knew it was miles away and I was tired. I did not want to speak to police or medics. I did not want to deal with their questions. I wanted to be alone, somewhere warm, in a soft bed. Everything I had witnessed collected into some vague cloud, the knowledge that something was wrong and that I had caused it.

This is your guilt. You are condemned.

The desert air cooled. I wore only jeans, sneakers and a t-shirt. I couldn't stay out all night. I decided to find a home with a phone and call it in as an emergency. I would offer no explanation other than *there is a woman and she needs help*.

I found myself walking again, through backyards, around and over low, split-rail fences set in brittle grass. I was looking for a light, some sign that another, normal person was awake, watching late-night television. I imagined a man like myself, a sort of laid-back dude who wouldn't scream when I knocked on his door and told him I needed to use his phone. He would be dressed in sandals and a polo shirt with barbecue sauce on it, would be on his third or fourth gin and tonic. He would listen to my story and nod in sympathy. Sure, brah, you can borrow my car. We'll sort it out.

But I found no houses with lights on. I saw no people through any of the windows.

It's a ghost division.

I decided to test the truth of that.

The house I chose was another stucco sprawl, its peach walls light in the night, with wooden beams extending from the façade like rounded cigar ends. It reminded me of the Alamo. I rang the doorbell, which gonged solemnly behind the thick wooden door. No lights were on and I knew no one would answer, but I used the heavy iron knocker anyway. The knocks echoed hollowly, and another five minutes passed. Once I was certain no one was watching me, I stepped to the left, and jabbed my right heel at the base of the foyer window. It vibrated. My second kick sent one thousand cracks through the pane. The third turned the webbed mass into a rain that seemed very loud in the night. I braced myself for the howl of an alarm.

No alarm sounded.

I turned sideways and slid through the narrow window frame, my feet crunching on pebbled safety glass and tile. Inside, I searched for a blinking alarm panel, but saw only dim walls and a wider opening into the sunken great room. I reached for a light switch on instinct, thought better of it, and waded deeper into the house with my hands in front of me.

'Hello?' I said, loudly. 'If anyone is home, I'm sorry. I've had an emergency and I need to use the phone. Please don't shoot. I just need to call an ambulance.'

I waited a while, but no lights came on and no one

answered me. My vision became attuned to the darkness and I realized there was not a single stick of furniture in the great room. The air carried new paint and carpet chemical smells. The house might never have been inhabited. I stepped down into the great room and looked up at the high-vaulted ceiling and the railing of the exposed second-floor hallway. No one watched over me. I looped around to the breakfast area and into the kitchen. I found a panel of four switches and flipped the first one up. A small recessed light came on, illuminating a desk area near a phone jack, but no phone. It was a bill-paying area just off the kitchen and the light was minimal. I did not think it would attract attention, and I doubted there were any neighbors on this street. The light boosted my confidence.

The refrigerator was empty, the yellow and black Energy Star tag still dangling over the door. The freezer's ice maker had not even produced its first cube. The unit was still warm, not even plugged in.

The house had a first-floor master suite. I arrived at it through a long, carpeted hallway, passing a laundry room and a bathroom on the right and a small den on the left, none of which had any furniture in them either. I threw the master bedroom light on and was confronted with a king-sized bed. My eyes registered sheets and pillows and a blanket with a south-western motif and my skin prickled as I jerked back, expecting someone to sit up and start screaming at me. But the bed was empty, the creased pillows and sheets square, unused.

Absurdly I lowered my voice and said, 'Hello?'

No, if someone was home, you would have been beaten with a baseball bat by now. A realtor staged it for showing, that's all. They just never got around to staging the rest of the house.

I went into the master bathroom and turned another light on. A large oval tub with dust and dead moths in it abutted a hexagonal shower stall with streaks of drywall dust on the glass panels. The low, almond-colored vanity featured his and her sinks. After making sure the water wasn't brown, I used one to splash cold water on my face and used my shirt to blot my face and hands dry. I turned off the bathroom light, but the darkness was too severe. I found the toilet alcove and flipped the switch. It cast just enough light on the end of the bedroom to put me at ease.

The walk-in closet was large and empty.

I stared at the bed. After a time, my legs felt rubbery and I sat on the edge of mattress, so firm it might have been designed to discourage actual sleeping. But it was softer than a sidewalk and cleaner than a lawn. There were no memories here. No one had lived in this house. No one cared about this house. Nothing could hurt me here. I would be safe for the night, for a few hours, just until the sun came up. I folded the sheets back and kicked off my shoes. I leaned over until my head touched the cool pillowcase. I pulled the covers up to my shoulder and listened to the house around me. It did not creak or shift. There was only silence and solitude. I bet myself that I could scream at full volume without drawing a response, and the thought was so freeing I almost did. Tomorrow I would steal her car and go home. Tomorrow . . .

I fell into a pleasant state of sleep without dreams.

Hours later, but still hours before dawn, I was awakened by the distant but distinct sound of careful footsteps crunching on pebbled glass.

SHE

The happiest summer of James's life took place at the house on Gaynor Lake. The small body of water was hardly a mile across, in a private development along the Front Range of Colorado. There were fewer than fifty homes lining the shore, and only two on the western side, where the Hastings and Tanner families vacationed. James and Stacey learned to water ski there, behind a low, sparkling red and silver boat with a Corvette engine. They swam all day, throwing the football over the dock and diving to look at each other in golden bands of sunlight above the darker plane below their feet. They got sunburned and his hair turned almost as light as hers. That August seemed to broaden his shoulders, put calluses on his hands and thicken his forearms. He became more than a boy and less than a man.

They played poker for bottles of her dad's Michelob, which she filched from the garage and stashed in her sun tote. She used SPF 4 and let the sand dry on her back. They rode the little Puch moped down the dirt county roads to the general store where you could still buy chocolate Cokes and stole a cigarette lighter to share their first joint. They smoked it on the other side of the lake, cavorted in the water for an hour and then rode home. To this day he remembers vividly, totally and painfully Stacey's wet green swimsuit sticking to the seat as she leaned against him, holding him as the cloud of dust trailed behind them, and the heart-shaped impression of moisture it left on the black leather when they got off.

He took Stacey out to where herons unfolded from the marshy north bank, taking flight over the bow while he paddled the canoe into the cat tails. There were garter snakes and leopard frogs, crawdads and skimmers, and, though he fished to impress her, he never caught so much as a sunfish.

There was a wooden dock and a boathouse at the end of the long concrete ramp, a great lawn with a sand vol-leyball court and a terrace with the grill and umbrella table, all leading up to the house. With the blinds raised over the wide sliding glass doors and the A-frame win-dows above, the den bedroom was the perfect place to lie back and watch strange things come over the moun-tains. Thunderheads that towered miles above like stacks of white balloons and gray-bearded titans. Branches of lightning that forked out in seven directions and doubled themselves on the black water mirror of the lake. Rolling gusts of eighty-mile-per-hour wind white-capping the usually placid surface of Gaynor before fat raindrops cupped it in a million places. Once, at the end of June, just after they arrived, baseball-sized hail splashed shingles from the roof like poker chips, pounding them off in a splintery rain.

They talked about how different time was here than in Tulsa, how strange that they had not been able to come together until their parents, old friends from church functions, lured them away from home. James remembered the time they had a playground crush-argument in sixth grade, and later that night ran into each other with their parents at Burger Chef & Jeff, stealing haughty glances and bonding subliminally over their fried chicken baskets. Stacey laughed about the time when fifteen kids from school went to see *Footloose* and how she called him Ren for weeks after, teasing him because he wore skinny ties and tried to make his hair like Kevin Bacon's. How even though she had other boyfriends and he had other girlfriends in high school, he was the one she called that time she ran out of gas. He drove out to the south side of town with a can to get her mom's Vega rolling again and followed her all the way home.

They had their first kiss on the dock, standing under the stars while their parents stayed up late playing spades and drinking gin around the dining-room table, listening to Neil Diamond. Under the pool table in the basement, she let him roll the straps of her one-piece down her shoulders and the taste of the lake was fresh on her skin. He kissed the triangles of white inside the darker lines of her breasts until the wide buds became firm in his mouth, making her laugh, her telling him they weren't popsicles. How tentative as he crossed the border of stubble along the inside of her thighs, testing the thick folds and her wetness for the first time. How clumsy her hand, a girl uncertain and a little bored, pulling him against her thigh, against her hip bone, his first orgasm with a girl. How strange and natural their fluid scents were, like the lake, as if it had been soaking into them for weeks.

Sneaking upstairs after, eating a late dinner of cold barbecue ribs and corn standing in the kitchen, amazed at their own daring, and finally off to their separate bedrooms, neither sleeping, the night sweaty and bug alive, they can almost read each other's minds in this moment, both knowing each is dying for tomorrow to arrive so they can begin again.

Tulsa was so hot in the summer, being in Colorado was perfect, and they always said one day they would come back. It was an annual tradition.

'When we're all grown up and married, think we can come back and live here and have babies?' Stacey asked him on the last night. They were swimming again, the water black around their gooseflesh skin. 'I want to live here when we're rich enough to own a lake house.'

And James said, 'I guess that would be cool.'

Stacey laughed.

It was the place they fell in love, the first time either fell in love. It connected their plain childhood to their unlikely future, and for that its power would hold sway over the rest of their lives. The parents never had a clue. They were very good at hiding everything, and, though it was only a month and went so fast, it lasted forever.

27

At first I did not know where I was. I raised my ear from the pillow and looked down to the foot of the bed where the faint band of light cut across the bathroom and I thought I was home, in the master bedroom in West Adams, looking out at my own hallway. The grinding sound was coming from the other side of the house. The space I inhabited felt disorganized, and the succession of recent events toppled forward like dominoes and I remembered I was in a stranger's house, the empty house in Sheltering Palms. I had broken a window . . .

The crunching noises continued a few seconds more and then the house fell silent. I thought of Annette, the alabaster form she had become. It did not seem likely – and I did not want to believe – she had followed me here. Whatever was wrong with her, she was not coherent enough to follow me. But no one else knew we had returned to Sheltering Palms. We had not spoken to anyone. Which meant that whatever had made the noises on the broken glass was either a curious neighbor who had seen a light on, the owner or owners who had come home, or, a preferable alternative, the thing in the entryway was not a person at all, but an animal. A deer or coyote, perhaps. But animals come searching for food. There wasn't any food in the house. If not lured by the scent of something edible, what other reason would an animal have for stepping over a ledge and sliding through a narrow window frame? None.

There were only two reasonable responses. I could get up, walk down the hall and confront them. Explain my situation, apologize, hope for the best. Or I could try to escape through one of the three windows to the right of the bed. I had not paid much attention to them before lying down. They were just three tall black rectangles behind the layers of drapes, the first a heavier fabric of light green or blue, and the filmy gauze layer against the windows. I could not make out any latches or cranking handles that would open them, but there had to be a way to do so. If someone came for me I could push the drapes aside, rip out a screen and leap into the night.

I rolled over and rested my head on the pillow again. I would wait them out. I had not heard another sound for at least two minutes, and I was banking on the possibility that the trespasser was another wanderer, like me. He might snoop around, realize there were no valuables, and decide to move on to the next vacant home. I positioned myself so that I was facing the doorway, which I had left open. The hallway beyond was dark, and the angle was wrong. I could see only a few feet into the hall, and only the left-side wall. If the trespasser chose to come into the bedroom, I would not see him coming; he would just appear in the doorway. My only other avenue of escape was not an escape at all, merely a hiding place. The walk-in closet to my left had a door, but I doubted it locked from the inside.

The next few minutes seemed very long. Five minutes might have passed, or half an hour. I imagined that I heard footsteps going up the stairs and along the hallways overhead, but the harder I concentrated the more ambiguous the sounds became. More silence passed, and my ears began to ring. I flexed my jaw until the ringing went away. At some point I caught snatches of conversation, faint but rhythmic, convincing me there were two or more of them. The voice or voices were low, not especially urgent. The words were indecipherable, mumbling. I pictured two uniformed policemen standing at the end of the hall, whispering into their shoulder mics and conferring with each other. They were getting ready to move on me. Then those voices stopped and the air grew heavy, closing around me in a pocket, until I could hear nothing but my own breathing. I felt as if I were in a bubble, my senses dimming. I kept blinking and popping my ears.

Something swabbed the floor. Or a wall. It was the sound of clean rubber, a new windshield wiper sweeping over moist glass. Someone laughed. It was disturbing in its casual release, the sound of a tired father having one last chuckle at a sitcom rerun before nodding off. After the tapering sigh of a laugh, someone said, 'Yeah, yeah, I know', and the volume of this voice was so low it might as well have been a radio in a car parked a block away.

You're hearing things.

Focus. For the love of God, what is going on here?

'Some kids,' I mumbled to myself. 'Just a bunch of kids out screwing around.'

Immediately I regretted speaking. As soon as I finished the half-whispered sentence, something banged loudly and vibrated at the end of the hall. It sounded like someone dropping a wooden dowel rod on the tile floor – *ah ha, he's down there, now put that thing down and let's go.*

This commotion finally snapped me out of my passive resolve to wait them out and I bolted upright. I shuffled my feet under me and backed against the wall. There was no headboard. I willed my legs to launch me from the bed, into the hall, the closet, out the window – anywhere – but they refused. I was trapped now, waiting for the inevitable footsteps and explosion of anger in the room. Any second now the lights would flash on and I would be caught. I stared at the doorway, and waited.

And waited.

The footsteps did not come. The hallway was carpeted. Were they creeping toward me in their stocking feet? What did they want? If I had angered them by coming into this house, why were they drawing it out? Why not just turn on all the lights and shout, demand I reveal myself, attack?

An interminable minute passed, then another. I pressed myself against the wall and forced myself to breathe through my mouth, into my cupped right hand. My eyes had adjusted to the darkness and I could see as well as I was ever going to see in here, at least until the sun began to rise. What time was it? How long had I been asleep? I was certain I had been out for hours, and that dawn must be coming soon. The promise I made to myself to get up and leave was repeated over and over, but, the longer I waited, the more times I told myself *in a minute*, the harder it was to move my legs. They began to cramp. A brave version of me kept daring the cowardly other, and the other shriveled at the challenge. My left leg was falling asleep. My back was stiffening. I knew someone was here. I had not imagined the grinding glass sounds in the foyer. I wanted to scream.

I believe I remained locked in this position for two hours or more. It seemed much, much longer than that by the time I finally realized I was spooking myself and no one was in the house. Or that if they had been, they were long gone now. The still silence had returned, returned and expanded in a torturous test of my ability to remain immobile, and nothing had changed. I almost burst into tears, but was afraid to show any emotion. I was tired, so exhausted I began to lose my fear of being found out. Nothing made sense. There was simply no logic that explained why anyone – the house's owner, a cop, teenaged vandals, or even Annette – would wait so long to make their presence known.

I caved in all at once, releasing a long sigh and allowing my legs to slide from under me. My knees popped and the blood began to flow back into my feet. I leaned back against the wall and wiped my face with the bedspread. I was very thirsty and I had to urinate. I decided

I would use the bathroom, have another drink of water and leave the way I came in.

I slid from the bed, onto my feet. The blood moved thick inside me, making my feet tingle. I walked into the bathroom and bent over the sink, cranking the cold water and cupping the flow into my mouth. I drank until my head ached and my belly was full. I stood and looked into the wide vanity mirror, wiping my mouth with my forearm. Next to the bed some twelve feet behind me was a boy with a white face under a black hood standing against the curtains, staring at the spot on the bed where I had been sleeping.

His presence was so matter-of-fact and perfectly still, my mind could not register it as fact and my body was gripped with total paralysis. He was staring at the bed, not me, and I could not move now in front of the mirror for fear of stirring his attention. I was aware of the hair on my forearm stiffening beneath my lips as I breathed into the crook of my elbow, but my eyes never left him. He was short, only as high as my chest, dressed in narrow black pants and the black hooded sweatshirt with a bulge at the lower front. I could not see his hands, and assumed they were in the pocket over his belly. His feet were bare, small as two decks of cards, white as Annette's stomach had been, nearly glowing in the dark bedroom. His shoulders were hunched forward, his neck cocked forward a bit, and the profile of his jaw and nose and chin were just as white as his feet.

My God, how long? How long has he been standing there? Half an hour? Two hours? Since I fell asleep? No, I'd looked at the window an hour ago. He was not there then. How did he get inside the room? He could not have come through the door-way – I would have seen him. Unless, while I was lying with my head on the pillow, I had not been able to see the floor in the doorway and at the foot of the bed. He very well may have belly-crawled down the hall and across the bedroom floor.

Or else he just materialized.

But what if he had been there all along and I couldn't see him until I looked in the mirror? Oh, Jesus, oh, Jesus Christ, this not happening.

He's not, he's not real. And that is what makes him so awful to behold.

He still hadn't moved. He wasn't even breathing. My shoulder ached from holding my arm horizontal across my chin. He had to go away soon. He had to, like the boy I saw in the backyard, wearing the blazer with the private school crest. It was him, I knew it, the same boy in different clothes.

At the same moment my memory made the connection, the boy in the bedroom lifted his nose as if catching a scent, then turned his head swiftly toward the mirror and the hood over his brow and ears cupped outward like the neck of a cobra as his reflection turned and came at me in a series of purposeful strides.

I turned on my heels in time to see him walking faster, everything moving too fast, and his hands came out of the pouch and reached up to pull the hood back, I knew, so that he could show me his face.

'No!' I shouted, backing into the vanity, trapped.

The white backs of his tiny hands came together over

his forehead and swept up without a sound, pulling the hood back and everything, his entire face, was flat white and his voice, if it was a voice, came through like a repeating snatch of overheard conversation whispered deep inside me.

. . . did look what they did look what they did look what they . . .

And I shouted, covering myself as he ran into me and I felt nothing other than the blood pounding in my ears, followed by a dull ringing, and finally silence.

I lowered my arms and surveyed the bedroom, which was filling with the blue light of dawn, but the boy was nowhere to be seen, and at once the room felt purged and dull. I was certain that I was alone now, mirror or no mirror. But I did not turn around to seek his reflection. Nor did I wait for him to return.

28

An hour and a half later, after stumbling upon the entrance gates and rotting swan statue in the septic fountain, I was able to recalibrate my bearings and find my way back to Annette's. The sun was up, the air inching toward the seventies, and yet I was cold, and tired beyond words. My brave decision to walk out of the SP had evaporated. Now I just wanted a hot shower and a familiar bed, even if it was hers. Whatever was wrong with her, she was a person, not someone who could appear and vanish through walls. She was sick, and a doctor would be able to explain how her freckles appeared to have vanished.

As for the boy, well, I was having a nervous breakdown, with the added bonus feature of recurring hallucinations. I was experiencing post-traumatic stress disorder, as Bergen had warned me I would. Better yet, some truant had decided Halloween came four months early this year, and I had let the little shit get the better of me when I should have grabbed him by the neck and frog-marched him home to his parents.

Daylight is at least one half the battle in restoring common sense.

The garage door was down. I walked up onto the porch and found the front door locked. The chalk circle was there, fading. I knocked, but she didn't answer. I cupped my hands and peered into the foyer, but there was no sign of her. I knocked a few more times. I walked around the garage to the gate, which was also locked. I was too tired to worry now. I was angry, and it felt good to be angry.

I went back to the front door and pounded. 'Annette! I'm locked out!'

I was about to kick in another window when I heard the soft crunch of tarmac gravel and the barely perceptible squeak of brakes. I began to turn, expecting to see her green Mustang.

'Morning sweetheart,' a man with a sophomoric cop-show voice said. 'Run and I'll put a boot so far up your ass you shit teeth.'

He can't be talking to me, I thought, too confused to be frightened, *and that doesn't even make sense.*

I turned. He was already halfway across the lawn, and, now that I saw him, I was afraid. He was big, maybe six two, at least two hundred and forty pounds, with speed bag shoulders and lineman thighs stamping black lace-up boots, the soles flapping paddles coming like comic strip exclamation points. His limbs were sausaged in sleeves of polyester: blue-black slacks and a matching lapel shirt that set off his wavy red hair and a mustache the size of carp. He had a hard paunch and his ogre hands were the throbbing white of cartoon gloves after the sledgehammer has landed. They were holding, almost burying, a .38 snub-nosed revolver whose black hole barrel underwent exponential growth spurts – dime, poker chip, wine bottle bottom – until it was a manhole cover hovering in front of my face.

'Hey, easy, whoa!' I raised my hands. 'I'm a friend of Annette's.'

'Like shit you are.' He was not wearing a badge or brass of any kind. Just before his shoulders blocked my view, I noted that his sedan was unmarked, an Interceptor deep red going to brown, spotlights over the side mirrors, with a brush guard and flat black rims. Undercover, in that not subtle way. 'Put your hands on that wall and spread your legs, cutie.'

My body still didn't believe this was happening. 'What for? What do you think I did?'

He knows about the broken window. He knows you were sleeping in someone's house. You're going to jail.

His eyes were reddened, huge and pickled in his fat face, like they weighed three times as much as the average human's. Looking into them was unpleasant, so I faced the stucco.

'Little B & E? Little sniff the panties while Mommy's away? That your thing?'

'I was just out for a walk and forgot my keys,' I said. 'I live here. Take it easy.'

'Shut it.' He holstered his gun. His belt did not have all the toys, but most of the important ones. He kicked my feet apart and patted me down, slapping my ribs and thumbing my crotch as he went south. 'You holding dope, faggot? Muling a little Tijuana brown up your

262

tailpipe? Tell me now before I find it, because if I find it first I'll take you down to the park and make you bob for apples.'

'What? No, Jesus, I don't have any drugs.'

He swatted my ass. 'Where's your wallet?'

'Inside. She didn't give me a key yet but she—'

'Shut the fuck up and turn around, puppy.'

I turned. He was standing with his hands on his hips, his dimpled, two-testicle chin nudging at me from under a mean little grin. He smelled of aftershave, the neon-blue kind that comes in a bottle shaped like the ace of spades.

'Name?' Now that he wasn't barking, his voice was actually a little high, not lisping but unexpectedly feminine.

'James Hastings.' Beat. 'Sir.'

'Panty wastings?'

'Hastings,' I said. *This one has studied all the shows.*

'Don't know any Hastings 'round here. Where you from originally?'

'Originally? Tulsa.'

He whistled. 'Tulsa! No kiddin'?' He smiled brightly, like he too was from Tulsa and now we were going to be friends, this was all just a misunderstanding. 'Tulsa, what?'

'Uhm, Oklahoma,' I said, then mumbled, 'pretty sure there's only one.'

'What did you say?'

'Nothing.'

'Did you say, "Pretty sure there's only one?"'

263

Okay, so he had the hearing of a bat.

'Look, with all due respect, officer, I have friends in the LAPD who would assure me I am entitled to see your badge.'

For a moment his eyes seemed to shimmy in their sockets. He leaned forward and shouted, dotting me with spittle. 'Wrong answer, retard! There's Tulsa, Oregon, and Tulsa, Oklahoma! You want to see my badge? Here's my badge!'

The heel of his palm went forward and retreated. I believe one of my ribs cracked, but I never found out. I fell to my knees, coughing. Oh, this asshole was going to pay. This was *good*. He was Sheltering's rent-a-cop, of that I was now certain, and I was going to sue the home-owners association for everything they had left. When I regained my sight, I noticed a bulge above his boot. Ankle piece, like Ghost used to carry. And then a funny thought came to me: what would Ghost do in this situation? Answer: the absolute worst thing you could do, of course. He would slug the cop in the balls, steal the cop's gun, jack the cruiser and go crash it into a Motel 8, order up two pros and a bag of blow.

'Howssat feel, Tulsa? That feel nice? You wanna see my badge again?'

'I live here,' I said, spitting to the side. 'With Annette.'

'Speak up. Sound like you got a dickey in your mouth.'

'Annette Copeland. She brought me here.'

'And who are you?'

264

'Her boyfriend.' I got to my feet. 'We just came back a week ago.'

'She didn't come back. Not possible, dickhead. Try again.'

'I was her neighbor. Her husband Arthur, I'm the one who—'

His mouth fell open. 'The fella lost his wife? The Ghost?'

I glared at him.

'Shit, you don't look much like a rapper, but then I guess you wouldn't.'

'I'm not Ghost. I worked for him.'

'Well, why the hell didn't you say so? I'm Rick, Rick Butterfield!' He slapped my back. 'Know 'Nettie from way, way back in the day. I'm sorry, guy, but you gotta announce yourself here. We got creepies and mopers and all kinds of termites.'

Now I remembered. She had mentioned him the night we had dinner and exchanged oral exams on Mr Ennis's patio. Rick Butterfield. Ex-cop. Her friend? She must have been exaggerating when she used the term friend. At least, I hoped she had been exaggerating.

'You know her,' I said. 'Okay. Right, I'm staying with her.'

He watched me with a combination of curiosity and hunger. 'Why won't she let you in?

'We had a fight. She locked me out.'

'Is that so?'

'Why would I lie to you?'

Rick nodded, something still troubling him, but satisfied for now. 'How's your gut?'

'Fine.'

'Sorry if I came on a little eager, but I learned my lesson the hard way. Had a greaser down on his belly last spring. Gave him the benefit of the doubt, didn't search him. I go to cuff him, but before I can get an angle he lunges, just quicker'n Dominican steals third base. Sliced up my thigh and opened my sack 'fore I knew what the fuck happened. Lucky my nuts didn't go rolling down the got-damned sewer hatch. Crossed a few wires, though. Street vasectomy. Couldn't dog my gal for a month. You better believe I showed that little prick his own private Gitmo.'

The man had to be on coke or speedballs. Something known to cause verbal diarrhea and general unchecked aggression.

'But since you're practically family now, trucey-ducey?' Rick Butterfield extended his hand.

I didn't know whether to laugh or run. 'Jesus. You're not playing, are you?'

'It's all a play, muffin.' Rick pumped my hand. 'Just good clean livin'.'

We sidled off the porch. I intended to climb the gate.

'So you're not doing anything?' he said.

'Now? No, but Annette's probably wondering—'

'Fuck that,' Rick said. 'I'm buying you a drink. Just comin' off the third shift, I ain't got anyone to drink with no more and I could use some stink on me.'

I began to protest but he was already steering me toward the car, one of his big mitts hanging over my neck. I realized this might be useful. Rick might be able to tell me a few things about my new girlfriend's history of mental illness, what Arthur was like. I was starving for perspective, any information.

No, the truth is I didn't want to go back inside. I didn't want to know what condition she was in, and after the last twenty-four hours I needed a drink. I deserved a drink. We stopped at the car, doors open, and Rick Butterfield looked at me across the roof like we were partners about to go on a patrol. He was grinning, his soup strainer wiggling.

'That figures,' he said.

'What?'

'She's already got you whipped six ways to Sunday.'

'Hey,' I said, my face coloring.

'Don't sweat it, Ghost.' He patted the roof. 'Isn't a man alive can resist that.'

I took the bait. 'Yeah, what?'

'Best pussy north of the border, *amigo*.'

Rick winked and ducked into his cruiser.

I looked up the vacant street, wondering what I had gotten myself into.

29

Rick Butterfield's basement was every high school kid's wet dream come true, minus the girls.

When he wheeled into the driveway of his unassuming but rather sprawling patio home on the edge of the SP's first wing tip, I said, 'I thought we were going to a bar?'

Rick finished mounting The Club to his steering wheel before answering. 'We are. Best one in town.'

I followed him inside. He led me through a cavernous living room that smelled like cat groins, through a small kitchen with a car engine and a cereal bowl full of gasoline on the breakfast table, to a stairway with a runner of baby-blue deep pile. As we descended into his walnut-paneled underworld, my host had to duck a neon sign bolted to the stairwell frame. Next to the pink palm tree, in loopy Vegas font, it said:

The Rick Room

There was indeed a bar, with all the main liquors (low-to-mid-tier brands) faced out in front of a large

Budweiser mirror. The bar itself was a ten-foot block of walnut with eight coats of varnish, silver quarters and buffalo head pennies trapped inside like bugs in amber. All three taps pumped regular Budweiser. Rick yanked us each a draught and handed me a frozen glass mug, the ice sheaths sliding like Superman's fortress at the North Pole.

'Make yourself at home, Ghost.'

'Just James,' I said. 'Ghost is the real one.' But he ignored this, busy as he was tinkering with two remote controls.

Shortly the ceiling speakers began to emit a steady stream of hits from Rick's favorite satellite station. Survivor, Journey, Van Halen, Asia, Toto. By this time I knew this was not a retro gimmick fad for him. I remembered a movie that had terrified me when I saw it in theaters as a child back in the early eighties. It starred Timothy Hutton and was about a caveman found frozen in a block of ice. He thaws out and comes to life, loses his mind and is pursued to a tragic death. *Iceman*, it was called. Yes, Rick Butterfield was like the Iceman, except he hadn't been frozen back in the Cro-Magnon age. He had been frozen in 1983 and he was never going to thaw out.

The basement was one huge room, all the walls removed, wooden beams holding up the main floor. I nosed around, too frightened to sit down; the tiger-striped couch might bite me. The three hulking antique safes were too large to have been lowered down the stairway. Rick did not tell me what was inside them, only boasted of having cut the foundation open to slide them in. One entire wall was a black lacquer cabinet holding stacks of VHS movies starring Burt Reynolds and a library of porn with all media formats represented. Classic issues of *Oui* and *Swank* and *Knave* were displayed in sealed plastic, as a kid would store Batman #2. Another wall featured a wood case with a glass front and a mounting board of red velvet, a track-lighted showcase of nunchaku, throwing stars and knives, balisongs, a dozen pistols, and a blowgun. The cork ceiling panels alternated with panels of gold-marbled mirrors, like a checkerboard. There were bean bags and a dart board and a regulation-size shuffle board. Budweiser lamps. Posters of hot rods and twenty-year-old calendars of bikini-clad women with Farrah hair, the winter months featuring purposeful protrusions of muff.

I won't belabor the first hour of conversation, our meet and greet before we got around to the interesting part of the morning. Suffice to say that, as he eased into his buzz, Rick Butterfield's contribution to the small talk revealed only the following:

He wasn't just obsessed with prison, homosexuality, fist fighting, pussy, violence, criminals, firearms, strippers, tiny breasted women, authority, anal sex and 'dropping massive loads' – all of which he referenced, peppered his speech with, or attempted to discuss in absurd detail, with alarming and then numbing regularity. No, no. Rick Butterfield seemed to believe the world, and all human interaction in it, had as its chief aim the seeking of, and revelry in, as many of these pastimes as possible, the *coup de grâce* of a life well lived being the arrival at some sort of miraculous locale where all of them happened in one night, Rick was the king, and everybody present looked like 'that real sexy hooch from *Charles in Charge*'.

I was all but certain Rick Butterfield was a true psychopath, and I confess that after my fourth beer and second shot of Beam I could not stop laughing at him and with him. He was in his own way as charismatic and singularly warped as Ghost. He just didn't have talent to mask his proclivities. I kept telling myself one more beer and then, if I hadn't learned anything useful, I would go home.

'So, how exactly did you two meet?' he asked from behind the bar. He was pouring another round into two new frosty mugs and had just finished his third anecdote from his time served as a security consultant at Chuckwalla, the medium-security facility in Blythe. That would be California's most remote, sweltering, middle-of-nowhere prison.

'She didn't tell you?' I was on a bar stool against the wall, afraid to turn my back on him.

'Nope.'

He knew I had lost my wife, and of course he must have known about Arthur's suicide. That would have been big news in the SP. Had Annette told him why Arthur killed himself?

'She moved in next door,' I said. 'It was strange because my neighbor, this old guy named Mr Ennis, died of a heart attack. I was beginning to think the place was, uh, sort of cursed when she showed up. Another week or two, I might have been gone.'

'Interesting.' Rick was staring at me again. He had a way of doing that, almost as if he were trying to decide if I was real, or the way a crazy person looks at an imaginary friend. 'So, uh, how'd you make your move? You lay the Ghost rap on her? I bet once she knew who you were she threw it right atcha, huh?'

'Rick, buddy,' I chuckled. 'I don't think you heard me earlier. I'm not Ghost. I had nicknames and we were . . . but you keep saying . . .'

I might have been speaking Portuguese.

I snapped my fingers a few times. 'I was his surrogate, a fake, a double. It was theater, man. You know that, right?'

Rick was bobbing his head. 'How long before she let you put it in her deuce hole?'

I reared back. 'Come on, seriously? This is what we're talking about?'

Rick looked hurt. I'd just put a ding in our new buddyhood. 'So, you're like one of those sensitive types, is that it? Used to rap about roofies, guns and bitches, but now you're a saint?'

I didn't bother correcting him this time. I was tired of trying to explain the difference. 'With the whole shop talk, already. Give it a rest?'

Rick laughed, his hard belly jostling. 'I'm just fucking with you, man. Jesus, she's really got your balls in a sling.'

It was like high school. Soon as I pushed back, I felt

like a jerk. 'I can take a joke as much as the next guy. It's just been a long week, all right? A fucking strange week.'

Rick was pouring two more beers, additional to the ones we were holding. I put a hand out and he cut me off. 'What's your hurry? Give her some time to cool off.'

I settled back onto my stool. 'She didn't tell you why we came back?'

'She didn't tell me you were coming back at all. Otherwise I wouldn't a ganked you.'

I decided to tell him. I don't know why. Maybe it was the alcohol. Maybe I just needed to say it again, the way I had told Bergen, considering things were getting worse.

'You're gonna laugh,' I said.

'Swear I won't.'

I told him everything that had happened since Annette arrived. The fall in the tub, the paintings, the signs of disorder around the house, the shoes buried in the yard, the phone calls. I told him about Lucy. Her total loss of sanity before running into traffic. The only thing I left out were the more serious changes in Annette since we came back. The lashing out in the furniture store, the foul tongue, the disappearance of her freckles. *The possession*, I thought drunkenly, wondering idly for a moment if I should consult a priest. Some things are too awful to say out loud.

'Most of it is attributable to Lucy,' I said, nearing the end. I took a long pull of the Bud. 'That makes sense, I guess. But I've seen things that can't be explained.'

'Like?'

'You have a boy running around the neighborhood?'

273

'A boy?'

'About this high.' I held my hand out above the barstool. 'Wearing a black hooded sweatshirt. Very pale?'

Rick stared at me, giving away nothing.

I continued. 'There's a kid's bike in her garage, little green BMX thing. Does she have a son? Did she and Arthur have a son?'

'Nope.' Rick dabbed his thumb in a bowl of salt and licked it.

'Are you sure?'

'I would know if she had a son,' Rick said.

'The other thing is, she's not really herself since we came back. She's always got a headache. She's turning mean. She's sick. Like bad flu sick.'

Rick nodded. 'She's moody.'

'No,' I said. 'It's worse than that. She's not well, Rick. Annette is not well. She says things no one else could know. No one but me and Stacey.'

'Stacey?'

'My wife.'

'Spooky, huh?' He laughed. 'You look like a fried egg. Have another drink.'

I felt stupid for talking too much.

'Listen,' he said. 'That business with Arthur. That was rough on her. She shouldn't be here. It's too soon. And I told her to sell that house a long time ago. This place is going to hell.'

I was exhausted. What else did I need to ask him?

He did another shot and then said, 'So, you plan on sticking around?'

274

'I don't have anywhere else to go. I miss my wife.'

'To the ladies,' Rick said, pouring. I did another shot. Rick did another shot. He went back to talking about women and cars and prison escapades. The music got louder. We found ourselves singing along to Steve Miller's 'Abracadabra'. Rick showed me a rare gun and fired a shot into his wall. I laughed and he let me fire another shot into his wall. The wood paneling smoldered. At some point I could not hold myself up on the stool and slid over to his couch. He was laughing and turning up the music. I nodded off to ZZ Top singing about legs and a woman who knew how to use them.

'Wake up. Wake up, Ghost. Yo yo, cornbread. You need to eat.'

I snapped out of my dead slumber, still drunk.

'I made a Tostino's.' Rick held out a paper plate with burned slices of gray meat and orange sauce.

My stomach roiled. I waved the slice away.

Rick gobbed it whole and spoke through a mouthful of mush. 'She hasn't called. You want a ride home or you gonna sleep here all night?'

I rubbed my eyes. 'It's night already?'

Rick laughed. 'You fucking pansy lightweight.'

I stood and made sure my pants were buttoned. They were, but my brain seemed to be gyrating. 'Holy fuck. What time is it? What have you been doing all afternoon?'

'Working on my car. I dropped by the house to see if she was around. She didn't answer the door. Won't answer the phone. You sure she came back with you?'

I did not understand the question.

'I would have seen her by now,' he said.

'You think I came here alone?'

'Maybe she's the ghost!' he said, and laughed. 'Maybe none of this is real.'

'That's not funny,' I said. 'I need to go home.'

Rick poured me a beer and I shoved it aside, then thought I might as well wash the sleep out of my mouth and took a gulp. It actually tasted pretty good.

'She's there,' I said. 'This was dumb. For all I know she might have killed herself by now.'

Rick kept shaking his head. 'I still don't understand how you got here,' he said. 'Where's your car?'

'Annette drove.' My head felt as though it had been run over. This made me think of Lucy. I almost threw up. Something was wrong. I looked around, feeling punked. 'Are you fucking with me? Did you slip something in my drink?'

Brah-haw-haw-haw! 'You're crazy, Ghost.'

My temper neared its boiling point. 'Maybe so. Fuck, man, you have no idea what I've been through.'

'Do tell?'

I turned to give him a mouthful about what it was like to lose your wife, but then I saw myself in the big Budweiser mirror behind his bar and almost screamed. My hair had turned white. It was standing up in a spiky mess and it was snow-white. Peroxide white. Ghost white.

Rick sipped his beer and nibbled at another slice of garbage pizza. 'What?'

'What did you do?' I shouted. 'What the fuck did you do to me?' I was up off my stool. I shoved my beer at him and it fell off the bar and splashed onto his pants before shattering on the floor.

'Hey, hey!'

I pointed at him. 'You motherfucker. I'll kill you!'

'Calm down, what is your problem?'

'Look at me! Look at this!' I yanked at my hair.

'What about it?'

'You dyed my hair? Are you kidding me?' I looked around for the evidence. A brown bottle of peroxide, a towel, anything. But I saw nothing, and my scalp felt the same as it always did. My hair was dry, a little oily, as if I had not showered in two days, which I hadn't. 'You think this is cute? What the fuck is wrong with you, man?'

Rick reared back. 'You think I dyed your hair? What the fuck is wrong with *you*? Your hair was like that when I met you this morning, dumbass. When's the last time you looked in the mirror?'

He was utterly calm. And I did not believe him.

'This is not – I'm not. Just get me the fuck out of here. I'm done. You, her, this whole scene. I'm done with all of it.'

Rick looked more frightened of me than I was of him. 'Fine by me. Take it easy, man. Jesus. I'll give you a ride home. Let me get my keys.'

It was night time again. Every third or fourth street lamp was on, as if the association were purposefully running them at twenty or thirty per cent to cut costs. As a result, the neighborhood was dark for long stretches, Rick's headlights sliding over abandoned houses and cars as we worked our way through the derelict maze. I felt far from civilization, the reality of the desert creeping in all around me. I had not eaten in some twenty or thirty hours and the beers and shots had gone straight to my blood. I felt sick in his company and it didn't help that Rick was doing almost sixty through the neighborhood. After a few minutes I didn't recognize any of the houses and sensed we were going the opposite direction of Annette's.

'Isn't her place back the other way?' I said.

'Gotta make my rounds. Sit tight, I'll get you home in a jiff.'

His rounds. 'You work for the association?'

'Association? Ain't no fuckin' association.'

'Oh.'

'I'm just a homeowner looking out for my investment.'

This was not going to be fun.

Rick hooked a hard right onto a steep road, his tires squealing and the undercarriage scraping as we jounced through the drainage dip and then climbed, the car roaring as if the engine had some kind of blower or four-barrel carb. *Whonh – whooOOOOOHNNNH!* We topped out quickly over the hill, floating on the cruiser's soft suspension. As soon as we nosed down, a little orange glow appeared up ahead and Rick killed the lights.

'Jackpot.'

He used a driveway apron to weave onto the sidewalk and quickly straightened out so that my half of the car was riding on the curb while he leaned toward the street. We continued this way, me dipping with every driveway and rising again, for about a hundred yards. I tasted Jim Beam and bile. The orange glow was in a house, now visible behind a garden-level window. As we approached, still pushing thirty, the glow enlarged and then snuffed out. Rick slewed onto the lawn, braked to a halt and left the cruiser idling, which it did in near silence.

I expected him to bolt immediately, but he just sat there watching the house through the windshield. In his blue pseudo-uniform, his acne-scar pitted face pasty with booze sweat, eyes glassy and low, he looked like a soldier of fortune.

I couldn't stand the silence, but as soon as I opened my mouth he threw his right arm across my chest.

'Shush.'

I shushed.

'They know,' he said softly. 'Now it's only a matter of how many will stay, how many will run, and which door.'

'Who?'

Rick looked sideways at me, his smile a red-lipped blade. 'The Crawlers.'

While I waited for an explanation, his left leg raised itself steadily and there was the sound of tearing Velcro. His left hand passed something over his lap and into his right hand, which extended to me.

Ankle piece.

I shook my head and whispered, 'I don't want that.'

'Yes.' The voice of the grave. 'You do.'

He saw the fear in my eyes, the need to understand.

'They crawl across the desert, into other kings' castles,' he said. 'Our mission is to let them know there's order in this kingdom, and make sure they never come back.'

A door slammed. We both looked up. It wasn't the front door; that was still closed. Another clamor farther away, footsteps bounding over wood, probably on the back decking.

'Rock 'n' roll, Ghost.'

The ankle piece fell into my lap. I hesitated.

He pointed his gun at my face. 'Stay here you'll die.'

Rick's door did not so much open as explode, ejecting the big man like a sprinter from the starting blocks. Except there was no grace, only raw power. He moved over the lawn with the frightening spurt of a buffalo startled from his herd. His boots threw a chunk of sod as he darted right and disappeared behind the house.

Stay here you'll die. Did this mean one of them would come out the front door and start shooting at me? Or that, if I didn't provide back-up, Rick would punish me?

I followed him. God help me I exited the car and, though I could have run away, I followed him. I would show him what happens to people who drug me and dye my hair.

Cool air in the desert night. My breath steaming alcohol fumes. Adrenaline rush across the yard and over the split-rail fence like a steeple chase, ready to pistol-whip any bitch, damn it feels good to be a gangsta.

Shapes and shadows weaving through trees, sod grid yards, out onto the expanse of the park with the dying baby trees. Two men ahead of him, using the playground for poor man's camo. Rick closing like he's got pupils big as eight balls night vision. Three, then four men and maybe a woman bursting from their hidey holes. Converging on the same narrow gap, a hole in the culvert wall. Into the wild, no more suburbs, just land. Weaving through rocks and cactus and dry river beds, pure terror.

My feet slipping, legs pumping, heart pumping faster, my lungs burning under enough moonlight to see their dark skin, his massive head jumping like an antelope.

The pistol swinging at my side, my finger inching closer to the trigger as I catch up to the black hulk of him cutting across the desert, the shouts of his prey as they realize there's nowhere left to go. One trips, another stops to help, the whole train piling up. He's shouting, they're surrendering like border jumpers, knees in the dirt, hands behind heads, and he's rounding them up, master of ceremonies now, Emcee Rick, huffing and puffing and waiting for me to bring up the rear. I'm ready to surprise them all.

The gun coming up, my gun, the tableau waiting to unfold.

The buffalope in my sights. His head exploding in a pink mist.

Psychological safety – off.

30

I didn't shoot Rick, though in retrospect I should have. It would have saved us both some trouble.

I did take the gun and exit the car, run around the house, trip over a plastic rain gutter and nearly slam face first into the grass before I emerged around the back. I heard him chasing them, shouting and firing his gun into the air (I hoped), and after another minute of running across the raw desert that lay just on the other side of all this false suburbia, I cramped up. The stitch lit up my side like a purple flame and I stopped, bent over and threw up into the rocky sand. I was dehydrated and lost and my head was throbbing like it had its own heart.

I wiped my mouth and walked back to the car. I thought of stealing it, but only slipped the gun into my waistband and wandered off down the street. I didn't want to know what Rick was up to. Chasing immigrants or squatters – the Crawlers, people like me the night before – was my guess, though why he cared I could not imagine. No one was paying him. It was probably simple blood sport to him, a hobby, a way to feel powerful and needed after being downsized from the prison. I knew guys like him from Ghost's security entourage. They were police academy rejects, looking for new, less regulated venues to exercise power.

The cool desert air cleared my head somewhat and I began to sober up, a little. I walked for ten minutes before I realized I was lost again. All of the houses looked the same as the ones on the streets near Annette's house, but I could not find her street. I couldn't even remember the name. I kept walking.

What was left of my internal clock told me it was maybe 9 or 10 p.m. But the fact that the neighborhood was once again dead quiet well before midnight only disturbed me further. I could not escape the feeling I was being watched. All of the houses had eyes of black windows, and it occurred to me that there is nothing so sad and uniquely abhorrent as an empty living room behind a window with no curtains.

How many are really still here? I wondered. How many are afraid to come out after dark? Were they afraid of Rick? Or just people in general? The country didn't used to scare me. I grew up in the country. There's that myth that the city is more dangerous, and I suppose it is, per capita. But at least when you start screaming, there's someone around to hear you. They might rush to your aid, call 9-1-1, or ignore you – but at least you will be heard. Out here, if someone chose to liberate my soul, my screams would be reduced to canyon echoes.

I had been walking for almost twenty minutes when the creeping suspicion that I was being watched became a certainty. I stopped and looked around. I focused on the spaces between the houses, the gaps behind bushes, under abandoned cars. I saw no one, but the nape of my neck was stiff and the flesh along my arms visibly prickled. I turned around on the sidewalk.

The boy was standing behind me. He was approximately a hundred feet back, on the same sidewalk, unmoving. He wore the same black sweatshirt with the hood up and pulled low over his brow. Black pants, hands hidden. He seemed very small, shorter and thinner than he had appeared last night. I stared at him for a minute, waiting for him to do something. He did not take a step or even raise his head.

I turned away and began walking, continuing as if he were of no concern. I listened for the sound of his feet slapping on the sidewalk, any sort of shuffling noises, but the only footsteps were my own. It seemed important to let him know that I was not going to be cowed again. I willed myself not to look back, but it was excruciating. I decided I would count my footsteps until I reached one hundred, and then turn back. My lips moved with the count. Somewhere around twenty-five, I revised my goal down to fifty. A light breeze swept by. I wiped my nose and kept walking. I stubbed my toe on a ridge in the sidewalk and kept walking.

'Thirty-six, thirty-seven . . .' I counted under my breath. At forty I stopped and turned around.

The boy was once again motionless, and had closed the gap considerably. He now stood less than fifty feet away, perhaps as close as thirty. I hadn't seen him come to a halt. His head was still down, the hood up, his chin the only suggestion of a face, but the jaw was clean white. His feet were close together, as if he were balancing on a flagpole, and the things protruding from his pant cuffs looked like two bars of white soap. The folds of his black sweatshirt revealed portions of white letters stamped across his chest. I made out an S and something near his shoulder that might have been an L or an I. I don't know why it mattered, but I needed to know what was printed on his sweatshirt.

He's either walking faster when I am not looking, or else he's not walking at all.

His hands were stuffed into the pouch, hiding something, and I felt certain it was related to his presence, something he wanted to show me. His apparent ability to find me wherever I was, indoors and out, was too complicated to rationalize right now, and the fact that I had Rick's ankle piece was of no solace. I was nearing my wits' end and there was nowhere else to go.

Let him come. Let him follow.

I turned and began walking again. He was close enough now that I should hear his footsteps, but I didn't. We had been climbing a hillock within the subdivision for the past few minutes and I refused to let the incline slow my pace as I crested the top. I glanced at the houses to either side in hopes of recognizing one of them, but I could not concentrate. I was descending again, counting paces. I decided to catch him off guard. *Sixteen, seventeen*—

I whirled. The sidewalk was empty. I scanned the yards in every direction. The boy was gone. I started to look away, but another shimmer of something on the ground made me stop. I looked down at the sidewalk. Seven black marbles, one white. Clustered in the form of a smile with two eyes – one white, the other black.

He'd left them less than six feet behind me.

Ten minutes later I found a familiar lane down into 'the pit' of more economical homes, and from there was able to make my way back to Annette's house. The door was unlocked. I went into the kitchen and hooked a right, intending to check the garage to see if the car was there.

'James?' she said from the living room. 'Is that you?'

I felt caught, full of the familiar dread I had experienced those last few months when I returned home from being on tour. The creeping unease of walking into our home, wondering how much worse Stacey had gotten while I was away.

I walked around the kitchen, into the living room. She was sitting on the couch, almost formally so, her hands flat on her thighs. Her white hair was parted in the middle and hung straight down, ragged at the edges. She was wearing a pair of pink flannel pajamas with chubby black sheep on them. Her skin was no longer the color of a trout's belly. Some or all of her freckles were visible, but I did not count them. She was still pale, but even in the lightless room she looked healthier, filled with some renewed vitality, as if the . . . condition . . . had passed.

'Hey,' I said. I did not turn the light on. 'You're up late. Feeling better?'

She wasn't looking at me. I could hear her breath

coming in and out, like she'd been running around the house until I came in. At first I thought she was crying, but her voice was steady and her cheeks were dry.

'I'm scared, James. I'm really scared this time.'

'What's wrong?'

'One of these days you're going to get hurt. You might not come back.'

'I'm fine. I was with Rick.'

'Rick?' she said. 'Who's Rick?'

'Pretend cop Rick. Rick Butterfield. Your friend who dyed my hair.'

She looked up at me with the eyes of a woman who has just survived a plane crash. 'But where are we?'

'What do you mean?'

'I don't know whose house this is. Is this one of his houses? Did you put me here?'

'Whose houses?'

'Ghost's.'

There was a moment when it finally hit me. The moment when Stacey turned the corner and lost the ability to hide it. When I knew it wasn't just a little too much 'partying' but a real mental illness, even if that mental illness was something as common as depression. The moment I realized *this is a serious problem*. It had hit me, not like a bucket of cold water, but from inside my veins. Everything in me thickened, hardening in self-defense. It was fear at first, then sadness, then loss. Because no matter how much I loved her I understood in a flash that a piece of her had died. That some or most of the woman I knew and loved may still be there, and what had been lost might one day come back, but that for now something, something as small as a toe or as large as her heart, had been stolen while I wasn't paying attention.

Days before she was killed in the alley, I had come home to find her standing on a short stepladder in the front hall, wiping down the shelf there with a moist rag. When I had asked her what she was up to, she had turned and looked down at me with a smile, and said, 'Cleaning.'

'The closet?'

'It has to be clean or else they won't come back.'

When I chuckled and tried to play along and asked who 'they' were, her smile fell off her face and she said, 'You know who.'

'What are you talking about?'

She had then descended the ladder and walked away as if I weren't even there. I followed her into the kitchen, out onto the back patio. She lit a cigarette and sat in one of the lawn chairs, looking at the backyard.

'Stacey? What's going on?'

She startled and looked back at me. 'Oh, I didn't hear you come in.'

'Yes,' I said, irritated. 'You did. We just talked in the hall. You were . . . Stace, come on. Really?'

'Does it really matter?' she had said. 'Wouldn't it be better if one of us just walked away?'

'From what?'

'It would be easier,' she said, her expression languid. Stoned. 'If you just left. Just go, James.' She laughed and it was an evil laugh. 'Go away. Go away.'

Had we argued? Had I gone to her and stood with her?

No, none of those things. I remembered now. I had stared at her a moment, staring into her bloodshot eyes full of magic pills, and I thought, *You're just like him. You're just like Ghost. A fucking addict. My wife is a fucking addict and I don't want her any more.*

'If you don't want to talk to me,' I said. 'That's fine. But the drugs aren't going to solve anything and I have a job to do.'

'Good, go do it. No one's stopping you.'

And then I walked out, got back in *my* car, the S5 I bought her, and I drove to Shutters in Santa Monica. I checked into a single room and pretended I was on call, expensing it to Ghost. I sat in the bed and hid from my wife and I knew that she wasn't crazy, that it might 'only' be depression at its root, but that by piling on the medications and trying to escape into a state of numbness she was killing herself slowly. Killing us, and for that I came very close to hating her.

How close was it? A week before? Three or four days? Or the day before she backed into that alley?

Did I call her family? Her friends? Lock her in the bedroom and sit with her?

No, I had checked into a hotel seven miles away. And stared at the television, resenting her, her biology, our lifestyle and life. Resenting myself.

'Who's house is this?' Annette had said. If she was still Annette.

Don't leave. You can't leave now. She'll die without you.

I sat beside Annette on the couch and took her hands in mine. They felt like refrigerated dough.

'It's your house, Annette. Home, in Sheltering Palms. You remember? We came back together just a couple weeks ago, sweetie.'

She gave me the same look I had seen in my bathroom. When she was propped up on the toilet, cowering from the rabbit paintings. After she hit her head. After something or someone made her fall. Was that when she began to change? Began to know me so well, what buttons to push? Yes, it had started as early as that. That might have been ground zero for it. That's when it – *she* – got into her.

'We're all right. I'm here. Just focus on me for a minute.'

'Who's Annette? Why do you keep calling me that? I don't like that name.'

Please don't do this. 'That's your name. You are Annette.'

'Why are you lying to me?' She turned her vacant eyes on me. 'Who's Annette, James? Is she your girlfriend? Does she go on the road with you?'

I let go of her cold hands and moved away.

'I don't know,' I said. 'I don't know what you want me to do.'

'I'm so cold. Aren't you cold? I keep having the dream. Every time I die in them, I try to sleep but I wake up dead.'

She was crying.

'Let's get you to bed,' I said, leading her upstairs.

Once she calmed down and fell asleep, I closed the bedroom door and made my way down the hall toward the second bathroom. I needed a shower. I needed to be alone. I needed sleep, but first I had to do something about my hair. She hadn't even noticed it. What if Rick had been telling the truth? What if it had been this way for days, weeks? What if I had never changed? When was the last time I had looked in the mirror? In the house, when I saw the boy? Had it been white then, or turned white? No, no, no . . .

I found the bathroom door, pushed it open, and arrived in a child's bedroom.

I stepped back into the hall and looked at the other doors. The upstairs hall had half a dozen of these generic faux-oak doors and they all looked alike, but this was the one that had been locked. Arthur's room. The Bluebeard room. Someone had been in here recently.

I glanced around and my eyes locked on a framed photo on top of the dresser. I went to it, holding up the 5 x 7. It was of Annette, younger, radiant, with redder hair. She was posed on a deck with the desert in the background. She looked beautiful and happy. Could have been two years ago or as many as seven. There was another photo on the dresser, fallen on its face. It was not in a frame, just a little wallet-size that had been propped against a wooden music box shaped like a sea turtle. I turned it over.

The boy was maybe eight or nine, with a crop of brown hair. He wore a white dress shirt and tie under a blue blazer with a private school crest. There had been an attempt at a smile, but his mouth still hung open in a sagging oval. There was a forced happiness about him, the kind that emotionally neglected children try so hard but ultimately fail to conceal. I flipped the photo over, returning to the tiny, blue ink scrawl at the bottom.

Aaron, Grade 5

He was the boy I had seen standing in my backyard just weeks ago. The boy in the black sweatshirt who had been in the empty house two nights ago, then followed me just hours ago.

Annette. Arthur. Aaron. A family of As.

The wife was sleeping down the hall. The husband was dead of suicide. What had happened to the son?

31

It was your average suburban boy's bedroom, but one that, at first glance, did not contain much in the way of personality fingerprints. I was not a homicide detective. The thousand ways in which this boy Aaron was unique were lost on me.

There was a poster of Big Ben Roethlisberger in a drop-back, arm cocked and ready to throw the pigskin to Neptune. A double bed with plain green cotton sheets and a thin peppermint-striped spread. Soccer cleats and mall clothes in his closet. Lots of toys, but I doubted they were much different from the toys of any single child born to parents with money. A science kit. A remote-controlled airplane and a space station thing hanging from the ceiling. Three dusty Track & Field Day ribbons from third grade tacked to a cork board. Plastic robots and manga books. Everything neatly displayed on shelves, waiting, preserved, nothing boxed up or stowed away. It was as if he had merely gone to bed a few nights ago and vanished before waking up.

What makes you so sure he's dead? That boy in the house and on the street was pretty lively. He gave you a handful of marbles, too. Maybe Aaron just ran away.

Yes, but his face . . .

A game system was tucked into a narrow entertainment center with a door of tinted black glass. Above it, an Onkyo rack with CD and DVD units wired up to a small, collapsible flat-screen monitor. On his desk was a Mac mini. Nice stuff, but I wasn't going to search his computer files, not now, not with Annette just down the hall. I needed something that spoke to him, about him. Most boys don't keep diaries, do they? I didn't find one in his desk, but I did find something else that seemed a bit of a coincidence. In the desk's shallow center drawer there was a single scrap of white notebook paper with numbers written on it.

22 38 44 06

And above that, written in the same stiff, pencil scrawl –

Middle combination

I kept the combination to Stacey's storage locker in my desk's center drawer, too. This must have been Aaron's locker combination from school. The numbers seemed excessive, though, and oddly familiar. Four of them instead of the usual three. I tried to distinguish a pattern to them. 22 38 44 06. What did they have in common? Anything? I looked up at his wall and thought for a moment, mumbling. 22 38 44 . . . I knew these numbers, could almost hear them. And then I could hear them, they came to me in a marching rhythm, a track with heavy base, a slow tempo, and a Bone Thugs set of harmonizing back-up vocals.

The 22 is for you
Cause I love my guns
The 38 is for hate
Treat 'em like my sons
The 44 is for whores
Cause I love my guns
The aught-six is for the pigs
Who sent my brother to the pen
Cause he loved his guns
The AK is for the State
Can you feel the white hate?
Motherfuckuhs grab yo guns
The Revolution's rising sun
They make me feel like a man
Join the Revolution, son

It was another Ghost song, 'From My Cold Dead Hands'. The numbers were guns. Gun calibers. A co-incidence? They didn't mean anything to me except for the fact that I remembered the song, and I doubted a kid would choose gun calibers for a locker combination. You didn't get to choose your locker combo when I was a kid. You bought the stupid lock from the drugstore and it came with pre-set numbers. I was closing the drawer when my eyes caught on something white and glossy – another photo. I turned it over.

A Christmas tree with bundles of torn wrapping paper. Aaron, younger, sitting on the floor in a pair of footie pajamas. Next to him, a large stuffed bear, the Kenneth bear, its eyes red from the camera flash.

The bear. She lied. Annette left Aaron's bear in my house. When? Why? What was she trying to tell me? And what if she didn't lie, but wasn't even aware of what she had done?

I put the photo back and closed the drawer.

Next to the entertainment center, on the floor and so innocuous I hadn't noticed it on my first pass, was a blue footlocker with leather handles. I had a green one just like it when I was a kid, filled with plastic Army men and Micronauts. Aaron's was latched, but I popped the brass flap open with a ballpoint pen I found in his desk drawer. Inside was Aaron's music collection. As I ran my fingers over the spines of the jewel cases, I became dizzy.

Ninety per cent of his collection consisted of releases from one artist.

The bad one.

I crouched over Aaron's footlocker, opened the copy of Ghost's first *Rolling Stone* cover, and found the review that introduced the monster to the world.

Parents, teachers and brain-dead celebs be warned – you're about to be bombed. Ghost, a white rapper cold as ice and anything but vanilla, has delivered a masterpiece in what is sure to become a hip-hop landmark of self-evisceration. Over the course of sixteen diabolical tracks produced by his mentor, PhD-Jay, *Autotopsy* combines terrifyingly nimble wordplay, no less than three personalities (alternately homicidal, comedic, tortured), and emcee-slaying splatter-crunk in genius and despicable ways. It may be the first rap album crafted equally for a generation of ADD tweens, Ivy League brats, desperate housewives and anyone else who prefers their audible pharmaceuticals, gonzo porn plots and Tarantino exploding heads served up on a bloodstained scratch-table smorgasbord of knives, ski masks, witches and farmhouse nightmares . . .

The review went on for another half-page. They gave it five stars. But, then, they gave all of Ghost's records five stars, except for *Snuffed*, the last one, which everyone knew was a tremendous hunk of shit and which even Ghost had started referring to as his *Godfather III*. There were dozens more such rags in the footlocker, the ones that had given my former employer top billing.

It didn't stop there. Little Aaron, at the ripe old age of eight (nine? ten?) had not been just another Ghost fan. He had the entire catalog. All five studio albums, the soundtrack to Ghost's movie, *Haunted Tracks*, the singles, even the imports. He also had the collectible Playa Cards and a pair of Ghost's signature Converse (size 5, never laced), a pint-sized white *Vaporware* tracksuit, as well as half a dozen concert tees, and – shrink-wrapped and autographed in green marker – a replica of the skull and bones wristband Ghost wore on stage to keep the sweat from shorting his mic. I could vouch for the signature. I'd seen it a thousand times and signed it a couple hundred more during those encounters when I was trapped into providing an autograph instead of just fleeing as the cameras began to click.

It was real, this was real.

The black hooded sweatshirt. The white letters across the chest spelled Ghost. The limited edition ones he had sold through his website. Of course, that's why I had almost recognized it.

Perhaps Aaron had died in it.

Or was this all a coincidence? I needed it to be. Ghost had millions of fans, after all. This footlocker did not mean there was a sinister connection between Aaron's world and mine, between Annette and me.

Even so, the guilt over Staccy that had reawakened during my encounter with Annette this morning now combined with Aaron's whispering – *look what they did, look what they did* – and this entire Ghost mess, and I knew it was all connected somehow, and that I was at the center of it, responsible for something worse than I ever imagined. The undefined guilt hung over me like a steel-spiked albatross, leaving me to dig for an explanation that would justify all I had dedicated to this man, this rapper who had become my alter ego and would not leave me alone, and I found myself sinking deeper into myself and defending him as if both of us were to blame.

The kid. Had Arthur and Annette condoned this? They must have known what their son was listening to. Had they caved in to incessant 'but all the others kids have it' whining? Or were they the kind of cool parents who understood that rap music, no matter how much it glorified violence and pornified women, was fiction and sometimes art? Did they accept that Ghost was a personality, an identity construct created out of a poor but fiercely intelligent trailer kid's imagination as a response to his nightmare childhood? Did they understand that the content of his music came from his environment and inspirations, his first means of escape: earlier rap music, horror films, his father's gun collection, his mother's medicine cabinet? Or was it simpler than all that justification? Maybe Annette was one of those moms who couldn't decipher the lyrics that rivaled De Sade's, the kind that hears only the catchy beats and rhyming sounds, and remained ignorant of what her son was giggling about from behind his bedroom door, from inside his iPod cocoon.

She and Arthur might have liked his music, I realized (which necessitated that she had also lied to me about not liking his music). The hate letters came from fundamentalists and censorship warriors: no surprise there. But Ghost's fan mail also came from Japanese schoolgirls, suburban American boys and girls of all colors and, yes, parents. Adults. Educated, cultured people. More than I would have imagined.

It wasn't just his music, which always had a pop hook to go along with the meat cleaver. There was something All-American appealing about Ghost's serrated honesty and charisma, his success story, the rise from poverty to empire, his very suburban appearance (read: white, clean-cut). He wasn't the Oakland Raider-clad, corn-rowed gangsta that had scared the shit out of the establishment in the eighties. He was just this guy with a knack for looking victimized, small enough you wanted to take him under your arm and explain it to him that it couldn't be all that bad.

They loved him because he tore himself apart for their listening pleasure. His demons and sins were their entertainment. Very few popular artists are capable, let alone willing, to open themselves to such an extent. But Ghost didn't know how to do it any other way. It was his calling card and philosophy. Music would heal him, but only after he had used it to destroy himself in front of the audience. It was right there in the title of his first album. *Autotopsy*, and he meant it.

But even Ghost fictionalized his self-image, exaggerated his wicked deeds. Of course he did. Otherwise he would be in jail by now. He could rap about making love to a headless woman – while her severed head used the voice of his mother to make fun of him from atop the dresser across the room – because it was too outrageous to take seriously. And the critics offered cover aplenty. Because he was literate, took poetry to another level. He had street cred because he flowed with exceptional ease and was his own worst critic. He used words the way Bobby Fischer used pawns and bishops, mixing slang and gutter talk with five syllable wowzers like some love child of Michael Chabon and Bushwick Bill. A guy who could cross-pollinate references to John Wayne Gacy with text excerpts from Pinske's translation of *The Inferno* couldn't really be a psycho in real life, could he?

No. Not at first, anyway.

Later, after his wife left him, when he became obsess—

There was something else in the footlocker, buried under the magazines. I set the CD aside. It was a black binder, a scrapbook full of plastic sleeves. I opened it. The sleeves were full of news clippings. The first headline said,

PARENTS CLAIM SUICIDAL SON
OBSESSED WITH RAPPER

My heart stuttered. *This is it, this is what happened to Aaron.* But, no, this article was about a boy of sixteen named Brian Jennings, of Dallas. I'd never heard of or read about him, and doubted Ghost had either. He didn't like to hear bad news. Brian Jennings had come home for lunch one day, painted his face white with clown make-up, and hanged himself in the garage.

I turned the page.

TEACHER ASSAULTED FOR
CONFISCATING GHOST

Carl Sanders, forty-three, of Newark. A high school social studies teacher who had taken an iPod away from one of his students. The iPod contained only one artist, Ghost's third album, *American Bloodland*. The student, who had been chanting the lyrics and making a nuisance of himself all week, went berserk. Mr Sanders was kicked and beaten savagely in front of his class. He spent three days in a coma, and, while a partial recovery was expected, Mr Sanders would never teach again due to the brain trauma he suffered.

On the opposite page,

PAROLED SEX OFFENDER USED GHOST TIX TO LURE SIXTH-GRADERS

I scanned the article. It made no mention of Aaron Copeland, and the pederast had been caught trolling suburbs outside of Indianapolis.

MADISON SCHOOL SHOOTER'S DIARY REVEALS OBSESSION WITH RAPPER

This one I remembered. Stacey and I had argued about it several times, and it had made international headlines, plastering the cable channels for weeks. A Hmong exchange student with a history of at least three mental illnesses had recorded video of himself at home in his basement, posing with Tec-9s while Ghost's chart-topping single 'Hot Lunch' played in the background. Thirty-two minutes later he had entered his high school cafeteria and shot eleven students and the custodian before turning one of the guns on himself. Neither the boy nor the media paused to reflect that the song was written as a eulogy, told from the point of view of a fictional girl who had survived the Columbine massacre, the unfolding horror of which, Ghost claimed, left an indelible impression on him when he was nineteen, touching notes of outrage and empathy in him from twelve hundred miles away. It was one of the first songs he ever wrote, before he even had a recording contract.

In 2006, Ghost performed 'Hot Lunch' at the Grammys as a duet with Sting, and later donated an undisclosed amount of proceeds from the single to the prevention of school violence. If you studied the lyrics, which were brutal but heartfelt, rippling with outrage and nuance that went far beyond sentiment and pop-culture references, you understood it was a work of art, an ingenious and haunting cry for honesty about America's love affair with guns, and a call for parental responsibility. Of course, the media took a handful of lines out of context and slapped them under the real killer's chilling self-video, turning Ghost into more fodder for the censorship warriors and a scapegoat for grieving parents. As the evangelists arrived outside his gated St Louis compound waving pitchforks, Ghost became apoplectic. He was hurt. He issued his only written response to this kind of thing, defending himself and the importance of music as a means to reach young people and help them consider society's ills, but he did so too late and it was buried beneath the next wave of national news, a political sex scandal.

I needed to find Aaron's hot lunch. I read on, hypno-tized by the paper clippings and articles printed from internet news sites.

FOUR YOUTHS SUSPECTED OF GANG RAPE
OUTSIDE GHOST CONCERT

TWELVE-YEAR-OLD CHARGED IN TWENTY-TWO CAT KILLINGS, CITES RAPPER

DORM MONITOR RAPIST USES 'GHOST' DEFENSE, CLAIMS HE WAS HAUNTED

BROOKLYN MAN BEHEADS WIFE WHILE SINGING GHOST SONG

MIDDLE SCHOOL GHOST-TEENS TORCH REPUTED GAY TAVERN

The lurid headlines throbbed before me. There were dozens of them, but none mentioned Annette, Aaron or Arthur Copeland. I wanted to leave, run downstairs, get in the car and drive to another state. But the secret was in here, I was certain. I had to find out what happened, why Aaron had collected these.

No, that was stupid. Of course Aaron had not been the one to save these. Annette or Arthur had. Why? Did they blame Ghost for whatever had happened to Aaron? Did Arthur kill himself out of guilt, or had she blamed his death on Ghost too?

I didn't even know for sure that Aaron was dead, or that he was her son. But why else would she preserve the room this way? Keep all this Ghost memorabilia? Why hadn't she told me about him? She had told me her husband was responsible for Stacey's death. That required some courage. What was so bad about Aaron that she needed to hide it? Pretend he did not even exist?

Nervous, wired now, I began flipping the pages too quickly. I stopped, went back to the middle, to read them more carefully:

PSYCHOLOGISTS SEE RISE IN PATIENTS TREATED FOR 'EVIL RECORDINGS'

I didn't have to read very far into this one to discredit the psychologist who provided the most provocative quote. 'It's not so much the content,' Dr Paul Brown of the Institute for a Brighter America said. 'This music presents extreme violence, pornography and drug abuse not as tragedies but as episodic cartoons, a sort of conse-quence-free funhouse where anything goes. It's destroying in forty-some minutes what parents spend years trying to instill in their children – namely, values and common decency.' Dr Brown was on the board of a right-wing lobbying firm that had been waging war on the First Amendment for almost two decades. He had simply moved on from Judas Priest to Ghost.

SALVAGGIO DEATH RULED SUICIDE, WIFE BLAMES HOUSING BUBBLE FOR HUSBAND'S DEPRESSION

This was different. There was no mention of Ghost but—

A soft but urgent scraping noise in the hallway whispered at me, disrupting the silence. I closed the scrapbook quickly, wincing from the slap of plastic. I started to close the footlocker's lid, then realized I had left the CD on the floor. I grabbed it as the scraping sound started again. I stood holding the copy of *Autotopsy*, afraid to move.

Scoosh-ush, scoosh-ush, scoosh-ush.

The sound of feet dragging along carpet drew nearer to Aaron's bedroom, but stopped short of entering. I didn't want to be confronted by Annette. She was supposed to be fast asleep three doors down. Was she sneaking up on me? I would not call out to her. She would have to break cover first. Maybe she was just using the hallway bathroom and had not realized I was in Aaron's room.

I waited, the guilt mounting exponentially. For being in Aaron's room and sifting through his belongings, and for whatever she thought Ghost had done. I had never robbed a grave, but I imagined the feeling being similar to this, the sense of being an intruder, of being watched by the dead.

The swishing footsteps started again, coming closer now.

The room was cold. I was dizzy, my legs stiff from crouching. It was morning and the sun was not high enough to warm the house yet, but Aaron's room was colder than could be explained by the time of day. The steps sounded too small and too light to belong to an adult.

Was he in the hall, peering around the doorway now? The energy in the room changed, grew heavier. I was certain he was already inside, standing behind me in his blue blazer with the private school crest, watching me with his vacant eyes. The room smelled like boy, an unwashed smell mixed with bubble-gum fumes and the stale earthen decay of his shallow grave.

Something wooden creaked. A door frame, the door opening a little wider. I turned around and was confronted by an empty bedroom. No one was standing in the doorway. But I *felt* him there. It was just like the street. When I turned around, he disappeared.

I turned back to the footlocker and he moved toward me with a sound like ruffling paper. I stared at the wall, seized. He was close enough to reach out and touch my back. The whole house seemed to be pressing down on me, as if we were in a submersible sinking deeper into the ocean.

Had he died here, at home? Is that why this was happening?

Delicate fingers slid down the small of my back, followed by a gentle tugging at my shirt tail. My left hand fell to my side, dropping the copy of *Autotopsy*. It hit the carpeting softly and fell open. Before I could focus on the case, his small hand took mine, palm to palm, squeezing, as if imploring me to go for a walk. His hand was stiff and cold and it held me in a pocket of his grotesque aura. He sighed with contentment, his little boy breath cold on my wrist. This was followed by the crack of plastic.

I began to turn, watching my toes sink into the carpet so that I did not have to look into his pale face, see his mouth hanging open. His grip loosed itself and the last of his touch slipped from my hand in a paper-thin draft.

There was no one in his room but me. I exhaled.

My mind was playing tricks on me.

I noticed the CD on the floor. The booklet with the liner notes had sprung free of the jewel case. It was bent open to the gatefold, its spine creased horizontally over the staple to keep it from flapping shut.

Ghost was looking up at me.

I remembered the photos used for this mini-spread, of course. The grotto shots of Ghost hiding in an alley, lurking behind a dumpster with a machete in one hand, his black hooded sweatshirt hiding most of his face, everything but a moon slice of white jawline and the demonic eyes. Just like the boy who had been following me, dressing up not as a Ghost fan, but like Ghost himself. I remembered the feelings I had when I began to work for him and revisited his albums, to study him. I had been a casual fan, but as his employee and double I needed to know his work like it was my own. I remembered comparing the photos of him to the man I saw in the mirror, now that I had acquired his look. The actor's urge to act. Could I go there? Be this dark personality? The strangely intoxicating sense of me in there, not him, our roles reversed, the monster he was pretending to be a real demon hiding inside of me. I remembered the drops of blood dripping from his blade, the little pool of red on the ground at his feet, shining like bar sign neon in puddles. But I did not remember the arterial streaks and splatters that escaped the main photo and splashed across the gatefold, the quantity of the blood.

I did not remember these cinematic touches because

none of the fourteen million copies of *Autotopsy* in existence had been printed with Photoshopped blood splatters *outside* of the photos themselves.

I bent over and plucked the booklet from the floor, careful to keep the spread open, pinching it by the edges the way a detective bags evidence. The blood was fresh, still wet. I dabbed it with my finger, right where someone with a tiny paintbrush, or very small fingertip, had defaced Ghost's hooded countenance with an accusation:

ghOst KilLer

I flexed my hand, opening the stinging smile in my wrist where the dead boy had cut me, and more of my blood began to spill onto the floor.

32

The cut along my wrist looked like I had tried to do myself in. I ran downstairs with it wrapped in my shirt, intent upon dialing 9-1-1, but it wasn't bleeding very much by the time I got to the phone, and I realized no veins or arteries had been severed. I washed my arm in the kitchen sink and kept a wad of paper towels around it until I located a pack of bandages under the first-floor bathroom sink. I used the largest square in the pack, the one you hope you will never have to resort to, and two smaller ones on the sides as tape, until the whole works seemed to be good and sealed off.

I was an exhausted mess. Dirty, hungover, running on almost no sleep.

Paranoia bloomed.

I locked the bathroom door and wrapped a plastic bag I had taken from the kitchen over my hand and stepped into the shower. I set the water as hot as I could stand it, and let it pound me until my headache began to fade. I tried to think my way through this discovery and everything it implied.

No one had been in the room with me. I had felt

Aaron's presence, but now I wondered if I had let the footlocker containing the evidence of Ghost's fame and infamy go to my head. I might have experienced some kind of panic attack and cut myself by squeezing the edge of the CD's jewel case. Those things weren't sharp enough to kill yourself with – barring an episode of total mania – but sharp enough to cut the thin skin at the wrist? Possibly. So, okay, it was a factory defect, and I had been squeezing the edge too hard while I imagined Aaron creeping up behind me.

Ghost killer.

But had I really written that word in my own blood? Was someone accusing me of murder? Of killing Ghost? Accusing Ghost of being a killer, more likely. Trying to send me a message. Aaron – had it come from him or was it about him? The album was full of media innuendo blaming Ghost for random crimes. Did someone in the Copeland family blame Ghost for Aaron's death?

Make yourself at home, Ghost.

Rick kept calling me Ghost. At first I thought it was a nickname, that he'd just been teasing me. He didn't believe me when I explained it to him, and then there was the matter of my hair changing color. I had to face this much – Rick Butterfield believed I was Ghost. And who is Rick Butterfield friends with? Where would he get such a silly notion?

Annette. Annette thinks I'm Ghost.

Oh, shit.

That could not be right. She knew me. She had been to the house. She knew about Stacey. She had talked with the police. Detective Bergen had been involved, he would have let her know I was me, James Hastings, body double and poseur. Not Ghost, millionaire rap artist and scourge. I hadn't played Ghost for over a year. After Stacey died—

Wait. Why hadn't Bergen mentioned Aaron? He must not have known. He might have missed it. Annette might have covered it up. Why would she?

Had Annette mistaken me for Ghost? Had she targeted me? Chosen to get close to me because of my connection to him?

I'm worried about you, Stacey had said in Laurel Canyon that day, begging me to quit my job. *What if you get hurt?*

I didn't get hurt. Stacey did. What if it had not been an accident at all, but revenge? What if Stacey was a casualty, like the news headlines in the scrapbook, that went unnoticed? Arthur striking back at me by killing Stacey . . . because he thought I was Ghost and that she was Ghost's girl. Was that possible? I had been ensnared in some form of conspiracy? But why now, a year later? Annette knew I wasn't Ghost. It didn't make sense.

I turned the water off and stepped out of the shower. I went back to the bedroom to throw on some clean clothes. The bedroom door was open but Annette was not in the bed. The bedding had been kicked aside.

'Annette?' I called out, walking to the top of the stairs. 'Annette? Are you down there?'

She didn't answer.

I dressed quickly and searched the rest of the house.

I went out back and checked the courtyard and pool area. The garage.

The Mustang was gone. Annette was gone.

If she wanted to get back at me, why had she fled? What the hell was going on here?

'She doesn't know who she is,' I said to the empty garage. 'Who is she, Arthur? Who is she now?'

Her head injury. Do you really think it's a coincidence she slipped and fell in our bathtub? That could have been staged, easily. Do you really believe she dyed her hair white, took up OCD gardening, and learned how to make love to you just like Stacey, all in a matter of a couple weeks? She's playing games with you. This is all part of her plan.

Except that there were too many unexplained phenomena. This was not a skit. This could not have been choreographed. Annette knew things and said things only Stacey knew. Annette was changing, that was certain . . . but into Stacey? Really? Why would she be worse now? Here, in Sheltering Palms?

Once we got here, way out in the boonies, the – call it the Stacey effect – got scrambled, or had been exacerbated. Annette was a wreck now. The effects of revisiting the scene of her family trauma.

Or.

Stacey knocked Annette down. She used the rabbit paintings to get into Annette's head long enough to cause her fall. She took Annette so she could be with me. She's not ready to let go. And maybe I wasn't ready to let go of Stacey. Maybe Stacey was protecting me, trying to stop Annette from doing whatever the hell she was doing to me. Maybe Stacey was fighting inside of Annette, surfacing, trying to warn me, keep the evil at bay. Difficult to accept.

Yes, but what did I believe? What did I feel when I looked into Annette's eyes? When we had sex? When Blaine screamed at the sight of her? It wasn't just her hair and the clothes or a few catchphrases. It was something inside her. A palpable thing, a wrongness others can sense.

Stacey. Stacey was trying to reach me.

But what did it all have to do with Ghost? Aaron? The footlocker?

I would never be at peace until I got to the bottom of what happened to Aaron – and how it was connected to Stacey. I needed to know what happened to this family before Stacey was killed. I needed to find out if Annette was running a game on me, trying to make me pay for what she perceived as Ghost's sins, or if she was for the love of God harboring the soul of my dead wife. And what I needed most of all was a good night's sleep. My mind was coming apart, and yet I was thinking clearly enough to understand this could all be a case of one severely deranged or damaged man, a grieving husband looking for an excuse to keep his wife alive. Only one other person knew Annette better than I knew her. One other place she might have run to.

I went back to Rick Butterfield's house.

33

The SP's ramrod answered the door in his grippies, one hand rubbing the shaving rash of his slab chest. His belly bulged obscenely above a purple marble pouch from which orange tarantulas of fur descended his thighs and blotted out his knees. His hair was flat, his eyes sagging, making him look even more *North Dallas Forty* than usual. His left big toe nail was yellow and standing upright like a matchbook cover, and he stank of cigarettes.

'Don't tell me,' he said. 'You brought back my gun.'

Shit. I had left the gun at the house. Probably not smart. 'Annette's missing,' I said. 'Is she here?'

He noticed but did not comment on the bandage on my wrist. 'What do you mean, "missing"?'

I explained that she had been disoriented when I came home, but had disappeared while I was getting dressed. I told him her car was gone.

Rick shook his head in disappointment.

'But I'm not really here about Annette,' I said. 'I'm here about Aaron.'

'Okay. And who's Aaron?' Rick was not a good poker player.

'I know you know,' I said. 'It's over. Whatever it is, it's over.'

Rick sighed. 'She's probably crying on Debbie Duncan's shoulder again, or down at the Rat Tail flirting with Luke. You want to come in for a drink? Wait it out in the Rick Room?'

'I didn't stick around to find out what kind of bullshit you pulled last night, but I have a pretty good idea. You think you are the sheriff in this little hamlet? Unless you tell me what the fuck is going on with Annette, Aaron and Arthur, right now, you'll find out who the real sheriff is. The LAPD will bring the hammer down on you so fast, by the end of the week you'll be back in Chuckwalla getting your salad tossed by the same cons you used to tickle with your nightstick.'

Rick remained unimpressed.

'Why does she think I'm Ghost? Are you both that stupid?'

'Oh, right,' he said. 'You're in retirement now, like Jay-Z.'

'No, Rick. Not like Jay-Z. You want my bank records? You want to see my contract for employment? For fuck's sake, grow up. I found the Ghost collection, all right? The footlocker in Aaron's room, the news clippings. It's a shrine. The only thing missing is the sacrificial chicken and voodoo doll. She blames Ghost for his death, Arthur's death, or both. And I guess since I was the one who played Ghost for three years, and since I'm the one standing here, that means Annette blames me.'

Rick leaned to the side and removed a Winston from

a table near the door. He lit it and exhaled smoke at my head. 'What makes you think he's dead?'

'I saw him two nights ago, in one of the empty houses,' I said. 'And last night, on the street. He followed me. He's here.' I waved my bandaged wrist. 'The little fucker cut me, but every time I turn around he winks out of existence.'

'Interesting.' Rick's façade was crumbling. 'What did he look like, this boy that supposedly cut you?'

I described Aaron, noting the black sweatshirt, his pale face. 'And his feet,' I said. 'His feet were bare. Bare and white as snow.'

'Are you queer? Can I go back to bed now?"

'Rick, listen. I haven't worked for Ghost in a year. Whatever happened, I am very sorry, but I haven't done anything. If there was a misunderstanding, I am a victim, too. I am trying to help Annette. We've been to the hospital together. We've spoken to the police. They know who I am. Do you understand? My wife is dead.' My voice cracked. 'Stacey's dead. I want to know what happened. I need to know, and I will not stop until I know the truth. I don't have a god damn thing left to live for, so let's get it over with, whatever it is, or else my next call is the LAPD.'

Rick was staring at me with a mixture of fear and sadness I would not have thought possible from him.

'Oh my God,' he said. 'You're not him. You're really not him.'

I sighed with relief.

'Oh, Christ.' He threw his cigarette onto his dead lawn. 'This is bad. This is . . . she told me . . . oh, man, look, I was only supposed to keep you entertained for a day or two. She won't return my calls. I haven't talked to her in weeks. She said she would let me know what to do once she was sure you – shit, hold on a minute.' Rick turned and opened his front door. 'I got to get my clothes. My car keys. Stay put.'

He left the door open. He leaned to the right, reached for something, then stepped out of view.

'When did this start?' I said. 'When did she first tell you about me?'

I heard vague fumbling sounds, a drawer opening and slamming. A zipper opening.

'Rick?'

'Sorry, can't find my keys.' He reappeared, still in his purple underwear. He was holding a syringe, flicking the base and then squirting a fine thread of clear fluid onto the sidewalk.

'What the fuck is that?' I said.

Rick glanced up and down the street again. 'She might need to be subdued.'

I took two steps back. 'Hey.'

Rick kept rolling it between his thumb and forefinger like a cigarette. 'Don't worry. We'll find her. We'll get through this together. Hate to do this to my own sister, but she's been through so much.'

He stepped down the porch, onto the sidewalk. He smiled at me.

His sister?

Before she changed. The red hair.

'How much you wanna bet,' he said. 'I can catch me a real live Ghost?'

I turned and ran. In three strides I was over his lawn, flying over the sidewalk. I was wearing sneakers. Rick was in his bare feet, carrying an extra seventy pounds of meat. There was no way he was going to catch me.

Yes, but the way he went after those crawlers last night. That buffalo can move.

But only for short distances. If he doesn't catch me in the first hundred feet, I will leave him in the dust.

I poured it on. I was in the street now, running downhill. Behind me, he grunted with exertion.

'C'mere . . . little . . . shit!'

I leaned into it, pushing my chest forward, bowing my back away from the fingers I imagined reaching for me. I cut a perfect line down the center of the road and I would not stop until I hit the ocean. My lungs blazed. I had him, I had the bastard—

My feet left the ground first. I thought I had been hit by a truck. The force against my back was too great to be anything less. And then we were flying forward doubledecked until I slammed into the asphalt, his two hundred and forty pounds smashing me flat as my left arm folded back, something in my shoulder popped and my face skidded across the road. I screamed and tried to roll him off. His knee staved my sacrum and sent an explosion of pain in all directions. Something crawled into my hair as I thrashed. My head was yanked back like a roped calf's. A nasty wasp stung my neck, very deeply, and I coughed out what little air remained. Heat swam into my throat. I could not breathe. The sunny morning shimmered and turned black.

SHE WHO

The last summer their two families spent August together at the lake house in Colorado, James and Stacey drove his dad's van out to Gerald's corn stand. His mission was two dozen ears of Silver Queen and Stacey rode along in the passenger seat, quiet as a field mouse. They followed the nameless gravel road from the driveway to the end of the lake and turned left on Anchor Lane, then on past the subdivision on the other side of the lake, up to Highway 287. A few miles later they made the light at Highway 52, turning left, and stayed northbound for fifteen miles, past tree farms and a gravel quarry and out into open prairie. They coasted for another two miles or so until they hit the four-way stop, where they were surrounded by acres of corn on three corners, and a white farmhouse with a dairy facility and grain silo behind it on the last corner. James backed into the driveway and parked in a wide patch of dirt next to a giant willow tree with a rusting, pea-green Ford F-150 in its shade.

'Where's the corn stand?' Stacey said.

'I don't know. Maybe they closed up early this year.' James got out of the van and walked around, opening the door for her.

'So what are we supposed to do, just go knock on the door?'

'Maybe holler. Keep your eyes peeled for Malachai.'

As she climbed out, the *ratatat* and squeaking bark of air-compressor powered tools echoed from behind the house. James followed the sound and Stacey followed him. They passed a small stack of hay and the scent of manure was strong as the wind blew over the dairy building off in the distance.

'Watch your step,' James said, weaving through stagnant puddles in the dirt drive that wrapped around the house. Flies and small clouds of slow mosquitoes jumped and followed their feet.

'It stinks, James.'

'It's a farm.'

On the backside of the house, the drive petered out into a broad oval of trampled grass. Two children, a boy of ten or eleven and a girl half his age, were playing on an abandoned tractor with tires taller than Stacey. Gerald's grandchildren both had thin black hair and wore dark jeans, collared plaid shirts and newer cowboy boots, as if dressed for church or class picture day. They stared at the young couple, the boy from the tractor's seat, the girl sitting on the ground with her legs splayed out and folded back like wings.

'Hello,' James said, loud enough for their parents to hear, should they be in earshot. Stacey smiled at them uncomfortably, as if embarrassed to be trespassing. 'Is your grand-dad around?' he said.

The girl pointed to the open barn.

'Grandpa!' the boy shouted, then hopped off the tractor and went trotting into the barn, slipping into darkness.

Stacey said, 'There's no corn. Let's go home.'

'Don't you want to see the rabbits again?'

Stacey shifted her weight, smiled a little. She remembered them, and though she was getting a little old to be charmed by them, there was some little girl in her yet. It was an old tradition on these corn runs.

James turned as a short man wearing matching green work pants and shirt came out of the barn with an air filter in one hand and a red, oil-stained rag in the other. He was bow-legged, with flat shoes and fewer teeth than he had four years ago, but he looked as innocent and dippy as always, his boyish black hair sweeping over his brow in an almost handsome wave. He carried himself lightly, as if he were ready to jump to the next task. He looked at each of them and tilted his head in polite curiosity.

'Hi, Gerald,' James said, remembering to pronounce it with a hard G. 'I don't know if you remember us. I'm James Hastings, this is Stacey. We usually come with our parents every couple years.'

Gerald squinted. 'Tulsa?'

James nodded, smiling.

'I remember your ma,' Gerald said. 'And the Oklahoma plates. Had a cousin in Tulsa who works for

Shell. Your ma didn't know him, but she always asked how he was doin'. Nice woman.'

'That's very kind of you,' James said.

'You all rentin' the summer house up in Loveland again?'

'Gaynor Lake, actually. But I'd drive from Loveland for a bag of your Silver Queen.'

'Gaynor, that's right,' Gerald said. He glanced at Stacey and frowned slightly. 'Sold off all my corn acreage across the road there, though, sorry to say. Closed the stand last year. We just do the cheese and some soybean now, but I'm fixing to sell off the soy parcels and switch over to goats next spring.'

'Goat cheese, then?'

'That's what people want. I gotta compete with the organic farmers now. God damned Boulderites want everything organic, don't realize most of it still gets shipped up from Mexico. Hell, I can put a label that says local on anything you want, don't make it so. Except, in my case, I guess it do make it so.'

He laughed. James laughed. Gerald Zurfluh had been bitching about the People's Republic of Boulder since James was eleven.

Gerald blew into his air filter, producing a tiny brown cloud out the other side. 'Sorry to disappoint you, Jeff. King Soopers back in Longmont's got pretty good corn now, or did anyway last time I was in. Wouldn't recommend the beef, though.'

'Oh, that's no problem,' James said. 'I just thought we'd say hello since we were out this way.'

''Preciate that,' Gerald said. 'How long you and – Stacey, is it?' He looked at Stacey. Stacey nodded. 'How long you kids plan on staying this year?'

'We should probably go, James,' Stacey said.

'Just a minute, sweetie.' James stepped closer to Gerald, until they were about ten feet apart. The daughter was hugging Gerald's leg and sucking her thumb, swiveling on the heels of her boots. 'I don't mean to interrupt your work, but I was wondering if you still have that condominium hutch. Out back there,' James pointed. 'Behind the barn?'

'Condominium?'

'James,' Stacey said.

'That's what we called it when we were kids,' James said. 'That was the tallest hutch I ever saw. You had ramps and little carpeted stairways. Loops and wheels. Remember, Stace? It was like bunny Disneyland.'

'Oh, ha ha, yap.' Gerald nodded. 'You got a good memory. Didn't know I showed you them. I built that for the kids long time ago. Don't have the hutch no more. Hell, I didn't know nothing about farming rabbits back then. Them's was just pets.'

'Grandpaaaaawww,' the little girl whined, tugging on Gerald's pant leg.

'Hush now, Deanie-Beanie,' Gerald said gently, scratching the top of her head with his red rag. 'Take your brother inside and fix yourself an ice cream.'

'I hate ice cream,' Deanie-Beanie said.

'Oh, you do not,' Gerald said.

Stacey said, 'He's busy, hon. Come on.'

'Aw, that's all right, Tracy,' Gerald said. 'She always gets upset but she don't know nothin' about it.' He faced James, a sly grin playing across his lips. "Mom-back. I'll show you our new set-up. Not quite Disneyland. Maybe more like rabbit suburbia – ha!'

James followed and Stacey lagged behind.

'Grandpa!' Deanie-Beanie wailed. 'I said nooooo!'

Gerald whirled on her, his face contorting in real anger. 'That is *enough*, young lady. I tol' you not to get attached! Now git in there 'fore I beat your bottom!'

Deanie-Beanie burst into tears and ran into the house.

Stacey watched her go. She looked like she wished she could go inside too, maybe to have some ice cream, but probably just to cry.

'Don't mind her,' Gerald said.

'Come on, Stace,' James said. 'You used to love this.'

Gerald's grandson jogged ahead and then turned back, walking on his heels. 'Can I take out Bronco?'

'Long as you don't drop him,' Gerald said. The boy ran off and disappeared into the barn. Gerald looked over his shoulder at them. 'You ever seen a Flemish Lop? Damn things get as big as a coon you feed 'em right. Ears long as socks. Bronco took first prize up the State Fair last September. Kyle's old enough he understands, but that little one, she still thinks they're all talking pets right out of her storybook.'

'What exactly do you do with them?' Stacey said. They had entered the barn. The space was dark except for a single propane lamp beside the Toyota parked a little ways past the doors. The hood was up, the air filter canister open. A tire was off, a jack raising the truck, with a rolling cart of tools beside the passenger side fender. The barn was clean, mostly empty except for the six or eight pallets of feed pellets stacked at the far end. Each pallet held something like fifty bags.

'Helluva thing,' Gerald said, walking toward the door. Though he wore a belt, the seat of his pants sagged as if he had crapped in them an hour or two ago. 'If you'd a told me ten years ago I'd be farming rabbits, I'd a told you you were shit nuts. Beauty of it is, not so much what do you do with 'em, but what can't you do with rabbits.'

Stacey took James's hand and squeezed it twice, then just clamped down on it as they reached the end of the barn and the door leading to the attached building.

'Italian restaurants,' James said. 'Rabbit's gourmet, isn't it, Gerald?'

Gerald stopped at the door. 'Rabbit might be gourmet, but I'm full up of it. I like me a porterhouse with that ah juice. Anyways, fella comes to me a few years ago and says, "I hear you got rabbits." And I says, "Sure, I got rabbits." And he says, "I'll take all you got." Well, hell, I told him I only had a few dozen, but they're coming on strong. "What do you want 'em for?" I says. He says, "I specialize in meat, but I got connections in fur, show bunnies, feet, pelts, gut string, bone meal, you name it." He says, "We use the whole rabbit." And by God he do use the whole rabbit. By God he do. We get three bucks per week up to twenty-four weeks, breeders and show ears go for more. A lot more. Rabbits what bought me that new truck there, and put the mortgage to bed for good. Yes, sir.'

Gerald held the door open and Stacey went stiff. James pushed the small of her back and she went forward grudgingly. He followed her, and the door closed. James thought immediately of plant nurseries, foggy white and half as long as a football field. But instead of plants and misting sprinklers, Gerald's nursery was lined with wooden hutches, a three-story Alcatraz with units ranging in size from shoebox quarantines to eight-foot breeding pens. The floors of the hutches were grated, and the pebbles fell through into steel troughs that were much cleaner than James expected. Behind the troughs and walls of cages, spaced out every ten feet or so, was a giant exhaust fan. It was like walking in a wind tunnel, but quiet enough to hear the rabbits nuzzling, the scamper of their feet.

The rabbits were white, black, black and white, brown, tan, cinnamon, spotted, roan, every color and pattern James could imagine. Rows and rows of red-eyed albinos. Some of the hutches contained whole litters, others had mating pairs, and others still were private residences for the prize adults, some of which looked freakish, not much like rabbits at all.

'Oh, man,' James said. 'This is a serious operation.'

Stacey had let go of James's hand and now walked to the opposite end, and he was so enchanted with all the floppy ears and strange, twitching and toggling eyes that followed his every movement, James forgot about her for a moment.

'Eleven hundred seventy-seven by last count,' Gerald said. 'But that was this morning.' He laughed. James laughed.

Stacey laughed too, harder, and her laughter went on longer than either of theirs, echoing back. She laughed and laughed and Gerald stopped and at stared at her. She was standing sideways facing the cages as Kyle rounded the corner at her end with Bronco in his arms. By the time she turned and saw that Flemish Giant out of his cage, her laughter had gone straight into hysterical screaming.

34

I woke to her screaming.

My first sense was one of being safer indoors, that I had found a haven from the monsters lurking in the desert. I had been dreaming, except that the dream had been a continuation of something we had shared, a single pearl set in a necklace of memories stringing back toward the lake house – and something beyond it that Stacey wanted to show me. Something to do with the rabbits. But I couldn't remember what happened – in either the dream or the real memories – and it was driving me insane that I couldn't remember, driving me out of sleep in a depleted panic.

The world I awoke to was gray, a dim room, still blurry and soft but taking shape, hardening over a period of minutes. For a moment – before I saw the wood paneling and the bar off to my left – I thought I was back in the hospital. I was very weak, as if I had been sleeping for days without food. I was warm, supine, thirsty.

No, not the hospital. I was on the tiger couch. In the Rick Room.

I felt no pain, and even my dream-state panic was fading quickly. Surely Detective Bergen would arrive any minute now to comfort me, tell me to keep my chin up and send me home.

He drugged me. He drugged me good. Well, at least he didn't kill me.

I looked down to find myself enveloped in a bright red blanket, velveteen. I squirmed, just to get a feel for my body again, and the blanket slipped against my skin. I was naked – no, just stripped to my shorts, I realized, feeling the waistband. My vision sharpened.

No, not a blanket.

I was wearing a red tracksuit. So shiny it seemed wet, a skin of blood. Ghost's signature threads, available in limited editions for nineteen hundred and eighty-eight dollars at Neiman Marcus, smoother than satin panties.

This is going somewhere bad. To a place we might not come back from.

I wasn't confined or bound, but my body felt as though it weighed six hundred pounds. Small patches of my arms and face burned coolly, not unpleasantly, the scent of menthol wafting from the collar of my zipped jacket. My feet were bare except for the smaller bandages around my toes. After prodding around for another minute, the first tendrils of pain radiated out of my shoulder, and from my lower back, and I stopped fussing. It didn't hurt as long as I remained very still.

A clinking noise directed my attention to the left, across the room. Rick was behind the bar, mixing something in a tall glass of bobbing ice. He stirred the concoction with a glass swizzle and carried it to me. He appeared nine feet tall.

'Drink this.'

My mouth was dry. The fluid was milky yellow with little white crystals eddying to the bottom. Rick was pale and showered, his curly red hair wet swept back. He was dressed in all black, the shirt something of a mock turtleneck, black jeans, a black leather belt with rows of holes and a buckle of silver nails. He seemed uninterested in me as he lowered the glass. I accepted it and sat forward to sip it, which took a long time. It was marvelously cold and bittersweet.

'Whazzit?'

He made a little 'up' motion with his hand. I guzzled the rest, spilling around the corners of my mouth. I wanted more.

Rick took the empty glass. 'Lemonade, vodka and valium. Best thing in the world for pain.'

I took a long look around the room. His display case of knives and Kung Fu weapons and guns had been emptied, of course. He had taken necessary precautions.

Rick pulled an ottoman over from the rest of the wild kingdom and sat facing me, elbows on his knees. In the dim light his red hair and mustache shined like amber and his eyes were dilated, the corneas thin rings of green around swamps of black. His rage had been sheared away, revealing something slow and dangerously resolved. He must have gone through a lot for her, I knew then. She was all he had.

'You love her,' I said.

He studied me for a moment. 'She's my sister.'

'Annette Butterfield,' I said, testing it out.

'Mmm-hmm, at first,' Rick said. 'Later, Salvaggio. Annette, Arthur and Aaron Salvaggio.'

Salvaggio. Even in my haze, the name sounded an alarm in my memory. Salvaggio, Salvaggio, where had I heard that recently?

News headlines swam up from the depths. The scrapbook. The Ghost headlines. *Salvaggio death ruled a suicide, wife blames housing bubble for husband's depression.* I had been scanning the article when the noises in the hall began, just before Aaron, or something in his bedroom, cut my wrist.

'Copeland is her maiden name?' I said.

Rick smiled. 'Ask your friend on the LAPD to sort it out.'

Detective Bergen would have known her maiden name. Copeland was a fake. An alias. Is that why he didn't know about Aaron? What else had she faked?

''Nettie wanted to be a nurse. She ever tell you that?'

'I don't remember.'

'She would have been a good one. She has a real touch. She should never have taken up with Arthur. Hotshot made her drop out. She kept her supplies, though. She gave me all this medicine and the little doctor's kit. Told me to hold onto it, we might need it someday. Yes, sir, she has real vision.'

Rick's eyes sparkled.

'Okay, you got me,' I said. 'Roll out the karaoke and I will turn up the flow.'

'Maybe later,' he said, as if he had been seriously considering just that.

Keep him talking. 'What happened to Aaron?'

Rick's mustache flattened and then began a slow bristling dance, an urchin moving across the ocean floor. He stared at me, waiting for me to answer my own question.

'You think Ghost is responsible for . . . whatever happened,' I said.

'What I think doesn't matter. The change you instigate in others is undeniable. You destabilize the impressionable. You've seen the evidence. The ones that made the news.'

The 'news' being the album in Aaron's bedroom. 'That's ridiculous. You can't blame an entertainer—'

'Aaron's story is the one that did not make the news,' he said. 'I made sure of that. To protect her. To protect us. And so you would never see us coming.'

We stared at each other for a full minute without speaking. I didn't understand what had happened. I only understood that Rick's temper was rising, filling the room, and soon would blow.

'He was a good boy. And you infected him.'

'No,' I said. 'Rick, no. I'm not Ghost. You can't – it doesn't work this way.'

'What else would make a ten-year-old boy creep into the bedroom in the middle of the night and shoot his father in the head? And then turn the gun on himself? What kind of boy is capable of that?'

I tried to think of an answer that would not further anger him. I couldn't.

Not quite singing, Rick began to recite a poem, employing the voice of a child in a cereal commercial.

There's a monster in my father and he makes
Me cry
There's a gun in the closet and it's just
My size
Daddy why'd you beat her with your boots?
Why do you do the things the things you do?
There's a creature inside me and it looks just
Like you
Daddy why'd you leave us all alone you make
Me cry
Daddy should never have come back here
To-night
I found the magic silver bullets you left
Be-hind
Daddy why do you do the things the things you do?
There's a werewolf inside me and it looks just
Like you
Kiss me good night one more time, Daddy, tonight you're
Going to die
Going to die
Watch me pull this trigger I got silver bullets now
Say bye bye
Say bye bye

The song was 'Silver Bullet'. The fictional one Ghost
had written about shooting his own father, after witness-
ing the old man beat his mother on Christmas Eve. That
little domestic abuse ditty reached #1 on the *Billboard*
singles and stayed in the Top 20 for eighteen weeks.

'Your words,' Rick said.

'No,' I said. 'That's not true.'

'In the form of a nursery rhyme. So that the children can understand. So they will follow you like the Pied Piper.'

'I didn't write that. I didn't write any of his music. Will you listen to me for—'

'Where is she!' he shouted, his face shaking, clenching his fists in a way that would have been comical if he were not deadly serious. 'What did you do with her?'

'Nothing. I told you, I don't know where—'

'She's not your wife! She's not Arthur's wife! You treated her like trash—'

Something in me snapped. I sat up and screamed in his face. 'It's just a song, you fucking animal! Jesus Christ, if you want him so bad I can find him for you! I'll give you his home address, his agent's number, we can arrange a meeting. All it will take is one phone call to prove I'm right. Think! Use your head! *You have the wrong man!*'

Rick closed his eyes as if meditating. He rocked back and forth until his breathing returned to normal. I swallowed a sour lump of something medicinal that had built up at the back of my throat.

'All right,' Rick said. 'All right. Since you refuse to accept responsibility, we'll just see. We'll just have to see about this.'

He stood and walked to the smallest of his three large antique safes. He spun the brass arms left, then right, left again, then right, running the combination. The safe door groaned and clunked open. He reached in and removed an unmarked disc in a clear jewel case. His back blocked the open safe. I wondered what else he was storing in there. He shut the safe, spun the wheel and returned to his cabinet of audio components in the corner. There was a click and hiss as he inserted the disc. The big plasma television mounted to the wall facing the couch came to life with a hum, but the screen was still flat gray.

'The windows are sealed,' Rick said, facing me. 'And there's a grate welded into the top of the concrete wells. Everything behind these walls is cement foundation, and the door will be braced with a steel rod and two deadbolts. Your back's probably broken. You're cut up. I saved a few stuck cons on the shithouse, but I'm not a doctor and I don't do stitches. Trying to bust out, running, these are not recommended. I'm telling you this to save you some trouble. I'm going to lock you in here now, and until I come back and open the door you won't be able to leave. You will hurt yourself trying, and I can't make you better. I won't make you better. Think about that before you decide to go Shawshank on me.'

He handed me a remote control and walked toward the stairs.

'What happens after?' I said. 'When you find her, can I go home?'

He watched me for a moment. 'I know who you are, and soon you will, too. So I suggest you forget about home. There is no more home for you.'

Rick shut the door to the basement. The doorknob clicked and latched, then something heavy slammed against the door, bracing it, I assumed. I listened to his big footsteps receding up the stairs until I was alone. The panic expanded in me until I thought I would scream and then expanded some more.

I barely reached a sitting position before my back spasmed and the first bolt of real pain lit up my every limb. No escape. All right. I would watch the fucking video.

What if there's something horrible on it? Stacey said in the dark of the basement. *What if it hurts you, honey?*

'How much worse could it get?'

Stacey did not answer. I situated myself on the couch so that I was facing the television. I leaned back carefully until I was supported by the cushions and the pain began to ebb. I considered the remote. I looked up at the blank screen and pushed play.

There is no more home for you.

The black screen filled with swarming lights and familiar music.

35

The compilation lasts only twenty-four minutes.

It begins in a club, the kind found in larger cities where global acts might deign to play three sold-out nights for a privileged two thousand fans. Art Deco sculpture climbs the walls, red velvet curtains on either side of the stage, racks of amps and speaker towers, a throng of waving hands, a stage with sickly orange lighting made dizzying by the handheld digital video camera that's capturing this. Green lasers stab the room. A mirror ball throbs silver and red. The footage quality is only marginally better than your average YouTube clip at first, and the large screen distorts it further. A cacophony of crowd cheer, drum machines, and of course the staccato, rapid-fire verse of the man himself. I understand we are at a Ghost show even before the camera finds him.

We go in at waist level, pushing through plastic cups, long sweaty t-shirts and hospital patient wristbands, shaking asses and flying elbows. The camera mic *fuzzes* and *whumps* as the operator is shoved and jostled forward. But persistence pays off and things come into focus.

The camera mic is too close to the stage; Ghost's spit is unintelligible, and I catch myself trying to decide which song is playing. It's not one of the dance numbers, like 'Bikini Lines'. It's 'Chloroform Dayz', maybe. The murder ballads are always dark and pummeling, surging, a primal assault of sidewalk-destroying beats, a verbal mugging you can't quite grasp how it's humanly possible, but as soon as it's over you want it to happen again.

The lens roves over a beautiful black woman lapping at the neck of a freakishly tall white guy who might be a Laker, up the wall, across the ceiling and settles on the other side, bringing into view a man most out of place.

He is older than the others, a serious person, not dancing, exactly, but moving up and down short, rapid spurts, shoulders rolling, arching his feet in time with the beat. He is wound tightly, his jaw set. He wears a vintage orange-brown leather jacket. His cheeks are pasty and sweat trickles from under his foppish hair and light, feminine eyebrows. He turns and looks at me and only now do I realize I have been watching Rick Butterfield.

The mustache is gone and he looks ten years younger and fifty pounds lighter – recent months have changed him for the worse. He reaches out, pulling the camera operator closer. A woman's voice produces something like, 'Come on, baby, let it out!' This encourages him, and I guess his date is the one holding the camera. He removes his jacket and looks around, shrugs and drops it to the floor. He is an awful dancer, but his eyes, the glee with which he allows himself to be drawn into the grind and pound of Ghost's relentless flow, almost fools me

339

into believing he is enjoying this, not merely putting up with it for her benefit.

The song ends like a recording studio on a flatbed truck with a bundle of dynamite strapped to the chassis hitting a brick wall. Fireworks rain. The camera goes up like a periscope and swings to the stage to capture the star. Ghost is standing with one foot on an amp, leaning forward like George Washington crossing the Delaware, his mic clenched in one brass-knuckled fist that jabs straight ahead and stops in a stark salute to the crowd. His head is down. The wife beater had been shredded right after the encore began, I know, and now he wears only his red track pants and red signature Cons. His torso is chiseled from ivory, his sweat streaming over the Emperor of Rap tattoo that adorns his abs.

He is exultant, beautiful, terrifying.

When he looks up and stares into the camera, right at me, there are tears flowing freely from his inflamed eyes. The tears are not of sadness. They are of rage and love and the ferocity he brings down from the gods. They are of poverty and fame, of black and white, of sex and death, of lust and addiction, of hunger and the endless appetite for their love of him. He cries because it cannot be contained. The ocean of emotion that ebbs and flows from them to him and back. It bursts him every time he performs. He stares into the lens daring all who would hold his gaze to try, just try and hold it, you can't ever hold this, motherfucker, I never look away first. I will never back down. You will have to kill me first, and when you come for me you better make it a passion play.

Then he cracks a smile and drops his head as the entire theater goes dark.

The applause is volcanic.

Rick, a silhouette in the darkness. He is staring into the space Ghost has vacated, his mouth open, eyes wide and glassy, wanting, wanting more of something that he did not know he came for. He is smitten. He has been touched.

She holds on him for an extra beat and the scene cuts to black.

A split second later we are on the street, the crowd almost totally dispersed. It might be Melrose or Sunset, but it's definitely Los Angeles. Ah – the El Rey Theater on Wilshire. I recognize the marquee now. Ghost had played two nights there as a favor to one of the studios. I was very likely backstage right now, turning off the TV in one of the entourage rooms, sitting on a couch with a bottle of beer, talking trash with the other members of his posse. I can't remember the date, nor what I did after. It was near the end of my tenure with Ghost, though, so I probably went through a standard decoy deployment out back where the usual crowd would be waiting while Ghost used a service exit.

The camera finds its subject on a side street. Rick stands on the curb with his jacket slung over his shoulder, looking short-circuited. In his other hand is a small brown leather case about the size of a cigar box. Ahead of him are a handful of teens not paying attention, going their separate ways. The street is quiet and two big

341

headlights come around the corner, then at us. A long white limo truck creeps, the windows tinted. It's a stretch UV, Ghost's limo. The limo comes to stop in front of Rick and he shifts the leather cigar box from hand to hand. He looks back at the camera, excited, *this is it*.

A solid black rear side window glides down. I can't see a face inside. The camera is lowered and I can't see anything, but their conversation is clear.

'You Ron Caspari?' a deep voice asks.

'The one and only,' Rick says.

'My guy says you got something special for us,' deep voice says.

'I do.'

'I saw the photos. Didn't look real. Is it here?'

'It is.'

'Show me.' Something unlatches. After a beat the man says, 'Ho-ly shit.'

'Oh, man, that is the heat!' someone else says. 'Where'd you get that thing?'

'I have friends,' Rick says. 'One of them is the warden of a state penitentiary where that was smuggled in by the former owner of a hedge fund. The warden owed me a favor.'

'Musta been a big favor.'

'The biggest,' Rick says. 'The only catch is he made me promise not to sell it, which is fine, because I'm not a dealer. Oh, and only five were produced.'

'Where are the others?'

'The man who developed the nano-polymer kept two for himself. The CEO of Blackwater bought one. The last one's going to a certain sitcom star who can't stop beating his wives.'

'Char—'

'Yes, that one.'

Someone whistles.

'That'll sail through any airport screener in the world,' Rick says. 'Our gift to you.'

'Why so generous, Ron?'

'Take us for a ride. My wife wants to meet the man.'

'She does, huh?'

'In the worst way,' Rick says.

'Cool,' the deep voice says. 'Hop in.'

I'd been there before, inside. Ghost's agent and manager and two or three of his bodyguard friends would be passing around bottles of Cristal and a blunt or three. There would be club music pumping, and very soon a collection of young girls more than happy to attempt their first lap dances free of charge. But as I watched the feet and the hands and the floor carpet, the camera temporarily forgotten, what was going through my mind was, *why them? What could he possibly have given them?*

Without the decibel levels from the theater overloading it, the mic captures the sound and we're still rolling. Everyone's hyped up from the show, talking over each other, four conversations at once. Shrill laughter. Hoots and hollers. When the lens lifts from the floor, they have reversed roles. Rick's filming the woman now. Even though I knew all along, it takes me a moment to recognize her in the black hair and silver gown that makes her look like a raven-haired version of Michelle Pfeiffer in

Scarface, but the freckles and her eyes when they look at me give it away.

'You look familiar,' a man says to her. 'Were you at the show in Oakland last week?'

'Nope,' Rick says.

Annette doesn't answer. She is focused on Ghost, sitting next to him in the back seat. Ghost's security supervisor and owner of the deep voice, Circus Mouse, is on her other side. So the back row is: a giant black dude, Annette, Ghost. Ghost is splayed out, taking up a lot of room with his legs as he opens the case and studies its contents. He holds the precious thing up, turning it from side to side.

'Damn, you are beautiful,' Ghost says, and kisses it.

It looks like every .45 I have ever seen but slightly smaller. Also, it's snow-white, as if made of porcelain. Not a single visible piece of the gun is metal. It looks completely fake, and for all I know Rick made it in his garage. Ghost puts it back in the box, latches the lid and passes it to someone in the opposite seat.

Ghost turns to Annette. 'You're beautiful, too, baby.'

Annette covers her mouth in mock embarrassment, spilling her champagne on the floor. Circus runs one of his gold-encrusted hands along her thigh and she throws her head back braying.

'Ghost. Yo, Ghost,' a man out of frame calls across the stretch.

Ghost is slow to react. He's watching Annette, shaking his head, as if sensing something here is off.

'I knew you'd appreciate that,' Rick says. 'Should look nice with the rest of your collection.'

Ghost nods at Rick.

'G, you're up,' someone says.

Ghost accepts a little gold-plated tray with half a dozen lines laid out. He hesitates, then looks at Rick.

'Turn that fucking thing off before I throw it out the window.'

'Oh, no, it's just my phone,' Rick says, his hands covering the lens. 'It's off. We're cool.'

The view goes black and buried for a few seconds, then Rick's hand slides away. The view is lower now, looking up, as if the camera is resting on the seat or between his legs. He's got balls, and I am reminded that high-quality digital video cameras no larger than a cellphone are now available for under five hundred bucks.

Ghost uses the gold tuning fork thing and inhales two lines at once. He blinks a few times and holds it up for Annette. She doesn't hesitate to hose down two of her own, coughs, and then steadies herself as someone refills her champagne glass, which she throws down like a shot.

'This is some hot milf shit up in here,' Circus says, then looks at Rick, above the camera. 'I think I'm in love with yo wife.'

Everyone agrees this is funny, including Rick, whose nervous laughter ripples forth. Annette shivers and then sort of luxuriates all at once, a woman who has just entered a warm tub of pulsating jets.

I look into her eyes and I see death.

This is all a ruse. She's waiting to make her move but she must know that if she tries to stab or shoot him, with this crowd, she's finished. She and Rick will never be seen again. She's got to get him alone. Does she think this is going to lead to a suite at the Mondrian? Is this the night Ghost vanished? Began his year-and-counting 'sabbatical' that really wasn't a sabbatical?

'Someone's having a lot of fun,' Ghost says to her. 'So what are you? Another collector?'

'No, baby. I'm just a fan.' Annette runs her right hand – the one not holding the champagne flute – over his still bare chest and kisses him on the mouth.

'Daaaaamn,' one of the guys says. 'Where you all from, anyway?'

'I know, I stopped trying to control her years ago,' Rick says. 'She keeps things interesting.'

Everyone laughs.

'We're cool,' Rick says.

'You cool,' Circus says. One of his hands is reaching around Annette's front, mashing her breast. 'But this pussy's hot. C'mere, lil' wife.'

Annette's giving Ghost the full-court press. Her hand goes over the waist of his red track pants, under, working him. There's no one else in the limo as far as she's concerned. Dudes are laughing and drinking and the music gets a little louder. I hear Rick breathing heavily in a disturbing way. Ghost is looking over her, at someone to Rick's right.

'We shoulda booked a third show,' Ghost says. 'That joint went *off*.'

'LA loves you,' a man says. I think it might be his publicist, Devon Wilson, a six and a half foot tall gay man who had been going with a kind of throwback rockabilly look the two times I had met him. 'We'll roll back in the spring.'

'I'll be in the studio in the spring,' Ghost says. 'Then we got the west, the south. I miss Atlanta. Atlanta's twenty-thousand stubs.'

'Summer, then. I'll call Beaux and tell him to bump up So-Cal.'

'Summer is them bullshit festivals in Chicago and shit. I hate those motherfucking festivals. Lollapa-jerk-me-off. Why can't we be the show?'

'Pretty sure you are the show,' Devon says.

Ghost just now remembers he's on the receiving end of a handjob.

Circus says, 'I think this track needs more bass.'

Annette's green party dress rides up as Circus lifts her by the hips until she is sideways on the bench seat. Circus's dick – a Snickers bar the size of my arm, bowing south – flops onto her ass. She stops administering to Ghost and looks over her shoulder – what the hell is going on back there?

'Knock it off,' she says without much volume. She tries to sit down again.

But Circus grabs her hips again and tries to reposition her.

'Easy, easy,' Rick mumbles, but no one else hears or pays him any mind.

Annette struggles, looking up at Ghost for help. He's not paying attention – someone's refilling his glass. She twists and Circus gets excited and pushes her forward too hard, throwing everything off.

Ghost says, 'What the fuck? Who's rocking the boat?'

Annette's dress goes way high, flashing the bald eagle. She looks back at Circus and says, 'I said not for you!' and pulls her dress down.

Circus looks angry for a moment, on the verge of pushing this too far, but gives up and haughtily puts his dick back in his pants. Annette turns back to Ghost, her hand returning to his pants as she leans in to kiss him.

Bored and rebuffed, Circus slaps her ass aside to fetch another bottle of champagne. The slap accidentally knocks Annette off the seat and she yanks Ghost as she topples to the floor.

'Hey, now!' Rick barks.

Ghost's eyes widen. 'The hell? This ain't Ultimate Fighting, yo.'

Annette gasps. 'I'm sorry! He keeps pushing me!' Her laughter is forced and embarrassing. Jesus Christ this is sad, awkward beyond words.

The moment has been spoiled. Ghost looks at Rick, down at Annette, at the other faces watching or pretending not to watch him. He snaps his track pants up higher and pulls his shirt down and casually uses his foot to shove Annette out of his way. She rolls out of frame.

'Everybody calm the fuck down,' he says. 'This shit ain't workin'. TK, I need some ecs. Let's go see your boy in Burbank.'

Annette pulls herself together and tries to wedge herself back into the seat between them. She glances back at Rick, embarrassed, trying to salvage the party.

She leans into Ghost and whispers something into his ear.

He rears back, genuinely surprised, maybe even disgusted. 'No way, you crazy.'

'Will you listen—' Annette says, pawing at him.

'Go home and please your man,' Ghost says. 'Like, seriously.' He scowls at the camera – Rick – as if to say, *can't you get your woman under control?*

'Aw, don't be that way,' Annette says. 'You don't know what I'm capable of.'

'It's cool, man,' Rick says, half out of breath, meek.

'Sorry, kids,' Circus says. 'It's past our bedtime.'

The music cuts off. The SUV rocks to a halt. A door opens. Ghost is looking away from them, tracing a design into the fogged window. I realize it's a happy face. He's done here, checked out.

Circus exits the truck. 'Party's just switching up. We got an early morning wake-up call. Thanks for the gift.'

'Out? You want us to get out?' Annette says. She looks back at Ghost for help. He ignores her.

She slaps his arm. 'What the fuck, *Nathaniel*?'

He turns to face her, his eyes wide. *Oh no, you di'hin't. No one calls me Nathaniel.* 'Sorry, baby, you're not my type.'

'Bullshit,' she says.

'Honey,' Rick says. 'Not tonight. Let's go.'

'I was your type five minutes ago,' she says. 'What's the problem? We're just having fun. Come on, baby, have some more champagne.'

Ghost scratches his chin.

She goes for him again.

'I said get your old ass out the car!' Ghost snaps, shooting a look at Circus.

Annette absorbs the insult. She is pierced, pale, and finally enraged. Circus grabs her but she slips free and goes at Ghost with her claws, raking at his face.

'The fuck off me, crazy ho!' Ghost yells. Their arms tangle and there is a loud slap. Ghost hit her, maybe. I can't tell. It was an accident, self-defense. Or not. Ghost's cheek is bleeding in tiger stripes, *Enter the Dragon*-style. His eyes are pinwheels of rage. He cocks a fist.

'No!' Rick shouts, his voice booming.

Circus Mouse lunges in and hauls her out. 'No way, darlin'. Not going to happen.'

Annette struggles uselessly in the huge man's embrace.

'The fuck you lookin' at, faggot?' Ghost leaps at Rick and swings an open hand. The slap of flesh is loud and clear and the camera tumbles aside, out of the truck, to the ground. The view is now of the chrome wheel and the curb, a line of parked cars and parking meters and darkness going up the boulevard. 'Don't even try it,' Circus says calmly.

'Whoa, whoa, it's cool, it's cool, we're gone,' Rick says. I can't see him but he sounds scared. Circus probably has a gun on him now. Or maybe Rick's just not that tough.

'Sorry, Dad,' Circus says. 'Go get a room and have some fun on the house.'

Paper, rustling.

'Money?' Annette yells. 'You think I'm a fucking whore?'

'Annette!' Rick yells.

'Fuck you, Ghost, you fucking faggot, can't even get it up, you fucking phony!'

A door slams and tires squeal as the engine roars and fades away.

'Don't touch me, you fucking coward,' she snaps. 'That was our chance.'

His voice pathetic, hurt. 'I'm sorry. I didn't know when to stop it. You said wait till after—'

Blackness.

A frame of dark shadows flickering, we're in a car, sitting quietly in a neighborhood of large homes on a block dense with mature trees. The silence and change of mood are unsettling. It's still night. The same or another I cannot tell.

'I'm so tired,' Rick says offscreen. 'I have to take a piss.'

'I know he's in there,' Annette says.

She doesn't sound tired at all.

The scene jumps. It's still night, the same street. The view is Rick's dozing face, out his rolled-down window. There is a large custom home with a rock façade set way back on the neatly groomed lot. Half a dozen European cars in the circular driveway. Only the single porch light on. The screen door opens. A man steps out, is obscured by trees as he walks to the end of the driveway.

'Wake up,' Annette says.

Rick makes a snotty, coming awake sound. 'What? Where? No, I don't think so.'

'Look at his hair. The suit.'

The guy crosses the street, under a street lamp, back into darkness. Red track suit. Peroxide blonde. The swagger, the slightly concave shoulders, a little hunching menace. He is Ghost and he is alone.

'Annette,' Rick begins, his voice tight.

'No, it's better. Wait until he's drives off.'

Ghost walks ahead of them, up the street, and the camera pivots, aiming through the windshield now. He passes two, then three cars, doubles back and shakes his head. Forgot which car was his. He slips into a sedan. The engine fires, headlamps brook the night, he rolls out.

'Do you even know what you're doing?' Rick says. 'Is this the coke talking?'

'Follow him,' Annette says. 'Or get out and walk.'

We catch up with Ghost five or six blocks later, at a light on Ventura, roll through a yellow light, can't lose him. An In-N-Out Burger off to the left, closed. A Del Taco, open. A darkened shopping plaza. A 7-Eleven serving late-nighters. Some kid busts an ollie on his skateboard, beefs it. An elderly Mexican woman on a bench at a bus stop. Then a few bars, people smoking out on the sidewalk. There are more street lights now. The road is getting brighter. We move closer to the target. There he is.

A white car. An Audi S5.

Stacey's car.

Cue the Sergio Leone score in my head, give me a key of Norman Bates. It's not Ghost they are following.

It's me, James Hastings.

The night comes back in a slap of memory. Mark Harris's party in Burbank after the show. A total bust with no action. Just a bunch of industry people sitting around talking about royalties and marketing campaigns. Rum and Cokes, I remember. I had six large Myers's Dark Rum and Cokes. Ghost came in, stayed for half an hour to score some ecstasy, and lit out for the clubs with the only three beautiful women at the party. I sat around drinking and playing poker with a couple of film producers and a visual effects artist named Doyle who told me Mexican beer is the safest way to go and proceeded to take three hundred of my dollars, perhaps proving his point.

I have no memory of seeing Rick and Annette, but I'm still sick and frightened by the knowledge that they had me in their sights. *Have* me in their sights, reality and time bending and folding within my head as I watch them now watching me as we head up Ventura, turning left on Crescent, wind up the hill, through the light at Mulholland.

A red light in the corner of the screen begins to blink.

'Shit,' Annette says. 'The battery.'

'That god damn thing's going to get us in trouble.'

'I have a spare,' she says.

The new battery brings us back on Venice Boulevard, then right on Arlington and left into West Adams where

Ghost – correction, the white Audi carrying James Hastings – takes the alley. They hang back between 20th and 21st, then crawl forward slowly, into the alley behind me. The Audi pauses, waiting for the door to go up, then noses into the garage, out of sight.

Safe, I can't help but think on Rick's couch.

They roll forward until the camera moves over the garage, up to the back of Whitey, which is dark inside every window. It's got to be three or four in the morning.

'This isn't a party,' Rick says. 'It's dead.'

'Oh, shit,' Annette says. 'What if he lives here? This is, like, his LA crash pad or some fucking thing. He's probably got some whore in there.'

'Annette, no. You're not going up there. He'll shoot you.'

'Oh, stop it.'

'And it will be legal. You're not getting out of the car.'

She doesn't say anything for a minute. 'But he has to come back out sometime, doesn't he?'

Daylight. A sunny morning, maybe eight or nine. The garage door is opening. We are twenty or thirty feet down the alley from the garage and fence that surrounds our backyard.

'Wakey wakey,' Annette says, and turns the camera to her brother.

Rick is sleeping in the driver's seat, his head leaning into the ball of his leather jacket. He looks pale, unwell. The rusty stubble along his chin is showing the first signs of gray. He does not wakey wakey.

'You're no fun,' Annette says. She turns the camera toward the windshield again and sets it on the dashboard, like a cop camera catching footage of a speeder who's just been pulled over. Up ahead in the alley I see the couch, the riot orange couch with sprung cushions, a shoe, some cinderblocks and a pile of rotting grass clippings. Every so often, but not often enough, a car or two passes the mouth of the alley, people leaving the neighborhood, cutting through side streets before they meet up with the real morning rush hour on Washington or Venice.

Annette opens her door and leaves it open. At first I think I am imagining it, but no. I can actually hear the faint sound of another motor growling. It's the Audi, hidden in the garage.

Annette walks ahead of her car, strutting in her dress and bare feet. For any other woman, this would be the walk of shame. Annette moves as if she is just now starting to have fun.

The garage door is up. The Audi's white trunk backs slowly into the alley. Annette prances out, blocking its path. The red brake light glows. The car doesn't move for half a minute. Stacey must be checking the rearview mirror, trying to decide what this means, who this woman is, what's wrong. Annette just stands there, arms hanging at her sides, feet planted.

Stacey emerges, on foot. She is wearing her vanilla cargo pants, a nice V-neck t-shirt with a chic tie-dye print, her hair pulled back in a loose tail too short to qualify as a pony's. Her yellow-framed sunglasses sit high up on her head. She approaches Annette slowly, and I know

355

from her posture she is concerned but cautious, willing to help this strange woman. Stacey stops about six feet away, both women in profile now.

Annette says something. Stacey doesn't respond. Annette keeps speaking, her lips moving soundlessly. Stacey is tensing, her shoulders bunching up the way they do. She crosses her arms defensively. Annette keeps speaking, her head now Oprah-thrusting, berating Stacey. She points at the house, stabbing with her finger, then at Stacey.

Stacey looks back over her shoulder for help, shakes her head. She steps forward, giving it back now, speaking forcefully. Annette slaps the sunglasses off the top of Stacey's head. Stacey recoils, putting a hand to her face. She disappears into the garage for a moment and reappears with her cellphone. Stacey shakes the phone at Annette in a threatening manner. Annette stabs her finger at Stacey twice more, then turns on her heels and marches back to the car.

Stacey begins typing something into her phone. She is theatric, looking at Annette's car, for a split second at me (and for a split-split second her eyes meeting mine are skewers through my guilty heart), then back down at the phone. She's getting the license plate, typing it into her phone.

Annette makes it back to the car. I hear but do not see her yank the driver's side door open, and imagine Rick toppling out.

'Move over!'

'Whuh? What happened? What's wrong?' Rick says, waking up.

'Get out of the way. I'm driving.'

There is a shuffling sound as Rick gets out of the way. The engine starts.

Up ahead, Stacey has put the phone to her ear and turned back to the garage.

'That fucking bitch is writing down the license plate,' Annette says.

'Who?' There is a pause during which I assume Rick notices Stacey. 'Jesus. Who the hell is that?'

'She says she doesn't know him, but she's lying,' Annette snaps. 'She's hiding him. He's not getting away with this.'

'What did you do?' Rick moans.

'Make sure you get this in case he assaults me. I want it on record.'

'Have you lost your mind?' Rick says, quietly.

'Do it!'

Rick picks up the camera.

Stacey steps back into the alley. She has the phone to her ear, possibly giving a description of the car. Or calling me. Maybe this is the 9.12 message. She paces, disappears back into the garage.

Rick says, 'You said only if he was alone. I'm not with you on this. Not with her.'

'All right, all right, screw it,' Annette says. 'We'll come back later.'

The car revs, pops into gear and speeds forward.

It's fifty feet from the garage. Then twenty.

Ten.

Stacey steps out and jerks back, her body going rigid

as they clip her with the right front fender. She spins out of view and Annette brakes. The sound of the impact is dull, the sound of an apple thrown at a barn.

'Fuck!' Annette screams. 'No!'

Stacey is nowhere in sight. No one moves or reacts.

'Where did she go?' Rick says very quietly.

Annette doesn't answer.

'For fuck's sake, back up! She could be under the car!'

'Don't yell at me!' Annette shouts.

Their car surges forward, then back, reversing with a whine. They stop a little more than half the distance to where they started. One of them is breathing hard. Stacey is not in the alley.

'Relax,' Annette says. 'We barely grazed her.'

Stacey staggers out of the garage. She is holding her hip and limping. I can't see any blood. She's looking back at them in disbelief and shock and, yes, I know that look, boiling anger. She's fucking steamed now, ready to throw down.

'You fucking bitch!' Stacey screams. Her voice is dim, far away, but still clearly audible from inside this car. 'You're dead! My husband's going to kill you!'

Rick babbles on. 'Too many people involved, can't clean this up, not in this—'

'You're already guilty,' Annette says. 'I'll give them your name, too.'

'Turn off the car and give me the keys.'

'Just let me think,' Annette says. She is no longer in a rage. She is calm.

Stacey's hand is shaking. She can't dial. She holds the

phone with both hands, concentrating, then staggers and covers her mouth. Wailing, she points the phone at them, then looks back to the garage. She's talking to someone. Help is coming.

Someone else is in the garage.

Rick yells, 'It's over! We have to leave!'

The white shade slides out of the garage, he's suddenly there.

Holding Stacey. A man.

'I knew it! That lying cunt!' Annette's voice goes guttural. 'He's dead, fucking dead.'

Ghost. Ghost in his red track pants and his bare feet, rushing to her side, holding Stacey up, and his hair is cowlicked, a bedhead mess, but blond, white-blond, and his arms and bared abdominals are painted with tattoos. She falls to his shoulder and he holds her. She's safe, she will be safe now. He reaches into his waistband and his right arm comes up with a gun in hand. It's his favorite gun, black and square-nosed, a Glock 27. He's turning, pushing Stacey back toward the garage but he can't stop looking back at the psycho people in the alley.

'C'mon!' he yells. 'Get out of the car! I dare you!'

'Kill her, fucking shoot the bitch!' I scream in the basement. My back is grinding bones of broken glass agony and I am ass-hopping on his couch, screaming at the plasma window to the world.

'I told you he'd have a gun,' Rick says, and the camera jostles. 'Back up!'

Annette does not back up.

The engine revs and everything lurches into gear.

Ghost is turning Stacey around with one arm and holding the gun at them with the other as the distance closes. The Glock goes off – *POP-POP!* – and Stacey shrinks into a ball, falling from his embrace. The windshield is cracked and two holes appear in it and Ghost screams and a third shot *POPS* and Annette screams and the collision is astounding. Stacey is just a dull sound and Ghost jumps forward, leaping head-first as if he is going to fly over the car like Superman, but he isn't, his head bounces off the top of the windshield and he crumples in midair, then folds over the hood before flying off it and disappearing under the front of the car. Annette slams the car into a telephone pole, smashing Stacey my love and the camera flies free and ricochets off the spider-webbed windshield and falls to the floor.

A man is moaning. The engine revs and the car reverses again. As it does, the camera view – of the seat or the carpet, I can't tell which – flips with a double bounce that makes someone scream grotesquely. They have just gone over a very large bump on one side.

Rick is moaning harder now.

'Be quiet!' Annette says, 'Or I'll fucking kill you too!'

The idle of their engine.

The screen goes black.

Steady on the ground, the weedy alley gravel and oil-stained dirt. Everything is quiet. Pan slowly. Ghost is lying on his back. He is bleeding from his ears and mouth and nose. His chest is not rising or falling. His eyes are blank, unblinking, looking up toward the sky, and one of them is filled with red, a pool of blood in and around the eyeball. A large black ant crawls over his chin and down his neck.

'Do you see that?' Annette says. Her voice is dull, heavy, sexual. No one answers her. 'Look who's a Ghost now.'

The camera slowly pans to the right. Stacey is arranged next to him. She is worse than he is. She is the Stacey of my nightmares. Stacey as I found her. They are shoulder to shoulder. They could be lying on a bed together.

'That's just a shame,' Annette says. 'That's what he gets for cheating on his wife.'

There is a sound of scraping somewhere. The sound of something heavy dragging across dirt. A roll of carpet flops over Stacey and Ghost and the weeds next to the orange couch. Rick's hairy hands withdraw.

'Ding dong, the Ghost is dead,' she says.

They stand in silence.

'We have to go now,' Rick says. 'This is a neighborhood.'

Annette makes a disgusting throat sound. A ball of white spit flies onto the carpet and skips twice dryly before smearing in the soot and dirt.

'That's for Aaron, you demon fucker.'

For a while there is only the faint humming of wind on the mic, a lament that rises and fades. Time elapses. The television goes black.

Everything goes black.

36

I sat in the darkness, feeling something irreversible leach out of me as I coughed on the choking bile of my tears. Stacey was gone and I didn't understand. Stacey was dead and I did not understand. There had to be more. Something was missing. I could not have seen what I had just seen. But I knew that I had finally been granted all, *seen the thing*, the missing support beam that had buckled under us, that was it, the end, my beautiful friend. Gone.

Everything gone.

Stacey is dead. Ghost is dead.

Except . . . and this was everything . . . Ghost didn't drive Stacey's car. Ghost didn't stay at the house with Stacey. Ghost got away.

James did his job. James Hastings took the fall.

James Hastings died with her in that alley.

That was me. That was me up there on the wall, on the TV screen. That was me in the alley, the star. That was me with blood running from my nose, my ears, my mouth. I am laid to rest.

I'm no longer here. I'm here no longer. I'm—

A series of heavy thudding noises came from somewhere above the basement and then down. Something
moved in the basement, off in the corner. A bright light
flashed, yanking me back from the abyss, blinking,
squinting.

Something moved in front of me. A man in black
pants. I squeezed my eyes shut, the echoes of her
screams and the moaning and gunshots overlapping in
my ears. I was floating, going to be sick.

'Do you see?' he was saying. 'Do you see?'

I opened my eyes. The man was standing in front of
me in the bright room. I worked my mouth around and
ground my teeth.

'The Hastings couple. Do you see what you have
done?'

'What?'

'They died for your sins. Like the boy. You are the
pale demon.'

He was dressed in all black, his face flushed, black
paint around his eyes.

'Who?'

'And now we have you.'

'Who?'

'There were two of you but now there is only one.
This is the inescapable truth.'

'What happened to me?'

'You got caught.'

'I was supposed to help her—'

His arm went back and when his hand came from
behind him a slim tab of metal gleamed briefly in the

light. His arm waved past like he was chasing a mosquito. He stepped back and waited.

I didn't understand what he was waiting for. I stared at him, my vision blurry.

'The pale demon bleeds,' he said.

Something on my chest began to itch. I looked down. The red tracksuit jacket was halved. A thin red line stretching from my left shoulder to my right nipple opened and a rake-shaped comb of blood began to flow. I scrambled away from him, up and to the side, my body clumsy, numb all over as I leaped over the end of the couch. I was halfway to the door at the bottom of the stairs when something small and quick sliced across my back, harder and deeper, down to my waist. The taut skin between my shoulders went slack. I grabbed the doorknob and it slipped in my clammy grip, unyielding. He roared and I turned around.

The man. The bad policeman was standing behind me holding something small and sharp. Oh, dear God, is that – it's a scalpel. He cut me with a scalpel. He cut me with a scalpel. He cut me—

His nostrils flared.

I feinted left, then bolted right, running past him, toward the far end of the basement, where there were no exits. His arm lashed out and my bicep opened like a fish's mouth. I screamed, wetness warm and sliding down to my wrist.

He walked after me, his voice slow. 'You can't get out that way, sport model.'

There was a bathroom at the end of the basement. I had used it the day we got drunk together. If I could get inside and shut the door, I could hide. The long shiny top of the shuffle-board table was beside me. I dragged my left hand through the powder as I ran until I got to the end and scooped up one of the steel pucks and I turned and threw it and it hit him in the chest and he laughed and the little metal blade cut sideways at my nose, just missing as I ducked and spun away. The sting bit into my ear and sliced across the nape of my neck. I hit the bathroom door and slammed it behind me. The door was light in my hands, too light, but it latched. I fumbled with the knob but my arms and hands were sheeted with blood sticky and slipping. I thumbed the brass tab to the vertical position and staggered back into the plastic shower stall.

A splintering hole blew inward and his fist followed, then his other fist, and then the door was tearing, the hinges squealing as he ripped the entire door from its frame as if it were made of Styrofoam. He turned and stamped on the bottom of the door, pulled his fists back through the hole, and flung the door into the two empty beer kegs leaning against the wall.

'Cool it down now,' he said. 'Before I cut your fucking eyeballs out.'

I did not understand why this was happening, who these people were, or what I was supposed to do. They killed Stacey. Was he punishing me for letting her die? Had he loved her, too? Is this where she had gone all those days? To this evil side of the world? I stood in the shower, shivering, and my blood pooled around the drain and bubbled, threading in.

'You're going to bleed to death,' he said. 'Come out and I'll give you a bandage.'

He stepped aside and invited me to pass. I couldn't make my body do anything other than shiver.

'I'm sorry, okay?' he said. 'This wasn't supposed to happen yet. Annette told me to take care of you until she got back and I got excited. Because . . . because *where is she!* Right? Okay, okay. I won't. Just come out.'

Everything was cold and I was bleeding and I turned and reached for something, a weapon, the towel rack, and my hand seemed to float out in front of me, someone else's hand, red up to the elbow. *That's my arm.* The shower was empty. There was nothing in here. I pawed at the rubber curtain.

'You can't stay in there,' he said. 'You're bleeding in at least seven places.'

He was enormous, his head filling the entire doorway. The scalpel he had used was not in his hands. He was holding his hands out, opening and closing them. He looked very worried.

'You have to come out, Ghost. You're dying. I promise.'

Ghost. Was I playing Ghost? Was this an act? I must be acting. I must be involved in something. This was planned, set up, another skit. Trembling, holding my ear, I walked out of the shower. My feet were slippery and cold.

'Please don't,' I said. 'Please don't hurt her, okay? Promise you won't hurt her again?'

'I promise. Let's go, let's go. We have to get you out, Ghost. The show's about to start.'

My feet didn't work right. I glanced to the side, then back at his face, the yellow moon hovering in front of me. I moved between him and the doorway, our faces less than a foot apart. I took another step and he winked and bit his tongue and three or four quick stings climbed my ribs and I looked down to see his fingers with the scalpel jutting from them prodding as if he were entering purchases into a cash register.

Noises came out of me as I ran making a trail of blood back to the bar where I tried to lift a barstool bolted to the floor. The scalpel went in behind my left knee and swirled around, raking bone. My leg buckled and I fell and the warden hauled me up by the arm and spun me around.

'Not her boyfriend now, are you, motherfucker! You're not anybody's boyfriend, you're mine, motherfucker mother fucker mother fuck fuck fuck—'

The scalpel made silver trails in the air around me as his face took on pointillist dabs of wet maroon and I lost the ability to scream or fight back or raise my arms to defend myself. I collapsed on my side, a wet, shivering hump. He screamed as he punctured my body again and again. The pain belonged to someone else and the house quaked around us and I knew she would be there to meet me soon. My senses misfired, strobed, shut down. The human body performs miracles and this was one:

My mind simply refused to allow me to witness the rest of what happened.

37

What I eventually recall.

I sleep a lot. I wake up on the couch again, day or night, in a cocoon of soreness, itching and nauseating drug high. I pat my arms and legs and chest, checking for more bleeding. I am dry and the gauze he wrapped me in before is now replaced or supported by an additional layer of cloth athletic bandages. I am constricted.

What is he waiting for?

Vague snatches of the conversation, talking about her again as he tends my wounds in the bathroom, kneeling at my feet and bracing me against the wall of the shower stall that is my slop trough. She's not at her house. *But I will find her. And you fuck, you better pray to God she's not hurt. You better pray she decides not to let me do it. Because I will do it. End this now if it were up to me. Cut your filthy fucking tongue out and mount it to my—*

Time slips.

Sometimes I am on the floor, sometimes I am on the couch. I bleed freely, at random times, no matter how he tries to patch me up. My back is a nova of pain shining light into every corner of my body. When the drugs wear off, I ascertain that my shoulder is dislocated, my ribs cracked, toes broken, face road-burned, throat swollen like a snake bite victim's. I cough and it is like being hit on the heart with a mallet. Too weak and in too much pain to get up, I lose control of my bladder several times per day. I itch. He adds blankets beneath me and the couch thickens. My piss nest. Chicken bones. Splinters in my lungs. My tongue fills my whole mouth. The needle. Sleep. Sleep and pray for death.

Time slips like a morphine drip.

Hands, the hands on me. Waking in the middle of a delirium in the dark and checking my body, under my shirt, under my pants. My hands. They are only my hands. But someone else's were here first. The bandages moist. The clothes stiff. My pubic hair shaved and growing back, itching. He can do this, he can do anything.

Time slips.

I never know if he will be gone for two minutes or three hours and his boot steps clunk above me at all hours. He paces holding conversations with himself about how much longer to keep me alive. Would be so much easier to dump me in the desert. Do it, fucking kill me you big redheaded cocksucker.

The side of my face is swollen and burning from the road, my body rejecting particles of asphalt through a yellow and purple glaze.

When he is upstairs, the activity varies. Often there is

only silence, but at other times the sound of power tools shakes the walls and ceiling. He sings songs to himself in the kitchen. He swears and shatters furniture. The water runs for six hours. One night I hear gunshots erupting in the backyard. Hundreds of them. When he comes down after, I can smell the powder on him from thirty feet away and blue smoke is rising from his hands and hair.

Slip. Slip. Slip.

He comes crawling across the floor on his hands and knees. Look here, look here. He opens the safe and shows me a nickel-plated .45 and calls it Aaron's gun. He says it was an accident. He was only trying to show the boy. He was only trying to teach the boy. He was always present. He weeps. How was he to know the boy would watch him, memorize the combination? He lost his temper, that was all. Saw the boy holding the gun, a circuit blew. He screamed and lunged and the boy wouldn't let go, he wouldn't let go. It was an accident, you can see that. He tried to explain it to Arthur but Arthur couldn't be trusted. They showed Arthur the music and said, see, see where he got the idea? It's a sickness, this music.

Arthur never liked him. Arthur had an accident, too.

He puts the .45 in my mouth. He weeps.

Time slips.

He misses another dose. Late at night and I am screaming in the dark, begging the warden. He comes down the stairs looking sleepy and sticks another needle in my shoulder. It isn't working. It might be vitamins. Or air.

370

My shoulder swells like a balloon. He pets my hair and says I should stop making those noises, the ones I don't know I am making. He sits with me through the night and calls me Ghost because James is dead and it has always been this way and that's the truth. I know what you're in for. I'm in holding, too. He says we are cell-mates, we will get through this stretch together.

Time . . .

He says all of the cuts are shallow. Except for the one that took the lobe of my left ear. I cry and ask about my ear, please, I want my ear back. No one is allowed to have my ear. I pat the ragged edge where it was and he looks for it for almost ten minutes before he finds it in the shuffle-board sand. When he brings it back to me it looks like a miniature ball of pizza dough rolled in flour. He asks me if I want it and when I shake my head he eats it like taking communion.

. . . slips.

In the dreams the boy in the black hood is chasing me, always chasing me. He can run forever and forever, his arms stiff at his sides as he runs, the white face floating after me, and no matter how fast I run he can always keep up with me. I run through fields and over hills, through empty streets and empty houses, and I lose him a mile back, three miles, ten. Having run for days I am in another state. I find the empty house and I find the closet and force myself to stop breathing and sink down into the corner silent and just when I think I have finally outrun him and found the perfect hiding spot, the closet door opens.

His feet are two baby doves on the carpet before me.

I am tissue paper delicate as butterfly wings. Please don't do it again. All it will take is the slightest tear and I will leak everywhere. His eyes are missing. His jaw is white and his hands come out of the pouch with the scalpel and it all starts again.

I can't stop screaming, even when I am awake.

He gave me cigarettes. He clipped my toenails. He let us watch *The Blue Lagoon* and said it was the story of Rick and Annette.

Someone laughed.

Their father was still in the prison in Gainesville for preying on children, their friends. Their mother died of a cerebral aneurism when they were still in elementary school. When Annette was fourteen he watched her body change. He followed her home from school and her friends laughed at him. He protected her from her boyfriends, making up for not protecting her from their father. They found the campground along the Kern River, where they could be together for days where no one would know, a place to rendezvous throughout high school, get away for a night or a weekend when times were hard. He had never been with any other woman, and never would.

Who's that man standing in the corner? He looks like

Aaron except bigger. He looks familiar. I used to look like him.

Come closer . . .

I'm getting bigger and stronger every day.

It's finally morning, the light is coming in. He has opened the curtains to let the light shine in. I wake up in a pleasant fog feeling nothing but the warmth on my skin, the sunlight pushing me up to the surface. There is no pain. I am flat on my back and naked and I lift my chin to see the red letters G-H-O-S-T freshly cut into the skin of my abdomen. The policeman is swabbing the cuts with clear fluid and cotton pads, admiring his work like a tattoo artist. I start screaming and he stops and looks up at me as if he has forgotten I am here.

James slips.

He brings me platters of food. When I can't swallow the food, he forces ice into my mouth. He recites lyrics from the CD booklets. He sits on the floor beside the couch and reads them to me in a monotone. When I forget the words he slaps me. When I forget why I wrote the song he slaps me. When I forget what the words mean he slaps me. When I sing it wrong he punches me and I gag on a tooth and swallow it and throw up on the floor and if he slaps me again I just might disappear.

Stacey? Are you in here?

The policeman comes home in a panic. He has had a scare. He has a measure of rope on his person. He uses it to make a necktie for me, loops it over a beam in the ceiling, and drags the long end until I jerk from the couch and swing suspended. My toes are four inches from the carpet. He is crying, yelling no, no, no. I fight and claw at it and it burns in my lungs. I can't see. I can't see.

It becomes beautiful in here.

In the blackness, James was alone. Everything that was him – every idea and thought and memory and image of himself and the world, and every sense of physical and emotional self that belonged to James Hastings – swirled down a black drain into an infinite spiral of nothingness.

Sixteen days after watching himself die on television, James Hastings died.

And I stepped forward.

In the vacuum of his death, I expanded, filled out his sleeves, took new breath into his lungs, opened his eyes, and tasted the salt of his blood.

I am not James. I am not a ghost. I am *the* Ghost.

Valium drinks and other drinks, and pills, injections and alcohol straight from the bottles. I accept them all without hesitation, gobble them down and roar my rebel yell. Dumbass has no idea I am Popeye and drugs are my spinach. I consume them and they taste good and they make me feel like a motherfucking god.

It's coming.

The warden takes the pills, too, and punches holes in the walls screaming where is she where is she where is she, and I laugh. I scream in his face and he doesn't know what else to do, gives in, laughs with me.

He shows me the Luger he used to gun down the A-rab crawler last winter. One shot from seventy yards. With a Luger. A god damn antique. How do you like that, Ghost?

I laugh.

This piece of smokin' white trash is going to feel God's wrath. Soon.

38

Ghost's stomach growled. Ghost woke up hungry. When was the last time he had eaten anything? Days ago, maybe even a week ago. Ghost looked around the room. There was the bar. The shuffle-board table. The dart board. The stereo cabinet. The large TV on the wall. His media case full of videos and magazines. There had to be a weapon in here somewhere. Ghost would find something. Ghost would rise.

The bar. A corkscrew. Maybe he had left some glass mugs behind. Break one over his head. Slit his throat. Drink his blood. Fuck his corpse and burn the house down.

I tried to sit up. The pain came like a shock wave and rippled from my waist, up and down. I fell back and breathed deeply until the pain faded.

You are a killer.

I counted to three and sat up again, faster this time and pulling myself through it. It wasn't so bad sitting up or lying down. It was the in-between that hurt.

The bar was only ten or fifteen feet away. My left leg did not respond properly. I put the extra weight on my right leg, leaning into it, hamstrings spasming. The back of my left knee went loose as I crossed the basement like a man on short stilts, hobbling on locked legs and falling forward as the bar floated toward me. I caught the thick edge of the top, swiveled onto the first stool, sweating, panting, and now the stinging was widening in lines along my back, the wounds were reopening.

The bottles of alcohol were behind the bar, against the large Budweiser mirror. I stared, dreaming of broken whiskey bottle necks, jagging the points into his neck, raking open his jugular as the pig's blood fountained onto the carpet and he fell like timber.

Something was dripping. I looked at the floor. A pool of dark fluid on the carpet next to my bar stool. While I was staring at it, another drop fell with a wet *plap*, and then another, and another, regular as my heartbeat.

Ghost was bleeding.

A surge of panic propelled me to my feet. I grabbed the bar for support and looked into the Budweiser mirror. My face was swollen, eyes hollow, lips dark and crusted. I averted my gaze down and to the right. The boy in the black hood was staring back at me from the corner of the mirror. He was standing behind me, the half-moon of his pale face gleaming in the darkness.

The door to the basement was still closed. He had been down there with me since I woke up. Or longer.

I limped around the end of the bar, trying to put a barrier between us. When I looked back toward the bathroom, Aaron was not there. I had heard no movement while my back was turned. The basement was almost too dark to see from one end to the other. I scanned the room from the wall and shuffle board on the left, going slowly to the right, trying to focus on the load-bearing pillars, the shelves against the wall, next to the cabinet containing the audio equipment . . .

He was standing behind the couch, in front of the middle of the three large antique safes, unmoving. His pose had not changed. His chin was still slightly tucked, his shoulders tight, hands hidden inside the pouch over his belly. The white block letters of his sweatshirt were crisp in the darkness.

GHOST

That's me, little man.

The letters blurred at the edges. The white faded out and the blackness of his sweatshirt deepened, almost as if disappearing, or he himself was becoming insubstantial. I blinked, focusing on the letters, and they changed, fading out, then focusing again. The whole process took me back to my third-grade classroom, memories of my teacher fiddling with the archaic film projector, the kind with the needle pointer that appeared on the white screen as images of Dutch farmers in their wooden clogs blurred in and out.

'Show me,' I said.

The boy's head snapped up and his hood fell back. Half of his face was alabaster-white except for the area around his left eye, which was bulging in alarm, the

378

green pupil radiant in the dark room. The other half, from the top of his cheek to the top of his forehead and bleached white hairline, was a ragged wound. The flaps of skin were blackened with old blood and stubbled with yellowed chips of bone. At the center, in the space where the right frontal lobe of his brain should have been, there was only a blackness deeper than the room, deeper than his sweatshirt, absolute and yet somehow glossy, lacquer-wet. His mouth opened all the way and his small flat teeth were very white inside black gums.

'I'm sorry,' I said. 'I can fix it.'

The letters of his sweatshirt flashed like a camera, winked out, the flash's echo lingering over the safe's door, my name printed on the metal, and then all traces of him were gone.

The safe. The safe where the video had been. And the .45. He had stood in front of the safe to draw my attention to it. The cop's storage lockers, like the one on La Brea, with all of Stacey's things.

Storage locker. Locker. Lock. Combination. Locker combination . . .

The numbers in Aaron's desk drawer. What had the little scrap of paper said? Middle combination? Yes. Middle. I was staring at the three safes. Aaron had stood in front of the middle of the three.

I let go of the bar and the pain shot up my sciatic nerve, cramping my legs. Each step was a cattle prod applied to my feet. I bit my cheek. I made it.

What were the numbers he had written down?

My song. 'From My Cold Dead Hands'.

379

The 22 is for you
Cause I love my guns
The 38 is for hate
Treat 'em like my sons
The 44 is for whores
Cause I love my guns
The aught-six is for the pigs
Who sent my brother to the pen . . .

22 38 44 06

But I could barely make out the numbers on the dial.

Heavy footsteps clunked above me, toward the stairs. I stopped, waiting, listening.

I couldn't wait any longer.

As I began to turn the dial, something thumped against the floor. The thump hit once, twice . . . then a long pause . . . and then several times, more urgently, an impatient old man tapping his cane on the kitchen floor. It stopped abruptly and then there was a horrendous crash of glass or crockery that made the ceiling shake.

Hurry, Jack. The Giant awakes.

I leaned over, trying to read the tiny numerals and grooved lines. They went from 00 to 99. When I turned the handle, the tumblers made no sound. No clicking came from within. The knob turned without a hint of friction. I focused, turned the arms clockwise first, all the way around three times, just in case it needed to be reset.

22 right, 38 left, 44 right, 06 left. Stop. I pulled on the door. It did not budge.

I ran everything again, slower this time. The door did not budge.

I tried the reverse, going counter-clockwise first. I pulled the arms. My back became molten steel, burning, screaming. My face broke out in sweat.

The door did not open.

I bent over, panting. I stood upright again, looking at the safe.

'Oh, you gotta be fucking kidding me.'

I was standing in front of the third safe, the one on the right.

I shuffled to the left. *Take your time and do it right the first time.*

Right, left, right, left. I stood, grasped two of the four prongs on the dial, and pulled. The door did not open – but something clunked inside.

Put some manhood into it.

I yanked harder, harder, until my molars ached. The hinges squeaked in protest, and the iron door clanked open. There were three thick shelves up high and a vacant space beneath those, large enough to hold a grown man folded over himself.

The safe was empty.

I sank to the floor and rubbed my eyes. Rising, my eyes caught on something dark, thick, all the way at the back of the lowest shelf. I reached in.

A gun. Not Aaron's .45. A revolver, heavy as a barbell, the cylinder fat with shells.

'Oh, Aaron, good boy.'

Time to rock and roll, Ghost.

Wait. The safe was still not empty. A little second layer of something had been hidden behind the gun, light and filament-soft, tightly bundled. I set the gun down. I swiped my hand over it and it fluttered in the air and settled into my palm.

A thin purple band squeezing a lock of her blonde hair. They took Stacey's hair.

My heart breaks. My mind races with the responsibility of it all.

Stacey is dead. James is dead. I have taken James's place.

I taught him how to be me. I put him to work. I sent him on the road. The road is a lonely place. I took care of his wife while he was away. She was lonely too, so sad. I gave her pills. Picked her up. Had a little pill party. Too much wine. A shoulder to cry on. Boo hoo, James is never home. How ironic. He's in Atlanta working for me; I'm in LA undercover, thought I'd stop by to say hello. I don't even know where he is any more. Haven't spoken to him in a year.

His wife is beautiful, pure. Poor Stacey. All she has is this dog, Henry. Let me rub your shoulders, girl. There is no James here tonight. But I can be James. He can be me. We can walk a thousand miles in each other's shoes.

Where did Ghost disappear to – the world wants to know. The media speculated I had retired, gone back into rehab, absconded to Bulgaria. No one really knew. My people don't even know. I didn't know. Now I know the truth.

James Hastings died so that I could live.

I am Nathaniel Eric Riverton, the artist formerly known as Ghost.

I am the pale demon. I took his wife. I got his wife killed. I got him killed. Snuffed on film. That poor bastard.

But no one knows what it's like to be me. If I hadn't dropped off the face of the earth, I would have killed myself. Burned out on the tour, the drugs that fuel the fire on stage every night. The fame, the public, the guilt. All those motherfuckers gunning for me. Five years is a career in hip-hop. I am done. I found my way out.

It's nicer this way. That's what my girl said.

Weeks went by, months. And can you believe my luck? No one knows what really happened. I was free. Shit, this was better than Tupac. I am a legend. My music will live on the mystery. I don't have to die to become immortal. I am already dead.

I escaped my own fate. I let my hair grow out, stopped coloring it. I threw away the clothes and bought new boring clothes, so I look like every other nobody on the street. I got me a pair of glasses. Laser tattoo removal – that shit hurts. I lived in his house. He died, and I awoke. But that house was fucked up. Once they were gone, there was no one there but me. And Henry. What was I supposed to do with a dog? Shit, I gave that puppy away. I learned to live it. Kicked it low. Stopped answering the phone. Ignored his family. Avoided their friends. Packed up her shit and just chilled. He was supposed to be in mourning.

It was perfect.

Except – why did I hear all those things at night? Why was that place always making noises? What was that sound in the ballroom? My shit always out of place. I could never find my car keys, my underwear. The maid gets spooked, like she knows, but she can't say nothing. Olivia looking at me like I am an alien, a body snatcher, and maybe I am.

Shit, I used to haunt him. Now he is haunting me.

Have another beer. Wait it out. The kid had enough of my money in the bank, wasn't goin' nowhere. I could do this.

I looked different and then, damn, I felt different. This act was working, working a little too well. It's like I am him. I felt him there. I felt her there. She won't let go. He won't let go. I started seeing things. Those rabbits, man.

I never meant for so many people to get hurt. Some people can't handle the music. All those teenagers who hurt themselves and each other. Their fucking parents should have paid more attention. I don't deserve this. I am an artist. I don't use guns. I use words. It's The Show, people. But that don't mean it don't hurt me. Of course it hurts. I got feelings, too.

I let Annette into my world. I knew she was crazy. But maybe I needed to be punished for my sins. And now I've served my time. James paroled me.

Except. Cover blown. The brother caught me, cut me up. They might be back soon to kill me for real. This shit cannot go on. Living in this prison homo's basement. Why the fuck didn't he fight back? What's a matter with you, James? Nut up.

Too late. He's dead.

I am Ghost, and I am so much stronger now. I wish I had known this a long time ago. I wouldn't have taken any shit from anybody. Rick? Rick Butterfield? You gotta be kiddin' me. I will eat that boy's heart from his chest.

Check it: all this time we was sitting in the basement, waiting for the motherfucker to come back with another tray of egg rolls to feed my sorry ass, the basement door wasn't even locked.

Fuck these bandages and fuck these back problems.

They can have my blood. I will always make more. I am the Emperor and I feel no pain.

I grabbed that gun and I hit them stairs and, kid, I *flew*.

SHE WHO WILL

Stacey was seventeen, the skin of her arms and legs deep brown from the summer, the cut-off jeans she had taken from him loose around her hips, her thin rubber sandals dirty from Gerald's farm. She was cradling a white rabbit with a black saddle, holding it in the cozy nook of her right arm and she scratched the top of its head with her left hand. The rabbit's ears were flat, its eyes closed, its whiskers twitching in almost murmuring pleasure against the safety of her warm body.

'I want to take him home,' she said, looking up at James as if asking his permission, and he was struck by the little girl that still existed inside of her, despite all they had done that summer. They had lied to their parents countless times, shoplifted, smoked weed and had sex a dozen times. Now she wanted a pet bunny.

'How would you take him back?' James was her age, and yet somehow older, the older James spectral, dying or dead, watching her through the eyes of memory. 'Carry him in your lap the whole way? Your mom's not going to let you take that thing home, Stace. You're moving out next year. You don't want a rabbit.'

She knew he was right. 'But he's so cute. I don't think I can put him back.'

She had bonded with him in the few minutes since Gerald, the farmer who owned the farm beyond the lake house, had taken him out for her. James was anxious. It was time to leave. They weren't supposed to stay so late. James looked at the sky. The sunny day was gray going to black.

'We have to go,' he said.

'You can't let her,' Stacey said, looking up at him with a sudden ferocity. 'You can't let her change the rabbit, James. Promise me you won't let her in.'

He didn't know what this meant, but he was chilled to the core by the growing sense that something had gone wrong, that this memory was wrong. Something in him was changing their last afternoon of that free month together, spoiling it.

'I love him,' Stacey said. She was crying now. 'I love the rabbits, James. Don't you remember how much I loved the rabbits?'

'Come on,' he said, hefting the bag of corn. 'We have to get back for dinner. They're waiting for the Silver Queen.'

Stacey put the rabbit back into his hutch, and she was sad, but not irrevocably so. *It's okay*, he thought. *It is the emotion of everything. The end of summer. Tonight is our last night at the lake.* They would be driving back to Tulsa tomorrow, in separate cars with their parents, and he knew she was crying because her childhood had ended.

They thanked Gerald for showing them the rabbits

and walked away holding hands, James swinging the bag with two dozen ears of Silver Queen in his left hand. And briefly, so briefly, he had time to wonder how. *How can I have the Silver Queen? Gerald said he'd closed the corn stand. This never happened.*

But he knew it had happened. Maybe it was happening again, in a different way, and maybe his memory was her soul.

Back at the van, James hugged her and kissed her neck and whispered in her ear.

'I love you, too,' Stacey said.

They drove onto the county road in a sort of daze, not speaking for half a mile, rolling, coasting, the air thick with humidity and the sky gray with a looming thunderstorm. He sensed her feeling a little better, until he saw the dark lump up ahead on the side of the road. A road kill. He braced himself, hoping she wouldn't see it, even as she leaned forward in her seat and set her hands on the dash. *She sees it too*, he thought, *and it's only going to make her worse.* He drifted into the other lane, giving the road kill a wide berth, and Stacey whimpered, turning her head as they passed.

'Oh, God,' she moaned, 'it's the rabbit, James. He got out!' She started crying again. 'Stop the car! Stop!'

'Stacey, no,' he said. 'It's too late. He's gone. It was just a jackrabbit. It's not him, it's not the same one. We put him away. He's safe.'

'He could be alive! He needs our help!'

He was torn. If the rabbit was alive, he should stop, put it out of its misery. If it was dead, stopping and letting her out to go see it would only make her miserable. He watched her pressing her face against the side window, turning as they passed, and he knew there was nothing he could do to help her. He had to do what she said, and she would grieve and there was nothing he could do to make it better.

The van floated . . . and he watched her, watched his girl.

A horrible whistle filled the air, a screeching tea kettle sound that jumped up from nowhere and then roared at them. He looked up to discover they had drifted all the way into the wrong lane, the oncoming lane. A semi-tractor trailer, a monster of a truck with a tall black flat face and teeth of chrome, was bearing down on them.

James yanked the wheel hard right and the van tires howled as they began to slide. Stacey screamed and he fought the wheel, overcorrecting now, back onto the road but swerving wildly, and he mashed the brakes, locking up as the truck passed, blaring its barge horn in his ear. They slewed sideways onto the soft shoulder and the van rocked to a halt and a cloud of dust rolled over them.

Safe. They were safe. James was trembling, clenching the wheel and trying to get his bearing when he looked over to find her seat empty. He looked in the rearview mirror and saw her running down the side of the road a hundred feet back.

He checked the driver's side mirror. The lane was clear. He got out and ran, chasing her down the road. When he caught up to her she was standing over the rabbit. He was small, black and white, but not saddled.

One of Gerald's had escaped, but not hers. Only his tail and face were white. The rest was black . . . and red, all red. He was covered in his own blood and there was no question he had been killed instantly. She was sobbing.

'Leave him,' he said. 'He's gone. Stace, he's gone.'

'He's not dead. He's not dead!' she kept saying.

James turned her away and hugged her on the side of the road, and she cried into his shoulder. He held her in his memory, the memory of them as children, and he told her it would be okay. He told her he would make it better and there would never be any more pain and he thought, *Stacey always loved the rabbits. That is why she ordered the silly paintings from the catalog fifteen years later, because the rabbits she hung on the bathroom wall were us, the couple from childhood. She had never been afraid of the rabbits.*

He's not dead!

His surroundings changed in a blink and he was no longer on the side of the road, he was no longer a child. He was in the bathroom with her, holding her as she cried into his waist.

Don't let the red rabbit get me, James.

He looked down. It was not Stacey. Annette was in his arms. Annette, red-headed and wet, cold and shivering on the toilet seat, her head bleeding. Annette had seen the rabbits turn red, the redness of death that had been seared into Stacey's memory, and Annette was terrified by them because Stacey wanted it that way.

Holding the towel around her, holding her upright, James backed away and made sure she could balance on her own. He turned and looked up at the paintings.

They were just two paintings, black and white and harmless.

And then Annette was gone and he was alone, standing in the bathroom weeks later, after he had woken up on the floor downstairs, after hearing Lucy's message, and all of the empty 9.12 calls from Stacey. He was staring at the paintings. The rabbit in the lower frame changed, her eye turned red. She was watching him, her eye toggling in its socket, following him as her body soaked through and turned red, everything red, the whole world turned red as if he were wearing tinted contact lenses.

Stacey trying to reach him, as she had reached Annette.

One was black and white, the other was red. Dead, red like the one Stacey found on the road when they were teenagers.

The other was alive.

The rabbits, the rabbits, one of the rabbits is dead and the other is alive.

From somewhere far away he heard a high-pitched piping sound, the sound of a tea kettle reaching steam, coming closer and louder until it cut off—

39

The kitchen floor was covered with broken glass and dishes. The window over the sink was a breeze of daylight and dry desert heat spilling in. The room very bright, shooting lasers into my head, dotting my vision with fuzzy red things that floated and faded. The roll of paper towels next to the toaster had been spun wild, leaving a long trail of perforated sheets pooled on the floor.

I looked over the car engine on the table. Rick was sitting in a chair with his back to the wall. His left arm was on the table, next to the cereal bowl of gasoline that had gone dry. He was staring at the kitchen sink or something just above it.

As I rounded the table and faced him I said 'for Stacey' and shot him in the chest. He jumped up an inch in his chair and then sat still. The gunsmoke curled into my nostrils and woke me up and I was ready to get it on.

I went closer and pointed the gun at the side of his face, said, 'Rick.'

His eyes batted slowly. His chest was swelling and deflating with long intervals in between. The bullet wound was above his heart, close to his shoulder, so I guess my aim was off. His lips parted and he began to form word fragments.

'Beg forgiveness,' I said. 'It won't help.'

Then I saw it and lowered the gun. The grooved, black- and yellow-striped handle of a screwdriver was standing out the other side of his neck. The shaft had been buried below his ear. Snug around the base of the handle was a swollen red lump of his flesh trickling blood down into his collar, over his back, onto the linoleum.

I reached for the handle.

'No,' Rick whispered, his eyes widening. 'No, no . . .'

I withdrew. 'Who did this?'

He breathed deeper, storing a good one up. 'She,' he began, and was unable to finish. Something in his throat gurgled. He swallowed, his neck bulging as he got his air back. I peered into the living room. The front door was closed and the room was empty. 'N-n-nuh-not . . .' His lips pursed and he flexed his jaw, straining to form the words. '. . . not uh-uh-n-nnn-nhhh-nette.'

While I absorbed the meaning of this, Rick's eyes rolled back. He began to choke, his body wracking as his face turned purple. He was suffocating. I placed my hand on his chest to steady him and took hold of the screwdriver handle. His big mitts clawed at my arms and throat. I pulled the handle sideways and it came away in a slide, easy as removing a thermometer from a chicken's thigh. It was a flathead, the largest one in the set, with a wide tip and nine-inch stem. Rick bucked in the chair and flopped onto the floor. Mercy undeserved, I shot him in the chest twice more and once in the forehead. His heart pumped some more of his blood out of the neck hole before it stopped beating.

My blood continued to flow, the cuts reopening as my legs gave out and I sat down on the kitchen floor. Our blood met like two small flooding lakes over a shallow isthmus and I held on. I settled into the vacancy of this little patch of world and the one inside of me, and we waited.

I could feel it coming back. It was almost here.

The sky was turning red.

She Who Will Rise

James is *there*, the most important place, *now.*

He is not in the bathroom or at the rabbit farm or the lake house or in Sheltering Palms. He doesn't know where he is. He is awakening as if from a dream, his vision returning before his eyes blink, because they are already open and staring up. The sky above is tinted red, and there are birds watching from telephone wires. The edges of the trees sway in a light breeze and he feels nothing. He hears nothing. He smells nothing. He remembers nothing. He doesn't even know who he is. There is no James Hastings. There is no Stacey. There is no Ghost. There is no information. The hard drive has crashed and rebooted, starting from nothing but scattered zeros and ones. There is only the red sky, the telephone wires, the trees.

He is on his back and something heavy and rough covers him, scratches his bare chest. He is frightened by an undefined menace and now the questions come.

Where am I?

Who am I?

What happened to me?

The sense of evil that pervades him induces a crawling claustrophobia and he throw his arms up and wrestles to shove the dirty thing off, the layers of scratching, stiff blanket, until it flaps to one side. He sits forward as if controlled by another entity, as if someone stronger has entered his body to save it, and this force wants him to get up. He is cold all over, cold inside his bones. The red is everywhere, and blurred in places. He sees the fences now, and the long lane of dirt, a shopping cart on its side, and the tops of the houses beyond the fences. There are dirty weeds and dust particles and trash. Beside him is a broken hulk of furniture, sour and rotting, and his senses begin to fire, sending their messages, the sensory sum of which amounts to:

This is a bad place.

He doesn't know how to move, but his body knows, it remembers, and though he is numb and cold all over, he is rising.

He staggers to his feet and the red world tilts and feels as though he is walking on a balance beam and will fall off any moment now. He walks until he is standing beside a small building with a car parked in its mouth. The car door is open. It's a low, sleek thing, this car, and when he wipes his eyes and moves closer to it some of the color returns and he sees white through the red, the car is white. He stares at the car and though he does not recognize it, it gives him a warm feeling, encouraging him, *yes, yes, come this way.*

The keys are in it. This car belongs to someone else. He should not touch it. He walks past it, through the garage – *yes, that's it, this is the garage* – and emerges into a yard of nice grass. Above the yard is a big white house that fills him with hope. He knows this place. He will be welcome here. He crosses the yard and enters the house through the door on the back patio.

In the kitchen the smells come alive, all of them familiar. This is his house, he is sure of it now. This is *home*, and every emotion and meaning that word contains fills him up. Happiness, relief, safety, food, warmth, love. He will be safe here. Whatever happened, this is where he belongs and he will find his way out of the nightmare, beginning here.

He is numb and things don't work they way they should. His neck is stiff. Walking is hard, slow work. His balance is off. He looks down and his pants are scuffed and torn. He is dirty, covered with sticky trails, not wearing a shirt, cold. He wants to be warm, clean himself off. A hot shower makes everything better.

He moves on instinct to the front of the house, up the stairs, over the landing, and up more stairs. He makes it to the top and down the hall, to the bathroom. It is dark with evening light and tinted red. He peels off his clothes and they stick to him in places. He looks in the mirror and is shocked to see that he has the red dirt streaked in thick lines from his nose, around his neck, from his ears and on his chin.

Oh, mother of God help me, it's blood—

He looks away and turns the water on very hot and steps into the tub and pulls the curtain around the hoop. The water feels so good, but most of all just because it *feels*, he feels it, it allows him to feel. He is increasingly sore and tired, bones throbbing, the him of him settling into his body again, his soul one hundred and sixty pounds of sand pouring back into its proper bag, returning, and he lets the water pound him, cascade over his head and drum against his neck and skull to stem the headache that has been growing stronger since he woke up, but it doesn't help. His head hurts too much. He washes the dried dirt from his nose and ears and corners of his eyes and by the time the water has run all the way to cold, his head hurts too badly to stay in and he knows he won't be able to stay on his feet much longer.

He steps out of the tub and looks into the mirror, wiping steam. He see colors now but the red lingers. One of his eyes, the left one, is red where it is supposed to be white, as if the eyeball is a bauble half full of blood. His hair is white and his head pounds and the bathroom spins. He turns away and moves to the medicine cabinet above the towels on the other side of the room and catches a glimpse of the rabbit paintings. They are in love. There is a boy rabbit and a girl rabbit. They are a couple and they live here and they are loved. The rabbits are black and white at first, but then the lower one begins to throb like a heart, like his swollen brain, bulging, turning red and fading, turning red and fading, and another spike of fear pierces him.

She is red because she is hurt.

Where is Stacey? Why isn't Stacey home with me? She is supposed to be home.

His head hurts too much to look at the rabbits. The room won't stop spinning. He staggers in a circle and throws his arms out, catching himself on the sink where he vomits. He throws up again and again and the pain and pressure behind his eyes is unbearable. Rods of steel are pushing through his frontal lobes and exiting his eyes. He coughs and washes his mouth. His head is going to explode. It does not seem possible that a human head can hurt this much and still be attached. He drinks some water and staggers, sliding along the wall to the other end. He holds onto the cabinet door as he fumbles for the aspirin. He finds the bottle and pops the top and swallows four quickly, dryly. He needs to lie down. He needs to close his eyes.

I've suffered a head injury. A terrible, terrible head injury. Something bad has happened. Where is she? Where is Stacey? I need my wife. I need help. I miss her so much . . .

He tries to walk and the bathroom door floats before him and he becomes untethered as his head floats away.

Time slips.

He wakes on the couch with no memory of how he got there. His head still hurts but it is better. He thinks he is hungover. He must have thrown down too many beers last night wondering where she was. He must have slept for a long time. It is afternoon already, almost sunset. Where is Stacey? Why hasn't she come home? He can't remember the last time they spoke. The last time he looked into her eyes. He can't remember why, but he is sure that she is mad at him. That she has been angry at him for a long time and he doesn't know why.

He sits up and goes to the phone and opens the phone book she keeps in the drawer in the little stand, the one in which she has penciled all the numbers with her delicate script, like the hand of another woman from another age. Why does she bother when every cellphone comes with an address book?

It's nicer this way.

He calls the Marina garden center and asks for her, but they say she is not scheduled today. He calls the art gallery in Culver City and a man reminds him that Stacey hasn't worked there for almost six months. He calls two of her friends, Rowina first and then Jessica, but they don't know where she is and he is left with the impression they do not much like him.

He sets the phone down and walks into the kitchen. He stands in front of the sink and drinks a glass of water. He is angry with her. She is always running away. She has been depressed and taking too many pills. She is so unhappy. Why hasn't he paid more attention to her? How did he let it get so bad? He is never around, always working, on the road. But that is no excuse. It's his fault, he knows. He has been avoiding his own wife.

The woman I love, and she needs my help. She can't do it alone. It is my job to help her. I will make it up to her. Next time I see her, I will hold her close and tell her we're leaving, we're going to start over, I quit, it's time to have a baby.

Where is Stacey?

Something bad has happened to her. I can feel it in me. I can feel it in the house. It is like a poisoned shroud, a toxic bubble that surrounds the house and all of West Adams. This was always a dangerous neighborhood and we've been lucky so far, but now I know. It's finally happened.

He looks across the yard and notices the garage door is open. It looks like a black mouth yawning. Deep inside, a pale white glare stares back. It is her car, he realizes. Her car is still in the garage. She left for work but her car never made it out of the garage. He is filled with a horrible premonition. He doesn't want to go.

He must go.

He walks across the backyard and the urge to run is strong, but he won't give in. For a moment the dizziness comes back and he feels weak, too weak to be on his feet, but he pushes past it. He walks into the garage and stands next to her car. The driver's side door is open and there is a cup of milky brown liquid sitting in the console's cup holder. Stacey's morning coffee. The creamer is floating in clumps. She always liked her iced coffee in the morning. The ice has melted.

To his right is the second garage door, also open, and the car's rear end is poking into the alley just a bit. Stacey must have gotten out to move something, something blocking her path.

But why didn't she come back? Why did she leave her car? Maybe she ran away with another man. Maybe she doesn't love me any more. Maybe he came to pick her up, to drive her off to a better life. Or maybe she has been kidnapped. Some sick fuck is driving her away in a van, on his way to Utah with her right now.

A fragment of an annoying pop song eddies through his head and he hums along, but the lyrics get away from him before he can carry the tune.

He walks through the garage and steps into the alley. The sun is low and the sound of the freeway on the other side of the sound wall is a growing hum. He turns and sees an orange couch. The savages have had at it, the cushions are destroyed. Next to the couch is a folded roll of scrap carpet, a dirty brown tortilla. There are weeds stuck to it, and drag marks in the dirt. Someone dragged this carpet in the alley, recently.

He follows the drag marks – and the other ones that look like skid marks from a car – back to the weeds where the carpet used to be. The weeds there are flat and bleached white from lack of sun. There are two sets of footprints. The ones made by the person who dragged the carpet – and another set. Clearer, made recently. This newer set is the set that begins at the carpet and walks away . . . into the garage.

Those belong to me. Oh, Jesus, those are mine.

He walks back to the carpet and rips the carpet away as easily as removing a clean, flat sheet from a bare mattress. In that split second before fear of the unknown becomes the assaultive horror of knowledge, he thinks, *this is where it started today. This is where I woke up.*

What really happened here?

Ghost or James.

There is only room for one of us in this vessel.

*

402

And now the rabbits help me see. Stacey's rabbits help me see.

The engine revs and everything lurches into gear. Ghost is turning Stacey around with one arm and holding the gun at them with the hand of the other as the distance closes. The Glock goes off – POP-POP! – and Stacey shrinks into a ball, falling from his embrace. The windshield is cracked as two holes appear in it and Ghost screams and a third shot POPS and Annette screams and the collision is astounding. Stacey is just a dull sound and James – James, not Ghost, me *– I jump forward, leaping head-first as if I am going to fly over the car like Superman, but I'm not Superman, my head bounces off the top of the windshield and I rock to a halt, then fold over the hood before flying off it and disappearing under the front of the car.*

I see.

When the light returns, the camera is held steady, aimed at the ground of alley gravel and oil-stained dirt. Everything is quiet. It pans slowly. I am lying on my back – not Ghost, James. I am bleeding from my ears and mouth and nose. My chest is not rising or falling . . .

. . . not at first glance. But even as I continue to watch, it is almost imperceptible, the shallowest swell of the ribs, but it is real. It was there in the video, I just didn't see it, and neither did they . . .

I am still breathing. My eyes are blank, unblinking, looking up toward the sky, and one of them is filled with red, a pool of blood in and around the eyeball. A large black ant crawls over my chin and down my neck.

'Do you see that?' Annette says. Her voice is dull, heavy, sexual.

403

No one answers her.

'Look who's a Ghost now.'

I see.

Stacey crying on the side of the road, crying over the dead rabbit. Trying to reach me, using my memories to show me.

He's not dead! He's not dead!

I see.

The man in the video, lying in the alley. Annette says, 'Look who's a Ghost now.'

But I'm not a ghost now. I should be, but I'm not.

I dove head-first into a speeding car. My head aches. It was my head. All this time it was not just in my head but *literally my head.* They put me with her. Dragged us to our deathbed together and whatever passed between us passed between us. And hours later, a lifetime later, I woke up. I went inside and cleaned up and lost consciousness again. Stacey didn't wake up and she didn't come home and I found her in the alley later without even remembering, all because of the damage to my brain.

There's no such thing as ghosts and haunted houses, Detective Bergen said.

Only symptoms.

I lost track of time. I lost my car keys. The forgotten trips to the storage locker. Things out of place in the house. Her image in the window, in Mr Ennis's house.

Symptoms.

The ability to remember what Stacey looked like, every lovely detail of her beautiful face erased from memory. The laundry I forgot I had folded. My damaged memory.

Symptoms.

Voices on the phone. Echoes from my grieving self. The gun Hermes gave me a year ago, not two months ago. Bergen caught on the gun discrepancy because time had become elastic, folded plastic.

The numbing. The gaps in memory. The constant headaches. The red rabbits.

Symptoms.

I'm not Ghost. There was no ghost in West Adams.

Only a damaged man. James Hastings reborn.

40

The screen door opened with a slow creaking and latched softly. When I looked up she was standing at the entrance, the afternoon sun from the broken window lighting strands of her white hair and dappling the soft, faded cotton of the violet and navy banded rugby shirt she stole from James in college. Seeing her caught so, my memory – *his* memory – dilated, inhaling her, devouring all we had forgotten before our anniversary.

Her small nose and low cheekbones and wide-set eyes of blue. The way her teeth set next to each other smooth and straight. Her thick lips pink over the clean line of her chin. The shape of her ears, so small, their lobes tight against her jaw. The hopeful tension in her small shoulders, the fullness of her hips. Her breasts pushing the fabric that contained them in correct proportion. The exact shade of her hair damp, clean and pulled back, her skin aglow. Her hands bunched at her sides and her eyes glassing over with tears, every part of her combining into the whole, filling the void in me better than a puzzle piece, as if my fingertips – the fingertips of his mind – were reading the Braille of her DNA.

Our Stacey.

'I had to,' she said, ignoring the corpse between us. 'He was going to kill you.'

I wanted to smile but I couldn't hold my head up or make my face work that way.

'I couldn't find you,' she said. 'He hid you from me and I was lost. I'm so sorry, my love. I came back for you. I won't ever leave you again.'

She came closer and kneeled beside me. His love for her inside me was like a flame feeding on every forest fire in California, and it engulfed me.

She kissed my neck, whispered in my ear. 'Come with me, Jameson. Let's go home.'

But here, up close, I could see the scars. Thread lines under her chin where another scalpel had been used, at her request. More healing lines behind her jaw and ears. The swollen, still faint blue-purple from her nose resetting, and the pink rawness around her eyes, the mask skin pulled tighter in every direction. The transparent ridges of her blue contact lenses.

Not our Stacey. The monster healing.

This was where she had been for the past few weeks while I was his prisoner. What had she told the doctor? Had she taken a photo of Stacey and said, this is the one? Make me look like her?

'I had to,' she said, seeing me wrestle with it. 'I couldn't stand the way you looked at her when you looked at me. I knew it wouldn't be real for you unless I changed the outside, too. I did the best I could. It's me, James. I'm in here. You know it's true.'

I wet my tongue. 'Why?'

'Why?' she said, her eyes glistening. 'You needed me. You would have taken your own life. I used everything to reach you. I took her for you. I got rid of Lucy for you. Look at me. Once I had Annette, I called Lucy every night. I went into her bedroom and taped her mouth and told her things. I told her what would happen if she didn't do what I said – but I did it for you. I chased her away for you. I got rid of them all so we could be together.' She looked at the dead man on the floor beside us. Dead Rick Butterfield. Her own brother. 'I set you free. Do you think Annette would be capable of killing her own brother for you? It's me, you know it's me. Don't you know by now? Don't you know?'

I didn't speak for a long time. Her eyes, the anima behind her eyes, was very convincing.

'James died,' I said. 'I saw the video.'

'No . . .'

'You never wanted him. You wanted Ghost.'

'*No.*' She held my face, shaking me, keeping me awake. 'You're not dead. It was an accident. She didn't know it was you. She thought you were Ghost. She never meant to hurt you. I tried to stop her. You're not dead. I can fix you. I'll make it all better.'

I raised the gun and pushed it between her breasts, hard against the bone there.

'No . . .' She leaned back on her legs. 'Please . . . *please.*'

I applied more pressure to the trigger. She looked down at the gun, then up at me.

408

'It's not natural,' I said.

Squeezing . . .

But what if it really is her?

What if Stacey's inside the monster and I kill her again?

Her eyes opened wide enough for me to see the whites all the way around.

Stacey would never hurt so many people. This malignancy killed your wife.

Kill her now.

My finger tightened and Annette lunged from the floor, shrieking. The pistol blasted overhead. She kept coming and I tried to bludgeon her with the gun and she slammed into me, pulling my arm straight until she had wrestled the gun from my grip. I kicked at her and she thrashed. I tried to cover myself and she went five notches insane all over me, screaming as she battered me and yanked my hair and dragged me bleeding across the floor. I twisted sideways and something in my back popped and the pain moved through me like electric eels. I screamed in agony as my entire body convulsed and went rigid. The room flashed by and the front door was kicked open and then I was falling down the front steps, hips cracking on concrete as she shrieked.

She hauled me across the front walk to the driveway and I had nothing left, but still I resisted her. I gnashed, my teeth catching on the bone of her wrist. When we got to Rick's car she used the driver's side door for an anvil and beat my head against it over and over until I stopped fighting back. I didn't lose consciousness this time. My head rang like a bell and I just stopped moving, half sitting up, my hands floating in front of me, the pain so severe I felt clapped between the hands of an angry goddess.

She wrapped her arms around my waist and with a grunt threw me into the back seat. She leaned in over me and pressed the gun to my chin and said, 'There are two bullets left. Fuck with me I'll blow a hole in your ungrateful stupid head and that will be it for both of us.'

She slammed the door on the flats of my feet, jarring my knees up. I curled onto my side and closed my eyes. She drove us out of Sheltering Palms.

41

The miles turned into hours and the day turned into night. By the time I was able to move without setting off a new round of spasms in my back and legs, we were well past Las Vegas and St George, Utah, heading northeast on Interstate 15, or perhaps we had already merged onto I-70. I could not sit up but I could read the terrain through the windows and the passage of time as miles. My best estimation was that we were out where the signs that say LAST GAS 160 MILES begin to appear, just before the real canyons swallow you.

When we first moved, Stacey and I drove from Tulsa up through Colorado to stop at Gaynor Lake for a weekend, before continuing west to Los Angeles, and then back and forth the two times we went home for the holidays, always preferring an extra day or two in the Rockies over the hotter, vaster and less scenic route through Texas. Annette had stopped for gas only an hour or two into this adventure. We were now some seven or eight hours outside of Los Angeles. I did not ask where we were going and I don't think she knew. What I did know was that after that sign for LAST GAS, there would be only scrubby desert, yucca plants daring you to take a shortcut, vertigo-inducing rock walls with pink and black candy swirls, and occasionally the mirage of civilization just a few miles up ahead, which were nothing more than strange clusters of stars playing tricks with your witching-hour brain. I needed medical attention and unless she stopped for gas soon, we were going to be stranded in the fuck-all nowhere.

I was very thirsty. My wounds were dry but only because I hadn't been moving. As soon as I acted out, the cuts would reopen. I tried to keep my back flat on the seat as I counted off miles and she ate another hour off my life. Even if the Interceptor got twenty miles to the gallon, which I knew it didn't, the tank would be no larger than eighteen gallons. If we had ten gallons left, and I doubted we had that much, we might make another hundred and sixty miles, tops. But we were climbing now and we would continue climbing in elevation all night as we approached the Rockies. We'd be lucky to pull sixteen miles per gallon, maybe even twelve when the inclines really kicked in. Added to the way she was whomping on the pedal . . .

'We're going to run out of gas,' I said at last. 'Do you have a plan or . . . ?'

She didn't reply for two minutes. Two and a half miles. 'It's summer. We have to go to the lake house.' Her voice was dry and tired sounding.

'What lake house?' *How did she know that?*

Annette laughed softly. 'Oh, James. What's it going to take to convince you?'

I didn't have an answer for that.

Ten or twenty miles later she said, 'Don't worry. We'll find a new car at the rest stop.'

Eventually the canyons released us onto the rolling hills again. She opened a window and the cool wind blew in smelling of childhood.

She means to steal a different car. She'll never pull it off. She can't keep carrying me. I'll scream. Someone will intervene. This is going to end soon enough.

The night closed in. Against my best intentions and all will power to stay wide awake, I dozed.

When I woke up the car was parked, the engine off. High road lamps lit the car with a dull bluish white light that felt like a hospital ward. It was late night, early morning. I was cold.

'Where are we?' I said, blinking up at the headliner.

Annette didn't answer.

I squirmed, testing the pain. It wasn't unbearable. I clutched the seat back and raised myself slowly. She wasn't in the car and the driver's side door was wide open. The two semi-trailers parked at an angle up ahead looked grainy, not quite real. Where did she go?

The needle on the gas gauge was below E.

I inched forward and nudged the door open with my foot. I leaned out and looked around. The rest area had the usual plain building of gray cinder-block walls and brown sheet-metal roof, a wide strip of grass with some picnic tables and a line of twenty or so parking places in the parking lot. Aside from the two semi-tractor trailers at the far end, there was only one other car. A small rusted-out silver Honda hatchback, empty, probably abandoned.

She must have gone to the bathroom. She's still carrying the gun. Get to the trucks. Get close first, then scream for help.

This is our chance.

I pulled myself to my feet. I leaned into the driver's side and turned the key in the ignition. *Click, click, click.* The battery was dead, too, now that she had left the door open and, most likely, the headlights on.

I shuffled a few feeble paces from Rick's police auction sedan. I looked to the bathrooms and saw no movement, then looked back at the trucks. A big guy with a bulging gut like a trash bag full of water was smoking a cigarette in front of his truck, rocking back and forth in a pair of heeled boots. He tossed his butt to the ground and walked around to the driver's side, disappearing for a moment. His door swung out, the dome light in his cab came on and he popped up into his seat.

I glanced back at the toilets and then began hobbling after him. The pain worsened with every step, but if he drove off without me I didn't know what would happen here. I trotted over the parking lot, onto the sidewalk, waving one hand. The truck was at least a hundred feet away. I couldn't tell if he was looking in my direction. I opened my mouth to shout for him before remembering that if she heard me yelling . . .

Get closer first.

A grinding noise kicked into the night and his engine fired, belching black smoke from the perforated vertical pipes. The diesel engine sounded like the world's largest dental drill. I was covered with dried blood and as I hobbled faster my clothes began to slip from my skin as warm wetness began to flow. God damn the desert at night.

As I approached, he bent down in the cab and I lost sight of him. I was short of breath as I walked around the front of the big white cab and stopped outside of his door.

'Hey!' My throat was as dry as if I had just run a mile. I looked back toward the bathrooms but she wasn't there, nor on the grass play area.

'Hey, hey, need some help here,' I called louder, straining over the drill of his engine. Six spaces behind me was the other truck, its engine off, the cab dark. This guy was my only chance.

I rapped on his door. 'Hey, can you hear me?'

He sat up quickly and looked down at me. After a moment, the window powered down.

'Help you?' His face was oddly thin for a man of such girth. The cheeks were pinched, the jaw askew. His nose hooked into a knob of loose flesh, as if he had contracted some rare disease that affected only his face. His neck skin was loose, baggy as a pelican's.

'I'm sorry,' I said, gasping. 'I need help. I'm – they kidnapped me. I need a doctor. Did you see her?'

He scowled and worked his lips around. He pushed the folded bill of his mesh cap back as he scratched his forehead. He looked across the lot, back to the car.

'What happened?'

'I'm . . . you have to help me. Call the police. You have to call for help, now.'

His chin shot forward. 'Call the police?'

'I think my back is broken. These people, they tortured me. I can't . . . do you have a cellphone. Can I come inside there with you? Please? *You have to help me, please!*'

'You want to get inside where?'

'It's not safe!' I realized my shouting was scaring him. 'Please, I can explain, but we have to get out of here first. You have to radio for help.'

'Who you traveling with didja say?'

'The woman. A blonde woman. Did you see her? She's crazy . . .'

He looked away, scanning the rest area, then back at me, frowning. There was about him zero sense of urgency. His mouth opened a crack and he snorted twice obscenely, as if he had a duck call in his sinuses. I waited for him to spit, but he just watched me.

'That your Interceptor?'

'Yes, that's her—'

'What'n hell you doing with a cop car?'

'She stole it. She had a brother – look, you don't understand . . .' I was dizzy, holding myself upright with my hands on my thighs. He was high up in his rig, safe. I was going to scream soon. 'I just need a ride. Will you *please help me*?'

He licked his lips. 'Well, I can radio the highway patrol. They'd run a can out to ya. Might take an hour or two but it'll get ya goin'.'

A can? He thought I was asking for *gas*? 'No, no, I don't want a can of gas! This is an emergency! Do you understand? She tried to kill me! She's got a gun!'

The man in the truck stiffened. 'A gun? Who's got a gun?'

'The woman who kidnapped me!'

'You on dope?'

'What? No! I'm injured—'

'Huh?' This came out like an accusation.

'I'm bleeding to death!' I screamed at him. 'Call the fucking police!'

'Okay, then,' he said. 'Sit tight, fella.'

I stared as his window went up in a smooth slide. I stepped forward with my palms raised, shouting. The loud engine got louder as he pumped the pedal and began to slide back, stopped, and then went forward again. His lights came on and a plume of black smoke belched into the night. The rig came at me, horn blasting as I stood in front of him. But he did not slow as he swerved lazily around me and rolled onto the interstate entrance ramp.

I screamed after him, trying to run, but I couldn't run and he was moving up through the gears now, rolling away until the orange lights across the rear doors winked and faded into the night.

I stared off into the dark distance where the truck had just been. No other cars passed. I turned in a circle. I was alone.

'Sonofabitch!'

I went numb. Motionless. The earth continued to rotate.

I was about to turn away and walk back to Rick's car when faint red spots glowed on the far horizon.

Brake lights.

He was at least a mile up the road now, but the fucker was braking. I blinked, waiting for them to fade out again, but they didn't. I took two hesitant steps, then three, and I never took my eyes off the brake lights as I began to move faster, ignoring the pain now, in fact feeling no pain at all, knowing any minute they would vanish.

I never looked back to see if she was coming after me and, eventually, I found the strength to run.

42

The headwind and exertion watered my vision, making the stars on the horizon oscillate. My feet slapped tarmac in a disturbing rhythm. Far beyond the reach of the rest stop lights, a hundred yards ahead where the red glow was thinnest, something low and moving fast crossed the road, blurring from the desert to the yellow lines and then back into the desert before I could classify it. It was too low and fast to be a person but larger than any animal I could think of. I kept running, my pace flagging, until I was limping in a desperate shuffle.

The truck was idling. I could see *and* hear it now. The engine seemed to vibrate through the road as I approached. The brake lights glowed red, faint but growing brighter as I neared, and my destination seemed another mirage, a vision that receded cruelly every time I closed another hundred feet, the black highway a giant treadmill intent on dragging me back.

Slowly, finally, the entire back of the truck came into clear view. My eyes adjusted and the road became a fixed position below the tall gray doors. I waved my arms and slowed as I reached the back, veering left, coming up the trailer's long dirty flank. I was out of breath, standing just behind the door of the cab, when I stopped.

Why hadn't he opened the door? He must have seen me by now. Surely his conscience had dictated that he call the highway patrol, stop, wait for help to arrive.

Unless . . .

For the first time I glanced back the way I had come. The rest area was now only a faint glow above the few trees alongside the road. There were no other cars coming at us. Even way out here in the middle of nowhere, someone had to come along soon . . . eventually . . . but where had she gone? Why hadn't she followed?

I turned back to the cab. The driver's door was now open.

Wide open. Inviting.

I hadn't heard it open. No voice had called out to me. And then I *knew*.

Annette had been in the cab all along. In the sleeping compartment behind the front seats. She had watched and waited at the rest area, waiting for the right prospect to come along. We were out of gas, and she was guided by the need to escape at all costs, in any shell that would have her. The trucker had left his rig to use the bathroom and she had crawled inside. She'd heard me screaming for help and she had stayed silent, hidden in the back. And as soon as he had driven off . . .

I was trapped again. Stranded. There was no escape in any direction. I simply would not survive out here.

Before I had made the decision, my feet were shuffling

forward, wide of the door. I walked out onto the center lane, pulled even with the open door.

The trucker was not in his seat. The front of the cab was empty. The seat was as high as my head, and behind it the cabin, an extended box behind the seats, large enough to conceal a narrow bed, a small table for eating, a cabinet above with a television and God knows what else bolted to the ceiling. The engine drilled the night.

I stepped closer. Raised myself on the balls of my feet.

I spotted a CB radio mounted low on the dash, to the right of the steering wheel. I could see the holstered hand mic attached to the spiral cord.

And next to that, a cellphone mounted to a plastic cradle. The lid was open, the keypad glowing blue. It would be so simple. Reach in and dial three digits. 9-1-1 . . .

But I could reach neither the CB nor the phone from the ground. I would have to climb in, lean over the seat.

I moved closer. I looked back and higher, between the seat backs. A breeze swirled through the cab, returning the aromas of sweat, enchilada sauce, and some kind of disinfectant. It smelled of death.

The dark porthole between the seats – the window leading back into the bunk – was a rectangle framed in splitting red vinyl, short but wide enough to crawl through.

A black mouth.

She was in there. I could feel her in the darkness.

I saw myself back away one last time, check the view to the road in both directions. I heard myself count to three, saw myself dance forward and scale the rig. Saw my feet mount the running board, the chrome step, my hand finding the steel bar behind the door, and then I was in the cab, my momentum almost pitching me over the driver's seat as I grabbed for the phone and a scream erupted—

I saw it all – and my feet never moved.

I had never stared into such darkness. I might as well have been looking into a mile-deep coffin. To enter would be suicide. I took one step back.

If he's not already dead, she'll kill him and then me. She took out her own brother as if he were a weed in her garden. If the thing inside was ever Stacey, it is no longer. They don't have names for what she's become.

Stop her. You have to stop her.

I went quickly, my feet sure, climbing, my hand on the wheel. I reached for the phone. I fumbled it from the cradle. My foot slipped and I caught myself, leaning over the seat. The wind was hot on my neck, hot as breath, but I focused on the phone. My thumb found the 9 and for a moment there was no response, not a sound behind me. Maybe they had already abandoned the rig. She could be chasing him into the desert . . .

I pressed the first 1.

A thick arm shot through the hole and waved, the fingers clinching above the driver's seat, grasping. He made no sound and his arm was grub-white.

I staggered back on my heels and for a moment was suspended, nearly vertical as I balanced, arms waving, the phone slipping from my hand.

'Help,' his tired voice whispered blindly. 'Oh, Jesus, help me—'

422

His words were cut off and his arm retreated and then he screamed.

I fell down, tumbling, just gripping the door handle before I reset my feet and landed on the road. I staggered back, my blood freezing in revulsion as the black hole filled with grunts and the hard knocking of a body slamming against a wall. I backed away, never taking my eyes off that open door, and caught my heel. I landed on my ass and my right elbow struck the tarmac, the force of my fear hitting me like a wall, making everything up to my neck tingle.

Someone screamed, and, while it sounded distinctly feminine, I knew it wasn't her. The metal side of the cab was shaking, flexing, and then there were no more screams, only a monotonous thudding, rhythmic and direct, the sound of a kid passing a basketball to himself off a gymnasium door. The pounding slowed, halted for nearly half a minute, then finished with a final sickening blow.

Everything was still.

I pushed off the ground and tried to stand.

She swirled out of the darkness, descending cat-like from the swinging door and dropped to the ground, coming for me with blood-soaked hands. There were more spatters of blood on her face and forehead, in her hair. Her shirt was torn open and one of her shoes – some kind of hiker-sneaker thing I didn't know she had been wearing – was missing. She was calmly striding after me without a word. She wasn't even breathing hard.

She stopped three feet away, looming above me. A knife wound some seven to ten inches long gaped white and fatty yellow along her thigh, the blood running down, soaking her socks. Her left eye was swollen shut. A globule of curdled blood and saliva hung from her chin and her teeth were red.

'I fixed it,' she said. 'We're going to Colorado. Everything will be better when we get back to the lake house.'

For a moment, in my obvious defeat, I thought of going. In the midst of her insanity I glimpsed her logic, the simple clarity of her vision. We would go to the lake house and spend the summer together, in privacy, and I would have another few weeks, perhaps even months, with Stacey. The illusion would be made real. To stay would be suicide, here in the desert, alone. To surrender all will would mean another few hours of warmth, and a lifetime of comfort in the seclusion of my lost mind, all for the low price of my cheaply bargained soul.

But I also knew she would never leave me alone. Wherever we ended up, she would never leave me in peace. It didn't even matter if she was Stacey, if Stacey had taken control of her long ago, or if Annette had been obsessed with human masks before she ever laid eyes on Ghost. She was possessed by tragedy and she would invite more; because she had suffered she would thrive on the suffering of others. If it didn't end here, she would possess me forever.

'No,' I said.

'Get in the truck,' she said, walking toward me.

'No.' I got to my feet.

'Get in the truck now, James.'

'You can't save Aaron,' I said. She stopped, her eyes full of fury. 'Aaron's dead. Just like Stacey. They're all dead.'

For a moment the fury was replaced by a broken sadness. 'You don't know what you're saying,' she said. 'You're lost—'

'I don't love you. I don't even care about you, Annette, whoever you are. You're rotten all the way through and you bore me.'

I turned on the yellow lines and started back for the rest stop.

'James?' she said. 'James!'

I kept walking.

'I'm pregnant, James. That's why we have to go. We can see it through. At the lake house.'

I shivered. I kept walking. Up ahead, more than a mile up the highway, headlights crested a hill.

'I'm going to have it,' she said. 'It's what we always wanted, isn't it?'

For every step I took, the car moved a hundred feet closer.

'I wanted it to be a surprise,' she said, her voice closer than it had been a moment ago. She was following me, as Aaron had. 'This is our chance to make it right. Don't you want it back? Don't you want everything you threw away?'

The car disappeared in a dip, then rose again, the crossbar of lights on top of the roof now visible. It would be the highway patrol. I could almost see his hat, the rounded brim and dented top, like a Mountie's. The image tapped a new reservoir of energy in me and I began to trot.

'You can't escape, James,' she said. Now she was out of breath, running, hurrying. 'I'll never let you go!'

The cruiser's lights whirled and flashed to life, lighting the road and the desert in every direction. A spotlight trapped us. He slowed and then, as if realizing the urgency of the situation, hammered the throttle. I put my hands up and turned around as the blue cruiser with its white stripe skidded around me.

The trucker fell screaming from the cab, collapsing on the road behind her, seeming to fold over some kind of metal stock. He was half naked and streaked with blood. She stared at me, pleading as the trucker rolled and got to his knees, his shotgun cocking and then leveling until both barrels were aimed at us.

He screamed and fired. The flash was a wide, white flame and I fell to the road, legs and arm stinging as the pellets tore into me. Annette's legs buckled. She swayed on her knees, watching me.

Howling, the trucker pumped and fired again, twice in rapid succession.

Annette's throat opened with a thick spray and her head rocked back, her body arced as if she were a bow and he had pulled the string. She sagged forward and her face slapped on the road. He lowered the stock, fired again and her body jerked. More shot peppered my ribs and skull. I rolled and covered my head, screaming for him to stop.

'Drop your weapon!' the patrolman shouted somewhere off to my left. 'Drop your weapon! Put it down right now!'

The trucker was in a glory all his own. The shotgun roared again and the patrolman unloaded over the two of us fallen until we were three.

Half an hour later a long orange Flight for Life helicopter set down on the road. By then there were red flares, horse barricades, ambulances and more state patrol cruisers, and the desert looked like a stadium, the end of a Ghost concert.

'Is she breathing?' I kept asking them.

The paramedic who loaded her said, 'She's gone into cardiac arrest.'

'She's pregnant,' I told him. 'She told me she was pregnant.'

He climbed into the chopper and looked back at me as I was being led away in the wheelchair, rolled to the waiting ambulance and police escorts. The paramedic was a blond boy with a good head of hair, but thin and young, and his eyes were old, glossy black, tired beyond words. His expression did not change as he regarded me a moment, then looked down at the bloodied bundle of rags before him. I waited for him to do something more, advance a judgement on us, but none was given.

The orange helicopter lifted off, billowing curls of road dust and sand, chasing me away, and I watched the machine rise into the black sky until my angel, the angel who had become my demon, was at last absorbed into the glittering heavens.

aftermath

This is home. This is where we live. This is where the dead belong.

If I had gone back to Tulsa, this chronicle of my sanity's erosion – and its eventual renewal – would never be done. I began after I left the hospital and it took me seven months. When I reached the end I saved the file to my email account and printed a single copy – which I deposited in the storage locker with Stacey's things over on La Brea, behind a new lock that utilizes a digital code and two keys. Then I did not write another word about my life for two years, and with sound reason, for that which has occupied me since is far more important than writing.

Three weeks after I finished telling my story, Eddie was born.

And I've got to say, being a single father has its benefits. Women who never used to bat an eye at me at Ralph's and The Coffee Bean, they suddenly couldn't get enough of us. We weren't on the market, though, so we smiled and played along and when we got home we threw their phone numbers away and went about our lives.

The first few months were hard, with my back surgery, the physical therapy, the blinding headaches that still paralyzed me for hours, the court paperwork, psychiatric evaluations, paternity tests, and all the rest that had consumed my first year. It broke my heart that Eddie had to go it alone in those early weeks that turned into months, a child ward of the state. But my friends on the police department and the lawyers my former employer loaned out helped push things along.

The first night I brought Edward Michael Hastings home, I took him upstairs to the ballroom, which I had converted into his playroom, and we spread out on the big square of purple shag carpet I had installed over the marble tiles. With my back against the blue bean bag and Eddie on my chest, a bottle of formula cocked in the crook of my arm, I told him the story of Jack and the Beanstalk, because it was the first story my father told to me. He didn't understand a word of it, but the sound of my voice put him under. And then I stared up at the skylights that had been installed and there must have been a good wind that night, pushing the smog inland, because I could see all the stars as I cried and thanked a God I did not believe in for delivering him to me.

Eddie's mother was not required to give permission for the adoption. Eddie has not met his birth mother, and he never will.

*

Blaine made a full recovery and Trigger went back to work on Project James with a Texas fire in his belly. He landed me some script work off the hope that I would one day offer up my story to the great crunching content machine, and I didn't bother to tell him that will never happen. Unless something terrible happens to us. Unless something irreversible and worse than death comes for me and someone were to discover it in the storage locker . . .

After two years of raising Eddie alone, I needed help. Euvaldo's niece, Celia, was looking for work. She watched Eddie during the afternoons and sometimes late at night, my two best windows for working. I am no longer an actor, I hope it goes without saying, but the writing thing sort of stuck.

One night I finished working on a bitch of an action sequence for a script – the pitch was *The Fast and the Furious* meets *Footloose* set in the world of rail-car graffitists – and I came out of my office in the sunroom, shocked to realize it was two thirty in the morning. Celia was sleeping on the couch with Eddie spooning against her, a black and white movie flickering over them. She had not interrupted me, even though she was only scheduled weeknights until ten, and watching my son in this woman's arms filled me with an array of emotions I was not prepared for.

Gratitude, that there were still good people around to help each other; a gentle but insistent lust, because she wasn't wearing a bra and this was not the first time that

I had noticed the generous swell of her breasts, the downward feathering sweep of little black hairs on the indentation of soft brown flesh covering her tailbone; possession, the certainty that these were my people, my new tribe; and finally the terror of my own heart's longing, because I did not know if I was allowed to have any of this.

She did not seem startled to see me there, hovering at the end of the couch. When I offered to take him she only smiled and carried him to the stairs. I followed. Eddie looked over her shoulder, briefly amused to be looking down at me, and then his eyes crossed with sleep and he returned to the land of beanstalks. After she set him in his bed and checked the wire connection on his walkie-talkie, I pulled the covers up and kissed his cheek. As I was leaving the room she caught my hand and without preamble or discussion led me into the master bedroom. As she disrobed, I asked Stacey's permission.

Are you at rest now? Are you safe? I tried to tell the truth. I'll never forget you, you know? Will you let me take another step tonight?

Before Stacey could answer, Celia kissed me and pressed her body to mine. I traced her curves without comparing them to any others. We slid into bed and she gave herself passionately without taking me too seriously, and it was good both times, all of which happened to be just what I needed.

She fell asleep in my arms and I could smell my son in her hair.

*

The one and only time I visited Annette Salvaggio at the Napa State Hospital, she did not attempt to communicate with me. She had been catatonic for ninety per cent of her waking hours since her apprehension and was deemed unfit to stand trial. The paramedics and surgeons had saved her life, but the scars were a series of scattered white slits up her chest and face, and the hollow of her throat looked like a child's fork drawing in mashed potatoes. Her hair was cut almost to her skull. She had lost a great deal of weight, rendering her cheeks concave, the brow and eye sockets simian in their stark contrast to the jaundiced skin. Several of the teeth that had been shot out from the back of her head had not been replaced.

I did not linger, only thanked her for carrying the child to term and wished her 'some form of recovery and a better existence than this'.

She stared at me for a long time, her once luminous green eyes now the flat gray of institution filing cabinets. She did not understand a word I had spoken or know who I was, and that was fine. I had not come for her. Though she had been upright, breathing and occasionally scratching her thigh or blinking as she wiped her nose, the event was little more than a casket viewing.

I don't have the nightmares any more. I haven't seen her lifeless eye or Rick's screaming, blood-dotted face in my dreams since Eddie turned two.

Ghost resurfaced with a full media blitz announcing his three-pronged comeback: double album, memoir and the launch of GhostVision, his music and movie channel.

He had been 'on sabbatical' in Buenos Aires for the past two and a half years, where, according to the press release, he kicked the white horse, became a vegan, wrote more than two hundred songs (and the memoir), and remarried and had a third child with his ex-wife, Drea-Jenna. His only personal acknowledgement of my ordeal was the parting remark on the phone when I called to thank him for the legal resources.

'Way to hang, J. Stay strong and hit me if you're ever in St Louis.'

I began this record by stating I hoped he was dead, and in the interests of accurately portraying my feelings at that time I chose not to edit or recant those wishes. But the truth is I was relieved. Having Ghost back at the top of the charts was another sign that the world had not totally slipped its axis, that reality – good old normal fucked up reality – had returned. I took comfort in the fact that the fire we once shared, however tangentially, still burned.

I blame him for nothing. Without Ghost there to take over when I was beaten down, without his fierce will to fight, I would not have survived. Ghost is the mirror, and some people don't like what they see in the mirror. Those who would mistake the mirror's reflection for reality can't be helped. They know damn well how to change the channel or turn the radio off. They just don't want to. They would starve without him.

I still see Aaron around. He is the boy under every hood, afraid to look adults in the eye.

*

I suppose it is obvious now why I picked this thread up again. I needed to remember the good things, too. But that is not the only reason. Celia and I have been carrying on this way for some months, and something strange happened last night. I don't remember the event, but she insists it happened, so I think it is wise to make note of it. It is important to keep a clear mind about these things, and the day may soon come when contributing to this file becomes impossible.

So, for now . . .

We were having breakfast this morning on the back patio. Celia had just finished feeding Eddie his scrambled eggs and toast and he was eager to be free of his chair, so she helped him down and let him run into the yard. He quickly submerged himself into an imaginary game involving his toy dinosaurs and the plastic fire engine on the grass beside us. I was half awake and staring into my coffee cup, thinking of nothing, but the words she spoke next roused me into full alertness.

'James, there's something we need to talk about.'

Celia had always been a morning person, but her face was drawn and her hair lacked its usual luster. She looked thirty-eight instead of twenty-six, as though she had not slept well, and I tried to conceal the little bolts of anxiety coursing through my veins.

'Do you – you don't remember last night, do you?'

I cocked my head.

'I woke up around three thirty and you weren't in bed. I couldn't get back to sleep right away. I thought you had gone to the bathroom, like you sometimes do.'

I said nothing.

'After twenty minutes or so, I was worried something was wrong with Edward, but I couldn't hear anything from the speaker, so I didn't think you were in with him.'

The coffee in my stomach turned to cold acid. I looked away, watching Eddie in the yard. The dinosaur had the firemen trapped in their rig and was battering the doors and windows with a taunting patience and taste for cruelty that was frankly disturbing.

'I checked the bathroom first,' Celia continued. 'But you weren't in there, so I went downstairs. The kitchen and living rooms were empty. I checked your office, but you weren't downstairs either.'

Please. Not in the ballroom again.

She squeezed my hand. She was smiling but her palm was moist. Moist and cool.

'You were in Eddie's room,' she said. Her eyes widened with encouragement, as if I were a bad student who had finally made good. Gold star for James.

'And?' I gritted my teeth. 'What was I doing?'

'Sleeping, silly. You were sleeping in his bed.'

'My God, how? Was I crushing him?'

'No. Your legs were hanging over the end. It was sort of cute. The way you were clinging to him.'

I don't know why, but my embarrassment bordered on shame. 'I must have heard him crying or something.'

'No. You couldn't have heard him crying, and I would have woken up if he had been. You know what a light sleeper I am. No, he was sleeping like a dog.'

'Like a log, you mean.'

'Yes, like you used to.'

I shook my head in an attempt to wake up. The morning sun was beating down on my face and I felt I was going to be sick.

'Hold on,' I said. 'What do you mean "used to"? I sleep like the dead. I've been sleeping so well I don't even remember my dreams.'

'That's what I'm telling you, honey,' she said. 'Don't get so defensive. I just wondered if you knew.'

'Knew what? Obviously I don—'

'That this wasn't the first time,' she interrupted. 'Last night wasn't the first time, James. The other times you were downstairs. On the couch.'

'How many times?'

'Oh, jeez, I don't know. Eight, maybe ten?'

I closed my eyes. The sun infected me like a fever.

'When did it start?'

'A month ago, maybe a little longer. I didn't think anything of it at first, James.' When she said my name again, her voice hardened. 'But after last night, I don't know . . . seeing you cling to Eddie that way, like you were trying to hide him, I couldn't help feeling like you don't want me to come near him.'

My chair seemed to be rocking on soft land.

'No,' I said. 'That's not true.'

'No?'

I forced myself to look at Celia. 'No. I promise.'

'It's just sleepwalking, then?'

'Yes.'

She watched me a moment. 'All right.'

We didn't speak for another minute and I relaxed.

'The only other thing, though,' she said. 'The reason you couldn't have heard him crying, even if he was, which he wasn't?'

Needle needle. Always needling me . . .

'You turned off the speaker in his room, James.'

I had turned off the wireless walkie-talkie?

'And the one next our bed,' Celia said. 'You turned that one off, too.'

'Why would I do that?' I said.

So she wouldn't hear the other voices.

'That's what I asked you last night, when you woke up. When you sat up and looked at me in the doorway like you didn't know who I was.'

She leaned back in her lawn chair and tucked a lock of her hair behind her ear, pouting. Her lips were thin, so thin and clean, not thin like the other's. I wanted to kiss them. Suck them and hurt them and bite them off.

She hiccuped once, and wiped the tip of her nose.

Inside I felt a familiar warmth I had not known for a long time. Years, years that seemed like only yesterday.

'You've never looked at me that way before, James. Your eyes . . .'

I looked at our son playing on the lawn, our beautiful boy that needed a real mother, not this . . . ingratiating *child*.

I turned and showed her my eyes, all of my eyes. 'And what did I say?'

I heard Celia's response before she spoke it. Heard it

inside the canals of my ears, in the folds of my gray matter mind, in the once empty and cold corner of my now warm, bursting soul.

It's nicer this way.

Acknowledgements

I'd like to thank Nikola Scott, my editor at Sphere, who offered scalpel-sharp insights into the early drafts of this novel, but wielded said scalpel with soft white gloves and plenty of intelligence, charm, and grace. We'll miss you. Also, my deepest gratitude to David Shelley, who believed in the project before I had written the first word. Without you and your team at Little, Brown, I would still be stuck in second gear. And to Dan Mallory, who embraced the final draft and applied his enthusiasm to the launch.

Many thanks to Scott Miller, who trusted me when I said I knew what I was doing and it would all make sense when I finished.

And finally to a VIP trio: Eminem, Slim Shady, and Marshall Mathers, without whose fearless forays into the dark side, addictive motherfuckin' beats, and lyrical genius this novel would not have been written. Another one, perhaps, but not this one. Your flow was the gasoline in the engine of my inspiration while I scratched this out, so thank you for having a killer relapse.